Turf

a novel

Darren E Laws

The first novel in the Georgina O'Neil trilogy

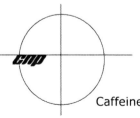

Caffeine Nights Publishing
Fiction aimed at the heart and the head

Published by Caffeine Nights Publishing 2008
Revised and reedited edition 2008
First published in 2003

Published in Great Britain by Caffeine Nights Publishing

www.cnpublishing.co.uk

British Library Cataloguing in Publication Data.
A CIP catalogue record for this book is available from the British Library

ISBN: 978-0-9554070-1-7

Book Design by
Mark (Wills) Williams
Photography by
Clint Spencer
Everything else by
Default, Luck and Accident

By the same author

Tripping
ISBN: 0955407001
Available from all good bookstores and Internet stores
www.cnpublishing.co.uk

Coming soon from Caffeine Nights Publishing

DARK COUNTRY

The second novel in the Georgina O'Neil trilogy

To Natalie
For persuading me that I can actually do it

Prologue

Smile, you're Dead

Max Dalton did not struggle nor fight; his body hit the water with a stinging embrace, though he did not feel any pain. He was past caring; technically still alive, but more than ready to welcome death.

The water was warm, inviting. Max had no real comprehension of where he was, and even less now of who he was. Slowly, he submerged. The warm fluid filled his mouth, the cavern enlarged by the removal of his tongue, lips and teeth. He breathed the water in through his nose; at first panic at the realisation that there was no way of expelling it, then only the comfort of allowing it to fill his lungs.

Part One

Hell waits

One

The alarm was ringing in his ears with a fuck you attitude that was sure to get Leroy LaPortiere out of bed, but on the wrong side. The heat was closing in already and his clock cheerfully told him that it was just after five thirty in the morning. His girlfriend, Lia, was lying on top of the sheets, her body glistening with perspiration like morning dew. Her arm outstretched touching his naked back.

'Go to sleep, hon.' Leroy wanted to roll on top of her and slip deep inside her.

'Be careful, baby.'

'Sure hon, nothing ever happens around here.'

And he was right. He was on the money one hundred per cent of the time, but a winning streak like that has to end some day.

After a cold shower, Leroy was ready to face another day. Breakfast, would consist of an artery hardening and unsatisfying stop at Wendell's Diner for an early morning mixed grill, hash browns and a gallon of extra strong coffee. The longevity of officers of the law on Turtle Island was not dictated by the rising tide of crime but by the accelerating spread of saturated fats through increasingly narrowing arteries.

'You gonna die.' A familiar voice came from behind.

'That is the most sense you've talked in a long time my man. We all gonna die.' Leroy didn't need to lift his head from his grease sodden breakfast to know his partner was standing behind him. The smell of Giorgio Armani aftershave followed Rick Montoya around like a dust cloud announcing his arrival. Montoya dragged a chair over the stone tiled floor and sat next to LaPortiere. He waited patiently for a passing waitress before ordering his morning meal.

This is Groundhog Day, TV, Football, Sex and living. The game plan was that they would meet everyday for the next twenty years, doing the same thing until they cashed their pensions, sold their homes and sailed around the world. Of course they were going to sail around the world; why wouldn't they?

Montoya, like his partner Leroy LaPortiere, worked for Missouri Police Department. LaPortiere for the past twelve years, Montoya, only one year in Missouri, twelve in Chicago before that.

Rick dropped a small brown envelope onto the table next to Leroy.

'What's this?'

LaPortiere opened the manila envelope, noticing that it was addressed to Captain Norman Frusco, his chief. He withdrew a small bundle of Polaroid photographs, knowing that it wasn't going to be Rick's holiday snaps.

'You know, I really thought that this sort of thing was confined to the big cities.' Leroy shuffled through the photos. 'This is the John Doe?' He studied the victim, or what was left of him. He stared into the white bloated face, the lifeless eyes; it was something a movie could never capture, no matter how good the actor. The mask of death was something that could never be faked even with the best special effects and yet here he was looking at a cheap Polaroid and the look was unmistakable.

LaPortiere shivered. 'Like I told you, we all gotta die someday.'

Narla Fleisher brushed her teeth vigorously while staring at her face in the bathroom mirror. She swirled water around her gums, dislodging toothpaste and various debris from last night's dinner. She smiled, thoughts of the previous evening still fresh in her mind.

'Honey, Don't forget it's parent evening tonight.' She called through the adjoining door.

An audible moan came from the en-suite bedroom.

'Harley's expecting us both, so try not to get tied up with work, okay?'

'Yeah, yeah.' Charles Fleisher rolled over in the bed onto his back and sat up.

The sunlight streamed through the window, which Narla had already opened to fend off the beginning of the day's intense heat. Charles massaged away the early morning fatigue from his face, sweeping back his dishevelled mousy brown hair. Narla walked into the bedroom, naked from her shower.

Charles admired his wife's body as much as when he first saw her naked.

Narla laughed and playfully threw the towel at her husband, all suburban happiness with no dark undercurrent. Charles leapt out of bed and grabbed his wife from behind. She enjoyed the sensation of his bare skin rubbing against her own.

'Hey, I thought you had enough of that last night.' She turned and immediately felt how excited Charles had become. 'Obviously not.'

She pushed his powerful frame away from her and he over-dramatically fell backwards onto the bed. His hands reached out and grabbing her arms, he pulled her on top of him.

'I've just showered.' Narla only slightly protested.

TWO

Leroy studied the pictures for hours. He searched through files on missing persons. He was wearing the face of a man that had spent too much time delving through the minutiae of boring details of boring people's lives.

'I think our break is only going to come when we find the body. The savagery of the killing…the mutilation, the killer wants us to be aware of his existence.' Rick broke the silence.

'Power games?'

'Something like that.'

Leroy looked at the photographs. 'D'you have a theory?'

'Curiosity, that's all. This guy really is pulling our chain.' Rick continued. 'Sending us the photos.'

'There might be clues here.' Leroy grinned

'He likes to play games.'

'Yeah, one big power game. The more we look at this, the more we might learn about him.'

'Ring Lia, it's going to be a long night.' Rick settled back in his chair.

'Shit man! Lia and I were goin' out tonight. She's gonna kill me and you're responsible. By morning you're gonna be looking for another murderer.' Leroy strolled away, tutting his disapproval. 'I need a holiday from this dump.'

'Harley really is an asset to this school, Mr Fleisher.' The grinning form tutor smiled flirtatiously at Charles. She crossed her legs, allowing her skirt to fall open briefly, exposing long tanned legs. Charles could smell her. The bitch was in season. Miss Fuller made no apology nor looked even faintly embarrassed. She stared into his eyes and pulled the skirt back to modestly cover her legs.

Narla coughed indignantly. 'Do you think she's making progress?'

Charles thought she was.

'Oh, most definitely.' Miss Fuller's southern drawl placed her somewhere between Missouri and Mississippi, what the 'Narla Fleisher's' of this world would have branded poor white trash, three or four decades ago, and even now only met at PTA meetings and on daytime soap operas. Mind enemas for the non-working classes.

Narla was impressed by Miss Fuller's simple beauty, her long, fine, sun bleached hair, her body, with only the merest hint of a tan, her smooth, moisture holding skin, wrinkle free and unblemished with a pair of green eyes to die for. Narla imagined a school full of pubescent boys with permanent hard-on's.

'Harley is top of her form in most subjects. She is a very bright young girl. Her maths still needs some work, but even here she has excelled against this time last year.' Miss Fuller continued

Charles looked across the hall at his daughter, Harley was sitting with a group of friends they were laughing and chatting the way ten year old girls do, with feverish excitement, possibly about the latest hunk boy pop group or an exchange of fashion tips which will come back to haunt them in future years.

Harley broke from her conversation briefly to look up and wave affectionately to her father.

Charles smiled back.

Later in the evening, Narla cornered Charles in a quiet moment. 'Miss Fuller wants to fuck you.'

Charles laughed. 'Do you blame her?'

Narla snorted. 'You smug bastard.'

'I love it when you talk dirty.' Charles continued to mock his wife, enjoying the frisson of the moment.

'Did you think she was attractive, I know I did?'

'Sure, if we ever have a son I'll send him here.' Charles pulled his wife closer. 'Seems our daughter is the school genius, though that's not surprising with our genetic pool.'

'Hey, Mr Modesty, be careful or we may have to widen the door frames.' Narla leaned up and kissed Charles gently on the lips.

Three

'Please, please don't hurt me. I promise I won't tell anyone, if you just let me go.'

Stephen England was lying face down on a mattress that smelled of car oil and stale urine. He was tethered by rope to his wrists and ankles. He was naked with his legs and arms spread-eagled, tied to the corners. He didn't even know if anyone was in the room with him or how long he had been there. He had slipped in and out of consciousness for three days, losing track of time. The black canvas bag over his head allowed no daylight to pass through and if it did, it would only confirm that he was alone in the dark. He listened for a reply, waiting to hear some confirmation, any confirmation that he wasn't alone. Silence greeted his plea, a silence that only heightened his fear. If he shouted would *he* come back and if *he* did, that would mean more pain, more humiliation, but what if *he* was gone, maybe somebody would hear him, come to his aid.

Stephen began to cry, the frustration of his predicament overwhelmed him.

The resonance of the heavy metal door opening suddenly focused his mind, the sound sharpened England's senses in a way that he really wished wouldn't.

Leroy crawled into bed at four thirty am; his mind was too unsettled for sleep, disturbing images from the Polaroid's infiltrating any resting moment.

'I hope she was worth it.' Leroy's girlfriend, Lia, said in the best sarcastic voice she could muster at such an unearthly hour.

'Nah, she don't do that thing you do with your tongue.' Leroy joked. He lay on top of the sheets, the sticky heat wrapping his body like a honey laced shroud. Unable to sleep, he watched daylight transcend from night. The few hours until Lia rose seemed like a lifetime. Leroy sat watching the ceiling change hue as the light filtered through brightening the paintwork. All the time he was thinking. The morning solace concentrated his mind perfectly, until the trill of the alarm broke his train of thought.

Devoid of light and disorientated in time, Stephen England found himself wishing for death. The last time *he* was here was the worst. The most painful, the most degrading. England tried not to think of the humiliation of being raped, urinated on, sodomised with everything from a beer bottle to a wire brush. The pain of the latter bringing blissful unconsciousness.

The door clanged open again and fear paralysed Stephen. Hands roughly turned back the black canvas hood on his head, exposing Stephen's mouth and nostrils. The rank smelling fetid air smelled fresh when free from the confines of the coarse hood. Fortunately, he could not see the hammer that smashed his teeth, shattering them and turning his gums to a bloodied pulp. He felt the second blow, but was unconscious by the third.

The sensation of his head being roughly jerked back woke Stephen. He immediately gagged on the blood in his mouth and coughed, spitting out blood and teeth into a mass gooey puddle on the mattress in front of him. His tongue tried to access the damage, pieces of pulped gum flapped loosely inside his mouth.

He screamed. 'Kill me now…please.' But it was unintelligible. Just a bloody gargled sound as his tongue pushed against air and gums.

There was a blinding flash, followed by another, then another. A voice whispered. 'Smile…you're dead.'

Four

Some things you never get used to. Paedophiles, child victims of murder, rape and sodomy; Brittany Spears singing, the phone ringing in the middle of the night. All of these things disturbed Georgina O'Neil, but tonight it was the phone that disturbed her most. Her hand automatically scrabbled for the phone receiver in the dark. The shrill of the ringing was obscenely loud in the quiet of the night. She wanted to quieten the noise before the dead awoke; sometimes it's just too late.

'This better be good.' She lifted the phone to her ear. 'Hello?'

'Agent O'Neil?'

It was a little after one o'clock in the morning, within two hours she would be on a plane flying south from Maryland, throwing up for the best part of the journey. Turtle Island...She had never even heard of it.

Jo-Lynn Montoya peered from under the bed sheet. 'Tell me it's Saturday.' Her voice has a raspy croakiness to it, brought about by the heat of the night.

'It's Thursday, hon.' Rick answered.

Jo-Lynn's sleepy face emerged into daylight. She squinted, allowing a gentle introduction to her eyes. Eyes that were as deep brown as her skin, her hair was dyed from it's normal black to a lighter brown and had been straightened with the help of a perm. The style softened her natural African-Caribbean look to a more Western-European look. A concession to fashion, and reluctantly; acceptability in a predominantly white Anglo-Saxon area.

Rick bent down and kissed his wife good morning. 'Hi, hon.'

'Don't you *Hi, hon* me. You missed Ray's match last night. He's as mad as hell and I ain't far behind him. We moved here to spend more time with Ray. He needs his father now more than ever.'

The recollection of his son's semi-final basketball play-off caused Rick to groan aloud.

'You know I wouldn't have missed it, if it wasn't for something really important.'

'I know, but *you* try explaining that to an eight year old boy.'

'I'm in the shit.'

'You got it.'

Rick took a deep breath. 'Did he win?'

'They lost by four points and he missed three baskets, two were penalties. You can wake him up.' Jo-Lynn sat up, her cream coloured floral print silk nightdress clinging to her body with a mixture of static and perspiration. She looked hot in more ways than one, though her body language warned him that for the moment, her body was going to be one playground that was out of bounds as a punishment; at least for today.

Rick stood up, dressed only in his white Calvin Kline shorts; Jo-Lynn secretly admired his toned, well-kept body, as he put on a pair of jogging bottoms.

'Be gentle with him. He cried himself asleep last night.' Jo-Lynn added.

'Make me feel great.'

Rick left the room and headed for his son's bedroom. He opened the door quietly and peered through the gloom. Ray was submerged beneath a light summer quilt. Posters of Michael Jordan adorned the wall. Attached behind the door was a mini basket ball hoop, the sponge ball he used to slam dunk was tossed on the top bunk once inhabited by his older sister, Jordan.

Rick sat on the bed. His son started to stir.

'Hey champ, how's thing's?'

A bleary eyed boy sat up and hugged his father. 'Hi, Dad.'

'I'm sorry I missed your game last night.'

Ray looked up. His brown eyes huge and forgiving. 'I'm glad... I stank.'

'I hear we have to work on your penalty shots.'

Ray smiled, embarrassed. 'Yeah.'

'We'll get out in the yard at the weekend.'

'Promise?'

Rick crossed his heart with his index finger. 'Promise.'

The telephone rang and Jo-Lynn called her husband from the bedroom.

'Gotta go champ.'

As he walked down the hall, Rick couldn't help but feel that he had let his son down. The sad truth was that he had.

Jo-Lynn had the phone to her ear and was talking to the caller when she saw Rick approaching. She cut her conversation and handed the phone straight to him. 'Here he is now.'

Rick took the phone; it was his chief, Norman Fusco.

Within twenty minutes he was behind the wheel of his Chrysler heading for Cape Gardeau. Someone had dragged up a body while fishing.

The roadblock and road closed sign heralded to Montoya that he was at last in the right vicinity. Murder victims cause 1.9% of traffic congestion, suicides 2.7%. The queue of cars ahead told him he was close. It was an hour's drive from his home so Rick was surprised to see Leroy LaPortiere's Volkswagen parked in the temporary make shift car park, which in normal times was the picnic area.

He parked alongside and headed out, up a hill, over toward the wetlands guided by a police officer's directions to where the body had been found.

LaPortiere was up to his thighs in water, wearing an overlarge pair of fishermen's waders. Rick recognised the tanned balding head that belonged to his boss, Norman Frusco. Frusco was standing on the drier bank by the marsh. Frusco waved recognition to Rick.

Rick acknowledged Frusco before shouting to Leroy. 'Hey, Leroy, mind the gators.'

'Very funny, Rick. Why don't you get your black ass in here?'

'You know I can't swim, otherwise...' Rick's sentence trailed away, noticing that Leroy's attention was firmly on events behind him.

Rick turned to see a young white woman, late twenties he guessed, dressed in a smart burgundy skirt and matching jacket, white blouse and Wellington boots.

Georgina O'Neil clumped over the brow of the hill and headed straight toward Frusco.

Her hand was outstretched to greet Frusco. Before she was within range, they made contact. Her grip was firm and the shake vigorous.

'Captain Frusco.' Georgina introduced herself. 'Agent O'Neil. My people informed you of my arrival.' She said as matter of fact, not debate.

Her hair was jet black, stylishly cut but more for practicality than fashion. In the field she had learned it paid to be pragmatic rather than vain. Her eyes were blue and lit with spirit, her skin Celtic white, inherited from her Father.

'Where's the body?'

'Over by the bank.' Frusco walked with Agent O'Neil down the incline. 'Did you have a pleasant journey down here Agent O'Neil?'

'To be honest, Captain, I can't stand planes they make me air sick. I would have driven but for the need to be fresh at the scene.'

They stopped by the body, which was encased in a bodybag.

'I gotta warn you; fresh is not a word I would use to describe the body.' Frusco crouched down and unzipped the bag. He leaned backwards as the aroma of decomposition wafted up.

Agent O'Neil held her breath, and then exhaled before breathing through her mouth. Some agents used tiger balm to keep the stench of putrefaction at bay; Georgina would have too but for an allergic reaction. The pungent aroma of rotting flesh permeated in to the air. O'Neil could taste the corruption.

'Where's the guy who found the body?'

Frusco looked around, spotting the fisherman on the bank side. 'He's over there…feeding the fish'

O'Neil turned and saw the man spewing the contents of his stomach directly into the river.

'Lucky fish.' O'Neil watched the heaving body of a man dressed in fisherman's garb with waders up to his chest. He wore an army camouflage jacket open to the waist, exposing a matured beer belly that strained the cotton material of his Budweiser tee shirt.

Rick moved down the bank side to talk with Leroy, some twenty yards away from Frusco and O'Neil.

'What do you make of that?'

'F.B.I.' Rick looked on as Agent O'Neil crouched down joining Frusco; she hitched her skirt up slightly, allowing herself to balance effortlessly.

She eased the body bag open.

'Phew! Quite a mess.' A bloated, swollen head greeted her, his skin was a grey, blue colour. The hair on his chest and around the genital area was matted with algae. There was a large tear in the stomach where the fisherman who found him had accidentally hooked into, but there was no blood, just loose flapping skin lying over exposed intestinal tissue.

'Looks like he's been fish food for some time. Vermiculation evident.' O'Neil scanned the body.

'Teeth and tongue removed, his genitalia has trauma, though I think that's mostly Gator related. These jagged marks here?' Her latex gloved finger probed and lifted serrated folds of skin where the victim's lips once were. 'These seem pre-mortem. See how uniform they are. It's almost as though the victim's lips have been cut off.'

O'Neil was zipping up the bag and telling Frusco to ship the body to the morgue for an autopsy as Montoya and LaPortiere arrived.

Divers continued to swim around the shallow marshlands; some policemen, dressed in waders like Leroy's, fished around with their hands, searching the silt bed.

'Agent O'Neil, May I introduce you to my two leading investigators on this case. Detective Rick Montoya and Detective Leroy LaPortiere.'

Rick smiled and offered his hand. He enjoyed the firm contact of Agent O'Neil grip through the latex glove she was wearing. She pulled at it and snapped it off to shake Leroy's hand. Leroy grinned like an imbecile, pleased to be one up on his friend and partner. The first to make physical contact with her flesh. Such little matters were all a part of a long playing game between the two men.

'Gentlemen, I am here from the FBI Behavioural Science Unit to help build a profile of our perpetrator.' She held up her hands. 'I am not here to tread on your toes or undermine any aspect of your work or the investigation. I think this manner of co-operation will best be suited to working together to achieve our common goal, i.e. catching Charlie Madman. Any questions?'

Leroy was rubbing his nose but secretly sniffing the perfume transferred from O'Neil's hand during their introduction. 'Is that Clinique?'

Georgina looked Leroy coldly in the eye. 'I think its rotting dead man.'

Rick allowed a smirk to spread across his face.

'Good, first things first, where can I get a beer and what's the best motel in the area that falls within a $50 a night budget?'

Five

She was expecting the knock at the door. One beer, a shower and a change of clothes later, Georgina O'Neil was ready for a hectic briefing session, even though it was late in the evening she felt it would give a good opportunity to become aquatinted with Detectives Montoya and LaPortiere. The air conditioning unit crackled and hummed annoyingly but it did at least alter the air quality to something more like that of her native Virginia. She pulled the door open and stepped in to the oven like furnace of a Missouri summer night. LaPortiere greeted her and walked with her to the car. Montoya was driving. She climbed into the back seat and was surprised when LaPortiere joined her.

'Things have been happening since this afternoon.' Leroy said 'It would seem our friend has already taken his next victim.'

Rick briefly looked over his shoulder and joined the conversation. 'Stephen England; reported missing by his girlfriend. He hasn't shown for work for six days. It might be co-incidence but nothing ever happens here. Nothing and now this.' He turned around and settled into his seat before starting the car. The Chrysler's tyres spun slightly on the shingle car park drive before gripping and pulling away; moving away from Turtle Island and back onto the mainland and Missouri.

'This may be the break we need,' O'Neil said 'unless he's had a change of heart, at some point he'll have to dump the body. So who was the John Doe we pulled out of the river earlier?'

'Still a John Doe, there's no local report of anyone else missing.' Rick replied, as he turned right onto the freeway. A large bug splattered against the windscreen, a small explosion of blood and green goo. 'But it's only a matter of time.'

'The preliminary autopsy report came through the system earlier tonight.' Leroy fished through a black folio bag and pulled out a folder, which he handed to Agent Georgina O'Neil.

The car sped along the highway passing thick wooded forests and wetlands. Georgina read the document. The two men continued the journey in silence both of them lost in concentration.

The car doors echoed as they shut in the near empty car park. Night staff was down to a minimum and what police vehicles remained were out on the streets patrolling. They took the lift up to the third floor where Montoya and LaPortiere shared an office.

Rick opened the blinds to allow the view of the city into his office. The night sky cast deep red with a few ominous looking clouds hovering overhead.

LaPortiere opened a small fridge. 'Beer?'

The fridge was one of the few concessions allowed for officers of their rank, one of the few luxuries that was always appreciated, there were no pretences about not drinking while on duty, the heat made it a pre-requisite. O'Neil and Montoya both nodded acceptance. Leroy threw a can to Rick and fished through his desk draw for a glass for Agent O'Neil. He took out a straight beer glass and opened the ring pull on her can.

Before he could pour, O'Neil replied 'It'll be okay from the can.'

Leroy smiled. 'Right on.' and passed her the can, which she immediately put to her lips.

'How do you put up with this heat, it's so ...muggy.' She gulped at the liquid then put the can down. 'Right gentlemen lets get to work.'

The smell of fresh bread baking assaulted Charles Fleisher's nostrils the moment he entered the house. There was the sound of talking and laughter coming from the kitchen, homogeneity painted in a thick syrup of emotions. Charles followed the enticing sensations, walking down the hall and turning the corner, where he found Narla and Harley in the kitchen

'Hi babe, come on in.' Narla beckoned her husband into the kitchen. Charles smiled, walking over to his wife; he kissed her, his usual greeting, warm, passionate, unaffected by his daughter's presence.

'You're drunk.' Charles noticed the nearly empty bottle of Muscadet on the worktop.

'Very nearly,' Narla smiled. 'but extremely happy.'

Charles breathed in. 'The bread smells nice.'

Narla sipped as she spoke. 'It's one of mother's Irish recipes, Harley's making it, I'm...'

'Supervising.' Harley chipped.

'Harley.' Charles greeted his daughter, he moved back to his wife, holding her by the hips.

Narla noticed a small speck of blood on Charles face. She wet her finger and wiped it away.

'Blood.' She explained

'Must have cut myself shaving.' Charles rubbed over the area with his finger then turned his attention back to his daughter. 'Come here short stuff, where's your greeting for your old man.'

Harley ran and embraced him, wrapping her legs around his waist and her arms over his neck. She placed a slobbery kiss on his cheek, covering the area just cleaned by Narla.

'So, you're baking bread, hey?'

'Uh-huh, Mrs Fuller set each of us a task for domestic science, I got baking bread.'

Harley smiled one of her heart-breakingly beautiful smiles; smiles that are designed to be extinguished by adulthood. Charles kissed her lightly on the lips. 'You are going to be a real heartbreaker honey, now give your old man a squeeze.'

Harley hugged her father tightly as she could, before being lowered to the ground.

'Better check your bread?' Charles patted Harley's bottom as she walked to the cooker.

'Mind now, it's hot.'

'Okay, daddy.'

'I'm going to shower, hon, then I'll come back down to entertain you lovely ladies.'

Narla finished of her glass of Muscadet. 'Don't be long now.' She watched her husband as he walked away.

Even though the world looks quiet and safe through your windows, you never know what is really happening out there…in the world. You know that there is pain and suffering but it's easy to ignore as long as it keeps a discreet distance, yet all the time you fear that it is going to walk right up to you, tap you on the shoulder and say. 'Excuse me, but may I have this dance.' Somewhere a file was being transferred via a modem from a computer to another computer miles away, via three different continents, and fifteen servers. This file was an image, a solitary image. A photograph of a man about to die, a man about to breathe his very last breath. And this image was about to change everything.

Excuse me, but may I have this dance?

Firefly's whizzed by, landing on the hollow reeds that grew from the rivers edge, the sound of crickets vigorously rubbing their hind legs, and the mellow scent of honey-suckle filled the air. Narla sat with her back resting against Charles chest; She continued drinking the wine, and was now subdued. Harley had long since gone to bed. The two of them sat watching the evening turn to night. Narla, unwilling or unable to move.

Charles had lit the outdoor candles that ran down the garden to the picket gate. A dog barking somewhere across the fields from the other side of the riverbank the only other sound apart from the gently moving river, the quietness and tranquillity of the moment soporific. The wine was taking it's effect on Narla, Charles never drunk to excess and was as sober as ever. Narla let the evening wash over her.

She tried to focus her thoughts, rarely had she felt so relaxed, so tired. She lifted the glass to her lips, her arm weighed a ton and the effort required just to lift it almost wore her out. Narla's eyes began to close; Charles felt her head grow heavy against his chest, then fall gently to one side.

Charles lifted Narla and placed her over his shoulder. She only mildly protested and felt the odd sensation of being carried upstairs, but was too tired to care let alone protest. Charles laid her on the bed, unzipped the cotton dress she was wearing and gently lifting her, managed to pull it off. During the summer she never wore a bra just plain cotton briefs. He scooped her up and held most of her weight cradled in one arm, while his other arm pulled back the sheet. Charles lowered her to the bed. From the bedroom window he looked out across the garden at the rising moon.

'It's ten thirty, I think we should call it an evening soon.' Georgina said realising that the plane journey down from Washington was catching up with her. 'So lets review before I totally flake out. All we know about this latest character, Stephen England, is that he went missing six days ago.'

'Yeah, his girlfriend reported him missing earlier today.' Leroy offered. He leaned back in his chair and supped the last of a can of beer.

'Seems it was not unusual for him to go walkabout a day or so, so when he didn't arrive home Tuesday, she didn't think it unusual. By Wednesday she was a little concerned, but his diary had him driving for a meeting in Chicago. My kinda town.' Rick cribbed the information from his notes.

'Has this man never heard of planes?' Leroy was genuinely astounded that anyone would ever want to drive the distance.

Rick referred back to his notes said, 'Phobia, he was scared of flying.'

'Needless to say he was a no show in Chicago, and then we get a phone call from his girl.'

'And *The Bulls* were playing too. Ray would have loved to have seen that.'

'You're a Bulls fan?' Georgina asked trying to catch a rare insight in to the detective's private life.

'Used to live there. My wife says I spent more time watching the Bulls than with her. I might add in my defence that, that was only true *during* the season.'

'And Ray is?' Georgina prompted Montoya.

'My son.'

Leroy groaned. 'Oh my God, he's gonna get his pictures out, I just know it.'

Rick opened his wallet and offered Agent O'Neil a photograph of his wife and son; she leaned across the table and took it, pulling another photo with it. She studied the first picture.

'He's a very handsome boy, you must be proud.'

'Just like his Dad.' Rick joked.

Leroy feigned being sick in the waste paper basket.

'Your wife is very beautiful.'

'She is.' Rick said with more than a little pride. 'She worked for the district attorney's office in Chicago. Now she shares a legal practice in Springfield, on the Island.'

Georgina looked at the second photograph, another family shot of the Montoya's but with an extra member. 'Oh, you have a daughter?'

Rick leaned forward and took the pictures from her. 'That's ...Jordan... named her after Michael Jordan... she's dead.'

'Oh I'm sorry, I didn't mean to pry.'

Rick remained quiet about the details. Georgina knew not to push.

'Okay, lets get on.' O'Neil said after a suitable break.

Rick and Leroy sat back in their chairs; they were as fatigued as the F.B.I investigator.

The fridge was empty; each of them having consumed three cans of lite beer, the daily allowance. An empty Pizza carton lay discarded save for a few crumbs and two dried pieces of Pineapple due to Leroy's dislike of the fruit.

'Our killer is probably white; though we are not precluding people from other ethnic origins at this stage. Male; probably mid-twenties to mid-forties. Although the preliminary autopsy shows anal trauma we must not assume he is homosexual. This is a man who wants to be in charge, raping his victim is, I think, a part of show of strength, not a sexual predilection.'

'Is that why a rubber was used, to avoid actual contact?' Leroy was trying to formulate a mental picture of the killer. 'There was no trace of semen, only latex residue and lubricant.'

'Partially.' O'Neil nodded. 'We cannot assume that the anal trauma is caused by penile penetration. This is probably the result of a prolonged attack using foreign objects.'

Leroy leaned forward stretching his aching back. 'Maybe he thinks this is safe sex.' He said sardonically

'He also didn't want to leave any semen, anything which could be used to trace him. So we can assume that maybe he might have some sort of criminal record or may have had a D.N.A swab taken at some time, although again this is purely speculation. Something…some trauma which happened to him is probably what is motivating him now.'

'Must have really pissed him off.' Leroy said. 'One dead and one missing is quite a statement.'

'Harboured grudges fester, it's usually better to vent your anger when you are initially aggrieved.' O'Neil sat back in the chair and rubbed the tension away from her neck.

'Again, this is a sign of repression which is now coming to the fore. He is probably quite intelligent. Research and history shows most multiple killers have an above average Intelligence Quota, many have no fear of God or religious belief though conversely there are a few examples who believe that they are doing God's work. Because all the victims are male so far, I think we can assume that he has no grudge against women.'

'No Oedipus complex, *that* makes a change. If he's not homosexual and gets along with women, then maybe he's married?' Rick offered.

'That's not uncommon; in many cases spouses have no idea of their husband's activities. Records show that some murderers often have a wonderful sex life. These attacks are not sexually motivated, this is purely to do with power, it's almost territorial. The male asserting himself.'

'Well, I think I have to assert myself now.' Leroy said standing up. 'Otherwise Lia is going to assert her foot into my black ass.' He cricked the knots out of his neck.

'Early start please gentlemen. I too have a home to get to, and the sooner we catch this guy, the sooner I get to see it. 8am here?' Agent O'Neil lifted the files and shuffled the papers, tapping them on the desk, before slipping them in the folder. 'Could I have a copy of the Polaroid's of the victim, Detective Montoya?'

'I think if we're going to be working together for some time then formalities could be dropped.' Rick smiled and passed O'Neil the photographs.

'Well, you can call me Georgina.' Georgina smiled back and offered her hand.

'Hello, Georgina.'

'Hello, Rick.'

'Before we go, I need the bathroom, could you point me in the right direction?'

Rick opened the door and pointed to a door adjacent. 'Go through that door, along the corridor and it's at the end, just before the elevator.'

'Thanks.' Georgina O'Neil picked up the folder and her small handbag and headed out toward the toilet.

'Call me Rick.' Leroy teased his partner.

Rick smiled. 'We'll, it's an improvement on the latex handshake.'

Narla moaned a slight protest, more of someone who was being slightly annoyed than anything else, but she was in too much of a slumber to wake. Charles shifted his knees around Narla's ribs, the mattress shifted slightly to support his weight. He called her name, the reaction was next to nothing. Then placed his hand against her face and stroked her cheek. She didn't flinch. He ran his hand down her neck, encircling it briefly with the span of his hand, his touch light, enjoying the sense of power he was holding. He opened his hand and let his palm rest on her breast bone, feeling the rise and fall of her chest as she breathed the breath of someone in a deep, deep, sleep. His hand moved side ways to the left, his fingers trailing lightly over her erect nipple, before moving on to her right breast, cupping the small breast, enclosed under his hand. Laughing to himself, Charles wondered what she would make of it if she was conscious now. How she would react if she woke and found him straddled over her. Both of them naked. The temptation to have sex with her was unbearable. A thin trail of semen had leaked on to Narla's stomach. Charles entered her, she was dry but it seemed to add to his excitement, he moved inside her gently. He moved back and forth very gently, lubricating her with both of their juices until he came. Narla moaned as his hot semen rushed inside her, but she did not wake. He climbed off her. The bed rocked gently, still she did not stir. Charles slipped on his jockey shorts and put on his white towelling robe, then picking his Polaroid camera up from the dressing table, took a photograph of Narla, laying naked on the bed. He pulled a thin white cotton sheet over Narla, the semi-transparent material clinging erotically to her. He took another picture and left the room. Charles waved the photos in the air impatiently, prompting the images to develop faster, a smile forming on his lips as the silver halide image formed. As he walked down the hall, the door to Harley's bedroom opened and a bleary eyed Harley stepped out rubbing her eyes.

Charles slipped the Polaroid's into his pocket and placed the camera on an occasional table, which held one of the six telephones house strategically around the house.

'Hello cup cake, what's wrong?'

'I had a nightmare.'

'Did you darling?'

Harley nodded. 'Can I kiss Mummy goodnight?'

Charles crouched down to her eye level. 'She's asleep, you wouldn't want to wake her up, would you?'

Harley shook her head. Charles picked her up and threw her over his shoulder, a squeal of delight emitting from her tiny lips. Charles carried her to her bedroom and plopped her onto the bed, before tickling her unmercifully. Laughter and shouts of delight filled the air until Harley pleaded for mercy. Her legs and arms thrashed trying to push her Father's fingers away from her. Charles pulled the quilt up over his daughter. 'Ssh, you'll wake mommy.' He put his finger to his lips bent forward and kissed Harley's forehead, she responded by kissing his lips. Her lips were cold and over wet, her arms clung around his neck and she hugged him tightly.

'I love you, cup cake.' He kissed her lips gently and almost immediately she closed her eyes to go to sleep.

Six

To Stephen England it was just a voice in the dark. He did not know who his kidnapper was; he did not know the man who had inflicted terrible pain on his body. He had never met the man whose incessant ramblings he had to endure for hours, between bouts of physical and sexual assault. It had just been his misfortune to be in the wrong place at the wrong time. Oh, what he would do now not to have worked late that night, what he would give to have left with Lorraine, his secretary. What he would do now to live his life to the full, as if every day were his last. But he didn't leave. He carried on working. Stuck at the computer, transferring and swapping files with other *collectors.* Now all he wanted was to die.

'He' hadn't been there for ages. Maybe, Stephen thought. 'This is to be my fate, left to die alone in the dark.'

Infections were beginning to set in to Stephen's wounds in his mouth, buttocks and internally. His own faeces an enticement to the flies. His wounds an invitation to the nest of maggots laid there. He pulled at the ropes using what little strength he could muster. The knots cut in tighter re-opening the raw skin. The pain was of little consequence. England screamed and pulled and screamed and pulled and screamed. He didn't know if it was his imagination, but the rope around his right wrist seemed to have gained a little slack. He stopped moving and concentrated all his effort, energy and thought on the one loose rope. If he could have seen the damage to his wrist, he would have stopped. The skin has ragged away, leaving the tip of his wrist bone exposed. He let his arm rest against the mattress; then gave an almighty jerk, followed by another, and another. Pain was replaced with hope. The canvas hood over his head started to restrict his breathing. His actions grew more laboured. The oxygen content in the hood dropped and was replaced with carbon dioxide. Images flashed through his head. The beginning of pain induced, oxygen deprived, hallucinations. He tried one last tug at the rope and to his surprise his arm came free, then he passed out.

Rick dropped Georgina back at her motel and finalised the next day's agenda before setting off to take Leroy home. Leroy and Rick talked on the short drive. Rain started to splatter on to the windscreen and the low rumble of shifting clouds above warned of a turbulent night ahead. Rick shifted the gear stick in to fifth, and turned on the wipers, the rain smeared like grease, temporarily obscuring his vision. Leroy now in the front passenger seat sat back and closed his eyes, confident of his partners driving ability.

'So what do you make of Miss Frosty Pants?'

Rick glanced at Leroy briefly, before returning his attention to the straight road ahead. 'I think you're pissed because she hasn't given you the green light.' They both laughed, knowing it to be true.

'You know something really bothers me about this case, we'll be able to ID the body real easy so *why* does he give remove the teeth and lips?'

Leroy stared ahead unfocused. 'Not only does this guy not expect to get caught, he's so sure of himself that he gives us enough information to build a case that he must know would involve The F.B.I. It don't make sense?'

'D'you think he has a grief against the Feds?' Rick slowed the car down and turned right in to a small road, which housed two tiered wooden structured houses.

'I don't know... killers seem to operate to their own agenda. Maybe he wants to spice things up by adding a chase element. Who knows?'

The car pulled to a halt outside a large wooden house, the main structure painted white with a small lawn that led slightly uphill to the porch. A light was burning in the main room. Leroy smiled. 'Lia's waiting.'

Rick watched a bolt of lightning light the sky in the distance. 'Storm's coming.'

The car wipers swished away the rain, which was now pounding tympani of sound on the metal roof.

Lia was curled up asleep on the sofa, tired of waiting for Leroy to come home.

The sound of thunder rumbling seemed distant and remote to Stephen England as he lay in the dark. He had no idea how long he had been unconscious and barely any idea how long he had been conscious. His mind had snapped into sharp clarity like the click of a switch. He moved his arm and began to remember. He was able to wriggle his fingers, lift his arm; move his hand. He fumbled for the edge of the canvas hood and started to pull it up, the coarse roughness of the material rubbed painfully against Stephen's swollen lips and mouth. He tugged it over his mouth, the effort sending sharp sensations of pain to his wrist. All the time he tried to remain focused, keep his concentration. One last tug and...darkness. The room was black. Despondent, Stephen lay there, hoping his eyes would soon adjust, but there was no light for them to adjust to. He began pulling at the rope, trying to get some slack so that he could pull his other hand free. Time in this void was meaningless but it took Stephen a further exhausting hour of pulling, tugging, and manipulating until quite suddenly and without warning his other hand slipped from its restraint. Stephen England sat crying tears of joy for ten minutes hoping he was only minutes from freedom. He shuffled backwards, trying to sit up and free his ankles; excruciating pain ran through him. Raw and open festering wounds protested against the sudden movement. The knot appeared to be some sort of slipknot, the more that he pulled against it, the tighter it constricted, much like a noose. England fumbled with the rope, his fingers slow and painful, but the ropes eventually slackened and he was able to pull one foot free and then the other. Again, the sheer effort exhausted him. Closing his legs together caused him to cry out, agonising pain mixed with the lack of use, bringing further unwelcome sensations. Still laying on his front Stephen England pulled himself forward to the edge of the mattress and he tried to stand. He crawled forward, waving one arm ahead of him, trying to feel out any unwanted obstacles, until his palm jarred off a wall. He pulled himself up using the wall for support and leaned awkwardly using his shoulders. His fingers searched for a door or light switch as he rolled against the walls. The relief felt when his thin bony fingers felt the square plastic mount with it's oblong rocker switch was as great as when earlier he freed his hand. The light blasted in his eyes, sending him reeling, falling to his knees. The hard floor jarring through his frail body, England's hands automatically shielded his face trying to block out the light that he was so anxious to see. Slowly he peered through tiny slats in his hands made by his fingers. He could see the mattress, he tried not to focus on the indignity of the excreta but tried to take in as much information as his disorientated mind could absorb. There was a hammer, the one -he guessed- used on his mouth.

Over in the far corner was a wooden workbench, with an electric drill and a jigsaw.   There was a roll of rope, still wrapped around its central core and many other tools. In the centre of the floor was what looked like a trap door. A set of dumb bells and weight's were lying against the far wall. To his right, a flight of stairs rose upwards. Stephen tried to stand; he hobbled back to the mattress and picked up the hammer. The weight dragging his arm. The fatigue-sapping effort of lifting it almost overwhelming. The stairs beckoned, sirens of freedom, hypnotising him. His foot stepped on the first runner and using the handrail he dragged his body up, ready for the second step. The door at the top grew closer and closer. His heart quickened, releasing endorphins blanking out his pain and giving him fresh impetus. He stood at the top and pulled down on the handle, now breathing hard, the air passed through his battered mouth, the sharp sensation of pain increasing his awareness. The door was locked. Rage quickly dispelled disappointment as he swung the hammer at the metal handle. The hammer sank in to the soft aluminium. He hit it again and again, until the handle folded to pulp. He crashed down on it one final time as the handle clattered to the floor. He pushed against the door; still it would not budge. His renewed energy began to drain and along with it any hope of escaping, he threw the hammer with frustration at the door making a small indent to the metal surface. Stephen trudged down the stairs, on the verge of giving up. He glanced at the workbench and spotted the array of power tools. The drill or the jigsaw would surely make easy work of the door, but he needed a long extension lead to reach it. He pulled open one of the drawers inset in the workbench. Twenty or so Polaroid photographs slid forward. Violent, graphic images of terrible deprivation. A variety of young men tied naked to the mattress, suffering obscene degradation. Implements of suffering and torture inserted into them. Close-ups of their bloodied toothless mouths. The reality that he was not the only victim began to dawn to Stephen, that he was only one of many unfortunate young men, started to sink in. The one fact that he was certain of was that if he didn't escape he was dead. The next set of photo's confirmed this to him. The blank staring lifeless eyes, the pale bodies, some missing hands or feet, one with entire limbs cut away, lying in a pool of his own blood. Panic and revulsion now began to motivate him, fearful that at any moment *he* could return. England threw the pictures, scattering them through the air, across the floor and opened the next drawer. Tin boxes housing nails and screws and various oddments but no extension lead. Stephen slammed the drawer shut, instantly regretting his action as the vibration jarred through his right wrist, he grabbed it with his left hand trying to sooth the pain and block out the image of the porcelain white bone exposed through the raw skin. One more drawer to go, the bottom one. Deeper than the other two; this offered hope. England opened it, closing his eyes through fear of disappointment. The fear confirmed; the drawer was empty. Despair swept through him. He looked around for the lead but there was no sign. With the door no longer an option for escape, Stephen's eyes fell upon the trap door in the centre of the floor. The door looked as if it opened into something below. He wandered around the room, bouncing off the walls looking for a control panel or lever to open the hatch. His eyes darted around the room. Hanging on the wall opposite was a bright orange, nylon rope, and just behind in a recess was a lever mounted on a panel. England grabbed the rope with renewed energy and headed for the lever. He pulled down with all of his strength using his left hand. The effort nearly lifting him off his feet. The lever protested mildly and then eased downwards. Stephen looked at the trap door. It was open....

The storm moved closer, the rain heavy, almost tropical.

Roads started to flood, torrents gushing down, filling storm drains taking debris, stones and earth with it.

Lightning flashed illuminating the bedroom. The air was heavily charged with electricity and sticky.

The voice inside grew louder.

'It's time, do it now!'.

The relentless splatter of rain against the window enforcing the voice, hammering home the message. Thunder exploded overhead, followed swiftly by the electro static crack of white phosphorescent lightning. *He* sat down. *He* was the one with the power, *he* was in charge, they couldn't question him. *He* made sure that they couldn't question him.

'Now' *was* the right time.

A klaxon wailed, the distress warning nearly sending him into apoplexy.

Stephen England sat on the edge of the abyss, his legs dangling into dark space, suddenly the sound of a wailing siren added impetus to his escape. He could hear running water below but could not see how far it was to the bottom. He lifted the hammer and let it drop in to the blackness, waiting to hear it land. The clatter of metal against concrete followed by a splash a second or so latter assured him that the drop was no more than fifteen to twenty feet. He secured the rope from the banister and let it fall in to the hole where the trap door was. Stephen guessed that there was at least forty foot of rope, hopefully, more than enough. It sounded like the end of the rope hit the water but he couldn't be sure. With no flashlight, no clothes and time running out until *he* returned, Stephen knew he had no option but to grasp the rope using what little strength he had left and try to climb down into the chasm. With a deep breath, he launched himself forward and hoped to have the strength to support his own weight. He swung sideways bouncing off the wall and held on tightly while waiting for the rope to steady. He tried to remember the correct way to climb down a rope, curling the rope under his foot, up his leg and across his thigh, so that his foot supported most of his weight and not his weakened arms. Slowly he started to lower himself into the unknown. After about ten feet he noticed the temperature began to drop, he looked up, the light above him was now inviting, below was only darkness and uncertainty. The further down he went the colder it became, the sound of the water increased. It sounded fast, rushing. England hoped it wasn't too deep; the prospect of having to swim was not one he relished in his current state of health. He kept looking up, expecting to see *him* at any moment towering over the entrance above him. To his surprise his foot suddenly felt the water and he allowed his arms to take most of his body weight. The water was cold, but fortunately not freezing, hypothermia was hopefully not going to be one of the conditions to add to his long list of ailments. He lowered himself to his waist, his feet were still unable to touch the ground. England's arms finally gave up their hold and he sank under the water. Instinctively he took a huge gulp of air before being submerged. Even though the water was cool it had a calming effect on Stephen. It supported his body, encompassing him in a womb like protective environment. If he died now -he thought- it would not be too bad, there would be none of the pain or suffering that was the fate of the other men in the photos. His body bobbed back to the surface and the instinct for survival quickly dispelled any thoughts of morbidity. England took a huge gulp of air and started to tread the water. Lights above his head flickered on and off before finally settling and illuminating the tunnel. The question now was, which direction to go in? Forward, to the left, right or backward? Cold air blew against his face, chilling his skin but giving him the answer. Forward it was.

Something brushed against his arms it was soft, fleshy. Stephen England started to move towards the direction of the breeze. Half-swimming, half treading water. Every now and then he would stop to check the breeze. The further he went the warmer the water became, even the breeze started to get warmer.

He opened the door leading to the sub chamber under the house knowing what he was going to find, there was no point in being optimistic about the situation. The room was empty. He saw the rope attached to the trap door and marvelled at Stephen England's ingenuity and fight for survival. He stood over the open chamber and gripping the rope lowered himself into the sewer system below. His journey down quicker and more assured than England's. Lights above flickered on, motion sensors detecting a mass greater than that of any sewer life than normally habituated the environment. He could hear splashing further down the tunnel, England was not far away…Oh this could be fun. He would follow from a discreet distance before pouncing. Oh yes, this could be fun.

The scream that echoed down the tunnel behind England cut through to his bones. *He* had returned. The shrill sound gave his legs and arms fresh impetus, moving him on at greater speed. Suddenly there was a flash of light up ahead, followed by another and the rumble of thunder. The current became stronger, making it harder for him to progress.

The lightning exposed the walls of the tunnel; Stephen figured he was in an underground river or storm drain. The entrance -his exit- was only fifty yards away.

Seven

Gillian Dace shifted the Subaru Jeep to fifth gear. Her husband, James, was sitting next to her asleep, as was her two-year-old son, Robert. They had been driving all day and it was her two-hour shift behind the steering wheel. It was their annual vacation, two weeks with Jimmy's mother – Barbara - on Turtle Island. Jimmy's mother and father moved there 15 years ago. George Dace -Jimmy's father- had died eight years ago and they have been holidaying there ever since. Now with little Robbie, it seemed even more important to have solid contact with Barbara. During the sixties it had been a place where artist's, writers, painters, photographers had flocked mainly to experiment with drugs in a certain amount of peace but a solid community had built up over the years and now it was more like a small insular outpost full of travellers who found their own Nirvana and decided to settle. It was a close-knit community with a real sense of purpose. Gillian loved it there and so did Jimmy; it was only their jobs that kept them from relocating and settling there. Gillian turned the wiper speed up a notch, the blades increasing their speed as they travelled across the screen vainly trying to keep her with a clear field of vision. She looked at the illuminated clock, only ten minutes of her shift left before Jimmy could take over the driving duties for the last stretch of the journey.

'Wake up, Jimmy?'

She took a hand off the wheel and shook his arm gently. He mumbled, moaning. Gillian shook him again. 'Come on, Jimmy, it's near your turn.'

Jimmy opened his eyes and blearily looked out at the rain lashing against the windscreen. They passed a signpost, it was illuminated by the Subaru's headlights.

Turtle Island 15km.

'Sure you don't want to carry on driving? We're nearly there.'

Gillian took her right hand away from Jimmy's arm and rubbed her neck. 'I'm bushed, kinda finding it hard to concentrate.'

'Okay, I'll just ring Mom, tell her we'll be there in half hour or so.' Jimmy lifted the handset from its cradle and dialled his mother's number.

'I hope she's still awake?' Gillian said looking at the clock; it was nearly two o'clock in the morning.

'She'll be awake...Yeah, hi mom...yeah, we're nearly there...just passing Campbelltown...Okay...see you soon.' Jimmy put the phone back in its plastic house attached to the dashboard. 'She said she hopes we're hungry.'

Gillian groaned, visions of a spread fit for an army flashed through her mind. The only thing she felt at the moment was tired and ready for her bed. She slowed the four-wheel drive down and pulled it to a halt on the verge.

'I'm not getting out in that.' Jimmy protested looking at the rain.

'Okay, shuffle over.'

The two of them made a simple manoeuvre look complex as they collided in the middle of the car, collapsing in a heap of laughter. After a few minutes they were back on the road, with Jimmy behind the wheel. Gillian opened a can of cola and sipped from it.

'Music?'

Jimmy nodded

Gillian passed her husband a can of coke while she opened the glove compartment and fumbled through a pile of CD's, until her hand rested on the one she was searching for. She opened the cover and popped the CD in the stereo. Iris Dement started to sing, filling the confines of the vehicle with her lyrical personal stories of America's heartlands and her life. The songs seemed to strike a chord of recognition with both Jimmy and Gillian.

Jimmy took a quick swig from the can.

'JIMMY!' Gillian's scream rose above the engine noise and the CD, waking her confused child and shocking Jimmy. She grabbed his arm 'STOP.'

James instinctively slammed on the brakes as the figure of a naked man, half bent over, holding his knee with his left hand and his right hand outstretched appeared through the blur of the rain. The ABS system stopped the wheels from locking but the vehicle skidded, veering wildly sideways on a blanket of water. Jimmy fought with the steering wheel to straighten the car. The Subaru aquaplaned as the tyres tried to form a bond with the tar macadam surface. The figure did not move, showed no sign of wanting to move. Gillian covered her eyes, fearing impact. They were almost on top of the man. Jimmy felt the tyres finally grip the road, he pressed down harder on the breaks, hoping the hydraulic system held up under the pressure. The wheels started to squeal a protest as the car finally shuddered to a halt but not before bouncing hard off the body of Stephen England, knocking him onto the grass verge.

'Oh my God.'

Jimmy stared at the naked figure of Stephen England., His hands were still gripped, white knuckled to the wheel. 'Shit...I never saw him....I'

James leapt out of the car, the rain immediately drenching him. Gillian turned around to comfort her son and found that the contact with him comforted her far more. She unbuckled the restraints and lifted the child from his seat. Gillian watched through the rain soaked windscreen as James took of his jacket and placed it over the man's body.

Gillian started singing to Robert to quieten him. 'Hush little baby don't you cry, mama's gonna sing you a lullaby.' In the background Iris Dement was singing about the death of her father.

Jimmy shouted through the driving rain. 'I think he's dead.'

He watched from the sanctuary of the darkened countryside. England was lying motionless in the road. Some poor sap was running around like a headless chicken panicking. He sat on the damp earth watching, willing the driver to get back in his car and leave. He could not help but laugh at the irony of the situation. Someone up there must really have it in for England. The driver returned to his car and used the cell phone. *He* waited until the ambulance arrived before getting up, turning and heading back towards the house.

Eight

The ringing sound was distant and annoying. The noise grew nearer and louder, until it registered in Agent Georgina O'Neil mind and her eyes snapped open.

Darkness.

The ringing again.

She scrabbled around the bedside table until her hand fell upon the phone.

'Yeah?'

Her eyes focused on the green illuminated LCD display. 4-35am. Somewhere down the other end of the line Leroy LaPortiere was imparting news that had just been relayed to him. His own mind was just beginning to assemble the facts through the fog of sleep. She placed the phone down and was tempted to crash back into the world of dreams and sanctity of darkness. Night was still pushing against the curtains.

Georgina sat on the edge of the bed watching the local TV station's news bulletin, while waiting for the kettle to boil. Her motel room was small and basic but at least provided the luxury of an electric kettle, two cups (one chipped.) and one saucer, some small packets of instant coffee, sugar and milk powder plus a portable television, which she had turned on, along with the kettle. Part of her morning ritual was to drink at least two cups of coffee before showering, because it was still the middle of the night Georgina saw no point in changing her routine. As she poured the boiling water onto the grouts that were meant to be instant coffee, her attention was drawn to an article on the TV. She saw Gillian Dace being interviewed.

'Well, we had been on the road all day driving to Turtle Island to see Jimmy's mother and all of a sudden I saw what turned out to be a naked man standing in the middle of the road, right about here.'

Gillian moved to a spot to indicate the exact position. *'He was kneeling in the pouring rain. Looked to Jimmy and me, like he had been beaten badly. He had no teeth, his mouth was a mess...I'm sure we didn't do that to him.'*

The phone rang again, interrupting Georgina's concentration. She answered it, turning the volume of the television down with the small remote handset.

'Hi Leroy... yeah I know, I'm watching. How come your boys didn't warn her away from the media?'

'It would seem Jimmy's mother works for the local TV station.' Leroy was sitting in his kitchen munching through a slice of buttered toast, talking to the phone via it's built in speaker, while simultaneously trying to shave with a battery shaver.

'What's that noise Leroy?'

Leroy chomped another bite of toast. 'Breakfast.'

'No, the buzzing.' Georgina said puzzled. 'Don't tell me if it's personal.'

Leroy laughed. 'I'm shaving.'

Georgina stretched the telephone lead to grab her coffee and swallowed a mouthful. 'How's is he, the TV says he's alive?'

'I've been on the phone to the hospital, the doctors tells me that he's in a coma. By all accounts he was a mess, unlucky to be alive.' Leroy replied.

Georgina swirled the grouts in the bottom of her coffee cup.

Leroy continued talking. 'Rick's down there at the moment assessing the situation. Making sure that even if he blinks we get to talk to him.'

'I think we should talk to...' Georgina read the name of the television. 'Gillian Dace and her husband. Can you meet me here?'

'No Prob.' Leroy put the phone down.

Nine

'Turtle Island is an oddity, 350 square kilometres, population somewhere in the region of 5,500. One of the last areas in the state to enter the union in 1822 a full year after the rest of Missouri.'

'Don't forget to tip the guide.' Leroy leaned to his side and joked with Agent O'Neil.

Rick ignored his partner and continued. 'The Island had a governor up until three months before joining the union; he was skinned alive by what we endearingly term *Native Americans* nowadays. This act was the primary reason for Turtle Island falling in line with the rest of the constitution. During the depression in the nineteen twenties, people moved away in search for jobs but a bootleg whiskey operation flourished during prohibition. The island had a large black community until the fifties. Mainly descendants from the slave trade, they all but left now. In the sixties it was a haven for artists, hippies and drugs. Now it's an idyll set among a mad world, populated by middle class wealthy whites and intelligent blacks, I'm pleased to say.'

'Yeah, that means Rick lives here.'

The Chrysler carried on down the decline toward the area known as Freemantle, Turtle Island's Main Street. One multi-plex cinema, eight restaurants including one Korean, one basic American, a small shopping mall and an edge of town general store. No police station, one small legal practice and a realty office. O'Neil tried to absorb her surroundings. The area looked affluent, there were no groups of kids hanging out, although it was still early in the morning. In many neighbourhoods where O'Neil had been called to work, it was not uncommon to find groups of delinquents bunking school and terrorising the locals almost any hour of the day. Montoya swung the Chrysler round a sharp left bend, causing O'Neil to fall against Leroy. The car then climbed up a sharp gradient, pushing them both back into their seats. The road was now almost dirt track, another sharp left past two derelict houses, wooden in construction, flaking paint and broken side panels. O'Neil noticed a mill house in the distance.

'This area is mostly owned by the realty office in the town.' Montoya offered 'Plans are to revitalise the properties and sublet them to tourists. You'll be pleased to know planning permission has just been granted to start the byway.'

'Amen to that.' O'Neil bounced around the back seat, her body battered by the dirt road. 'So where do you live Rick?' She asked more to pass the time than real interest.

'Near town. Jo-Lynn gets phobic if she can't see some concrete.'

'I'll get phobic if I don't see some tarmac soon.' Leroy said looking pale.

They bounced along for another five kilometres before joining a stretch of tarmac and what appeared to be a better-preserved area of the Island. Montoya halted the Chrysler outside a large detached brick built house. There was a Subaru parked on the drive and a 'M.R.TV.' van behind. The double garage next to the house was open and residence to two more vehicles.

The home of Barbara Dace was comfortable; Georgina O'Neil guessed they paid well in TV land, even if it was only the local station. They were welcomed into a large hall. There was a staircase slightly adjacent to the front door. Barbara Dace put her fingers to her lips.

'Ssh! Gillian and James are just finishing a spot for the next bulletin, hopefully it'll be going network.' She whispered. 'Follow me.' Barbara led the three detectives through the hall into the kitchen. 'That's better, we can talk here.'

O'Neil opened a calfskin wallet and showed the silver haired woman her identification.

'That's all right dear, I know who you are, I received a phone call from Captain Frusco. He's a nice man…a rare breed these days.'

The words nice man and Frusco were rarely used in the same sentence and brought a smile to both Leroy and Rick's lips.

'Oh my, look at my manners. Would you like drink?' Barbara Dace continued. 'Tea or coffee, or maybe something cold?'

Rick was going to decline but when Agent O'Neil immediately accepted a coffee he reconsidered and asked for one too, Leroy plumped for tea. As Barbara filled the kettle the detectives sat on kitchen stools placed away from the walnut breakfast bar. 'I'm sure they won't be too long. Is there anything you'd like to ask me?'

Georgina stiffened her back and sat upright on the chair. 'I presume the police officers warned you against doing that last night?'

'Of course they did.' She smiled patronisingly. 'I am a reporter Ms O'Neil, this is what I do for a living. It quite simply is the biggest thing that has hit our little island in nearly two hundred years, probably ever will. Anyway, I preserve the right of my family to the Fifth Amendment, besides James and Gillian are being paid $15,000 each for their story.'

Rick interrupted. 'Their story? There is no story. All they did was run over some poor bastard.'

'Oh, but were that true detective. If there was no story then what are you doing here and what is the F.B.I. doing here in my kitchen? It is no secret that a killer may be at large in our small community here on Turtle Island.'

O'Neil, LaPortiere and Montoya looked at each other with a certain amount of surprise.

'Don't try denying it. As soon as the story went out on the air this morning the television station had phone calls from six families reporting missing people plus one person claiming to be the killer.'

'Yeah, an probably five UFO sightings and Elvis Pressley about to jump from Independence Bridge.' Leroy tried to dilute Barbara Dace's reporter's intuition. He studied Dace. She was of average height, slim and fashionably dressed; silver-haired. He guessed she was in her late fifties. There was no attempt to dye her hair but she had it cut short with a modern style that was attractive and flattered her features. Her skin was slightly weathered, tanned with a few wrinkles, though again not unflattering. She filled three cups with hot water, the liquid turning various shades of brown. 'I hope you don't mind instant.' She stirred each cup, adding milk as she did so.

A tall, black haired man appeared at the kitchen door. 'We've finished, Barbara.' He smiled at the detectives then returned to the lounge.

'John Keller, my cameraman.' Barbara explained. 'You can see James and Gillian now.' Barbara walked in to the lounge. 'You can bring your drinks.'

James and Gillian were sitting on a sofa; two camera lights were on stands in front of them, extinguished. John Keller was putting away his Camera into a large canvas bag. Rick and Leroy pulled chairs from under the dining table and sat in front of Gillian and James.

Ten

He lifted the weights above his head, his arms straining, pumped up, veins standing proud, sweat pouring down his face. He held the weight steadily, swaying slightly before letting it crash down to the ground. Dust rose into the air in plumes, refracting against the strong light. He lifted the dumb bells and started arm curls, grunting with each laboured exercise. His arms hurt but the pain was somehow nice. His voice drove him on warning him of the dangers. He knew what had to be done now. His thoughts were clearer than they had ever been before. Exhilaration replaced pain; flowing through his body like the blood being pumped by his heart. There could be no more mistakes now. He stared appreciatively at his body in the full-length mirror attached to the wall. Every muscle was defined, glowing with health. He placed the dumb bells down on the floor and sat on a thin mat, towelling himself dry.

'The others won't be so lucky.' He thought to himself.

He showered and dressed and read the newspaper before pushing out a further one hundred press-ups. Lunch was light, mostly fresh fruit, some poached eggs and a slice of wholemeal bread toasted on one side. The television had been buzzing with stories and assumptions about a man found wandering on the highway from Turtle Island. One intrepid reporter even managed to link the man with two out of the other three missing locals, speculating whether a serial killer might be at large in the small island community. *He* sniggered to himself, spurred on by his newfound infamy. There was a need for release burning inside of him. A wanton lust that need fulfilment.

As soon as he saw the television early that morning, Gary Clarkson knew it was going to be a busy day. He wandered through the stock room of the general store looking for maps, films, sun block, cold drinks and snacks, in fact anything that he thought might possibly sell to the curious, the morbid and the media. He whistled as he plucked items from the racked metallic shelving; every cloud has a silver lining. The door rang. A customer.

'Ma.' No answer. 'Ma.' Again.

Gary groaned as he placed the armful of stock on the floor and made his way to the shop. A man was standing at the counter, newspaper in hand. Gary recognised Charles Fleisher instantly, he was a regular, not the sort of regular that would make Clarkson rich but a steady reliable spender.

Fleisher was reading the front page.

'Charles.'

'Gary.' Charles answered but continued reading the paper, seemingly absorbed in the story. Gary did not need to ask what he was reading about. It was the talking point of the year…hell, of the decade.

'Seems we're going to be famous.'

'Seems so.' Charles answered flatly.

'Going to be quite a circus trudging through this little island.' Gary Clarkson was excited at the prospect; he looked at the headline on the morning paper, bad news for some was always good news for others.

'D'you have a packet of mints?' Charles never looked up from the paper.

'Got a viewing?'

Charles proffered a five-dollar bill. The bell to the shop rang again. Gary and Charles both watched Karen Fuller walk slowly down the shop. Gary leaned forward and whispered to Fleisher.

'Never had teachers like that in my day.'

Charles Fleisher turned and watched appreciatively as Karen made her way toward the counter. The morning light reflected around her, silhouetting her. Occasionally as she moved part of her would be exposed to strong sunlight and her skin became porcelain. She stood right next to Charles, as close as she could. Charles wanted to reach forward and touch her face. Just stroke it.

'20 Marlboro, Gary. Please.'

Gary turned his back to fish the pack of cigarettes from the racking behind him.

'I should really be quitting.' She said to no one in particular. Her hand rested briefly on Charles hand. Karen Fuller's index finger stroked the back of his hand before moving away to her handbag.

This was easy, everything was easy. *He* scanned the images one by one. The bright fluorescent tube passed back and forth over the images, the terrible craven images. Later on he would upload the images direct to his web site and then when he became confident, through a live feed and then for greater action, for greater excitement there was high quality web cams, but this was the start…the beginning. As the images were transferred via the ftp program, he sat back with a feeling of accomplishment, a sense of achievement and excitement, then he closed the program. He typed DEATHCAM.NET into his browser and there they were for the entire world to see; his masterpieces.

Eleven

T'he humidity to the morning was made stronger by the sun's desire to absorb all the moisture from the ground from the previous night's storm. Agent O'Neil unbuttoned her jacket letting it flap open as she walked back to the car. Rick was dressed in a short sleeve shirt and Leroy held his jacket draped over his shoulder. James and Gillian followed.

'It was just up here, about one hundred yards ahead.' James pointed to an undefined point in the road. 'I marked the spot by leaving a full bottle of 7up there on the verge.'

Rick stopped by a green plastic 2-litre bottle full of clear liquid, there was the temptation to open it up and drink down the whole two litres but it had been baking in the morning sun for nearly five hours.

Georgina scanned the horizon. A bank ran to her left lined with hickory trees, to the right more trees. She walked up the bank, her foot slipping slightly on the damp grass. She steadied herself, placing her hands on the bank to stabilise her body, before continuing up the small incline. At the top she asked. 'What's beyond these woods?'

Leroy shrugged his shoulders.

'Could you get a map, I've got one in my folio in the car.'

Rick had started to climb the bank, Leroy looked behind him. The cars were parked on the verge a couple of hundred yards away. He turned and slowly traipsed away mumbling to himself. 'Yez boss, ize goze and gets it for ya.'

'Hey, Leroy, bring the camera too?' Rick yelled after the detective. Leroy continued walking. 'Okay, Masser.' He passed Gillian and James who stopped at the foot of the bank by the road.

Rick called down to them. 'And you didn't see which direction he came from?'

'He was just standing in the road. But *this* side as though he had come from the direction of Turtle Island.' Gillian offered. 'He was that tired, I don't think he would have changed directions once he got to a road, though I could be wrong.' She smiled apologetically.

Leroy came running back down the road with the map in his hand. 'You're gonna like this.' He stopped and caught his breath, wiping a bead of sweat that trickled down his forehead. 'About two miles south.' He continued between breaths   ' ...is the river.' Leroy started to walk up the bank, still talking as he went. 'And a further three miles east is where...we... found the first body.'

'Do you need us? Can we go now?' James called up the bank.

Georgina nodded. 'Yes, you can go now. Thank you very much, you've been very helpful.'

James and Gillian walked back to their Suburu Jeep, the fatigue of their adventure catching up with them.

Leroy unfolded the map and pointed to the river. ' We found the John Doe here and Stephen England here.' His finger then moved along the river to Turtle Island. 'But with the information from the Dace's, we can assume the tidal flow carried Dalton from somewhere on the Island. My guess is Stephen England somehow used the river to escape, it gets quite shallow up here.'

'Shall we go for a walk gentlemen?' Georgina strode away in the direction of the river.

The trees magnified the humidity, and stole the daylight. Georgina O'Neil was silently thanking her good sense at choosing comfortable footwear as she walked through the thick forestry. Leroy hung back behind her, occasionally studying the map but mostly studying the rhythmic sway of O'Neil's hips as she walked with Rick by her side.

The forest was alive with the sounds of indigenous birds and with the humidity it felt tropical.

'Leroy?' Georgina called behind her, feeling his eyes boring into her as she walked.

'What?' Leroy replied puzzled.

'Stop staring at my ass, you're giving me a complex.'

Leroy blushed, his dark skin reddening, almost invisibly. 'You got eyes in your ass?'

'Only yours, Leroy, only yours.'

Rick turned to his partner laughing 'Oh man, you are sorely em-bar-rased.' He exaggerated the three syllables of the last word in a mock West Indian tone.

'So Rick, what made you want to become a cop?' Georgina asked between pushing back low, thick growing branches.

'I kinda stumbled in to it. There never was a master plan. Left high school graduated at college and was at a loose end. Then my dad suggested it. I can honestly say that I had never seriously considered it until then. Joined the Chicago P.D. became a beat cop for a few years then for want of a better word, *stumbled* into homicide. As I say no great plan...What about you? How does an intelligent young woman end up working for the Feds?'

'I always wanted to be a university lecturer but there was too much competition in the family, I have an elder brother who's a university professor. So I looked for another area that would be a challenge, then a friend of mine went missing...'

'I'm sorry.'

Georgina continued. 'We were best buddies for ...oh, I'd say the best part of six years. Used to sleepover, go camping together, take holiday's, you know that sort of thing. The sort of friend who only comes along once in a lifetime, even shared a couple of boyfriends...not at the same time.'

'Hey, I didn't say anything.'

Georgina briefly smiled. 'Then one day she didn't turn up for work. At first I guessed she was taking time of ill. A week passed and no word, then the rumours started, finally the police showed up. Her body was found in a dumper truck. She had been raped and strangled. They never caught her killer...I guess I'm trying to redress the balance.'

They walked on in silence for a minute before Georgina turned and asked Leroy. 'Leroy, what made you join the force?'

Leroy jogged along a couple of steps to catch up, slipping slightly on the grass. 'Me, I was a big fan of Shaft. Never saw him walking through this shit though.'

The dark moment was broken.

Her hand was clasped tightly around his. Doctors passed by every now and then, popping their heads through the door opening to check Stephen England's progress. Cara Morton had been awake ever since Stephen was brought in. She sat by his side talking to him, unable to comprehend why somebody would want to do this to her fiancée; unable to understand how someone could do this...period.

The doctors had operated on his mouth and were going to have to carry out more surgery on his bowel and large intestine, but for the time being, they kept him under heavy sedation to let his body recover from the shock of his ordeal.

By the time she had arrived at the hospital, Stephen was already in surgery. Cara looked at his face, his mouth a mass of stitches, bruised and swollen beyond recognition. His right arm was bandaged from the elbow to the wrist. He was lying on a support frame to relieve the pressure on his back and buttocks. Dr Martinez told her that 'Stephen must have had great strength of will to survive his ordeal.'

England was being intravenously hydrated and fed; various monitors were keeping his condition in check via bleeping tell-tales and electronic graphs. He slept and he dreamt. In his dreams he had still not escaped. In a corner of his mind he never would. But for now the effect of his drug-induced coma held him prisoner, his eyes darted wildly under their lids, moving left and right. The read outs on the monitors became a little more animated, scribbling informative lines on graphs. A nurse entered with a doctor and adjusted the drug feed in to Stephen's system, clouding his mind even further, sending away the demons. He started to settle again, Cara looked imploringly at the doctor.

The trees opened out into a small open expanse of grassland and the river ran sublimely past. The gentle sound of water moving within a peaceful environment. Georgina O'Neil stopped by the bank watching the current flowing toward Turtle Island.

'The river splits about five kilometres down stream and circles Turtle Island. If England came this way at night, during the storm, injured as he was, then I'm a member of his fan club.' Leroy said as he emerged from the woodland.

'How deep is the river at this point?' Georgina asked turning toward Rick.

'Deeper now than last night. Tidal flow and the storm will have swollen the level by four or five feet. I'd guess that it would have been knee to waist high last night, maybe deeper at points.'

Leroy opened the map and followed the river toward the Island. 'It could even have been lower, storm drains are pinpointed at various places near the Island to take the overflow and stop the Island flooding.'

'Can we get some boats to circumnavigate the Island?' Georgina asked

'Yeah sure, Ned Freeman runs tours of the Island by boat. I'm sure we could give him a call and get him down here.' Rick sat down on the bank. He pulled out a small cell phone from his inside jacket pocket, pressed a button and waited while the connection was made. 'Yeah, hi, it's Detective Montoya. Look we're out at the river, bout five kilometres from Turtle Island heading out toward Cape Gardeau. Could you give Ned Freeman a call and get him down here to give us one of his tours?…Okay' Rick closed the phone.

Leroy sat next to Rick and looked up at O'Neil. 'So what do you expect to find?' Leroy asked the F.B.I agent.

'I don't know.' Georgina studied the lush green countryside. The woods were some one hundred yards from the riverbank with the land between wild and overgrown. 'I just want to get a feel of the place.' She continued. She walked along the riverbank, absorbed by her surround, trying to imagine Stephen England's escape. Hot air rose from the ground, bringing drifting scents of damp earth, grasses and wild flowers to her nose. Georgina pushed back her short hair, some of it matting and sticking against the sweat on her forehead. The water looked cool and inviting. The sound of Rick's phone buzzing broke her concentration. Rick flipped the phone open.

'Yeah...Make sure Ned's stocked up with plenty of cool drinks...No. Any word from the hospital...Call us if...yeah, Okay.' Rick closed the phone. 'Ned's on his way.'

Twelve

After one hour there were two thousand hits, after four hours it was twenty thousand. He watched with relish...now he had their attention, soon the world would know his name. He stood and stretched his arms above his head. He felt restless, caged.

The shop door rang constantly. Gary Clarkson was right, Christmas had come early. Many of them people he had never seen before, all of them had a hunger in their eyes. They were all after the same thing. They were the sort of people who slowed down at an accident in the hope of seeing tragedy unfurled and splattered across the freeway. The blood-hungry, seeking ghouls whose thirst and desire for death would not be quenched until they had experienced it first hand. Gary didn't mind, he'd take their money, hell, he'd take anyone's money. Photographers, journalists, tourists, body hoppers, ambulance chasers, they were all fair game. There was even a contingent of priests, nearly stripped him out of wine. The door ran again. An old lady took her time entering. She looked frail but it was obvious when you came within earshot that she was far from delicate. Clarkson looked up from behind the sanctity of his counter.

'Afternoon Martha.'

'Good afternoon, Gary. Is your mother ready?'

'She's not going today. Says she worried about this here murderer that's been all over the papers.'

'Nonsense.' The old lady brushed past Gary without hesitation and walked through the back of the store to the living quarters. 'I lived through the war in Europe, ain't gonna let no murderer come between me and my daily swim.'

During the week the old ladies always took the afternoon bus to the mainland for an afternoon filled with swimming, saunas and shopping. Within minutes Martha was brushing Gary aside, making way for his mother. He watched their backs disappearing out of the shop.

'Have a good time ladies.' They were gone before he had finished the sentence.

Rick, Georgina and Leroy sat on the riverbank watching Ned Freeman's boat, *'The Ingénue'* move majestically, almost silently toward them.

The boat was an old converted fishing vessel about twenty-five feet long powered by a Cummins diesel engine. The maximum river speed barley tested the boat's engine. Ned dressed the part to please the punters, silver side-burns ran down his ruddy weather beaten face from his ears to his cheeks, the sort of lamb chop side burn that Elvis would have been proud of. His fisherman's hat covered the disappearing but matching silver thatch underneath. Blue eyes sparkled beneath the rim of his cap, eyes that had seen more life than most. Nobody knew his age, nor would he tell if anyone asked, but he had been around as long as most folk cared to remember.

The boat pulled alongside the bank, chugging to a slow, seasoned, halt. Ned's dog, Nemo, barked a greeting to the detectives. The small, wiry, Jack Russell scampered around the boat, his paws slipping on the wooden surface. Ned stretched his arm out and pulled Rick, Leroy and Georgina on board, his grip still powerful and firm.

'Hi, Ned.' Rick had been on Ned's boat many times, taking Ray and Jo-Lynn out on Sunday excursions and the odd holiday. He bent down and stroked Nemo who gathered excitedly at his legs. 'Hello boy.'

'So, who do we have here?' Ned asked.

Georgina showed her I.D

'F.B.I.'

'Hi, I'm Leroy La Portiere, Rick's partner.'

Ned shook their hands. The hand shake as firm and powerful as before, nearly too strong.

'Pass the map, Leroy?' Rick took the map and unfolded it. 'Can you take us on the full tour, Ned?'

'Don't mind where I take you, as long as you're paying.'

Georgina handed him a form, P114ex. 'Fill that in and send it to the address at the bottom of the sheet. Don't worry it's freepost, you'll be fully reimbursed for any expenses you incur.'

'Sheets ain't money, honey.' Ned said smiling

Rick opened his wallet. 'How much Ned?'

'Full tour could take anywhere up to four hours, I could be picking up paying customers.'

'How much Ned?' Rick repeated not particularly wanting to play the game.

'$150.'

Rick had a fifty in his wallet. 'Leroy, what you got?'

Leroy searched through his pockets. 'Forty five and some pennies.'

'Give us the forty five, bro.' Rick took the cash added it with his own then looked at Georgina.

'I gave Mr Freeman the official P114ex form.'

Rick nodded at Georgina beckoning her away from Ned. 'Look, if you don't pay the man, we don't get no nice trip up the river. 55 bucks and we are on our way.'

Reluctantly Georgina fished inside her purse and pulled out a fifty.

Rick smiled and handed the money to Ned.

'I owe you five.'

Within two minutes the boat was turned and they were heading toward Turtle Island.

Even at such a slow pace *the Ingénue* offered the detectives the chance to catch a cooling breeze on the deck. The blue grasses, tall grass and reeds that grew along the river were home to a rich variety of wildlife. Thrush and Oriole flew overhead resting in the trees and prairie grasses. Georgina breathed in; relaxing momentarily, wondering how such violence could be brought to such a quiet and peaceful place. The killer was obviously deeply disturbed but it never failed to fascinate her how that even in such tranquil idyll's the most evil acts were perpetrated. She could understand why people go off their heads in New York or L.A…but here?

'Peaceful, ain't it.' Leroy joined her by the port side of the vessel.

'You read minds too.'

Leroy looked at her, enjoying her beauty, enjoying being close to her. 'Sometimes.'

The breeze created by the boats movement flattened Georgina's hair, parting it in the centre. She tried vainly to push it back but gave up after three futile attempts.

'So, what's the story here?' She asked casually, hoping the relaxed atmosphere would enable Leroy to be a little more forthcoming about the events of the past few weeks.

'You mean the case?'

She nodded.

'Just checkin. Ain't much of a story other than what you already know.' Leroy turned and rested his back against the handrail. He watched Nemo scurry around following his master, Ned, who in turn was busying himself tidying the mooring ropes. Leroy looked into the bridge and saw Rick steering *the Ingénue.* 'I want to do that.' Leroy sounded genuinely envious of his partner's promotion to Vice-Captain or whatever they had on boats. 1st mate, yeah that was it, 1st mate. As Ned passed by walking to the stern of the boat, Leroy called to the Captain. 'I'd like to do that, drive this boat.'

Ned stopped in his tracks. '*Steer the ship*, detective, *Steer the ship.'*

'Yeah, whatever, boat, ship, steer, drive.'

Ned called to Rick. 'Ten minutes, Mr Montoya, ten minutes.' and continued with his business checking the condition of the ropes.

The Ingénue maintained its course against the tide moving toward Turtle Island.

'Kinda touchy.'

Georgina smiled, a rare event, but one that Leroy was glad to witness. 'Probably seen Jaws too often.'

'I wondered who that guy reminded me of; it's that Irish guy in the film.'

'Robert Shaw. He played Quint.'

Georgina smiled again; Leroy was hoping it was going to become a habit.

'Yeah, he was great, shoulda got the Oscar, great film. So, you a film buff?'

'I'm an only child, my dad used to take me every weekend.' The memories of afternoons and evenings spent with her father in darkened cinemas rekindled fond memories of their relationship

'You're very close to your old man.'

'Yeah. You?'

Leroy thought about his father, the relationship they had was good. Together they covered most aspects of what would be deemed a closely bonded relationship, it still would have been today had his heart been stronger. For such a large man, -he stood over 6'5'' and weighed in at 17 and a half stones-everyone thought he would live forever. He was strong as an ox and never complained of illness, bar the one day he took to his bed never to get out. 'My father was one of the best. I don't know how my mother coped when he died. I was 24 years old at the time, and had had a lifetime of memories and fun with him, but I had younger brothers and sisters. I was the eldest of five children, ages ranged from 24,' Leroy pointed to himself with both hands. 'down to eight, my baby Sis' A smile came to Leroy's face just thinking of Merrill, his younger sister.

'Your father must have been quite young when he died?' Georgina turned around and rested against the hand rail, like Leroy

'He was forty-eight. My mother had just turned forty; my father was her first and only man. She was thirteen when they met and sixteen when she fell pregnant with me. Fell pregnant isn't that such a stupid phrase. Makes you sound unwanted, unloved, nothing could have been further from the truth.'

'Your father...was he Dominique La Portiere, the centre for the Philadelphia Warriors?'

'Yeah, that was my old man, he played NBA for five years, until he busted his knee in a...'

'Coach accident. They were returning from playing the Celtics. The bus ran off the road.' Georgina searched her memory for the details.

'The driver had been drinking and fell asleep. Your dad and the driver were the only casualties.'

'You really are a fan.'

Georgina nodded. 'I saw your father play once. Long time ago when I was a little girl.' Georgina held up her index finger with her thumb closed close to it. 'Very little... I must have been around eight years old. He was great.'

'Yeah.'

Ned walked past Georgina and Leroy. 'You can see Turtle Island from the bridge. Tell Mr Montoya that you are to relieve him at the helm.'

Leroy saluted. 'Aye, aye Cap'in.'

Georgina laughed as they strolled to the bridge. For a few moments this was summer in the country, it wasn't searching for a killer or trying to find clues, it was something happy couples do. She reflected on the moment.

Leroy took control of 'The Ingénue' and steered her against the flow toward the Parlandale fork, where the river split into two, circumnavigating Turtle Island. Rick studied the map with Georgina, his finger tracing possible routes from the various tributaries that fed in to the river.

'If we take the right fork we pass the storm drains and the old mill plus a whole load of dwellings built on the river.'

'What are these?' Georgina pointed to three marks constructed across the width of the river.

'They're called the Three Wise Men. Bridges built about seventy years ago, they used to link to the mainland, they're unusable by car or just about any other vehicle now.'

'So the only way on to Turtle Island is over Independence Bridge...or by boat.'

Ned sat close by petting 'Nemo', watching and listening to the detectives. He slowly peeled an orange, cutting the rind with a sharp knife before splitting the segments revealing the fruit's soft fleshy contents. He popped a piece into his mouth, speaking as he mashed the segment to pulp. 'That's not entirely true.' Ned stood, casting Nemo to one side as he joined the detectives. Rick looked puzzled

'There are a host of tunnels leading from the storm drains, some are merely excess water chambers which drop one hundred to two hundred feet to underground rivers, but others are access tunnels used during construction.' He offered Georgina and Rick a slice of the orange, which they both took.

'Left or right?' Leroy shouted from the bridge, slowing the boat at the fork.

Thirteen

*H*e showered, dressed and read the newspaper before pushing out a further one hundred press-ups. Lunch was light, mostly fresh fruit, some poached eggs and a slice of wholemeal bread, toasted on one side. The television had been buzzing with stories and assumptions about a man found wandering on the highway from Turtle Island. One intrepid reporter even managed to link the man with two other missing locals, speculating whether 'a serial killer' might be at large in the small island community. He laughed, spurred on by his newfound infamy. There was a need for release burning inside of him. *There would be no escape this time, although even that mistake served a purpose.* The computer screen flickered and buzzed. *He* moved the mouse and the screen saver of two men torturing a boy disappeared, to be replaced by a list of names. The first two were highlighted in red, number three was flashing on and off...waiting. *He* highlighted the name with the cursor and clicked the left hand button on the mouse, the screen changed once more and a picture along with the resume of his next victim appeared.

Charles Fleisher sat behind his desk in the Office of Bradwell, Shawsted, Fleisher; Real Estate Agents. As a senior partner of the small Island business, Fleisher's association with the company stretched over ten years since joining the then fledgling company. It took time until he was trusted enough to be brought on board as a partner. As time passed so did the elder partners, some into retirement, some relocated to busier areas where the action was faster paced and some to the Green Pastures Memorial Gardens outside Campbelltown, Charles though was happy where he was. He liked certain things to be predictable. Fleisher felt good, pumped up. A lunchtime workout always managed to get the adrenaline flowing, if he was true to himself (which he often was) he felt horny. The day was quiet. He didn't have an appointment until 4-30 in the afternoon. Three and a half hours to kill. Charles flicked through the roller deck, stopping at Harley's school. Visions of Karen Fuller, Harley's teacher, formed in his mind. His fingers were dialling the number before thoughts of the consequences were able to stop him. It was nearly one. She'd still be at lunch. Two minutes of hanging on the line listening to a Phil Collins medley were rewarded with the sound of her sweet voice on the end of the receiver.

'Hello, Miss Fuller.'

Karen Fuller didn't take much persuasion before succumbing to an offer of dinner, she never did. Charles knew where it would lead, exactly where it always led. He put the phone down and breathed deeply trying to control the surge of adrenaline. Sometimes he felt as though he would explode. His mind went back to Narla and thoughts of last night. He phoned Narla. 'Hi, darling. Got to work tonight...probably til 11 or so, hopefully gonna tie up selling the Kingsley plot...Yeah , put the champagne on ice...I love you too. See ya later hon.' He put the phone down, it was that easy. The deception made him buzz.

The Kingsley plot was just about done and dusted. At four thirty he would meet with representatives from 'Harper Pellum' at five he would be shaking hands and taking his usual ten per cent rake off on top of their normal fee. *Easy money.*

Beep! An incessant tone registered Stephen England's every breath. A tiny pulse monitored his life in static green flashes on the small screen above his head. Cara Morton sat patiently by his side, holding his hand and talking to him. The doctors told her that under the medication he had been given, Stephen was likely to remain unconscious for some time. They wanted to give his body time to repair and his mind more importantly time to adjust.

Dr Martinez opened the door to the private room and poked his head through the gap.

'You still here?'

Cara looked at the Latino doctor. 'I want to be here when he wakes.'

Martinez pushed the thin wooden door open further and entered. 'You know that could be some time, you really ought to get some rest.'

'No, I'm alright, anyway this is hardly strenuous.'

'Not physically.' The doctor walked toward the bed and stood beside Cara 'But mentally it can be quite exhausting.' He rested his hand on her shoulder as a sign of compassion for her plight and gently squeezed. Cara appreciated his strength and encouragement, and knew the doctor was right. She had been at Stephen's side for almost ten hours and apart from the occasional bout of activity on the monitors, which the doctors assured her was nothing to worry about. 'Probably nightmares'. He had not moved or shown any sign of waking. Cara yawned and stretched. The sterility of the room and the temperature were beginning to have an effect.

'Maybe I will have a break, get a coffee.'

Dr Martinez picked up Stephen's chart and noted his body temperature and pulse rate before signing his initials and logging the time. 'Tell you what, we have a private room for relatives, it has got a bed and a telly, picks up cable.'

'Wow, cable hey?' Cara mocked, smiling for the first time in ages.

'There's no one in there right now, why don't you get a coffee and something to eat and rest in there for a while.'

The prospect of a few hours rest appealed to Cara.

'And you'll call me if Stephen wakes?'

Dr Martinez crossed his heart with his index finger. 'The very minute he wakes, I will personally call you.'

'Okay.'

Ned pulled *the Ingénue* to a halt by the side of a quay and leapt onto the wooden platform with impressive agility. He tied the ropes to a mooring ring and called his dog. Although equally aged, Nemo leapt with similar impressive style.

'That completes the tour, you've circled the entire island.'

Georgina O'Neil felt disappointed. She didn't know what she expected to find but felt somewhat cheated as to gaining anything new, except for a greater acquaintance with the lay of the land. She had studied and noted the location of houses, both empty and occupied. She had made notes of possible places that were more likely to be where she would choose to, if that way inclined, kidnap and torture people. Singular, isolated properties close to the river. There were three in particular that she wanted to have a more detailed look at. Two of them, Rick informed her, were vacant; the third occupied by Chris Hurley, owner of the local radio and television stations.

It was four o'clock and the sun was still high in the sky, Rick and Leroy were both of the impression that they had wasted a day; that the world was moving apace without their presence. This was not how they liked to work, but Frusco insisted they co-operative with O'Neil fully. There were worse ways of spending an afternoon other than sightseeing around Turtle Island with a beautiful woman.

'Your cars should be about half a mile beyond the trees.' Ned said, watching the landlubbers disembark. Georgina had phoned ahead and asked Frusco to get some deputies to move their vehicle to their new location, just by Independence Bridge. Rick thanked Ned; Leroy swigged on his bottle of coke and saluted the captain and his dog.

The trees Ned pointed at were Oak and Tupelo, the wild grasses that ran to meet them were waist high and peppered with wild flowers. Agent O'Neil nodded a curt goodbye to the smiling seafarer and was already strolling through the maize fields toward the thick clump of forestation.

'Frosty.' Ned informed Nemo. 'That's why I don't like women.' He rubbed his faithful friend's head. 'Only whores and dogs.'

Nemo barked approval.

Fourteen

It was a rare moment, the house was totally silent. Narla Fleisher sat drinking black coffee enjoying the tranquillity. Harley was visiting friends after school and Charles was working late, so she contemplated an evening reading by the river with a bottle of wine and a Korean take-away from the village. She breathed in quietly, listening to her heartbeat, the sensation of beginning to drift away made Narla sit up sharply and shake her head. God, she'd have to go easy on the wine tonight. One glass, two at the most. Narla stood and gulped down the last of her black, sugar free, coffee and decided that she had to wash her face to shake of the after effects of last night. As usual, it was only now, some nine hours after she woke that the full force of her hangover kicked in. She made her way to the bathroom, where she threw cold water over her face, enjoying the coolness from the oppressive mugginess that pervade the long hot days. Water from her face ran down on to the silk blouse she was wearing.

'Shit.' She grabbed a towel and dabbed it, the droplets formed tiny circles on the fine material, which unless immersed in water would dry to a stain. Narla quickly undid the buttons and filled the sink before immersing it, she watched the material absorb the water, slowly sinking under its mass. She envied the blouse and a cool bath now seemed a priority. With just her skirt to loosen, Narla was soon duplicating her blouse and immersed herself in cool clear water. She rarely wore underwear on really hot days, except for when Charles requested it. Some days they would meet for lunch and take a stroll in the country park or across the fields, which invariably led to them making love alfresco, the danger of getting caught by passers-by really gave Charles a thrill and her to, if she was honest. His erections always seemed harder, longer, their lovemaking more frenzied, passionate. She smiled as she lay in the bath, memories of close encounters turning her on.

The sound of a voice calling out, '*hello*', downstairs, sent Narla into a panic. 'Fuck.' She remembered that it was Friday, the groceries were always delivered on Friday and Mr Johnson would expect paying too. She looked around for a towel. 'Damn.' All the towels were used, lying in the laundry basket. She stood and let most of the water drip from her body before deciding to streak across the hall to the bedroom. She grabbed Charles towelling robe and wrapped it around herself. She quickly brushed her wet hair, slicking it back, and making sure she was not about to give the septuagenarian grocer an eyeful that would surely kill him and ran down the stairs to be greeted by his wizened features.

'Hello, Mrs Fleisher.' George Johnson smiled, handing Narla the bill for the three bags of groceries that were sitting on the floor next to the old man. Narla took the receipt from his shaking wrinkled hands, the bones around the knuckles, arthritic, stretching the thin waspish skin almost to breaking point.

'Have to be a cheque, George. Fool husband of mine's taken all the cash.' She instinctively put her hands in to the pockets of her husband's dressing gown. Her fingers wrapped around two thin pieces of what felt like card. 'Hang on a moment George. The check book is in the kitchen.'

George nodded.

As Narla walked to the kitchen she pulled out the pieces of card from her pocket. The black backing surrounded by the white border told her instantly that they were Polaroid photographs. She flipped them over and visibly staggered when she saw the images of herself naked on the bed.

Fifteen

Rick, Leroy and Georgina entered the office to find Barbara Dace waiting. She was smoking a cigarette; patiently waiting for their return. She had been there for over an hour. Barbara stubbed out the remainder of her cigarette and stood to greet the three detectives. She lit up another cigarette and pulled sharply on the long stick, orange embers raced towards her lips. Her gaunt cheeks sucked in, causing hundreds of thin lines to gather around her eyes and mouth. She exhaled a bank of blue smoke, which she directed to the rotating fan in the ceiling, where the swirling blades dissipated it. Barbara sat on one of the chairs that faced Rick Montoya's desk.

Leroy opened the refrigerator. 'Cool, the fridge fairies have been.' He pulled out a cool beer from the freshly replenished appliance. 'Beer anyone?'

Georgina raised her hand.

'Mrs Dace?' Leroy thought it only polite to ask. She surprised him by accepting. Rick already had his hand out ready to receive. As the sound of beer cans being opened filled the office, Barbara began to answer.

'This story is big.' She drew down to the filter tip, whilst pouring the beer simultaneously. 'It's the sort of story that if you worked in a major city like LA or New York comes along every other week but you'd still kill for, pardon my choice of words. But to happen here in a small community like Turtle Island, this is my one shot. I know what you're thinking; *who is this middle aged woman?*...but... something happened this morning.' She stubbed the half spent cigarette out on the rim of her beer can, letting the smoke escape from her lips as she spoke. 'I received a package to my house a couple of hours ago...' Barbara put a Jiffy envelope on the table. It was A4 in size and the addressed to Master Robert Dace in purple ink, hand written, delivered by courier.

'As you can see it was addressed to my grandson. I've advised my son and family to go back home until this thing sorts out...I think it will be safer.' She lit another cigarette.

Georgina pulled on a pair of latex gloves and opened the envelope. A videocassette fell out. 'Have you played this?'

Barbara drew hard on the cigarette. 'You see these?' She held forward her trembling hands, smoke from the cigarette was drawn upwards by the rotating ceiling fan. 'I recommend something stronger than beer before you view it.' She stubbed out the remainder and immediately lit up another.

'Mrs Dace, I'm going to have to ask you to give us your fingerprints and a DNA swab. Although I very much doubt it, there *may* be a chance that our killer may have left some incriminating evidence on the cassette or envelope, it will cut out confusion.' Leroy tried to be sympathetic asking an awkward question.

'Yeah, sure.' The smoke drifted into Barbara's eyes stinging them.

'Was there anything else, notes, messages?' Leroy was eager to view the video; he needed to make a connection with the murderer.

Barbara shook her head

'Has anyone else seen the cassette?' Georgina asked.

'Chris, that's all.'

'Chris Hurley?' Rick asked.

'Yeah.' Barbara sighed expelling a vast amount of smoke.

O'Neil exchanged bemused glances with Leroy.

'Did he make a copy of the tape?' Rick asked before downing the last drop of cool amber beer.

'I don't know, ...I mean he could have. I took the tape to his office. We watched it there. It's possible he could have ran a duplicate simultaneously.'

Georgina picked up the cassette, carefully holding it by its edges, mindful of any prints that could get smudged by her latex gloves. 'It's Showtime.'

'Should we run the tape down to the lab first for prints and analysis?' Leroy said somewhat nervous of exceeding protocol.

'That will take them the best part of two hours, maybe longer.' Rick argued 'I say we watch it now.'

'Send the envelope down to forensics, get them to check the gum for DNA.' Georgina said.

Barbara stood. 'If you don't mind, I've no desire to push it into the Nielsen's by viewing it again. Once is more than enough. Before you play it, I think I should warn you that there is a message directly aimed at the investigating team right at the end. I'll be waiting outside if you need me.'

'Go down to the second floor and get printed. It's gonna save a whole load of trouble later.' Leroy said. 'You gonna be all right?'

Barbara Dace shook her head. 'I seriously doubt it but thanks for asking. Thank God I've got a bulletin to get together for the six o'clock to keep me occupied.'

'You sure?' Georgina reiterated.

'I'll be fine.' Barbara said. She walked out of the office.

Georgina span around. 'Right, let's get it on.'

She held the tape in the mouth of the eagerly waiting jaws of the V.C.R. The tape was snatched from her hand and consumed into the stomach of the black box. The telly screen was awash with dancing static until the cassette slotted home and began to play. Montoya, LaPortiere and Agent Georgina O'Neil sat in the darkened room holding their breath.

Narla didn't know what to do. Should she ring Charles and question him? She looked at the pictures once more. Sitting on the lounge suite in the living room with a glass of brandy in one hand and the photographs in the other, she tried to understand the significance of the images. Although she was naked in one of them, she appeared to be asleep. A thought flashed through her mind. What if there were other photographs hidden around the house? Maybe there was other women?. The thought had never before entered Narla's mind during their entire relationship, it was a giant leap but the photographs disturbed her. The thought came like a sledgehammer; her mind began to think about Charles's *late* work, his long hours, and his business conferences away from home. Suddenly Narla's life was unravelling in front of her. His study and gym, that's where he'd hide anything from her, he knew she rarely entered his domain. It seemed to Narla to be the obvious choice. Charles had specially converted the old summerhouse at the foot of the garden by the river. He *'needed somewhere where he could train and study in peace'*. Narla knew the summerhouse would be locked, there was a spare key somewhere, now where was it?

Charles washed and shaved in his small but well appointed personal office suite. It was handy to keep fresh after strenuous gym sessions or other strenuous sessions with female clients. Half an hour till his date with Karen Fuller. The Kingsley deal was wrapped up as he'd expected. Charles was feeling good, he was going to give 'Miss' a night to remember? He brushed his teeth, grimacing wide-mouthed in front of the mirror, studying the two perfect rows of white tombstone teeth for unwanted debris. Dining in one of the local restaurants would be too risky, so Charles had booked a table at *Palacs*, a quiet restaurant outside Missouri in Campbelltown. He had used it many times before and felt comfortable there. The staff were discreet and the atmosphere conducive. An expensive dinner there had always brought its rewards later in the evening. Though tonight, Charles knew there would be no doubt about the consequences. Karen Fuller was the find of his adulterous life, a borderline nymphomaniac with an insatiable appetite for wild uninhibited sex, almost paralleling his own. The meal was merely foreplay, something he knew Karen would find torturous.

The door finally gave way to the pressure Narla inserted on it with a large steel screwdriver. She had pulled back on the handle with all her strength and weight, watching the steel shaft of the driver bend, hoping it wouldn't break. She no longer cared about the damage to the door. If she had to she would have used an axe to gain entry. Charles had been careful enough to take the spare keys with him. This only confirmed to Narla that he was trying to hide something. She stepped into the summerhouse. The white pitch board walls on the outside deflected the sun, making the interior cool and dark. Charles had boarded over the windows '*to help keep the temperature down when I'm working out'*. 'Sure.' Narla said to herself. She switched the light on. A neon tube flickered. While the light was strobing, Narla imagined Charles walking toward her. A dull ache had begun to throb in her temples, she promised herself two migraine tablets when she got back in the house. She felt uneasy entering *his* domain, even though she knew Charles would be home late. *'Was that another of his little secrets, was he meeting secretly with someone? They could even be making love right now.'* Her mind conjured thoughts that were unimaginable.

Weights were scattered around the floor. His desk was over the far side of the room. Slowly, she walked toward the old oak writing bureau. She held on to the screwdriver; the bureau would be locked but not for long. Narla tugged at the writing flap with her fingers just in case it had been left open, but its refusal to budge confirmed the need for the screwdriver. She wedged it behind the lock at the top of the flap near the centre and pulled back sharply. It gave way with a lot less protestation than the door. The flap bounced down. Papers, pens, a book dealing with real estate law, some property sheets from his office, advertising Turtle Island's hottest properties and a photograph of Narla with Harley were the desks only contents. Narla began to wonder if she was being paranoid or oversensitive. Her period loomed, which always made her a little edgy, and now with her head aching she began to think there was a perfectly innocent explanation for the Polaroid's. 'No, No, No!' Narla shook her head. She rocked the bureau back and forward frustrated by the lack of incriminating evidence. Something inside a secret compartment jingled. Narla shook the desk again. There were *always* secret compartments on old writing bureaus. Her fingers ran along the flat seam edges of all the joinery, hoping to find a false panel or tiny door. She never heard the footsteps behind her, creeping closer, stealthily, so as not to be heard, so intent was Narla at finding out the key to her husband's betrayal.

'Mum?'

'Jesus.' Narla turned her heart racing. 'Harley, you nearly scared me to death.' She clutched the screwdriver to her breast, feeling her heart pound fiercely inside her chest and her head. Harley stood still, looking admonished, holding her school bag.

'You never came to collect me.'

'Oh my god, is that the time? I'm sorry *Lamb.* I kinda got caught up in things. Did Mrs Pearson drop you home?'

'Yeah. Is it alright if I go to Leigh's for dinner tonight, Mrs Pearson said I could sleep over.'

Narla looked at her daughter. 'Of course it is.'

Harley turned to run away, but before leaving kissed her mother and said. 'Thanks, you're really cool.'

'Don't forget to bring some clean clothes for tomorrow and ring me?' Narla called after her daughter who was already half way up the garden heading toward the house. She heard Harley reply 'Yeah, okay.' before her daughter disappeared inside the house. Narla sat against the wall and slid down until she was sitting on the floor. She felt physically sick and mentally drained. Her nerves were jangling. Her arms pulsed and felt heavy. After a few moments, she had calmed sufficiently enough to resume her search. Narla rocked the bureau again, trying to pin down the exact source from where the noise was coming from. Lattice carved wood shelves that housed paper and envelopes took up two columns, which ran from the right and left of bureau, separated by an arch. Narla felt around the arch. Two thin joinery lines ran to the back of the bureau. Her fingers pressed upwards and there was a small click. She pulled her hand away and in her palm was a little wooden drawer with two keys rattling around the bottom of it. She lifted the keys from their sanctuary and looked around the room for somewhere to fit them. Her heart beat a little faster; expectation and trepidation were implicit pals. She could feel the pulse in her head throbbing. Thud, Thud, Thud. Sweat tricked down her back, her palms were clammy. The heat seemed to engulf the room. There was no obvious door, maybe it wasn't in the summerhouse; maybe Charles liked to keep his secrets far away. She pulled the bureau away from the wall. Set into the wall behind the desk was a small square door about twelve inches by twelve. It had been painted over to blend in with the rest of the room's decoration. Narla inserted a key in to the tiny aperture and twisted it. The key jammed, the door did not budge. She jiggled the key, freeing it before inserting the second key. This time the key span in the barrel and the lock pulled back, releasing the door from its frame. There were two shelves in the tiny cubbyhole; on the floor of the cupboard were three rows of videotapes. Tiny black mini cassettes, each labelled in Charles handwriting. H in bath, H in bed, H with C, H mouth C, T and G C-h-tel, M C-h-tel. The list went on. Narla counted over twenty of the miniature videocassettes. On the shelf above were rows of neatly stacked Polaroid's, and a small cash box, metallic green and locked. Narla picked up the cash box and shook it. She placed it down on the ground next to her knees and took a pile of the photos, so neatly arranged.

As she thumbed through them her entire life began to crumble. She had steeled herself for her husband's betrayal but nothing prepared her for the images on the tiny squares of paper. As she looked at her husband defiling their daughter, it slowly dawned on her what the 'H' might be on the videocassettes. Narla's stomach turned. 'Why didn't Harley say something to her? How could *she*, as Harley's mother, not have noticed what was happening to her daughter?' Narla took the videos marked 'H' and left the summerhouse. Her legs, both laden and jelly-like at the same time. For a moment Narla thought she was going to be sick, her vision blurred over.

The tape was even worse than Barbara had indicated. It was evident that she was shocked by the contents, but nothing, not even Dace's warning about the message at the end of the tape, prepared the detectives for the pure evil savagery played out for their 'entertainment'. Georgina O'Neil sipped from a cool glass of water. Her throat felt tight and her stomach was queasy. Leroy closed his eyes and held the bridge of his nose between his forefinger and thumb. He breathed deeply. 'Man, I've seen it all now. Don't worry, Rick; I am sure the department will pull all of the stops out to catch this sick son-of-a-bitch. Jo-Lynn and Ray are safe.'

Rick sat staring at the TV screen. Shock was painted on his features with a broad brush. 'I…I…what has he got against me?'

'Guards will be getting there right now, Rick. Even as we speak.' Leroy's hand on Rick's shoulder did nothing to control Rick Montoya's deep sense of ill ease.

'How does he even know I exist?' Rick said.

'The threat is non-specific, Rick. We are just taking precautions.'

'He'd have to be mad to try anything now. He would know we would post troops all over your house.'

Rick turned to face Leroy. 'Tell me, Leroy, did they look like the actions of a sane man?'

Leroy's silence amplified what everyone in the room was feeling.

Sixteen

Norman Frusco rocked back and forth on his office chair. This was not the sort of job for a man with his patience, then again what was? Captain, was the moniker on the door but it hardly began to tell the story of twenty-five years service to the Missouri police. His once resplendent head of hair was now a memory, his slim athletic figure gave way to middle age spread; the curse of *promotion* to a desk job, though he still liked to get out in to the 'war zone' occasionally. The war zone, used to be the city, used to be areas of deprivation, where tough living forced tough choices on to people with no choice. God, he and his wife had talked about retiring to Turtle Island. Frusco watched the news on the slim portable T.V that was sandwiched between a row of unread books and the trophy his division won three years on the trot for the highest arrest and conviction rates. The trophy was now tarnished but then again what wasn't? Barbara Dace was looking at him from the tiny TV screen, reading the *major story tonight*. In Norman's mind, she was not tarnished. Norman Frusco during honest moments with himself, found Barbara Dace very attractive, he always had done. They went way back far too long for Frusco to care to count. It seemed that Norman and Barbara were always destined to be on parallel courses that were designed to cross. He pressed the intercom in front of him.

'Where's Montoya and LaPortiere?' he let go of the switch before anyone would be foolish enough to reply.

It was eight o'clock and it had been a very long day. All Frusco wanted to do now was go home relax with a beer and take a month off. The chances of taking a month off were as remote as was relaxing, unless of course he got totally drunk. As his finger depressed the intercom switch again the door to his office opened, Frusco looked up. It was Montoya and LaPortiere.

'Don't you guys ever knock; I could have been having a private moment. Sit down.'

Frusco neither had the patience nor the will to further this line of conversation, knowing that for every jibe LaPortiere would repost with two, at least.

'Where's O'Neil?'

Rick sat. He answered his boss. 'She's still analysing the tape.'

'Yeah, the techno boys have got their computers and microscopes out.' Leroy chipped in.

Frusco leaned forward on his desk. 'Rick, I want you to know that we have already placed an armed guard outside and inside your house. Ray and Jo-Lynn are perfectly safe.'

'What I want to know is, how does that sick freak-show know anything about me?'

'I don't know but he seems to have made a link with you for some reason, but we can use that to our advantage.' Frusco tried his best to sound confident; truth was he was worried.

8-55pm. Another long day. Agent O'Neil removed her reading glasses and rubbed her eyes. The static flicker of the television was causing her pupils to hopscotch. She scooped the cold remnants of fried chilli beef between her chopsticks and force-fed herself. If the job didn't one day kill her, the diet certainly would. She longed for home, a cool bath, and a massage. The thermometer read a sticky 74 degrees that in actuality felt more like 94. She rewound the tape, now a copy, the lab boys were scrutinising every micrometer of the original. She decided to watch it one more time before leaving for the 'comfort' of her motel room. The tape whirred and locked. Georgina pressed the remote. The screen went blank, before an out of focus image of a man sitting tied and bound to a chair slowly sharpened. A figure dressed in black walked behind the bound man, his face was not visible. A hand removed the carpet tape that had been stuck across Max Dalton's lips, ripping roughly from his bloodied mouth. His mouth was a mess. The teeth had been crudely hammered out, the lips split, swollen and pulpy.

Off screen the killer spoke one word.

'Read.'

Even this had been electronically disguised. *He* pushed the bound man's shoulder. The words were barely audible spewing out of the mashed orifice that was once a mouth. Agent O'Neil turned the volume up and began to write down Max Dalton's last words.

'By the time you receive this; things will have progressed. I have a plan.' Max is interrupted by the sound of the killer laughing; again it has been distorted, making it sound more grotesque. All the time *he* is pacing back and forth in the background. *He* tells Max to 'Continue.' and strikes the back of Max's head with a stinging blow using his knuckles.

'Mr Max Dalton is already...' Fear is etched so deeply in Max's eyes that a shiver runs up Georgina's spine even though this is the seventh time she has viewed the tape. 'Dead.' Dalton's voice quivers. 'And now

Detective Montoya, you will be looking for...' Max Dalton stops reading and breaks down crying. 'I can't...I can't do this.'

The killer walked around to face Max Dalton, *his* face still remaining out of shot. Slowly he began to beat Dalton's body with a Hammer. The blows were carefully aimed at the bound man, designed to break a rib, shatter a collarbone, chip his elbows, pulp an eye socket. Georgina looked away from the screen as the hammer pummelled into Max Dalton's groin. His screams distorted the sound recorded by the microphone. The screen went blank. Georgina guessed Dalton must have become unconscious at this point. When the image came back on, the date recorder on the bottom left hand corner of the image had moved on by two days. Dalton was still bound and looking like shit. He was crying uncontrollably mumbling his way through the rest of the message.

'And by now Detective Montoya... you will be looking for Stephen England, or maybe even...someone else...'

At first nobody saw the photographs that were carefully placed behind Max Dalton, it was only on the third viewing that Agent O'Neil noticed them, the camera briefly but purposefully focused on them for no more than a second before the tape ended. The unmistakable images of Jo-Lynn Montoya and Ray. Photographs taken of Jo-Lynn kissing Ray goodbye in the morning, as his nanny was about to take him to school. The images were sharp, though taken with a telephoto lens, probably from a car parked nearby. The screen finally went blank, fading to black. Georgina let the tape run as her mind tried to absorb the information. As she leaned forward to turn the cassette off another piece of the puzzle revealed itself.

The killer's voice rasped. 'Tell Detective Montoya, I'm changing the rules of the game.'

'You know, I feel very, very wicked.' Karen Fuller smiled. She leaned across the car seat and kissed Charles Fleisher slowly, passionately on the lips. Her tongue parted his lips and entered his mouth, probing searching, tasting, licking. Charles responded equally passionately, sucking, biting, savouring. They had parked outside one of the properties that Charles was letting and knew to be unoccupied but lavishly furnished.

Karen pulled at the front of her loose fitting dress, exposing her delicately small but pert, tanned breasts. 'It gets so hot, some times it's hard to breathe. Don't you think?' Her southern drawl tried to excuse her actions on the weather but Charles knew better. 'This does not look like the home of a real estate agent. Are you going to seduce me, Mr

Fleisher?' Karen kissed Charles again, this time she let her hand fall on to Charles groin, where she felt his already hardened penis.

'No, I'm going to fuck you, Miss Fuller.'

'Why Mr Fleisher, what would Harley say?'

Charles knew the answer to that, but somehow thought that the teacher wouldn't understand about his relationship with his daughter, instead he put his hand on her breast and whispered 'I want to fuck you.' He said it with such passion that it didn't even sound crude; to Karen's ears it somehow sounded romantic, and it was just what she wanted to hear. Charles put his hand into his jacket pocket and withdrew a set of keys.

'Charles, I'm going to give you a night to remember.' Karen flicked her head back just as the main beam of a passing car exposed her cool beauty.

On the journey back to the motel Georgina thought over the developments of the day. She was tired and her head was beginning to pound. The bright lights from the oncoming traffic did nothing to soothe her pain and she was regretting not taking a couple of Advil tablets to ease the sharpness of the constant ache when she had the opportunity. She tried to think of brighter things, maybe she would phone her father when she got in and question him about the case, or take that bath like she had promised herself. As tomorrow was Saturday and one of the few foreseeable days where they might be able to sneak a little free time, Rick had invited her to his house for a barbeque.

'Jo-Lynn wants to meet you, accept a little southern hospitality. It's more of a barbeque actually, I hope you eat meat?'

She gratefully accepted, the prospect of another fast food meal and her stomach would surely rebel? With the afternoon off it would be a great opportunity to get to know the other side of the detectives, the private world of real people. Rick invited Leroy and Lia too. Georgina looked at the illuminated clock on the dashboard. 10-58pm. She briefly envied the girls in the typing pool with their nine to fives, *briefly*. Her job infringed on many aspects of her life, too many, the social part being the greatest intrusion. It was three months since she had been on any sort of a date, she could not remember the last time that she had made love to anyone but herself. She kept telling herself the sacrifice was worth it; that it would pay off with promotion. She laughed to herself in the car, wondering who she was trying to fool. Younger, less experienced men gained promotion above her; she stared at the soles of their shoes through the glass ceiling. If she complained she knew that was be a one way ticket to obscurity, relocation to some god-awful field office. Georgina knew the options, tough it out and be *so* much better than the rest so that *they* had no option to ignore her, or loose ambition and stay in the field, eating shit, taking shit and having shit fired at her from every angle.

The motel came within sight, its garish neon illumination buzzing quietly, proudly, to the world, praising its very existence. Insects battered off the windscreen in a kamikaze duel, harbingers of another muggy night. For another twenty bucks a night she could have rented a hotel room with air conditioning, instead it was another night listening to the vibrating swirl of the fan blades as they fought valiantly to redistribute the humid, heavy air and the noisy lovemaking of the hookers in room 22. She pulled the rented Lincoln to a halt outside number 24, turned the lights off and sat alone in the dark for a few moments. Letting her mind start to unwind a little, she closed her eyes and saw the hammer swinging toward her. Her eyes snapped open. Relaxing tonight was going to be a little more difficult than normal.

Narla needed the drink. She had slumped from the settee to the floor. Physically and mentally she could not reach a lower point. The images that bombarded her eyes were such a shock that she had to stop the tape on three occasions because she could no longer see the television through her tear streaming eyes. Her husband, the man she had vowed to love until parted by death, was stripping their daughter naked, even though she was crying and obviously distressed. He kept forcing her. She could hear his voice on the tape. 'Mummy wants you to love Daddy, you do love me don't you.'

The confused child nods. 'You have to kiss Daddy to show him how much you love him...Kiss me.'

Harley sobbing leans forward and gently kisses her father cheek, the innocent way a child would kiss her father. 'NO!..I TOLD YOU...' Charles raises his voice. 'On the lips.'

Narla stopped the tape, unable to watch further. The date on the corner of the tape made it over four years old. She scrambled through some of the other tapes retrieved from the summerhouse and found the latest tape. Six days old. She put it in the VCR. The image that appeared on the screen reviled Narla. Charles had obviously progressed in his corruption of their daughter. Straddled across her father, both of them naked smiling, laughing as though they were partaking in an innocent game. Narla hung her head and vomited on to the floor, she pushed away the tapes at the last moment. Totally drained of every emotion, Narla slumped backwards and lay there, listening to her daughter being raped by her husband, listening to Harley's soft whispers, listening to Charles low moaning. The sound of his breathing becoming laboured. The grunting noise she knew all too well, the noise that he always made just before he comes. The noises mingled in her head, mixing, and growing louder and louder, until they were a spinning cacophony, a crashing symphony of defilement. Narla started to scream to make the noise go away, above it all she could hear Charles breathing and Harley saying 'Yes, I love you Daddy.' Narla needed to get away from the television. She placed her hands over her ears and continued to scream at the top of her voice until it echoed inside her head. She couldn't hear the doorbell ringing. Life outside her head no longer made sense. All that made sense was the screaming white noise inside her head. She staggered forward and fell against the television set. Tumbling over it, pushing it backwards. Just before passing out Narla thought she saw someone standing in the room with her.

Leroy opened the door gently, trying not to wake Lia. He crept in the front room and noticed that there was no sign of her,

'Must have gone to bed.' he said to himself.

Not that he blamed her, waiting up night after night with no promise of when he'd be home was not what he would call fun. Leroy hit the remote control lying in the chair and flopped exhausted on to the seat. He lowered the volume of the TV set and scanned the channels thinking to himself how Bruce Springfield had got it right when he declared 'fifty-nine channels and nothing on'. The shopping channel tried its best to sell Leroy a singing Marvin Gaye memorial doll, Leroy tried his best to stay awake, both failed. Sleep swept over him without protestation, Leroy kicked back on the reclining mechanism and within seconds succumbed. The faint drone of the ever present shopping channel salesperson receded and all was silent in Leroy's world, save for the approach of dreams.

SATURDAY

'Uh...What the …'

Someone was screaming. Leroy woke with a start, confused, disorientated. He looked around, trying to obtain his bearings, trying to fix on the noise. It wasn't screaming. It was loud, very loud talking.

'AREN'T THESE DOLLS BEAUTIFUL. GET THEM WHILE YOU CAN, THESE BABIES ARE GOING TO BE WORTH TRIPLE WHAT YOU PAY FOR THEM NOW IN JUST THREE YEARS TIME. ISN'T THAT RIGHT KIRSTIN?'

'YOU'RE NOT JOKING, BOB. REMEMBER OUR LIBERACE MEMORIAL DOLL, EIGHTY-FIVE BUCKS TWO FALLS AGO? ONE SOLD AT AUCTION IN MICHIGAN FOR OVER FIVE

HUNDRED DOLLARS AND THAT'S NOT ALL; OUR MARVIN GAYE MEMORIAL DOLL COMES COMPLETE WITH A CERTIFICATE OF AUTHENTICATION AND THIS UNIQUE PRESENTATION BOX. WE ARE CONFIDENT THAT YOU WON'T BUY A BETTER INVESTMENT THIS YEAR THAN THE MARVIN GAYE MEMORIAL DOLL.'

Leroy stared at the screen finally comprehending where the noise was coming from; his arm had fallen asleep and gone numb, pressing his weight on the remote handset's volume button. He shook his arm trying to get some life to return to the dead limb. The remote fell to the floor as a rush of blood brought pins and needles along with restored feeling.

He bent down and reduced the volume. He stared at the plastic facsimile of Marvin Gaye.

'Brother, you better off dead than seeing this shit.' Leroy rose from the armchair. Daylight flashed a tentative eye through the small gap in the curtains. The clock on the wall told him it was 7-50, Leroy knew that it must be later than that because the battery had been running down for the past six weeks, it had been losing up to five minutes a day, though Lia usually reset it at least once a week. Leroy had been meaning to buy a new battery but it was way down a long list of things that he meant to do and never seemed to get the time to get around to. He ambled to the bathroom quietly, not wanting to wake Lia up, not just yet. He showered and shaved and put on his towelling robe, ready to make breakfast. Breakfast in bed with Lia sounded good to Leroy, and after breakfast maybe a little love. Leroy certainly felt the need of a little comfort after the past few days. He stood over the stove, shuffling the bacon rashers back and forward, trying not to weld them to the non-stick pan. He flipped the eggs over and let them rest against the blistering surface for only a minute before removing them and placing them carefully onto the hot buttered waffles. As bad a cook as he was, Leroy's stomach was doing a tango in anticipation of some sustenance. He poured some orange juice and two cups of freshly brewed coffee, placed them all on a tray and walked down the hall to the bedroom. The door was pushed too, as usual; Leroy opened it with his back while keeping the tray in front of him.

'Hey, sleepyhead, time for breakfast.' Leroy turned and faced an empty bed. The smile faded from his face. 'Baby?' He put the tray on the bed and moved swiftly down the corridor, knocking open the second bedroom door, empty. The bathroom, the kitchen, the lounge, the toilet, all-empty. And it slowly dawned on him that 'empty' was the correct adjective. How he didn't notice until now baffled him. Even when he was in the bathroom he failed to spot that all of Lia's wash things had gone. Leroy went to her wardrobe and pulled it open. The clanging hangers echoed around the house, sounding the death knell of a home whose very heart had been removed. Stuck with sellotape to a shelf where Lia used to keep her winter woollens was an envelope marked *Leroy*. He snatched the envelope and sat down on the bed scattering the orange juice and coffee, sending the liquids hurtling together in to an undrinkable concoction before they finally came to rest on the waffles. Leroy pushed the tray back toward the centre of the bed, leaving a trail of orangey-brown fluid on the crisp white sheets. The envelope was not sealed, the flap springing open almost too obligingly. Leroy pulled the neatly folded piece of paper out. A waft of Lia's perfume, 'Jewel', a waft of Lia…a memory.

Leroy,

I have tried to talk to you on many occasions but it seems that time is our enemy. We just don't seem to have enough of it to spend with each other. I know that things will not improve because you love your work so much, maybe more than me. I know that sounds harsh but I really believe that you can live without me; I wish the same could be said about your work. I have waited and waited and waited; I can see my life passing me by. I need to find life before it's too late. I have stocked up on groceries for you and the freezer is full. Don't try to find me. I have taken two thousand dollars from our savings account to get me by. Don't hold harsh thoughts about me, my heart is breaking but this is something I have to do.

Love Lia xxx

Leroy felt lost, an empty pit opened in his stomach, which he felt his heart would surely drop in to. A feeling of desolation and rage swept over him simultaneously and he could do nothing but sit on the bed and cry.

The police arrived within ten minutes of Narla's phone call. A detective, fattish, going bald, got out of the car with surprising agility for his size. Narla watched through the lounge window sitting wrapped in a blanket. She was holding a cup of sweet tea. A sense of relief at seeing approaching safety made Narla sob quietly. Narla dreaded Charles returning during the time spent waiting for the police, breezing in with his usual cheery disposition and his 'Hi, Honey I'm home' falseness.

Norman Frusco stood at the door and rang the bell. Before the chime had finished, Harley had the door open and welcomed the detective in. His first impressions of 14162 Harpenders Grove was that the owners were far from poor. On the way down, Norman had the station run over any details that they may have had on the owners. Apart from two unpaid parking violations the Fleisher's were model citizens.

'Come in, detective.' Narla's voice was trembling as much as her hands. There was a hot sickness in her stomach. The image of Harley curled up on the bed wouldn't leave Narla's mind. She wondered about the damage both mentally and physically to her daughter and was amazed at how she could manage to keep the abuse a secret. To Narla it seemed too much of a burden for a girl to have to carry, it was too much for anyone to carry.

'It's Captain Frusco, but you can call me Norman.' Norman smiled trying to put Narla at ease. He wasn't fully aware of all the facts but knew enough for a little gentle diplomacy. A policewoman entered behind Frusco, they followed Narla in to the lounge. Frusco admired the decoration of the house. The simple colour scheme, the tastefully arranged but expensive furniture. The paintings on the wall, not by famous artist's but originals. Aesthetically pleasing, gentle on the eye without being pretentious.

'I've brought along Policewoman Reynolds, if there is anything you feel uneasy about telling me, you might find it easier.'

Narla was nodding, already ahead of Frusco. Guilt adding to the plethora of mixed emotions swimming around in her head. Frusco and Reynolds sat opposite Narla occupying different ends of the three-seat settee. Norman Frusco placed a voice-activated tape recorder on the glass table that separated them. 'Whenever you're ready Miss O'Connell. Whenever you feel fit enough to tell us.'

Narla cleared her throat, coughed and swallowed nervously.

'Daddy?' Ray shook his fathers arm gently, trying to rock his father from a deep slumber. 'Daddy, Uncle Leroy's on the phone...He sound's strange...Daddy.' Ray shook his father once more. The words began to filter through to Rick Montoya's sub-conscious; his son's voice was miles away, like a sonar, getting nearer and nearer until it breached the boundary between dreams and reality.

'Daddy, Uncle Leroy's on the phone he sounds weird, I think he's crying.'

Rick woke up. The bed was empty, Rick's mind instantly started to assemble information, he looked at his son, standing in front of him in his Spiderman pyjamas.

'Okay, Ray. Tell Uncle Leroy I'll be there in a moment.'

Ray trotted off outside the bedroom and down the stairs. Rick could hear his son telling his partner that 'Daddy would be right down.'

Rick sat up in bed and rubbed his face. Today was barbeque day. Jo-Lynn would already be at the supermarket buying provisions. He stretched his legs and inhaled a lungful of Turtle Island's finest air. The air conditioning unit hummed, breathing out cool air, making the environment a little more liveable. Rick stood and briefly glanced outside the window. Clear blue skies and the sun already hammering out a fierce heat, *'today's gonna be another hot one'* Rick said to no one but himself as he pulled on a pair of shorts and headed out for the phone.

'Yeah, what's wrong, you an Lia not comin to our little wing ding?' The smile on Rick's face shrank as Leroy told him that Lia had left him *'for good this time'*

'I'll be right over...you stay cool.' Rick put the phone down and called his son who was happily ensconced in front of the T.V. watching cartoons. 'Ray, call Korjca and see if she'll look after you until mom comes home, I gotta go to your Uncle Leroy's. I'm leaving a note for Mommy attached to the fridge.'

Ray continued watching the toon; his hand stretched out and grabbed the receiver of the phone in the living room. He pressed one of the automatic dial numbers stored in it's memory without even looking. By the time Rick showered and dressed Korjca was ready to take charge of Ray. Rick kissed his son, pinned the note to the fridge and was heading over Independence Bridge within twenty-five minutes of the call. Lia leaving Leroy was not a huge surprise to Rick, she had confided to Jo-Lynn on numerous occasions how unhappy she was with Leroy working all the hours that God sent. Jo-Lynn sympathised and made sure that she told Rick, certain that the message would get back to Leroy, which it did. But *the job* was worse than a mistress; it broke marriages and relationships indiscriminately without infidelity.

Seventeen

'**I**'m watching you,'
Jo-Lynn Montoya moved her trolley around the aisles, picking up various groceries.

His heart thumped, the excitement was almost too much to endure. The feeling of light-headedness virtually consumed him. *He* could take her at any time...any time at all. As *he* approached her, each step became a tiny orgasm, closer and closer. The feeling, exquisite. *He* so much wanted to feel her warm blood over his body.

'All good things' became *his* new mantra. *He'd* make them pay; *He'd* make them all pay.

The door to Leroy's home was open; Rick didn't wait for an invitation. He found Leroy sitting watching some home movies on the video.

'She's gone...it's like she's dead, it's like I'm dead.' Leroy turned to face his partner and was not ashamed to show the grief etched on to his tear stained face.

'What are we gonna do with you?' Rick sat down next to Leroy and hugged him, while his partner sobbed uncontrollably.

'Jeans and a tee shirt, or shorts and a vest? I don't know why I'm asking you, you're not much help.' Georgina threw the clothes at her reflected image in the mirror. She had been awake for two hours, placed calls at the station and hospital plus one back at the bureau to see if they had come up with anything fresh. All the calls drew a blank, it seemed that she would be able to take her half-day's leave after all. A half-day off during any investigation was a luxury, one after only a couple of days was almost unheard of, it was a sign of what little progress had been made despite the evidence. A fact that depressed Georgina, but she would take her time knowing the next free day might be a long way away.

'Shorts and a vest plus plenty of sun block.' She finally made up her mind, dressed and put on a pair of *Nike Air's* on her feet. She looked sporty and fit; neither attribute was a lie.

Georgina decided to take another tour of the Island, this time by car before going to Detective Montoya's. She threw some cold sodas into a rucksack along with her camera, donned a white baseball cap and headed for her rented Lincoln. She pulled the soft hood of the convertible back and decided to drive semi alfresco rather than breathe the manufactured cool air of the car's air conditioning. Sunglasses on, she hit the highway toward Turtle Island.

Dr Martinez bounded up the steps two at a time rather than use the elevator. He spoke into his cordless phone and listened in breathless excitement.

'Good...and what are his vitals...excellent.'

The news that Stephen England was out of his coma was the first bit of good news that day. Some days were totally devoid of good news. On those days Martinez seemed to spend his entire shift handing out bereavement counselling numbers and crisis support cards.

He thought he heard a noise, a creak on the landing. Thirteen-year-old Dolan Cooke quickly pressed his mouse and the screen in front of him changed from a lurid pornographic photo of a young girl barely his age giving head, to something far more innocuous. God, he hoped it wasn't his mother again. He shifted in his seat, pulled his tee shirt over his groin and listened...nothing. He hadn't heard the car return, it was just guilt-ridden paranoia. His heart throbbed; his cock throbbed. He clicked back on to the porno site, hoping to download an mpeg, something he could really get his teeth into and saw the small inviting advertising banner constantly flashing. A red skull and crossbones. Underneath the banner an eighteen-inch prosthetic penis was being gorged by three young women, another site was offering the best in animal sex, an equally naked woman appeared to be engaged in coitus with a horse. So much to choose from. Dolan's hand hovered between the adverts, undecided. He clicked on the red skull and crossbones, 'DeathCam.net'. The page opened with a flashing Skull interspersed with a picture of Max Dalton's crushed and bloodied face. Curiosity drew him deeper into the web site.

'This is so cool.'

Another creak on the landing, this time Dolan, already too absorbed by the images of violence in front of him did not turn, his eight year old sister watched over his shoulder as image after image after image loaded, each worse than the last. He turned his head.

Georgina O'Neil decided to take another look at the houses that ran along the river. The victims were both held for a period of days before their murders, maybe longer. Both of them had made their exit via the river, one alive, one very much dead. Georgina surmised that these houses would be as good a place as any to hold the victims. The location was certainly quiet enough; you could torture, kill or maim in the open, let alone locked away within the confines of a house and nobody would hear you scream. She had parked the car on the grass verge, which ran along the main highway in Turtle Island then walked a mile or so, following the river where she could. Stopping only to view through a pair of binoculars at the numerous houses that were dotted along the banks. Any one of them could hold the answer. She watched a boy, his father and grandfather pitching balls and practicing batting, in a makeshift baseball diamond outside one of the houses. Memories of her tomboy childhood flooded back. Shooting baskets with her father whose rudimentary knowledge of the game wasn't too bad considering his Irish origins. The sun beat through her cap causing beads of sweat to form on her brow and run down her face. She wiped her face dry using a small towel taken from the motel and took a long cool swig of coke before continuing on her journey. Georgina carried on walking for a further half mile and had counted five agents boards 'for sale or let' in the one and a half miles covered. Three were on the river; two set a little way back, one bordering the forest. She had barely completed an eighth of the rivers circumference around the island. Viewing the empty properties would be heavy on manpower and time, especially with such a small local force. She sat briefly, to rest in the long grasses, enjoying the sun beating over her, realising that a house search of the empty properties could also prove to be a futile waste of time if the killer was a local, happily ensconced in marital bliss. For all she knew, it could have been the father playing ball with his son or even the grandfather. She shook her head trying to clear the jumbled mess of thoughts, hoping that one solid idea would stick that could lead them to their man. Her growling stomach told her lunch was not far away and she remembered the barbeque.

Georgina looked at her watch 12-53, 'time to go' she spoke to the field, almost with the expectation of a reply.

She stood and walked back to her car. As she walked she swished her hands through the long grasses playfully pushing them to one side, suddenly beginning to relax for the first time in weeks. She promised herself a holiday when this case was over. Two weeks in this field with a supply of drink, good food, some choice reading and maybe a friend, sounded just like heaven at the moment. She stopped to take another gulp from her bottle; the soda was starting to get warm. Taking her bearings, Georgina wondered to herself whether the killer had been in the very field where she stood, maybe in the very spot. The notion uneased her, leaving her feeling vulnerable. Not easily spooked, she had the feeling that eyes were boring in to the back of her head. She quickly swivelled round. Her hand instinctively reached for her weapon a 9mm Smith and Wesson. More of an up close and personal type of weapon but she was an expert shot and felt confident with the gun's relative lightness. Only this time the weapon was back at the motel locked away in the room safe. Her car was little more than six hundred yards away but her legs suddenly felt paralysed and as rational as she thought she was, Georgina could not help but feel vulnerable and exposed. The feeling made her uneasy, it went against every piece of training that she had learned. Instinctively she knew she was being stalked, something primal was awakened in the field and her intuition was telling her to get the hell out of the field. Georgina started walking toward her car, she knew it lay just beyond the field, parked on the verge. She dipped into the rucksack and searched for the key while she walked. Her pace quickened then suddenly she was jogging. The edge of the field was getting closer and closer. All the time she was looking, scanning every tree, watching for possible hiding places, every nook and cranny. The long grass by its very nature was the perfect cover, Georgina knew she could be running straight into danger, into the arms of who knows what. Panic was now beginning to replace any levelheaded detachment she should be applying to the situation as a professional. Her behaviour was completely irrational, but she kept on running until she left the field and headed down the grassy bank to the verge where her car was parked. She already had the key in her tightened grasp and plunged it into its waiting socket and twisted. The central locking popped reassuringly. She pulled the door open and dived into the seat, gasping for air. Quickly, Georgina looked over her shoulder and checked the back seats then pressed the interior locks on the doors. She finally began to relax, tilted her head back, resting against the head restraint and briefly closed her eyes, trying to regain her composure and make some sense of her unreasonable behaviour. She breathed deeply, her hand automatically fumbled for the radio cassette. A little music might help. Some lead singer from a heavy metal band was singing *bring your daughter to the slaughter*. Her fingers pushed home her cassette, and the gentle sound of Alison Krauss singing came through the speakers. Georgina's lips started to mime along with the words on the overplayed tape. A feeling of normality was returning. She opened her eyes, and there it was, on the dashboard inside the car. A child's tooth; a solitary, white, tiny milk tooth. The tooth appeared to be old, it certainly didn't look fresh, there was no trace of blood or tissue and the root was dry. Georgina opened her rucksack and pulled out a transparent evidence bag. She picked the tooth up with the tweezers she had in her make-up bag.

The drive back to the precinct was tense but without further incident. She left her car to be dusted for prints and other DNA matter the intruder may have left behind. After a brief phone call to Norman Frusco, she borrowed a car from the car pool and drove out to Rick's for the barbeque.

Stephen England was sitting up in bed. His eyes had blackened, his nose and jaw was broken, as was every tooth in his mouth up to his molars. His cheekbone was shattered and his skull was fractured in two places. From his neck down to his waist he had another fifteen broken or fractured bones, including his elbow. Stephen England was very unlucky to be alive; the living nightmare to which he was trapped made a life spent in this condition nothing to be envied. He did not know how he got into this condition and found comprehending anything other than the fearsome memories that flashed through his mind impossible. Who the strange girl was who was holding his hand?

Dr Martinez shone a torch into Stephen's eyes looking for pupil dilation, only the left eye dilated the right was blown. Indecipherable words spewed rambling and incoherently from his pulpy mouth. Cara Morton sat quietly, waiting patiently for the doctor to finish his examination. She had a thousand questions that were burning down the length of a fuse.

Eighteen

The temperature on the thermometer read 97 Fahrenheit, Georgina looked at her watch it was a little after three in the afternoon. Police guards sat discreetly across the street watching the house. She recognised the large ginger headed man from the precinct as Detective Walhberg and his partner as Officer Collins, both of them were assigned to protect Rick's wife and son. She waved to them before pressing the doorbell. Walhberg lifted his coffee cup in salute to O'Neil. She watched Collins lean over and whisper in his partner's ear. Whatever he said made Walhberg smile. Georgina couldn't hear but had worked long enough around a predominantly male workforce to guess that the content of his amusement probably involved her body. The shorts that she wore, while not tight were short and the vest was loose and baggy, neither items designed to flatter, but O'Neil knew that most women could wear a sack and invite sexual abuse. Walhberg's tongue snaked and this time it was Collins turn to laugh.

'Come on, come on; open up.' Georgina was pleading with whoever was going to reach the door first. She never did like being in a shop window and it pleased her even less to give letches like Collins and Walhberg a hard-on. She could hear noise and the sound of footsteps running to the door. Small feet, the sound of a child.

'I'LL GET IT.' A wee voice called.

Ray opened the door and his face became a Christmas tree whose lights had just fused.

'Oh.' he said not bothering to hide his disappointment. He turned ignoring Georgina and called. 'It's some woman.'

'Some woman.' Georgina thought to herself, feeling the juxtaposition of her sexuality from the males of this world whose hormones had yet to kick in. From the North to the South Pole in a matter of seconds, another eight years and he would be tying his dick to his leg to keep it down. Ray trotted off without another word.

Georgina called after him. 'Hey Ray, you not gonna say hello?'

Ray stopped. 'How'd you know my name?'

'I know lots about you.' She lied. 'I'm a friend of you dad's. I work with him.'

'You a policewoman?' Ray turned his head to face Georgina.

'Something like that.'

A woman came from the kitchen.

'I'm sorry, has little Ray not invited you in?' Jo-Lynn Montoya was holding out her hand as she walked down the hall. Her grip was firm and warm, her eyes smiling.

'Rick has had to go out. A bit of a personal crisis but he said he won't be long.'

'Oh...I'm sorry. Is everything alright?'

'Yeah, come on in. Don't look so concerned. You're Miss O'Neil right?'

'Georgina.'

'Well the problem's Leroy, Rick's partner.' Jo-Lynn began to explain. 'Leroy is having the crisis actually.'

'What's wrong?' Georgina said. She followed Jo-Lynn through to the kitchen. Ray ran ahead of them.

'I guess I can tell you, considering you're a work colleague an' all. Leroy's girlfriend Lia has upt and left him. The big old softy is pretty upset. So Rick's over there doing his '*she was no good for you anyway*' speech.' She laughed 'Not that that's true. It's quite ironic, Lia *was* the best thing that could happen to Leroy.'

As Georgina entered the kitchen she noticed another woman standing near the sink. She was preparing salad, washing vegetables and dicing tomatoes and onions.

'Georgina, let me introduce you to Korjca. Ray's nanny.' Jo-Lynn explained 'I am a working mother, so Korjca here helps keep my *little one* in line during the day and school holidays.'

The young white woman turned around and said 'Hello' her accent was eastern European. She was 19 or 20. Slightly overweight but the weight flattered her features, her hair was dark brown, pulled back, secured with an elastic. She wore a straight skirt, which touched her knees and a crisp white blouse, which nearly matched her complexion.

'Her second name is something unpronounceable.' Jo-Lynn smiled.

Korjca laughed. 'Piekarska.'

'See I told you.'

Georgina shook Korjca's hand.

'Hello.'

Korjca smiled. 'Hello...I'm from Poland, so you must forgive my English.' She seemed to be apologising, there was unsureness in her voice, even though her English was far better than Georgina's Polish ever would be. 'So my English is still not too good, but I am learning.'

'Yeah, I teach her.' Ray sidled in to grab some attention.

'We were going to eat outside but I think it may be too hot.' Jo-Lynn was standing at the open rear door leading in to the garden.

'I like the heat, it can get a little sticky but when you're raised in Maryland you learn to appreciate the hot days.' Georgina joined her at the door and looked down the length of the garden.

A paved patio area was home to a sun lounge and a table. To the left was a hardcore area with some familiar looking painted markings and a basketball hoop. Further up was a large lawn with a huge hole being dug at the very foot of the garden.

'Good, I like the heat too, I was just saying that so as to be polite.'

'It's a nice garden.'

'Don't you mind the mess at the end there. That's where we're having a pool built, come down I'll show you what we have planned.' Jo-Lynn stepped into the furnace of heat outside; Ray pushed past Georgina and ran down the garden shouting at the top of his lungs with his arms outstretched pretending to be a plane. Jo-Lynn and Georgina walked up the garden toward the construction area. The sun was high in a cloudless sky and for a brief time the world seemed at ease.

'I don't blame Lia for leaving Leroy. The job takes too much from relationships; time, energy...don't you find that?' Jo-Lynn spoke as she walked.

'During training they prepare you for everything except the sacrifices, both personal and mental. You seem to be coping though.' Georgina replied.

Jo-Lynn laughed sardonically. 'Yeah, I'm coping but I feel I shouldn't have to cope. Ray suffers. He misses his father. I try to be here as much as possible but there are times when it seems I don't see my son for days. That's not unusual for the both of us because of our work commitments; there was a time last year where I never saw Ray for nine days. Korjca is invaluable, I don't know how other families cope, families that can't afford to buy help.'

They reached the large hole; mounds of earth were piled to one side of the rectangle ditch. A small digger lay dormant a few yards away.

'The compensations for our sacrifices, the loss of time and family against a nice house, a new car every other year, a pool and a foreign holiday. We truly are children of the new millennium.' Jo-Lynn sighed.

'A beautiful son. Some people would swap the world for a child.' Georgina was watching Ray bounce a basketball on the hardcore. He was throwing the ball up to the hoop.

'Yeah, I know, it would seem that when you have everything you never realise what you truly have, only what you don't. I should thank God. I know how precious a child's life can be.'

Georgina knew that Jo-Lynn was alluding to Jordan. 'I was sorry to hear about your loss.'

Jo-Lynn stared into the freshly dug pit, remembering a day three years previously when she was staring into a different pit. 'Yeah, everyone's sorry.' She turned and looked at her son trying to shoot a hoop. 'His father said he'd help him practice today…another broken promise.'

'Put your weight on your back foot, then lean in to the shot.' Georgina shouted to Ray.

Ray did as told and put the ball clean through the hoop. He yelped with delight.

'Rick promised, hand on heart, that he would shoot some baskets today.'

'But he wasn't to know about Leroy?'

'No....but there is *always* something.' Jo-Lynn began to walk back to the house.

'Do you think Ray would allow me to practice a few shots with him?'

Jo-Lynn stopped. 'Are you serious?'

'Deadly. I may be white but I *can* shoot hoop.' Georgina threw an imaginary basketball at an equally imaginary hoop.

'No, that's not what I meant...I mean of course you can. Ray has been on to me an' Korjca all morning. Ever since his father left this morning. Tell you the truth I may be black but I ain't no good. Korjca plays with him sometimes, but right now she's more use to me in the kitchen, another place that's not really my domain, I'm happier in court.'

Georgina and Jo-Lynn walked together back up the garden toward the hardcore area where Ray was practicing shooting.

'Rick mentioned that you were a partner in a practice just out of Springfield.'

'Yeah, it's just small. Mainly divorce work, lord knows there's enough of that, and a few local issues, planning that sort of thing, nothing too exciting but that's the way I want it. My partner Phillip Galloway, had to defend a man charged with murder about a year ago, domestic violence, but most of the big stuff goes straight to the attorneys in Missouri.'

They stopped at the edge of the miniature basketball court.

'Hey, Ray?'

Ray looked sideways at his mother and totally missed the shot.

'Ah, mom.'

'What you say if Miss Georgina here wants to practice with you?'

Ray looked Georgina up and down disapprovingly, while bouncing the ball.

'But mum, she's...'

'White.' Georgina chipped in

'A girl.' Ray said with disgust.

'Now Ray, you know what your Mama says about working with minorities.'

Okay.' Ray groaned reluctantly giving in.

Georgina smiled and stepped onto the court

'Ray, like my husband and myself, never see colour in skin, only the heart that beats behind it. Good or bad.'

'I guess that's twice that I've put my foot in my mouth today.'

'Nonsense.' Jo-Lynn bent down to her son's level and spoke to him sternly. 'Ray, I want you to play nice. No rough stuff.'

Ray smiled his best, most mischievous smile

'Pass me the ball, Ray?' Georgina called. Ray passed the ball straight to the detective. Georgina caught the ball expertly and in one fluid movement twisted and shot the ball straight through the hoop. Ray stood open mouthed.

'WOW.'

'I am impressed, Miss O'Neil. Would you like to be my son's personal coach?' Jo-Lynn said obviously impressed. Georgina ran over to the hoop and collected the ball.

'Okay Ray, how about a little attack and defence? You try to score and I'll defend. One on one.' Georgina passed the ball to Ray, bouncing it off the ground. Ray caught the ball and immediately went on the attack, bouncing the ball, moving forward, shimmying to one side, trying to faint a dummy to throw Georgina off her stride. She stood in front of him, arms flapping trying to block any potential shot. They were in front of the 'D' ring. Ray took two quick steps to his side and launched a shot, which ricocheted of the hoop board.

'Good shot, Ray.' Georgina praised the boy's effort.

Sweat was beginning to run down her back, she used the bottom of her vest to wipe her forehead. Ray watched fascinated, studying her stomach, looking at the half exposed cups of her sport bra. Something caught the light, dazzling reflecting from the sun.

'What's that?' Ray pointed to a shining object that appeared to be growing from Georgina's navel.

'A stud.' Georgina explained. Ray still looked puzzled. 'You know like ear rings, but I've had one put in my tummy instead.'

'Why?'

Georgina thought back to the drunken night she decided to have the stud inserted. She had been working on a case in L.A, during part of her training. She was teamed with an experienced female investigator and their enquiries had led them to a tattoo and piercing parlour. She watched a young girl, no more than nineteen having her stomach pierced. The girl already had her tongue pierced and was talking quite frankly with the piercing artist about how her *girlfriend* got a kick out of the small silver ball. With their enquiries complete, Georgina thought no more about it until, celebrating the successful conclusion of the case, she found herself lying on a chaise lounge having local anaesthetic applied to her navel. The rest was a blur. She woke the following morning with a bruised stomach and the beginning of an infection that took three hundred dollars of drugs to clear. Having suffered so much for the dammed thing she decided to keep it.

Georgina pulled her vest down. 'You know, Ray, I really don't know why. Sometime adults do strange things. Come on, you try defending, I'll attack?' She grabbed the ball from his hands and tried to make a sharp dart around him but Ray was quick and blocked her attack shot by jumping and parrying the ball with his hand. The ball bounced once and Ray was on to it, bouncing it and leading it away from Georgina. He turned to attack, running down the court, dribbling the ball expertly like a miniature Harlem Globetrotter, as he drew near, his eyes lit up and he called 'Hey, Dad?'

Georgina foolishly turned and within an instant, Ray had passed her and had a free shot at goal. He steadied himself, aimed and leapt, launching the ball against the rim board. The ball hit the rectangle marking and bounced against the hoop, rolled around the rim and fell through the net. Rick was nowhere to be found. Ray fell to the floor laughing, celebrating his victory.

'Hey, that's not fair.' It was Georgina's turn to complain, though she was laughing as much as the boy.

Jo-Lynn and Korjca watched from the kitchen window. Salad, vegetables and fruit were washed, sliced, cooked and prepared. Four huge mounds of fresh steak were lying on a cutting board, waiting to be cooked on the barbeque.

'I hope Rick's not too long, this food ain't gonna stay fresh forever.'

Korjca finished drying her hands, watching Georgina play with Ray. 'She's very good.'

'Yeah.'

'She's also very good with children, Ray has taken to her very quickly.' Korjca knew it had taken her about three weeks to reach the stage that Georgina had achieved with him in little over an hour. Three hard weeks of tantrums and cajoling and trying to win over the barrier that Ray had imposed.

'I think I should bring them a drink maybe?'

As Jo-Lynn watched Korjca give her son and the detective sodas, she felt a twinge of sadness that Jordan wasn't out there with them playing.

Jordan's premature death had hit the whole family with such a jolt that it threatened at one point to devastate it. Moving away was their salvation, but somewhere left in Chicago were tiny fragments of family life that could never be stuck back together.

His hands moved closer, closer. Fingers outstretched, ready to wrap around her neck. They moved around the base of her neck feeling the smooth brown skin.

'JESU...' Jo-Lynn started to turn around but the fingers loosened their grip and slid to her collarbone.

'Hi-ya, babe.'

'Jesus! Rick you scared the shit outta me.'

Rick laughed. 'You were miles away. We came into the kitchen banging an' a crashing around, but you were out there in a world of your own.'

'*We?*' Jo-Lynn turned to be greeted with a kiss from her husband. Over his shoulder she could see Leroy standing three feet away, looking awkward. He waved 'Hello' and smiled.

'Where's my little man?'

Jo-Lynn nodded out of the window. 'On the court, playing basketball with our guest.'

Rick leaned against his wife, peering over her shoulder. He saw Ray, Korjca and detective Georgina O'Neil, shooting penalties. 'Hey, Leroy, you gotta see this? A white girl playing basketball.'

'Don't mock, Rick. She's good.' Jo-Lynn informed them.

All three were leaning forward looking out of the window, while Georgina aimed a shot at the hoop. The ball glided through the air and went clean through the basket.

'Good shot.' said Leroy, clearly impressed

'I told you she's good. She's been teaching Ray a few moves too.'

Ray took the ball it was his turn. The kitchen fell silent. As he lined up, Georgina, tapped his feet. Ray moved his legs, spreading his feet slightly. She stood behind him coaching him through the shot, moving his arm down a little and motioning to him to stretch up before letting go of the ball. As he released the ball, Georgina looked into the kitchen window at the anxious faces. She didn't bother to watch the ball as it fell through the hoop, just their faces. The cheer that erupted from the kitchen told her all she needed to know.

Rick, Jo-Lynn and Leroy walked in to the garden cheering and whooping to join the celebrations.

'Hey, Agent O'Neil, that was some fine shooting.' Rick called.

Georgina nodded.

'How about a match...Ray, Korjca and my good self against you, Jo-Lynn and Leroy?' Georgina asked

'Are you kidding? We'd wipe the floor with you, it would be embarrassing.' Rick replied laughing with Leroy.

'Don't include me, you know I can't play.' Jo-Lynn tried to back away.

'Don't worry babe, trust me we're gonna win, but we need you to make up the numbers.'

'Well, I'm a good loser, I promise you.' Georgina bounced the ball at the detective.

'Okay, but to spice it up the loser gets to be barbeque chef.' Rick smiled a mischievous grin

'Hey man, I'd end up killing most of you with my cooking.' Leroy scoffed but before he could protest further, Georgina's hand was slapped in Rick's, shaking it hard

'Deal, I love it when a man cooks.'

Nineteen

'No way…' Wesley Timms jaw dropped. 'No fucking way.'

He looked over his shoulder. No one could see him, and even if they could they would not pay any interest. They were all too busy wrapped up in their own work to notice. Too busy selling advertising space to major players by the inch, by the yard, by the foot, on billboards, on TV, on the back of bus tickets, even on a grain of rice. Wesley once made one person into a permanent walking advert, when a seventeen year old boy had a well known clothing brand trademark tattooed on his face to help pay for his university education. The boy got the money but was promptly thrown out of the university. Wesley didn't care. Wesley didn't care that the boy took his own life three weeks later when his girlfriend dumped him, though the advertisers were pretty pissed. The united colours of grief.

He clicked on another page. This was just too good. He looked at the page counter 11,185,000 hits since…Wesley quickly looked at the calendar on his desk…yesterday.

'No fucking way.'

'Harley must have suffered for so long...I can't believe she managed to keep it to herself.' Narla's hand trembled holding the cup. She felt dead, hollow. Sitting in the forensics room dressed only in a white gown, a pair of paper slippers and an elastic rimmed paper cap, which was cutting into the skin on her forehead. 'How long before I will know the result?' Narla handed a nurse a small vile filled with a sample of her urine.

'Not long, but we will run other checks to make sure. At the most three hours.' The nurse was sympathetic. 'But it would pay to be safe and have a further test later in the month.' She marked the sample bottle N. O'Connell.

'What about Harley?' Narla asked anxiously.

The nurse looked through the glass partition that separated the two rooms, at the young girl sitting on a trolley bed swinging her legs.

'She remarkable, I don't know how she's managing to cope so well. I'm a little worried that she may be blocking everything out. A skill she could have developed to help keep the abuse secret.'

'Do you think she could be pregnant?'

'She hasn't begun menstruating yet. As far as we can tell, she seems to be in the clear. We're testing her just to be on the safe side though.'

The door to the small room opened and Captain Frusco walked in. Narla guessed from the look on his face that he wasn't about to impart good news.

'I take it you haven't found Charles yet?'

Norman Frusco shook his head. 'Not a sign of him yet but events have just turned again.'

Narla could feel the pit of her stomach turn. 'What is it?'

'Harley's teacher, Karen Fuller failed to return home last night. Charles credit card was used last night at Palacs, a restaurant in Campbelltown. We checked and he was with a woman answering her description. Her friend rang in early this morning to report her missing. At the time she was only six or so hours overdue, the desk sergeant figured it was some sort of domestic and told her to give it another couple of hours. Needless to say she hasn't shown.'

'It's too much of a coincidence. Do you think they could be together?'

'I think we have to assume something along those lines Mrs Fleisher.'

Narla's put her cup down and gripped the chair she was sitting on for support.

'O'Connell, please use my maiden name…I am no longer his wife.' She stood and ran to the sink in the corner of the room. 'I think I'm gonna be sick.' Her stomach retched but nothing other than coffee and phlegm escaped. Frusco steadied her, supporting her weight. Between gasps Narla fumbled for reason. 'You think that Charles is this guy the TV are talking about?'

'Its too early to say.' Frusco guided Narla back to her seat.

'I can't believe it.' She shivered as the thought of him pawing over her daughter's body fought its way through her sub-conscious. 'Poor Harley.' Narla looked through the glass partition at her. Harley waved back

'We have a team of investigators who are going to find him Mrs…Miss O'Connell." Frusco reassured Narla hoping the words didn't ring too hollow. First though, he had to find his team of investigators.

Twenty

The sound of Georgina's phone ringing broke her concentration, she was determined to score from the three penalty shots she had. Leroy had blatantly fouled her, pushing her from a good scoring chance. The game had become competitive, the testosterone levels rising with the heat and the deficit of score against Rick, Leroy and Jo-Lynn's team. They were six points down; scoring these three penalties would put the game almost beyond their reach with only one-minute left to play. Georgina had rolled over on the hot hardcore surface, grazing her knee. As she stood in the penalty 'D' she could feel a trickle of blood run down her shin. Leroy was mortified. His charge, while illegal was only meant to have been a playful knock to unbalance her. He had been 'booed off' and was sitting out a penalty suspension in the sin bin, a wooden bench seat erected with a bench and umbrella for the purposes of eating the fare that followed the game. The phone inside the house started to ring, so did Georgina's mobile. The detectives looked at each other, they knew something was breaking. Georgina gave the ball to Ray.

'You better shoot the penalties, champ.'

The boy looked bemused.

'Go on, I'll be watching from the bleachers.' Georgina explained. She handed him the ball and ran to her phone, Leroy had already disappeared inside the house to answer the Montoya's phone.

Georgina sat down on the garden seat, opened her phone. Ray ran over to her.

'Remember what I showed you, don't be afraid of the hoop and don't be afraid of missing.'

'Thanks for coming today, Miss Georgina. It's the first time I've managed to play with dad since, since…I don't know when.' Ray's voice had a sadness that children of his age shouldn't know.

'Well, you show him how good you are. Go on champ, I'll be rooting from here.'

He leaned forward and hugged her, before running back onto the court.

She watched Ray, while the case developments unfolded through the ether into her ear.

Three out of three penalties went in, much to the delight of everyone including Rick, even though it meant he lost the game. Korjca hugged Ray. Then he was smothered with kisses from his mother, much to his disdain as it encroached his street cred. Thankfully none of his friends were there to witness such an outpouring of emotion but he didn't complain. Secretly, he loved being cuddled, enjoying the security of his mother's embrace. She always smelled nice and her skin was so soft. He smiled.

'You are a real champ, son.' Rick ruffled his son's compact, wiry hair. He was watching Georgina's face. The relaxed expression was now gone, replaced with a taut seriousness. As her phone call ended, Leroy shouted from the back door.

'Looks like the game's over.'

Korjca blocked out the light as she stood in front of Georgina. 'I'll get you a plaster for that cut.' Before Georgina could say anything the Polish nanny was disappearing into the kitchen. She returned with a first aid box. Korjca crouched in front of Georgina. She was slightly flushed from the physical activity and was sweating as much as Georgina who had been playing for over twice the amount of time. Korjca applied some antiseptic lotion to a wad of cotton wool and started to wipe the line of blood that was beginning to dry on Georgina's leg. The lotion was cool and pleasant, Korjca's touch gentle. She wiped continually folding the wad of lint. 'You have to be careful of germs... no?'

The cut, once cleaned was small. Korjca held Georgina's knee while she put a plaster over the wound. Her hands were tiny but gentle; she smoothed the plaster with her thumb, securing it to Georgina's leg.

'Come on we've gotta go.' Leroy shouted once more.

Georgina drove back to her motel to shower and change while Rick and Leroy showered in the house then headed straight for the station. Within twenty minutes she was back on the road to join her colleagues.

Twenty-One

Stephen England was aware of the pain in his mouth and all over his body but he sat in silence, imprisoned in his own torture. Though his eyes were open all he could see was the nightmare of his abduction. Somewhere in the distance was a voice he recognised, but it seemed the owner of the voice was locked away in a room far, far away. The hammer kept reigning blows on his face. Hitting him violently, smashing bone, chipping, splintering, disfiguring. Dr Martinez shone a small pencil light torch into his eyes. Martinez wasn't even sure if Stephen England could see out of it. The torch's beam was a mild annoyance to Stephen. An intruder from another world, a world where pain existed, he could keep the pain locked out if he stayed where he was, if only he could keep the memories at bay.

'As you can see, he's pretty non-responsive. There is brain activity but the trauma he has suffered may be irreversible.'

Barbara Dace nodded, taking in the doctor's prognosis.

'Mr England's fiancée has given us permission to obtain some film footage of him in the hope that it will lead to the capture of his abductor.'

'This is highly irregular and I'm not sure that I can see how it will help.' Martinez waved a hand in front of the non-responsive patient's eyes. England didn't blink; he was too scared to ever close his eyes again.

'It could help the police catch the person who done this…you never know. Might jog someone's memory or conscience.'

'Whoever is responsible does not have a conscience and if someone is hiding that person, well…' Martinez left the sentence unfinished. Dr Martinez's beeper shrilled calling him to the nearest phone. 'Look, just be quick.'

'Less than five minutes, I promise.' Barbara Dace crossed her heart.

'Make it three.' Dr Martinez said as he passed Barbara. He stepped in to the corridor and turned right. Walking away at speed

Barbara nodded to her cameraman who was waiting outside. An unlit cigarette placed between his lips.

'Okay, John, we've got permission. Ten minutes, let's hurry it up before the good doctor changes his mind.'

John Keller picked up a large canvas bag, which housed his camera and portable lighting set-up.

Barbara waved to Cara Morton who was sitting on one of the hard plastic bucket seats that lined the wall along the corridor. Her earlier optimism had been replaced with the bleakest depression. A severe jolt of reality had come knocking. She felt angry, wanting vengeance for the unfairness that was being heaped on her life. Filming Stephen's plight gave Cara hope; hope that the monster who inflicted the terrible injuries on her boyfriend could be flushed out. *Flushed out,* that was a good metaphor she thought for a piece of sewage that carried out such atrocities. Cara drank the dregs of her twelfth cup of coffee. The murky brown liquid was cold but Cara was past caring.

Barbara closed the door.

'Right John, I want to get some close-ups of Stephen's injuries, plus a long shot of him propped up in bed. We need to convey the appalling tragedy and viciousness of the attack. I'll do a voice over when we get back the studio.' Barbara thought twice about plumping up Stephen's pillows to make him sit straighter

John Keller looked at his injuries. 'I don't think we're going to have too much difficulty in conveying the brutality of the attack.' He switched on his lights. Stephen didn't react. 'This guy's face is an *'R'* rating.'

The almost silent whirr of the camera was the only sound in the room. John focused on Stephen's face, the camera lens pulling sharply into focus on his red raw toothless mouth.

'God, what sort of person could do this?'

'I've known one or two directors.' Barbara was hot on sarcasm. She drew on a freshly lit cigarette

'Hey, you're not supposed to smoke not in here.' John's own unlit cancer stick dangled precariously between his lips.

'Who's gonna tell...Him?' Barbara pointed to the semi comatose patient. An alarm started buzzing and the door to the room opened. A nurse entered demanding that all cigarettes be extinguished. She took the cigarette from Barbara's lips and in passing snatched John's unlit prop.

'Cigarettes are not aloud in any part of this hospital.' The nurse was about to launch in to her routine 'no smoking' statement, when she realised what Barbara and John were doing

'I'm going to have to ask you to leave, please stop filming now. This is totally against hospital's protocol.'

John continued filming.

'We have permission.' Barbara said undaunted.

'I don't care. I know hospital protocol and the policies of good healthcare, and nowhere does it state that it is in the patient's best interests to be filmed while in no fit condition to make a valid judgement. If you don't stop filming I'll have no option but to call security.'

John raised his thumb, indicating that he had obtained enough footage and lowered the camera.

'Good.' The nurse said. 'Thing's are bad enough here tonight with the police swarming all over the place. I want you out of the hospital in two minutes, Mrs Dace.'

'Oh, you're a fan.' Barbara said sarcastically.

The nurse glared.

'Okay, we're as good as gone.' Barbara raised her hands in surrender.

'Now.' The nurse turned on her heel and left as abruptly as she had entered.

'My God, what was she...The Tobacco Police?'

'I've got her down as suspect number one. Does she do dental?' John laughed

'Come on, if we hurry we'll make the eight o'clock bulletin.'

Barbara and John rushed out of the tiny room, leaving Stephen continuing to stare through the wall, searching for a place of quietness, of peace.

Outside the small room, there was a row of empty chairs. Cara Morton was gone.

As Barbara Dace and John Keller hurried along the sterile hall toward the exit, Barbara lit up another cigarette and passed it to John before lighting her own.

'Boy, this would taste better on the back of a good brandy.'

Barbara nodded. 'Too damn right.'

They hit the exit doors and the warm evening air

Twenty-Two

'We now have a name, Charles Fleisher and more importantly, a suspect that fits Agent O'Neil's profile.' Frusco spoke. 'That's the good news. The bad news is that a teacher from the island has been reported missing. Her name is Karen Fuller and it just so happens that she teaches the Fleisher's one and only progeny. Fleisher was last seen yesterday. He was in the General store, along with Karen Fuller. Seems he may have been having an affair with Karen. She is well known to most of the people on the island. She was reported missing yesterday by her flat mate, about the same time Charles locked up shop and disappeared. General store owner, Gary Clarkson, recalls seeing the couple in his store yesterday but they weren't together to his knowledge.'

Georgina should have been happy that the real estate agent fitted her resume of the suspect but something nagged in the back of her mind. She kept mulling over the case, trying to find the cause of her concern. Norman Frusco's face loomed in front of her.

'Something wrong, O'Neil?'

Georgina jerked her head back, distancing herself from Frusco.

He continued. 'You seem to be miles away.'

'I was wondering, has there been any information about the tooth found in my car.'

'Only that it is a child's tooth. To be honest it could have come from anywhere.' Frusco answered, but Georgina wasn't paying attention. Her brain was trying to logically understand the killer's motives. Nothing made sense.

'With due respect sir, I was thinking..,' O'Neil began.

'There is nothing to think about. Turtle Island is a small community with a mad man hiding out on the loose somewhere out there. His name is Charles Fleisher. All we have to do now is hope that we catch him and pray to God that Karen Fuller is still alive.'

'Sir, why change now? Why go after a woman now?'

'You heard the tape Georgina, he said he was changing the rules. I guess this is what he meant.' Rick offered

'No, I don't buy it. Something's not right.'

'Too fuckin' right. The man's a psychopath. *That* ain't right.' Leroy gave the room his usual concise opinion. 'All we gotta do is find the sick fuck.'

'I think Leroy's right.' Rick offered support to his partner's theory, such as it was.

Georgina was beginning to feel manoeuvred out of any chance to express any alternative hypothesis. The ball had started to run down hill and it was gathering pace, she knew she had two choices. Keep up with it or bail out.

'So, where do we look?' She motioned toward the map pinned to the chalk board.

Turtle Island was distinctive, ringed by a circle of blue that isolated the small community from the mainland but still surrounded by 69,000 square miles that comprised of the state of Missouri.

Norman Frusco threw a folder in front of each of the detectives. 'These are the properties that Charles Fleisher has keys to. Seven of them skirt the river. An area I think that we are all agree is most likely the location that he would be working from.'

The detectives opened the folder and nodded agreement

'Good. What I propose is that we take a helicopter and buzz around these seven and see if there is any signs of life. It will be dark in an hour, unless Charlie-boy likes sitting in the dark. I think we should have a good chance of finding him.'

'If he's in.' Georgina added.

He sat alone in the dark with just the flicker of the computer monitor lighting his face, files were slowly transferring from his computer via an FTP program to a server that was sitting, for the most part dormant, in another continent. It really was that easy. After the files finished uploading he clicked onto his browser and checked his web site. DeathCam.net. The new images were there and so was something else, something he wasn't expecting. A message had been added to the main page, something he had not uploaded.

WANT TO TALK…MUTUAL BENEFIT. A FRIEND

His lips parted, initial anger turned to a grimace, then a smile. Somebody wants to talk. Somebody had hacked into his server. Quickly he went back to work, opening his web editing suite and composed a reply for his erstwhile hacker.

DEAREST FRIEND, INTRIGUED. SEND E-MAIL TO INITIATIVE@HOTMAIL.COM. ACCOUNT WILL REMAIN ACTIVE FOR NEXT TWENTY MINUTES ONLY.

He knew it was a risk, but that was half of the fun. Somewhere in the distance, sirens were wailing.

The police cars raced along the highway, sirens blaring, lights flashing, demanding a clear road and getting it. Georgina sat in the back next to Leroy. Frusco was driving, Rick sat in the front passenger seat next to his superior. Leroy was staring fixedly ahead, concentrating on the events that were hopefully about to be drawn to their conclusion.

'Are you all right?' Georgina asked Leroy.

'I'm a bear.' Leroy smiled. 'But thanks for your concern. I'll be okay.' Even he didn't buy the tone in which he sold the lie, but Leroy hoped the darkness would hide the pain in his heart and on his face. 'Gotta work.'

'And what happens when you stop working?' Her voice was low. She wanted to keep the conversation between herself and Leroy.

'I'm gonna get drunk and then I'll drink some more. Apart from that I haven't really made too many plans, you know.'

'If you need to talk?' Georgina left the offer open.

Leroy raised his hand and rubbed the stubble on his chin with his thumb. 'I know...gotta lot of thinking to do. Lia is my life.'

For a second or two, Georgina could see nothing other than a lost child sitting next to her.

'Airport's ahead.' Frusco called back.

Leroy immediately snapped out of his trance. Eyes alert once more ready to work. The car squealed past wire-fenced gates that ran parallel to a runway. Ahead, a helicopter sat impatiently, rotor blades whirring cutting dark skies. It's bright halogen spotlight, a beacon leading the way, lighting a white path for Norman Frusco to follow. Georgina dreaded the journey ahead of her; not yet on the aircraft and her stomach was limbering up. The prospect of low, night flying filled her with terror. She tried to talk her way out of coming, saying that she would be back up in a vehicle but Frusco wouldn't allow her, arguing that if the search proved fruitful there would be no time for anything else other than a direct assault on the property. No time to call for back up. He needed every fully trained professional at his disposal.

'Got the search warrants, Rick?' Leroy leaned forward.

Rick waved them in his face bouncing the small wad of paper of Leroy's nose. The comic moment broke the tension briefly but the feeling wasn't to last. Everyone in the car knew that this would probably be the last light moment of the night. Frusco pulled the car to a halt some twenty yards from the chopper, another police vehicle pulled up aside. Frusco was first out followed by Rick and Leroy, Georgina took a deep breath and joined them. Four uniformed officers, dressed in black, suited with Kevlar body armour and helmets with toughened bullet protecting visors, ran to another waiting helicopter. Their faces painted with nightstick to dull glare from greasy, light reflecting skin. They entered the other copter with a graceful ease that suggested that the manoeuvre was born out of practice. Georgina put her foot on the landing board and was hoisted inside by Leroy. Before she had sat down, the helicopter had left the ground and was already twenty-five foot in the air, starting to veer into a sharp right turn. A manoeuvre, which helped Georgina locate her seat quicker than she anticipated. She thumped onto the cushioning of the seat with little elegance, much to the amusement of Frusco seated opposite.

'You really do hate flying, don't you?' Leroy's deep voice boomed over the noise of the helicopter engine and rotors and into the headphones Georgina had just placed over her ears.

Georgina didn't answer, choosing to spend her energy and thoughts on securing herself with the safety belts instead. She sat back and gripped the black harness, which criss-crossed her shoulders, tugging on the black meshing and generally checking her safety.

The chopper raced along, nose slightly down, allowing the detectives an excellent view below. The night sky was clear with perfect visibility. Georgina breathed deep, trying to calm her nerves. She was aware of each breath, long and shallow.

Within what seemed to be seconds, Rick spoke into the small mic connected to the cans on his head. His voice sounded metallic.

'Turtle Island up ahead.'

Even in the darkness, Georgina could see the river snaking around the Island. The moon's glow reflected off the river's surface, highlighting its progress, circumnavigating the landmass. She opened her map and found the mouth of the river. The first house was no more than a mile in. As the two helicopters swept past, it was obvious that the property was abandoned. The house was old and left in a state of disrepair, broken windows and no door with much of the roof's slating missing. Frusco told the pilot to carry on.

He could hear them coming. He watched the bright searchlights weaving, scanning the fields. Searching, searching for him.

'Come and get me.'

Karen Fuller tried to move her tongue. Pushing it against the towelling robe belt that Charles had used to gag her. She wanted to swallow, finding it almost impossible. Saliva dribbled out of the corner of her mouth, leaving a damp patch on the pillow. Sober reality cast a shadow of degradation over the past twenty-four hours. But she couldn't deny she had done things that even thinking about them now, hours later, had given her a massive thrill. The thrill of pain, of pleasure, of being helpless. It was dark once more, between fear and uncertainty lay hunger. Karen had not eaten since their meal the previous evening. She hadn't seen Charles for hours, but the uncertainty was part of the fun. She tried to move her arms and legs but to no avail, fishing wire cut in to her wrists and ankles. Spread-eagled and naked, secured to the bedposts, Karen Fuller wanted to shout for Charles but the gag blocked out any sound she could muster. Had Charles simply forgotten about her? Dark thoughts ran through her mind, visions of being left alone. She tugged at the fishing line once more but there was no way it was going to break. The cutting effect on her wrists gave her the impression that her hand would sooner be amputated than the line would break. What little she knew about fishing drew her to the conclusion that the breaking strain of the line must have been greater than her body weight. The need to urinate now occupied her thoughts. Somewhere in the distance she could hear a low buzzing hum. The noise was getting closer.

Georgina marked a dark blue ring from a thick tipped felt pen and ringed a circle on the map. A big black X obliterated the red circle of the house they just flew over was.

'Over half way there, three to go.' Georgina said to herself. 'Don't barf now.'

The copter swooped in a sharp upwards motion, leaving Georgina's stomach on the floor; she leaned nearer the open door, allowing a little fresh air to hit her face. A bright light was burning in the near distance, like a beacon it drew the two helicopters toward it.

'Fifth time lucky maybe?' Frusco said to know one in particular.

Georgina hoped so, just so she could be on the ground. As they drew nearer it was obvious that the light was emanating from what should have been an unoccupied property. The house was a large two story wooden constriction; white slatted bargeboards covered the facia. Frusco asked the pilot to sweep past low, circle and land in the field adjacent to the house, some 60 yards from the river. They needed to get in quickly on foot.

Frusco, Rick, Leroy and Georgina were going to go in through the front, while the other team in the second chopper were going round the back. Adrenaline was starting to push away Georgina's phobia; this definitely had possibilities. The helicopter hovered briefly before setting down on the soft ground. Georgina stepped from the helicopter; the rotor blades had shifted enough air to cool the immediate temperature by about 15 degrees. Rick and Leroy were already running

ahead, Frusco lagged a little behind. Georgina soon caught up with the portly detective. They were now running at top speed toward the door of the house. The ground was uneven with the grassed lawn overgrown. Georgina was very aware of her footing. The second team were already in position around the back of the house, awaiting instruction. Frusco made the door last, puffing heavy, seconds after Georgina. He composed himself and nodded to Rick and Leroy
'Lets go.'

Charles Fleisher had been watching the television when he heard the sound of the two helicopters landing nearby. He quickly rose to his feet and walked to the window. Pulling the curtain back, Charles saw the two vast machines taking off again and flying back toward Missouri.
'Strange.'
He headed to the bedroom; she would be ready now for another session. Karen was still tied to the bed, small traces of blood appeared around her ankles and wrists. She was moaning, it was hard to tell exactly what she was saying. All Charles heard was moaning. Karen lifted her head and saw Charles standing at the entrance of the room. He was holding a knife. She dropped her head back to the pillow, struggling was painful and a useless waste of energy. The fear was exciting, she felt incredibly aroused. Charles walked toward the bed; with each step he took, Karen's excitement grew. She had enjoyed the pain. At first she was sceptical. The lack of freedom, the humiliation, the sheer raw pleasure. Together they had done things that she had never in her wildest moments dreamt of doing. Sex before was purely perfunctory with men and boys who had no imagination, the focus was always on them, on what they wanted and was often over so, so quickly. She wasn't sure if she would like games, but once the boundaries were withdrawn, Karen was introduced to another world. A world where pain and pleasure walked hand in glove, where humiliation enticed with fear heightened their lovemaking. Charles stood naked in front of Karen. His right hand gripped the handle of the carving knife. Its stainless steel blade sparkled. He straddled across her body, his genitals brushing against her stomach. Charles shimmied down her, tracing the knife's blade between her breasts, trailing it down her stomach, stopping at the small mousy blonde coloured mound of hair between her legs, before gently entering her with the tip of the blade. Karen gasped as the cold steel entered her body. Karen wanted to move, to struggle, but the knife inside her kept her still, stiller than she could ever imagine being. Charles removed the knife and placed the tip of the blade in his mouth. His eyes closed tight as though with pain. The blade jerked further in to his mouth with each cry, until Karen saw

104

a trickle of blood run down his chin and splash on to her thigh. Karen's need to urinate now was overwhelming, brought on now through fear though. She wanted to scream but all she could do was watch this crazy naked man eating a nine-inch carving knife. Charles coughed and pulled the blade from his mouth.

'Don't struggle.'

Blood ran from Charles mouth down his neck and chest. He slashed the knife to his right and at once one of Karen's arms were free. He raised the knife and was about to slash out again to free her other hand.

Leroy pulled back his size eleven boot, aiming it at the middle portion of the flimsy door.

The door gave way with the first kick and within seconds Georgina was entering the house behind Rick and Leroy. Frusco was on the radio as he entered ordering the team at the back of the house to enter. With quick succession they entered and cleared all the rooms on the ground floor. Rick ran up the stairs gun ready, in front of him. Georgina followed. Her firearm raised, pointing to the ceiling. Leroy and Norman Frusco took the steps that led to the basement. The door to the room ahead of Rick and Georgina was ajar. Rick pushed straight through. Any procedure learned through training, discarded. Georgina feared the worst; being three steps behind Rick she was too late to pull him back. She grasped outward with her hand, reaching for his jacket to pull him backwards, but he was gone.

The door flew open and Charles Fleisher turned to see a man pointing a gun, shouting at him. Charles was sitting straddled across Karen Fuller. His right arm continued to slash through the catgut, which tied Karen's left arm. Fleisher saw the flash from the barrel of the weapon and briefly felt a stinging sensation. Karen Fuller's free hand was fumbling with the gag around her mouth, desperately trying to free it, when the side of Charles head exploded, showering her in blood, bone and brain tissue. The dead weight of Charles body collided with Karen pinning her to the mattress. Charles dying body convulsed, flailing wildly, the knife in his hand scoring deep flesh wounds across Karen's face, neck, arms, stomach and thighs, until a second shot rang out, stopping Charles in his tracks, leaving the knife embedded deep in Karen's bare chest.

Georgina lowered her smoking gun.

'Jesus fuck, Rick!' She ran past a motionless Rick Montoya and started to pull Charles Fleisher from Karen Fuller's body. Helping hands arrived, reaching out, pulling the dead estate agent away.

Georgina looked up to find Leroy there, ready with a sheet to cover the teacher's nakedness.

'An ambulance is on its way.' Leroy touched Karen's arm, while Georgina untied the gag around Karen's mouth.

'He...He was going to...kill her.' Rick finally said.

Karen rasped, wincing through the pain. Her voice gurgled as though she was swallowing water while talking. 'No...no.' Blood seeped through the white sheet, spreading outwards like blotting paper eating ink.

'Where the hell's the ambulance?' Georgina shouted knowing that they were helpless to the teacher's plight. Karen raised her arm and gripped Georgina's sleeve. She coughed, vomiting blood, then breathed in as deep as her lungs would allow, but never breathed out. Her body stiffened, convulsing in a brief shudder before falling limp. Georgina shook Karen, trying to get a response. She quickly lay her down on the floor and pinched Karen's nose and blew air into her failed lungs. 'Pump her chest Leroy.'

The large detective knelt by Karen Fuller's side. 'The knife? I can't.'

'Pull it out...she going to die.'

'She's already gone.'

'Just pull it out, Leroy.' Georgina didn't wait she leaned across Karen's body and grasped the handle of the knife and with one quick tug pulled the blade from her chest.

'Now, pump her chest.'

Leroy moved forward and started to decompress Karen's chest. Georgina waited for him to stop and pinched Karen's nose again and breathed into her mouth, only one side of Karen's chest rose. Georgina breathed again, repeating the process another three times. Her own lips suddenly felt wet, sticky warm fluid painted her own mouth as Georgina tasted the teachers blood, returned to her mouth via Karen Fuller's filling lungs. Leroy stood and dragged Georgina away. 'She's dead.'

Georgina stormed over to where Montoya was glued. 'What the hell were you playing at? You know procedure for entering a room, *especially* where a kidnap or hostage victim is being held.' She grabbed Rick's lapels shaking him violently.

Rick stared blindly. 'He...had...a...knife, I saw him slashing across the girl with it. I thought he was killing her.' Rick repeated himself. His voice was monotone, as dead as the body of Karen Fuller.

'Come on.' Frusco pulled Rick out of the bedroom allowing some of the uniforms in.

The distant wail of sirens announced the arrival of the paramedics and back up. The siren grew louder and louder and then stopped.

Forensics moved into the house once the bodies were cleared for transport to the pathology lab for post mortems. Georgina and Leroy hung around, trying to uncover anything fresh, searching the house for fresh evidence to incriminate Fleisher. Georgina moved from room to room searching methodically, taking her time, lifting and moving every conceivable object. She entered a door, which lead to the basement and found a full video-editing suite with monitors and scores of videotapes.

'Leroy?' Georgina backed out of the room and called up the stairs to the upper half of the house.

Time ran quickly into the morning and an entire night had been spent on the search for evidence for a case that was now closed as far as the state of Missouri and Norman Frusco was concerned. Georgina knew she was wasting her time, Frusco had his man; the media had their story. She would rather have spent the time asleep in her motel room but for the nagging lingering doubts that pervaded her thoughts. Leroy moved from room to room, intrinsically searching for anything that would take his mind off Lia.

The press and TV were banging at the door within an hour of the incident. Barbara Dace heading up the long line of reporters vying for exclusive access. Barbara stood on the door demanding to the police guard that she spoke with either Captain Frusco or the FBI agent, Agent O'Neil. Georgina was within earshot, she recognised Barbara Dace's voice. She came to the door.

'What can I do for you Mrs Dace?'

'I was hoping for a little payback for the help I gave you.' Barbara was her usual assertive self; even so, her voice had an edge to it tonight. Dace's cameraman John Keller was waiting behind her, looking tired and in need of a long vacation.

'Mrs Dace.' Georgina's voice was firm; there was no way she was going to be intimidated by either Barbara Dace or any of the other reporters standing line. 'When forensics have finished here, I promise you will be the first and only reporter allowed inside the house, but until then would you kindly fuck off.' Georgina's voice didn't change pitch or tone but she knew it had the desired effect when Barbara's jaw hit the ground. Georgina smiled and closed the door politely.

'Hey, that was cool.'

Georgina turned to see Leroy standing, laughing.

'Have you ever thought about working in public relations?'

'You know those leeches really crawl on my skin sometimes.'

'I guessed. You kinda gave that away.'

The letterbox to the door opened and Barbara called through. 'So, when do you think forensics will be finished?'

They watched totally enthralled. The small community of Turtle Island was unexpectedly thrown into the limelight and their attention had not been captured so collectively since the Oklahoma bombing or that dark day in New York, September 2001. Images filtered through the air, through cables and broadband telecommunication lines. Riveted, the populace never moved from their seats, choosing to watch the news unfold in front of their eyes, and then the beginning of the exodus of the curious and the morbid as they began their pilgrimage to the house on the far side of the Island where Charles Fleisher kept Karen Fuller captive and eventually killed her. It was a trickle at first, then a continual steady flow of people ready to pay homage, then a rush. Each of them curious to see first hand, to feel and breathe in the air, the very same air Charles Fleisher breathed. A group of inquisitive onlookers encamped outside Fleisher's realty agency, though what they expected to find was as much a curiosity, some even settled outside the Fleisher household. Narla Fleisher watched the whole event unfold via news broadcasts. Their daughter, Harley watched with her in stunned silence, at first disbelieving, then finally relieved. At four in the morning she finally slunk beneath the covers of her duvet. Harley Fleisher would sleep soundly for the first time that night in years, there would be no more interruptions and no intrusions in the middle of the night.

Twenty-Three

Georgina lay on the bed in the bare surround of her motel room, exhausted. The only light in the room was coming from a small table lamp that sat on the locker by the bed. She noticed the sheets had been changed for the first time since she arrived. Even though she desperately wanted to close her eyes and sleep, her mind was still racing. The *'coming down'* period after a case's resolution always left her drained but restless.

The horrible feeling that she had taken a life stuck in her claw, even if it was a lowlife like Charles Fleisher. Somewhere inside his twisted mind there must have been the fragments of a decent person and to have extinguished anything that may have once been good unsettled her, redemption is always for tomorrow. Charles Fleisher was the first person she had ever shot, let alone killed and she had to come to terms with it, figure out in her mind what it was now that separated her from him. Both of them were now killers, even though the government sanctioned her, it didn't address the internal moral battle. She had stopped someone from living, snuffed them out, stopped them...Full stop.

Georgina sat up, leaned across the bed and opened her small attaché case. She pulled out a large A4 pad and pen and began to write her report on the case. She was angry that she was compromised into killing Fleisher. If anyone were going to break that night she would have laid a month's salary that it would have been Leroy but if anything he was more focused than usual. Rick Montoya had acted like a rookie, a bad one at that. Georgina was in no doubt that if Rick had aimed better Karen Fuller would have lived to tell the tale. O'Neil worked on until 4-30in the morning, when finally she succumbed to sleeps hypnotic potion. She fell asleep holding the biro, still writing the report with the pad resting on her raised knees.

SUNDAY

At twelve thirty, Georgina called into the office. The day was overcast and considerably cooler than of late. Rain threatened and the stormy clouds that held it were moving fast towards Turtle Island. She had watched the morning news and wasn't surprised to see Barbara Dace reporting from inside the house where Charles Fleisher and Karen Fuller had died. The media were spinning their own version of events on Turtle Island. It would seem that everything was straightforward and Barbara's report appeared to be with the police department's blessing, it certainly coincided with Captain Frusco's thinking. Seeing Norman Frusco interviewed by Dace confirmed Georgina's suspicions. The case was over and the only thing left for Georgina to do was to file her report, which out of courtesy she felt obliged to show Frusco, even though she knew his reaction would be far from one of pleasure. She waited outside his office occupying one of the seats that was usually kept for interrogating suspects. The well-worn leather seat was unsupportive and for the few minutes she had been sitting on it, found it extremely uncomfortable. With luck she could be on her way home by Monday, Tuesday at the latest. She had no desire to be drawn into a lengthy post mortem of the case, not that for one moment did she believe there would be one. This case had all the trappings of an irritating acquaintance and the chances were it was going to be swept under the carpet and forgotten about. It was not the sort of thing that the people of Turtle Island wanted hanging about, it stank as bad as the unknown corpse they fished out of the water at the beginning of the case, lowering property prices and scaring prospective tourists. Hence the sunshine and roses report from Barbara Dace.

'…the nightmare ended last night and now residents of Turtle Island can return to the idyllic lifestyle they shared before Charles Fleisher began his short reign of terror. Tonight we can sleep safe. Barbara Dace, M.R.T.V Turtle Island.'

Georgina waited patiently in the office, looking at the hive of activity unfolding in front of her. Missouri Police were dealing with the daily running of their state. Norman Frusco was lunching with Barbara Dace and the desk sergeant couldn't give a time, approx or otherwise, of his return. She said she'd wait.

Georgina waited an hour before accessing a photocopier and leaving a Xeroxed copy of the report on Frusco's desk. She couldn't shake the image of Karen Fuller lying dead on the bed under the prostrate figure of Charles Fleisher. She wanted to go somewhere to clear her head, do something positive. She found herself driving down the highway towards Leroy LaPortiere's house. As she drove, she began to question the sacrifices she had made for a *career* and wondered about the psychological damage to her mental welfare. The scars usually materialised in the form of nightmares, sleepless nights, or as now, trying to find some sort of mental release. After a mile or so Georgina couldn't understand why she was having difficulty seeing properly, when she looked in the rear view mirror she saw the reason; both her eyes were clouded with tears. She pulled the car to the hard shoulder and spent a confusing twenty minutes controlling large shoulder heaving sobs. She could see Karen Fuller in her mind, lying perfectly still, perfectly dead. Georgina had been close to death on many occasions and was at a loss as to why one more death should affect her so deeply. Georgina had seen worse, dead children, murdered babies, old folk robbed and brutalised; why should the death of a middle class school teacher move her to tears on the hard shoulder. She wiped her eyes dry and tried to compose herself, before putting the car into drive and pulling away.

In the daylight, Leroy LaPortiere's house showed the signs of neglect that Lia had so often complained. Cracked and flaking paint around the windows and doors allowed rain to seep through the unprotected surface, swelling and splitting the exposed wood. Georgina looked for a bell, two bared wires hung impotently from a small hole which once was resident to a push button bell. She rapped on the fly screen with her knuckles hoping that if he were in, he would hear her. Georgina waited for a minute, before pulling open the fly screen and knocking hard on the glass panelled door. Leroy's lumbering frame moved toward the door behind the obscured glass panel. He opened the door, unshaven and reeking of alcohol, eyes hanging out of his head. He looked bewildered, lost.

'Hi.'

He seemed unsurprised to see the detective standing at the door and stepped to one side to let her in. Georgina noted that he was still wearing the same clothes as when she last saw him.

'Sorry the place is a bit of as mess.' Leroy apologised as Georgina entered the main room.

A home video was playing in the VCR, Lia was running around in the garden, spraying water over the cameraman, whom Georgina guessed to be Leroy. Lia was laughing, filmed during happier times. To the side of the armchair that Leroy had obviously been sitting in lay an empty bottle of rum and five cans of beer. The image on the television froze, Georgina turned. Leroy swayed unsteadily, the VCR control held in his wavering hand.

'Been watching old films.' Leroy said almost apologetically. 'You know, I've been walking around the house spraying an old bottle of Lia's perfume, just to pretend she was still here...'

Georgina spotted the bottle of *Jewel* lying amongst the empty bottles.

'I spent 50 bucks on a bottle of her brand of perfume just to spray around the house, yet when she was here I never bought her a bottle. She always used to buy her own, 'cause I was too busy...pathetic isn't it?' Leroy dropped into the armchair, his foot kicking the empty bottles out of the way.

'I don't know what you want me to say Leroy. I know this job eats too far into all of our lives, but no matter how much, it always come as a complete shock to us as to the damage it is doing to others.' Georgina sat opposite Leroy, placing her report folder down next to her. Leroy scratched his head then rubbed his face with his hand. He stared at her, through her, for a moment completely lost in his own world.

'You know I had all the warning signs, just ignored them...' Leroy raised his large hands in a dismissive gesture. 'She...was...just the most beautiful woman, did I tell you that?'

Georgina smiled. 'Leroy, she still is, she is not dead.'

'Then why do I feel as though I am mourning her. She has gone and I miss her so...' Leroy's voice trailed away, cracking slightly. '...much.' There was a vulnerability to the big man that was hitting home to Georgina's heart. She wanted to console him, take him in her arms and ease away the pain, maybe she felt that would help relieve her own burdensome anguish or would that just be calculated self reciprocation. Part of her wanted to mother him, part of her wanted him to father her, part of her, the trained self reliant woman wanted to step back and not get emotionally involved. That side of her was saying in her head. 'Keep your distance.'

'All I have is this video, she didn't even leave a photograph.' Leroy paused the video, Lia was laughing, holding a hose, water gushing from its spout spilling onto her face. 'Hey, I'm sorry. I must really be dragging you down.'

Georgina stopped herself from going over to Leroy and hugging him. 'What are you going to do?'

Leroy shook his head and looked out through the window. 'I don't know yet.' He sighed. Then added. 'Have another drink, then maybe drink some more until the pain eases.'

'Sounds like a good idea, maybe we should get drunk together.' Georgina didn't want to leave him alone to drink. As always, there is safety in numbers.

'There's a tumbler beside you in the bag. She took all the glasses, so I bought some from the gas station last night.'

Georgina felt inside the plastic bag lying next to the sofa she was perched on and grabbed a plastic tumbler. She threw it to Leroy who, though his senses were dulled by drink, managed to catch it.

'Only got brandy.' He said unscrewing the cap of a bottle.

'Fine.' Georgina shrugged not really caring what she was going to drink as long as it was alcohol.

'So, you know my problem, what's yours?' Leroy filled Georgina's plastic tumbler to the brim. 'Sorry, no coke left.' He handed her the full glass, their fingers touching briefly. Georgina realised that was what she wanted now more than anything; human contact. Leroy held onto the glass, spilling brandy down their fingers.

Georgina took a deep breath. 'My problems pale in comparison to most people I know, present company included.'

'A problem is a problem is a problem.' Leroy raised the glass in salute to Georgina and took a large gulp from the plastic tumbler. Georgina passed the brown folder to Leroy.

'This is one.' Georgina handed Leroy her report.

Leroy's eyes focused on the A4 pages of type.

'You pick your times.' Leroy said trying to concentrate. He began to read Georgina's case report, he sat back in to the seat, while she swallowed back the contents of her tumbler then topped up both glasses.

Frusco closed the folder and pressed the intercom on his desk.

'Get me Agent O'Neil, Hannah? She's staying at the Motel off highway 14.' He let go of the button, not waiting for a reply and dialled a number on his phone. The phone, eager to please as usual, rang in his ear. Frusco waited for Rick Montoya to answer. The phone rang three times before a child answered.

'Hello.'

Frusco knew Ray's voice and asked to speak with his father, he heard the phone being placed down and the child saying. 'Okay' followed by his little voice booming. ' DAD, PHONE.'

There was a scrabbling sound and Ray spoke quietly into the receiver. 'He's coming...'

Frusco could hear the child breathing and chomping something, probably gum. Then from nowhere the boy said. 'I gotta bike today.'

Norman felt uneasy speaking to the boy, having missed out on the whole child rearing process. It was not that he didn't have any, he had a boy and a girl, it's just that he was too busy working while they were too busy growing up.

'That's nice.' Frusco lamely offered.

Fortunately before Frusco had to indulge in any more 'small' talk, Rick picked up the extension. 'You can put the phone down now, son.'

Norman heard the click; Rick asked 'What's up?'

'I need you to make a full account in writing of what happened last night, it seems O'Neil is going to name you as being incompetent and endangering the lives of other officers, including herself.'

Rick listened in silence.

'I'll eh...I'll...come in...right away.'

'You know the procedure once a complaint has been issued by an FBI agent against a Police officer, Internal Affairs are going to be all over you and the station, plus...' Frusco didn't like saying what he had to say next and took a deep breath before continuing. 'Plus, I'll have to have to suspend you until any investigation is completed.'

Rick felt his stomach flip. He stood pole-axed. He placed the phone receiver back in its cradle without saying goodbye to Frusco. Rick put his jacket on. Just as he was leaving the front door Jo-Lynn caught him.

'Where you goin', hon?'

'I gotta go in.'

'But you said you got time off time to be with Ray and me.'

'I know, I know...It's just that something...unexpected has just occurred.' Rick kissed Jo-Lynn on her lips and walked straight to the car and sped away without further explanation. Jo-Lynn stood at the door baffled.

'Is something wrong?' Korjca's voice gently asked, sensing her employer's distress. Jo-Lynn put on her fake smile- the one that she usually reserved for clients that she didn't much like. 'It's nothing to worry about, I'm sure.'

'I see that the protection men have gone.' Korjca's broken English added a greater hint of danger. Jo-Lynn peered across the road, the darkening sky hovered overhead cutting visibility. An empty space occupied the place where the twenty-four hour police protection vehicle had stood guard for the past two and a half days.

Leroy closed the file. 'Are you sure you want to do this?'

'You saw the way Montoya acted. He may as well have been holding the knife himself.'

'I know that he's been under a lot of strain. The threats may have clouded his judgement.' Leroy tried to defend his partner.

Georgina wanted to believe that, but if that was the case then he should have distanced himself from the investigation. 'Anyway, I thought I would show you.'

'Frusco won't be too pleased that's for sure.'

'What about you, what do you think?'

'Me, I'm nearly past caring...' Leroy emptied the remains of the rum bottle in his glass before resting it down next to the other empties. 'But Rick is a friend. One of the few true friends I have at this moment. I'm not happy...but he did jeopardise our lives.'

'Do you think I'm being unfair?' Georgina pressed for Leroy's opinion.

'Does what I think really mean that much.' Leroy rested his head against the curve of the chair. The effects of the rum slowly driving home.

'I don't know, I always seem to be on the outside...on the periphery, looking in on the real world, that kind of detachment doesn't always make you the most popular person in the room. It's kinda hard to judge whether I'm being too...' Georgina searched her mind for the right word but Leroy found it first

'Objective.'

Georgina smiled. 'Something like that...So?'

'So...' Leroy took a breath. 'My opinion for what it's worth. Rick Montoya is a friend and a good detective. He's been there backing me up, supporting me and I have never had cause to find him lacking in commitment...'

'But?' Georgina could sense a 'But' was coming.

'But,' Leroy cleared his throat, making room for a confession Georgina thought. 'But he arrived on Turtle Island under a cloud of suspicion. Now I wouldn't tell you this under any other circumstances because he's a brother...'

Georgina was getting impatient, wanting to know Leroy's secret.

'But?'

'But there were rumours that followed him here.'

'What sort of rumours?'

'Lets just sat that he had a brush with Internal Affairs back in Chicago. I don't know the full account, Rick's never entrusted me with any confidences from those days. I do know it's something to do with Jordan's death.'

'His daughter.'

Leroy nodded. 'I looked into it, he doesn't know though, but I thought that if I'm putting my ass on the line with this guy then I need to know about the rumours and dispel any harbouring doubts I had about his...'

'Commitment.' It was Georgina's turn to complete a sentence.

'Yeah...Something like that. Commitment.' Leroy paused, drank a little. 'So I dug a little and I found some things out.'

Georgina sat forward on the edge of her seat, willing Leroy to reveal whatever he knew about Detective Rick Montoya.

Leroy closed his eyes, tried hard to remember the details, the names, and the places.

'Rick had been on the tail of a small time sociopath, Fortune something, was his name, something like that anyway. As I say mostly small stuff, a robbery here, extortion there, nothing much, but all of a sudden Fortune's name was linked with a kidnapping. A wealthy young business man, Patrick Multhorne.' Leroy took another sip from the tumbler before continuing. 'Whether Fortune had Multhorne or not will probably remain a mystery. It seems that on the day Jordan died Rick was taking her home from school, when he caught sight of Prentice Fortune, yeah that was his name Prentice Fortune, driving a beat up ol' Mustang. A chase ensued. The rest is history. Rick somehow managed to clip Fortune's Mustang; his jeep rolled killing Jordan instantly, breaking her neck. Fortune's Mustang mounted the kerb and shot straight through Garland Bach's front window.'

Georgina looked puzzled. 'Who?'

'Garland Bach.' Leroy continued. 'They're high fashion retailers. Fortune had his girlfriend with him at the time. She was all but decapitated when a scaffold pole used as part of a display went through her head. Three people in the shop were injured, one person was left paralysed under the wheels of Prentice' car. Prentice was arrested but the Chicago PD couldn't nail anything on him...muchacho embarassmento.'

'Surely Prentice had a strong case for compensation?'

'Yeah, sure he did, would have won too, but you know how the system works. Chicago PD stood by their man, Rick had lost too. They dragged the case out and started to counter sue Fortune's estate on behalf of Rick for the loss of his daughter, which just about financially crippled Prentice Fortune. He dropped the case, had to sell house and just about everything else. Meanwhile Rick took a sideways *promotion* to...'

'The Missouri PD.' Georgina raised her glass and polished off it's contents.

'Correct, but allegations followed him here. *IA* was all over him for about two months, then they seemed to disappear, things went quiet, returned to normal. Fortune Prentice vanished; Patrick Multhorne was never found. So as you can see, another round with Internal Affairs is going to dig up a whole can of worms.' Leroy finished his glass and sank back even further in to the armchair. 'Shit man, I'm outta booze, why is it that when you want to get steamin' you can't?' He tossed the plastic tumbler to one side.

Georgina could feel the effects of the brandy beginning to take hold.

'I don't know what to do.' She waited for a response from Leroy but he just stared at the ceiling, remote, lost once more.

'Life's a bitch.' Leroy whispered.

Georgina woke, it was dark. She was lying across two seats of Leroy's sofa and had a thin blanket wrapped over her. Her shoes had been removed though she had no recall of taking them off herself and her jacket was lying folded over the back of a dining room chair in front of her. She sat up in the darkened room and tried to focus. The armchair opposite was empty. Her eyes stumbled around in the darkness trying to pick out familiar objects; there was no sign of Leroy.

'Leroy.' Georgina whispered through the dark, though she didn't know why. It was as though she didn't want to break the fragile tranquillity of the night. The only sound was that of the promised rain running down the windowpanes, that and her breathing. She walked to the window and looked out. Not a soul stirred on the street, the only activity, that of droplets of rain bouncing hard from pavement back toward the sky, fighting gravity, refusing to yield to it. The world was empty tonight. The aching loneliness in her, depicted so clearly on the streets. She turned, wondering where Leroy was, whether he had driven off in a drunken stupor to find an open liquor store, or whether he had sobered up and had gone off in a mad search for Lia. Georgina walked down the hall to find the bathroom. On the way back she passed an open bedroom door. Leroy was lying sprawled across the bed with just his 'CK's' on. She stopped in the doorway and watched him sleep. Tonight they were both vulnerable. She entered the bedroom, stripping down to her underwear and curled in tight to Leroy.

He mumbled. 'Love you baby.' and continued his sleep.

She sat awake for a few moments feeling his body so close to hers, enjoying the comfort of his body until she closed her eyes and slept.

MONDAY

Georgina woke with her arms still wrapped around his stomach. She was drenched with perspiration, her underwear cold and clinging against her skin. Realization slowly emerged through hazy memory as Georgina remembered where she was. She tried to pull her arm free but his arm and side trapped it. As she pulled away, her fingers brushed against him. Waking him. Charles Fleisher turned smiling. Georgina woke screaming to an empty room. Lost for a second she tried to gather her thoughts, everything was alien, strange. She scoured the room; her clothes were in a pile on the floor by the bed. As the confusion of nightmares gave way to the certain reality of day, Georgina smiled, chiding herself, more through relief than anything else though. Leroy appeared at the door, panicked, and dressed in a robe with shaving foam covering half his face.

'JESUS.'

Georgina looked suitably apologetic. 'Sorry...bad dream.'

Leroy entered the room and sat down on the bed next to her. 'Are you alright?'

Georgina pulled the quilt up to cover her breasts, even though she was still wearing her bra, she felt a little awkward with the situation.

'Yeah...sorry if I scared you.' She looked around for a clock. 'What time is it?'

The sound of the phone ringing delayed Leroy's answer. 'About...who can that be?' He stood. As he was leaving the room to answer the phone he said. '10-45.'

Shocked that she had slept for so long, Georgina threw the quilt off and stood. Almost instantly regretting it, as her head pounded a samba rhythm that was a characteristic of drinking too much alcohol. She swayed for a second, gingerly holding her head, waiting for the room to become motionless. Leroy appeared at the door again, this time Georgina made no attempt to cover herself, more concerned with remaining vertical and holding down the contents of the previous nights consumed brandy.

'That was Frusco. He wants to see me.'

Georgina opened one eye, then slowly the other. Her hand was still trying to stop her head from rolling off her neck.

'And he said if I manage to bump in to you, he'd like a word with you as well.' Leroy smiled. 'I've nearly finished in the bathroom, looks like you could do with a shower. I'll put out some clean towels that's if she's left me any. And when your ready, breakfast will be waiting.'

The thought of food was the last straw and Georgina rushed past Leroy hand held firmly to her mouth, bouncing off him in the doorway, running toward the bathroom.

'I must be losing my touch.' Leroy said to himself. The sound of retching from the vacuous bathroom confirmed another lost battle to drink. Georgina staggered out of the bathroom looking considerably worse than a few moments previously.

'Sorry.'

'You go ahead and take the shower now, I'll finish off later.' Leroy wiped the remainder of the soap from his face. 'I'll put some coffee on.'

Georgina slunk back in to the bathroom.

Leroy heard the shower start as he filled the kettle with water and placed it on the flaming gas ring on the hob.

The pressure of the water on Georgina's face and body was therapeutic as it slowly began to wash away the grogginess. The shower gel was a man's sports gel, but at this stage it was the least of her worries, besides it smelled nice, comforting. She lathered her short black hair and rubbed the residual soap in to her face, blinking out the invading bubbles before they began to sting. She stayed under the powerful jet of water for fifteen minutes before she felt fit enough to face the world and Leroy. When she pulled back the mottled screen a fresh pile of towels had been placed on the closed toilet lid, with a robe draped on the top. She hadn't heard Leroy enter, but the towels and robe were not there before she stepped into the shower. She wrapped a towel around herself and began to dry quickly. Georgina then put the robe on and began to dry her hair, which because of its length was a short task. Georgina placed her bra and knickers in her pocket and taking a towel with her, continued to rub her scalp as she wandered down to the kitchen. Leroy was putting the finishing touches to scrambled eggs on toast with fresh coffee and orange juice.

'Thanks for the towels.'

Leroy looked up. 'No problem.'

Something unspoken passed between them for a moment. Leroy was the first to break the silence. 'I've laid some deodorant and a brush and some other bits and pieces I thought you might need on the bed. They're mine so you might smell a bit testosteroney. Breakfast will be waiting when your ready.'

'Thank you, Leroy.' Georgina paused. She turned and walked to the bedroom. As promised arranged on the bed was a can of deodorant, two hair brushes, her clothes and the remnants of the perfume Leroy had bought to remind him of Lia. She sat on the edge of the bed and dressed, combed her hair, applied some make up from her handbag and began to feel human again. She sprayed the perfume on her wrist and breathed in its heady aromatic scent.

'Lia used to do that.' Leroy's voice startled her. How long had he been standing there?

'To answer your question, not long. I just came down to say breakfast is served.' He smiled a genuine smile.

'How did you know what I was thinking?' Georgina smiled back, feeling comfortable in his presence.

'I get paid to know what to ask.'

Frusco was in better form than Georgina hoped, but he still applied a lot of pressure on her to get her to modify her report. She sat at his desk staring into the face of the cat that had *his* cream last night. O'Neil wondered who the Milk Maid was. Georgina reluctantly amended her report, withdrawing criticism of Montoya or the department, more for Leroy's sake than anything else. She didn't want to blot his copybook. The post mortem results on Max Dalton were sitting on Frusco's desk addressed to Georgina. She noticed that the envelope had been opened. Frusco argued that his secretary opened all the post and had overlooked that it was not addressed to her boss. She slipped the report from the envelope and began to read what was obviously now second hand news. The water in Dalton's lungs was that which matched the river sample, no surprises there. Lips and tongue were removed with pinking shears a short time before drowning. He would have died from massive blood loss or trauma had he not drowned. Anal trauma was caused by penetration from a projectile of some sort, definitely not penile. There was no trace of sperm or DNA material other than that which was his own. At the time of death Max Dalton ejaculated, a not too uncommon occurrence. Semen was present in his urethra. The report concluded that Dalton had been kept hostage for approximately three weeks before his eventual death. Georgina closed the report. Certain in her mind now more than ever that Charles Fleisher did not carry out the Turtle Island murders, but she also had no proof to the contrary, only instinct. She looked at Frusco.

'Case closed.' Frusco took her case report and offered her a ride to the airport, which she declined until Leroy offered to be the chauffer.

Georgina asked Leroy to make a detour to Rick's house. Korjca answered. Her hair was pulled back and she was wearing a flattering tight fitting tee shirt and jeans.

'Mr Montoya is upstairs; I will call him for you. Come in.' She bounded up the stairs. Leroy and Georgina walked through to the lounge and sat waiting until Rick appeared.

'Hi, what brings you out here?' Rick Montoya was dressed in a pair of baggy training bottoms and a vest. Sweat ran down his chest from his weights session.

'Georgina's going home, thought she like to say goodbye.' Leroy spoke for the detective.

'Would you like a drink, tea, coffee or something stronger?'

'Coffee.' Leroy and Georgina answered simultaneously.

'I just wanted to say...' Georgina just wanted to say the opposite of what she did say. 'I just wanted to say the case is officially closed and to thank you for your hospitality.'

Rick knew what she *wasn't* saying to him and was relieved. 'I know I messed up...and it's me that should be saying thank you. I don't know what happened...I guess I just froze, never happened before.'

'And it won't again.' Leroy was quick to say.

Korjca entered carrying a tray with coffee mugs and a steaming pot. She poured the coffee and handed a mug to each of the men before handing Georgina hers with a serviette. Georgina noticed a phone number written in tiny lettering, Korjca's thumb brushed against Georgina's hand, the slightest touch. Georgina drank from the coffee and wiped the corners of her lips with the tissue before placing it in her pocket.

'I've taken a month's leave, try to sort things out.' Rick said, looking downwards, trying to avoid eye contact with Georgina.

'Good.' Georgina looked at Rick, trying to read his guilt. She wondered whether she was seeing the real Rick Montoya.

'You know it will haunt me for the rest of my life. The fact is that had I killed him Karen Fuller would still be alive.'

'What do you want me to say?' Georgina couldn't hide her feelings any longer.

'I know...I know.' Rick was wringing his hands together, still looking down.

Georgina finished her coffee. 'Gotta make a move, 8-45 flight.'

It was only 4-17pm but she had to be driven back to the motel and pack yet before the drive to the airport and the dreaded flight.

By five twenty she had packed. After a quick phone call to Leroy she was ready and on the road to the airport. Leroy was quiet, never prompting conversation and only answering in monosyllables until they reached the departure lounge. He was carrying her bags; the last call for her flight had been announced.

'Well, it looks like it's time.' Georgina smiled weakly. She hated goodbyes nearly as much as she hated flying. She leaned forward on her toes and kissed him tenderly on the lips. 'Thanks for looking after me.'

'I could say the same. It's me who should thank you.'

'What about Lia?'

The tall detective leaned forward and kissed Georgina. Then he let her go and said. 'I'm still working it out.' He breathed deeply and looked away for a moment 'I'm...I'm making plans, don't know what I'm gonna do yet though.'

Georgina's flight to Maryland was called over the tannoy.

'Gotta go.' Georgina needed to get away before she totally cracked. She squeezed his hand.

She took her bags from Leroy and made her way along the gateway to the waiting plane.

PART TWO

With the waiting comes the fear

Twenty-Four

Six Months Later

*H*e had waited for a long time, had been patient, let life return to normal on Turtle Island. Now was the right time to strike…now that no one expected it. That would show them, show them how wrong they had been. He watched them from the comfort of the swimming pool. The neatly housed pool was ideal to watch them, a blessing, especially now the winter nights were drawing in. Every night for the past fortnight he had lodged in the poolroom and watched them through his binoculars. The perfect family, playing, laughing, he had even watched them making love in their bedroom, through the open curtains. The garden backed onto nothing other than more open land, *they* often walked around their bedroom naked. He watched them do all the things he had been denied and now was the time to stop it, now was the time to regain the power. He knew that the time was right. There could be no other way, succession and relinquishment. He was always right. He put down the binoculars and rummaged in the rucksack for the pistol and knife. He hoped to use the knife, get up close and personal, feel the warm blood through his fingers; it gave him such a rush. He would wait until the last light went out, and then wait a further twenty minutes. He was almost giddy with excitement. Tonight was to be the night. No more waiting.

Maryland. Portmorion

The piece of paper was crumpled and tired looking. A little frayed at the edges, just about the way that Georgina O'Neil felt. She had just returned from a kidnapping in Boston, a three-year-old boy, taken by his estranged father and held for ransom; three million dollars from his ex-wife's wealthy family. Five weeks taken from her life trying to bring the case to some sort of resolve. Hunting down the father and boy.

Covering thousands of miles, searching every lead. Having her worst fears confirmed when the mother received the boy's toes, before, and against instructions parting with the ransom just to find the boy dead, lying face down in a puddle of diesel in a lock up garage, seventeen miles from the family home. The father escaped the country with the money and little or no chance of being caught.

The world had been beating Georgina up for the past year and feeling at an all time low she sank exhausted into the comfort of her bed vowing never to get up. The piece of paper turned up as a reminder of the past, a time only briefly forgotten. There were times when she had wanted the company of a friend, a companion, someone to talk to, whinge to about her job, cry with, when like tonight things looked black. She had dialled the number only to hang up before connection was made, or just to hear Korjca's voice say *'hello',* at the last minute Georgina lost her nerve and hung up. She hated herself for being so pathetic, why did friendships and relationships cause her so much anxiety? Eighteen hundred dollars of psychotherapy had failed to find a reason, the only thing she did know was that the longer it went on the harder it was becoming for her to form anything close to a friendship, let alone relationship. She worked hard, always got on well with her colleagues but remained detached, or rather, kept a detachment. Preferring to keep work colleagues at arms length. She picked up the phone and dialled the number, willing herself to say talk, just say hello. The phone rang twice before Korjca's voice mail system cut in, informing Georgina that her phone was either busy or not turned on. The tone to leave a message beeped. Georgina waited for a couple of seconds, deciding whether or not to leave a message. Her mouth began to form a word as her hand placed the handset back in to it's cradle.

'Closer, closer, closer.' He mumbled the mantra, girding himself, steeling himself for the moment as he placed the hunting knife in its holster, strapped to his calf. He moved stealthily from the pool house across the grass toward the house. He had waited for thirty minutes after the last light was turned off. Waiting in the dark, watching for any movement, thirty long minutes where each heartbeat thumped, where every movement he made was physically sensual, almost sexual. The feelings inside him were certainly close to those with which he would compare to making love.

'Closer.'

He reached the French doors. Opening a zip pocket in the upper arm of his black blouson jacket, he checked the syringes lying dormant wrapped in a small cloth. The needle tips covered with small rubber stoppers. The Dormicium inside the syringes looking innocuous, but he knew the drug was powerful enough to send a rhinoceros to sleep for a fortnight when administered in the right volumes, too much and the sleep could be permanent, not the outcome desired tonight though. Not tonight. As expected, the French doors were locked but they were worth a try anyway. He moved along the outside of the house to the rear door from the integral garage. The garage, like many, was used as a storeroom. Mainly for the boy's toys, it had probably never seen a car since it was built. He had watched, from the fields behind the house, through binoculars, watched the boy playing on his bike, shoot a few hoops, and leave the door open, as he always did.

'Closer.'

He pulled the knife free from its holster and entered the house. Switching on the small torch housed on his black beanie hat, he stepped cautiously over the scattered toys toward the door that bordered the inner sanctum.

12-30am. Georgina couldn't sleep even though she was exhausted. She lay awake. She wanted to speak to someone, call her father, have someone to talk to. She looked at the clock again that sat on her bedside table. The green illuminescent glow radiated 12-33am. She had called him later than this early hour, usually to the chagrin of his wife, Cally, her stepmother who, aged 34, was only three years older than herself. She did not deny her father happiness with a much younger wife, because Cally had stepped into the picture when Georgina's father was on the brink of an abyss. Barely managing to hold himself together after the sudden death of his wife and her mother.

Georgina thought about her mother, she missed her as much as any one would miss their mother but it was always true that she was closer to her father in many ways. They both had a joy of the academic; Georgina had toyed with the idea of teaching or lecturing after her degree. She never dreamed for one moment during the years at university that she was to follow in her father's footsteps. She was daunted by failing or more precisely not living up to measure. The thought of not being able to fill those footprints almost decided an alternative career. After she had enrolled with the FBI and passed training at Quantico, her bond with her father deepened. She shared thoughts and ideas about cases with him, usually the ones that had her stumped. He enjoyed the challenge and the closeness they shared through the secrecy of the work. They thought their dependency on each other was their little secret, thought it was not a secret, certainly not to her mother. If anything, it was Cally who had a hard time accepting the closeness of their relationship; sometimes Georgina sensed Cally's jealousy over the time Wynan O'Neil gave his daughter.

As Georgina was about to dial her father's number, the image of Harley Fleisher appeared in her mind, she wondered about the relationship the little girl had with *her* father. There was a feeling of unfinished business that haunted Georgina, not just her curiosity over Korjca and the piece of paper she was holding. There was not the feeling of satisfaction with the case that usually accompanied the successful resolution of her work. She dialled her father's telephone number. The phone rang twice

'Hello daddy. It's Georgie.'

The boy was asleep in his bed.

He could have danced in front of him and would never have woken the somnambulant child. A thought passed through his mind as to whether he would actually need the Dormicium for the boy, or whether he would just live with the thrill of him waking as he took them to the secret place. The needle pierced his brown skin by the neck, drawing a tiny prick of blood on its removal. The boy didn't even wake.

'Closer, I'm getting closer'

He wondered what it would be like to draw the knife's blade across the boy's throat. He would pay a fortune to see the boy's father react to finding his son lying in a pool of blood, with fear etched in the darkest pools of his eyes..

'No one is innocent.' He whispered, before leaning down and kissing the boy's forehead. 'No one.'

The room was like that of any child. The walls adorned with posters of basketball players and pop stars, and a set of bunk beds. The empty top bunk. Part of him hoped that when he entered the detective's bedroom, that Rick Montoya would be awake, part of him wanted the confrontation now. He had to suppress those urges. Knowing that Montoya would be strong, who knows, maybe even stronger than him, especially when he would have to fight for the lives of his family? He left the boy's bedroom door open and crossed the landing. There was no light from under the door, no intimate sounds coming from the room behind the closed door. He turned the handle, the door opened. His heart felt as though it was going to rip right out of his chest, such was the excitement he felt. The waiting was nearly over.

'Closer and closer'

He wanted Montoya to wake briefly, just long enough to see *his* face, before injecting the Dormicium; it really didn't matter if his wife woke. She'd be no match. He put the needle to Montoya's neck. Perfect.

Rick's eyes opened, unseeing in the dark, until they adjusted, focusing on *his* face.

He breathed the words 'Hello, Rick' into Montoya's face then pushed the plunger.

The sound of a mobile phone ringing in the room next door woke Jo-Lynn.

'That girl and her phone.' Jo-Lynn moaned through bleary, sleep-filled eyes.

The ringing stopped. The phone answered.

He stood completely still, hovering over the drugged detective.

'I'm sorry to ring you so late, but it's.... I. I don't quite know what to say. It's Agent Georgina O'Neil of the FBI. I get the feeling that you wanted to talk to me. I know a long time has passed but...' Georgina hated answering services. An inherent fear of sounding monosyllabic slowed her delivery subconsciously. Suddenly lost for words, Georgina hovered with her finger over the receiver.

Korjca's mind was trying to interpret the message through her sleepy fuddled mind. Her hand automatically reached for the handset, knocking her bedside lamp in the process. She put the handset to her ear.

'Hello.'

But only heard the static buzz of a disconnected line.

'Shit.'

Korjca slapped the phone back down in its cradle and sank into the pillow. Her eyes open now trying to adjust to the room. The room was lighter than usual and Korjca wondered whether it was later than the time set on the phone. The realisation that the curtains were open solved Korjca's mystery. She swung her legs out of the bed and blearily wandered over to the open drapes. The moonlight bathing the room in silvery luminance. *He* watched excitedly, almost beyond restraint from the shadow fallen corner he occupied near the door. Only the tip of the knife glinted in the moon's radiance.

Korjca closed the curtain, turned, eye's half closed ready to return to the sleepy world of dreams. The bed was a giant vat waiting for her to plunge into its welcoming arms.

The scream of madness was not heard by anyone else but Korjca as *he* ran toward the sleepy nanny. Korjca felt a blow to her chest, the attack so fast, so unexpected, she briefly wondered if she was dreaming, or if she had somehow merely fallen in the dark, but there was somebody standing in front of her. She could see the whites of *his* eyes glowing brilliantly in the moon glow. There was a person standing in front of her, close, so close.

Korjca felt the pain in her chest. She was confused, her thought process's suddenly sharpening as she began to understand what was happening.

He pulled the long, serrated knife from Korjca's chest. The jagged edge opening flesh and snapping bone on its retrieval, blood spread out through the print of a teddy bear on Korjca's nightdress. She fell to her knees, her hands grabbing at her attacker for balance, her breathing laboured. Korjca felt hands push her backwards. The nanny slumped, falling onto her back with her legs pinned underneath her. Her body folded back like a collapsible chair. Unable to move, Korjca could only stare at the ceiling and the shadowy outline of her attacker. A face appeared in front of her. Korjca saw the glint of the knife before it was placed under her chin. She could feel the cold tip pressing into the soft fleshy skin of her neck, followed by a stinging sensation as the tip of the blade sliced through skin and tissue, then a soothing warmness flowing down her chest. The face moved closer and closer. Korjca felt warm lips pressing on her mouth as the last breath of air from her lungs was literally sucked away by her attacker. She tried to breathe. An act so instinctual, now taking every last ounce of her effort, of thought, of will power. But it was like breathing in a vacuum. She was extremely aware of the last few minutes of her life, aware even after the last gasp of air had left her lungs, aware of her bladder betraying her, aware of the silvery moonlight in the room, aware that she was dying. She wanted to see the room, keep her eyes open until the very last moment. Feelings of who attacked her did not enter her mind, she never questioned why?

Coldness started to spread from her fingers moving up her arm and down her legs; the tightness in her chest gave way to a feeling of numbness. The remnants of oxygen in her brain began to diffuse into carbon monoxide. Korjca closed her eyes.

He pulled the van into the garage driving over or through the clutter that Ray left scattered. There was blood on his latex gloves. *He* was charged with electric excitement, his heart pumped so hard that he had to will his arms and legs to move. Adrenaline coursed through his body, surging in swathes of stimulation that was as close to pure pleasure as he had ever experienced. *He* was in control now.

Rick was to be the first; bounced down the stairs, his head striking off every step. *He* had grip of the detective's ankles, pulling him along the carpet. Rick's naked body offered no protection from the harsh surfaces he encountered as he was dragged to the van. Once in the garage *he* bound Montoya's arms and legs with carpet tape, stuffing paper into his mouth and sealing it by wrapping tape round his head three times. *He* rolled Rick's motionless body onto the lowered hydraulic ramp at the back of the van before raising it and pulling the unconscious form into the empty cargo area. That was the hard one; his wife would be much lighter; easier to carry. *He* knew that *he* would be able to carry her body with ease. As for the boy… he was small potatoes. *He* ventured back into the house. Jo-Lynn lay sprawled across the bed in the same position, where a brief struggled ended with a small quantity of Dormicium flowing through her veins. Jo-Lynn was hoisted onto *his* shoulders. She weighed no more than nine stones, maybe eight and a half. On the way back down to the van *he* stopped at the boy's bedroom and grabbed Ray roughly by his pyjama top, carrying the small boy with one hand. *He* felt empowered. With every step toward the van his strength grew. *He* stopped only to bind the detective's wife and child with carpet tape. With all three secured in the back of the van *he* returned to the bedroom of the nanny for one last look at his power. Korjca was prostrate on the floor, eyes closed. The moonlight turned her blood black. *He* bent down and dipped a gloved finger in to the inky liquid pool that was starting to congeal around her throat and wrote the word 'CORRUPT' across her forehead.

The drive was short… so short; that was part of the fun though.

Twenty-Five

Rick could hear crying coming from somewhere, the sound invading his brain, stirring the dormant thought process. As his mind began to whir, starting to function, he recognised the crying child's voice, it was his son. Rick opened his eyes to total darkness. Cold water lapped around his thighs and for the first time with it the realisation that he was cold, very cold. He tried to call out to calm his son but a gargled cacophony filtered through the tape. Rick was aware that his arms and legs were bound and that he was secured to a chair immersed in water of some sort but how he got there was a mystery. He wondered if it was some sort of nightmare. The fact that he knew he was awake made him shudder because it meant this was real. Rick tried to move his arms but they were bound so tightly he knew it was a waste of strength. Whoever was doing this to him would make themselves known soon; otherwise he would already be dead. The water around his legs lapped gently over his thighs. Rick could hear a muffled sobbing coming from somewhere near his left.

Jo-Lynn woke first, the drugged haze in her head now clearing. Her understanding of what was happening even less clear than that of her husband's. She too, could hear Ray's sobbing but was helpless to either reply or give any form of comfort to her son. Jo-Lynn had waited with her eyes open for over ten minutes before hearing Rick's struggling. In that time her eyes had not adjusted to the dark. No chink of light entered the place where they were being kept. The cold water that came up to Jo-Lynn's stomach gave her a sense of foreboding that frightened her almost beyond reason but most of all she wanted to be close to her son, if *she* was frightened she dreaded to think what her son was going through. Right now all she wanted to do was hug and reassure him, tell him that everything would be okay, even if she didn't quite believe it to be the truth herself. Jo-Lynn tried to move forward but the chair she was secured to rocked uneasily in the dark. The prospect of plunging head first into the water soon stopped any attempt to free herself.

He watched them slowly wake through his night vision glasses. First the woman, then the boy and finally the detective; the reason they were all there. *His* enjoyment was all encompassing. *He* felt the embodiment of that joy soaring through his body. The pleasure, a palpable tingle that coursed and surged and grew greater as each member of the Montoya family woke from their drug induced sleep. *He* watched from the safety of darkness, a voyeur observing a sacred moment, one *he* had prayed to God for. A moment that was finally answered, God does indeed move in mysterious ways. *He* moved closer, into the water, stirring the stagnant liquid, until *he* was inches away from the detective's face. *He* whispered in Rick Montoya's ear.

'Soon.'

Wesley Timms opened his e-mail program. The always-on connection heralded each new arrival with a trumpeted fanfare, which pissed everybody in his office off, but he didn't give a fuck. He never really cared about any of them, except maybe Chelsea Drake; yes there he could give a fuck…given the opportunity. Wesley spent most of his day peeling off layers of her clothing with his eyes, but knew she wasn't interested in him. He'd have to find other ways to make her interested and he never doubted his own ingenuity for one moment.

He read the e-mail.

Some time ago you contacted me with a business proposition, now is the right time to talk seriously, go to www.deathcam.com now and see if you think the time is right. Click on the web cam link. Password 'CORRUPT.'

This e-mail address will remain active for one hour.

A Friend

Wesley felt his throat tighten. His fingers jabbed at the keys on his keyboard, misspelling the web site address twice in his clumsy eagerness. As the site began to load Wesley imagined Chelsea Drake fuck naked, straddled over him, dripping lust.

The first image that loaded on his screen was a picture of Korjca. As Wesley typed the password, the letters appeared on Korjca's forehead, written in blood. She was obviously dead. The picture disappeared, replaced with a new image. A night cam offered grainy views of a cellar, three figures were strapped to chairs and a counter was set on the screen counting down. 59:59:40. In the darkness a figure moved toward the camera, covered from head to toe in black with just two slits through a mask highlighting the killer's eyes, which in the weird lighting looked like red pools.

'Hello Wesley…feel honoured?…You should. This is a premiere, just for you.'

Rick didn't know what time it was or even the day. The darkness had stretched the hours. He tried to wriggle his fingers and toes. The immobility coupled with the cold water had numbed them and the only sensation he felt was a dull aching that was spreading from his feet upwards. It had been ages since he had heard the voice and in the hours that had passed had spent his time trying to match a face to it. Hoping to make sense somehow of why he and his family was being tortured in this way. A blinding flash suddenly illuminated the room, the bright, startling explosion, momentarily stunning Rick.

'Smile you're dead!' The voice said.

The command was followed by another flash. This time Rick saw a blurred outline of his captor. He briefly saw a Polaroid camera in the split second that it took for the flash to expose the film. His brain took in a lot of background detail and for the first time he was aware of where he was being kept.

'Once more, this time with emotion.' The voice called again.

Rick felt a stinging blow to the side of his face.

'Profile.'

Rick turned his head and the flash popped once more. In the far corner of the chamber he caught a glimpse of his son, head slumped down unconscious, asleep or...Rick didn't want to think of the worst.

The Polaroid camera whirred as it spat out the print.

'Other side.'

Another slap, pushing his face to his right. The flash this time illuminated his wife. Jo-Lynn was sitting up in the chair, bound in a similar fashion to him. Her eyes wide open with fear. Water soaking through her nightdress, a small smattering of blood smeared down one arm. The horror images were relayed to Rick's brain, absorbed in the fraction of a second of light. Suddenly the darkness seemed to be a preferable option. It was the markings on the wall behind Jo-Lynn that confirmed Rick's dread. He had seen them before, and in the split second it took to illuminate them, his brain had searched and recollected just where. The videotape sent to Barbara Dace's grandson.

Twenty-Six

October mornings in Pormorion, Maryland, are crisp. Georgina loved them when as today they were bright and sunny. The prospect of winter loomed around the corner and she hoped to be able to spend some time at home decorating and making her house more habitable. For the past fourteen months it had been no more than a place to rest her head in between cases, no more than another motel but off a familiar highway. She hadn't yet given the old half-brick, half-wood, constructed house her own sense of identity. She stood at the kitchen window and looked out onto the overgrown lawn, promising to cut it at the weekend, if she could wrangle a day off. Two brightly coloured fake magnetic tropical fish flipped about in their water world fish tank. The buzz of the roving magnet -that enticed and seduced the metallic clones, drawing them to all the corners of the tank- no more than a faint hum in the background, soon to be consumed by the radio. Georgina filled the kettle. She hummed along with the tune, a song by Radiohead. She wasn't sure of the title but thought it to be 'Karma Police'. Her suspicions confirmed when the chorus started. After drinking a cup of strong coffee she changed into her running gear, long grey sweat top and baggy jogging pants, a pair of Nike Air trainers and went for a five mile run around the streets of her hometown. Pormorion was a small, quiet fishing town, somewhere away from the hustle of Maryland and the bustle of the city. It was the ideal retreat that Georgina sought. A sanctuary away from the horror and madness that often was a big part of her work. Running through the small lanes, past the old colonial houses, she could quite easily get away from the stresses and strains of the day she left behind, and the day that was to come. She turned inwards to the coastal road. The slight incline was especially tiring as it came near the end of the run, but it was worth the final burst of effort just to take in the view of the Atlantic Ocean. A view which always managed to take her breath away with greater ease than the endeavours of her exercise. As she neared the top of the hill the sea came into view. A benign smile spread across her face. Georgina breathed deeply, the air slightly salty, blowing in on an easterly wind that although light, still managed to blow her short black hair backwards. As often during a run along the coast road, Georgina felt a surge of joy spread through her body. She knew all about *runners high's* and the endorphins that were released into the brain and bloodstream and guessed that she was a little luckier than most experiencing that sensation almost every time she ran that route. She stepped up the pace for the final mile, the cool morning chill dissipating under the warming autumn sun. Her breath bellowed in cloudy vapour trails, she could feel the sweat under her running top, cooling and clammy against her skin. Another part of her morning ritual that she enjoyed would be the steaming hot shower when she arrived home and the breakfast that followed. 'Probably scrambled eggs or French toast' she informed herself. She turned off the coast road and headed down the last five hundred metres. Soon her house would come into view, a sight that always brought a smile to her face... but not today.

The blue flashing light was a part of her daily life, something she saw every day. Something that she should be immune to, but when Georgina saw a police car parked outside her house, the momentary feeling of dread spread through her the way it would anyone else. Thoughts of her father entered her head, memories of her mother and how the news of her death was broken. Georgina was unaware that her speed had picked up to a sprint, her mind concentrated solely on the black and tan with the blue flashing light. Her breath bellowed in white clouds from her nose and mouth. As she drew nearer the car she saw a familiar face sitting in the back of the car. Leroy LaPortiere allowed a grin to spread across his face on seeing her approach. He opened the door and stepped from the warm interior of the car into a cold Portmorion morning. Georgina instantly recognised the detective's anxiety and put aside worries of personal tragedy. She knew this had to do with work and also from the look that now occupied Leroy's features; she could tell it was serious. Georgina stopped in front of Leroy, her breath now coming in sharp bursts; she doubled over to catch her breath. Crouched over, her hands resting on her knees for support and recovery, she looked up at him. Leroy's expression remained sober.

'Hi.' His greeting flat, another ominous sign. 'We need to talk.'

The inside of Georgina's house was not far off the mark as to how Leroy had pictured it in his mind's eye on the flight from Missouri. She was a neat and tidy person whose tastes ranged from the homely dresser in the kitchen with it's myriad of plates, cups and saucers, to the slightly modern, with a glass topped wrought iron legged coffee table that stood conspicuously in the centre of a lounge, full of older furniture. None of it fashionable but by the same token not too hard on the eyes either. Rather like Georgina herself, Leroy thought to himself, watching her as she entered the lounge holding two coffee mugs in one hand and a plate of chocolate cookies in the other. She had a towel draped over her shoulders and her hair was tousled from a vigorous rub. She had discarded her sweatshirt and just wore the sweat stained tee shirt, which hung loosely over her jogging pants. Georgina handed Leroy the mug of coffee and placed the cookies by his side on the sofa. She sat down opposite him, the way she had six months previously in his house. Leroy took a sip from his mug; the steaming liquid lubricated his dry throat. Georgina waited for him to speak

'I got three weeks left in the force...three weeks and then I'm out. That's the plan. Gonna move up north to Washington, join Lia. We talked the other night for the first time since she left, really talked, you know. About six weeks ago I finally tracked her down. She's livin' with her Aunt...' Leroy left the sentence unfinished. Georgina could sense there was another motive to his visit other than to impart the news of his personal life. 'Rick and his family have been kidnapped.' Leroy blurted the line out. He moved back in the chair and rubbed his hands wearily over his face. 'Oh man, this is bad.'

Georgina sat stunned for a moment, allowing the information to filter through her shock.

'Korjca's dead.' Leroy continued.

The two words sledgehammered into Georgina. The blood drained from Georgina's face. Her lips opened slightly allowing a few words to escape.

'What happened?' For a moment Georgina felt dizzy, as the shock began to register. She grabbed the edge of the chair for support.

'Are you okay?' Leroy asked.

'I'm alright...it's just the run...it's just the run.'

'I'll get you a drink.' Leroy walked to the kitchen and opened the refrigerator door. A carton of opened grapefruit juice, three pints of skimmed milk and an orange soda bottle, half empty, greeted him.

'Remind me not to come for dinner.' He said quietly to himself. His eyes cast over to the draining board by the sink. An empty glass with a transfer on the clear surface saying 'DRINK ME!' was lying on its side waiting to fulfil its purpose. Leroy filled the tumbler from the faucet.

'Tap water good?' He called in.

'Yeah.' Georgina's voice sounded broken.

Leroy entered, holding the glass.

'You sure you're okay?' He repeated.

'This job, I get too involved sometimes. I always hate death.' She sniffed, wiping her eyes with the corner of her sleeve. 'Oh God, I think

I'm gonna be sick.' Georgina straightened and steadied herself, breathing deeply.

Leroy handed Georgina the glass, cold beads of water clung to the surface of the tumbler like the tears that Georgina wanted to cry but would only cry during the quiet moments alone.

Georgina looked at Leroy. The sadness evident in her face. She shook her head. 'It's just so sad...Korjca was a nice person. What about Rick and his family, any leads?' She changed tack.

Leroy grabbed his coffee and took a long slow gulp. 'Your hunch was right. Frusco and Rick...all of us I guess, except you, were too keen to close the case back on Turtle Island.' Leroy paused. 'Charles Fleisher wasn't our man, sure he was a bastard who got his thrills by tying up and fucking his daughter's teacher, pardon my French. But he wasn't the *Dentist* or whatever name the media wished to give him. *He's* still out there.'

'Fleisher was part of something bigger.' Georgina knew the implications ran deeper than the surface impression. Apart from having to return to Turtle Island and try to find the perpetrator of the original crimes as well as find Rick and his family, she also knew that there would now be a full enquiry by her superiors into her actions in resolving the original case. Georgina shook her head.
'Shit.'

'I know, it sucks.' Leroy sympathised with modest understatement.

Twenty-Seven

The flight back to Missouri was as bad as Georgina had expected. Air pressure played havoc with her sinuses, causing excruciating pain, and bad turbulence only added to her misery. The sudden drops in altitude churning the contents of her stomach, which already had a higher than usual acid content brought on by the anxiety of flying and bad news. She gripped the steady handle in the toilet and hung her head over the open bowl, trying to force the contents from her stomach, but to no avail. It seemed she was destined to spend the entire flight suffering discomfort. Leroy sat watching the in-flight movie, headphones secured over his ears. A squeaky clean, edited version of 'Along Came a Spider'. Leroy liked Morgan Freeman as an actor; the man has a quite, stately grace that many in his trade would do well to inherit. In all the years that Leroy had been flying it always amazed him how the airline industry managed to mess up so many good films with just a pair of scissors and a morality that was slightly higher than that of God. The plane hit another bank of clouds, Leroy remained oblivious, engrossed in the feature, nor did he notice that Georgina had been out of her seat occupying the mid-cabin toilet for the best part of half an hour. A stewardess knocked for a second time on the door and called through.

'Are you alright in there or do you need some assistance?'

Georgina looked at her sallow complexion and splashed water over her face once more.

'I'm alright, I'll be out in a minute.'

The plane rumbled through the cloudbank. Georgina gripped the handrail tighter and wished that the plane would either hurry up and land, or crash. In her present state of discomfort either option would have suited her fine.

'There are people waiting out here for the toilet, Miss O'Neil.' The stewardess voice called through the door once more.

Georgina wiped her mouth with a paper towel and stared once more at her reflection in the mirror. Tiny blood vessels in the whites of her eyes were rupturing, streaking tramlines of blood toward the iris and pupil. The pain in her head increased as she felt the aircraft rise in altitude, leaving her stomach floundering. A third knock at the door prompted her to reach out and unlock the latch. She opened the door to be greeted by the exasperated face of one of the passengers. A young man with a serious attitude problem. He 'dussed and tutted' as he barged past Georgina, before she could make her way out of the small cubicle. She staggered back to her seat, using the headrests to steady her progress and slumped down next to Leroy, who remained unaware of her discomfort.

'This is a good film.' Leroy said without breaking eye contact with the screen on the back of the headrest. Georgina reached forward for the sick bag, hating every second of the flight. She rested her head back, closed her eyes and prayed for sleep, while gripping on to the small white bag. Every noise, every whine of the engine, every voice that talked, from whiney children to arguing couples, entered her head, nothing escaped. Her senses suddenly seemed to be on hyper alert and try as she might to sleep, she couldn't. The blackness of closed eyelids was not a sanctuary as purple and blue flashing spots invaded the darkness. A menagerie of thoughts and images started to play games inside her head, memories of her time at Turtle Island six months previously. Faces, Korjca's smiling slightly rounded face, her pure white skin. The sight of Karen Fuller's dead body lying sprawled and naked, under the dead weigh of Charles Fleisher. Georgina had her own in-flight movie on constant play.

The sound of the cabin bell resonating broke the images. Georgina opened her eyes. The film on the screen had finished and been replaced by a map showing an animated aircraft moving over an area marked *Missouri*. The no smoking sign was illuminated and the captain spoke over the address system informing her that they were about to land in approximately ten minutes.

'You been asleep.' Leroy informed her.

Somehow she had managed to fall asleep, but how and when, like most sleep, would remain a mystery. As the plane started its descent to the airport, Georgina gripped the armrests tighter, her discomfort now displaced by her fear of crashing. The landscape of Missouri came into view through the small window to Leroy's left. The plane would pass over Turtle Island before landing, Leroy watched out for the small enclave surrounded by water. Georgina eyes were clenched as tightly shut as were her hands encompassing the rounded ends of the armrests. As the plane lowered, cars came into view, milling around, carrying people making their way home after a long day at work. The aircraft followed the highway that led to Turtle Island. Independence Bridge appeared, the link to the Island. Car headlights were being switched on as dusk began to settle over Missouri. Within three minutes the plane's tyres were touching down on the airport runway and Georgina's heart rhythm began to settle to a more accustomed pattern.

The air temperature was warmer than Pormorion but much more comfortable than her previous visit. Early 60's Fahrenheit, Georgina guessed. Leroy loaded her small case into the boot of his car, while she pulled a cardigan around her shoulders just to keep the coming night chill away.

Jo-Lynn tried to move her legs; the cold water was doing its level best to numb them. She curled her toes constantly to keep the circulation of blood moving in them. She no longer had any idea how long she had been kept tied to the chair. The darkness and the cold water were the two constants that remained unchanged throughout her ordeal and both played havoc with her senses. Time was irrelevant; it became suspended, like her senses. The tape over her mouth was uncomfortable at least she could swallow and breathe with ease though she didn't know how much longer she could last before hypothermia began to set in as the cold began to seep through her bones. She prayed that Ray was no longer immersed in the water. If he was, she feared for his life. The thought of him sitting in the cold water, alone and afraid, was about the only thing spurring Jo-Lynn on, keeping her from crumbling, she needed to be strong for Ray. She promised herself that she would take any half chance, any opportunity at all, to escape. Jo-Lynn tried to call through the tape, she desperately wanted to hear from her son, some sign of life, a noise, a muffled cry, anything would be welcome but her effort was left unanswered. She tried to move her legs, break the tape that was binding them together.

He watched her struggle, fascinated by the maternal bond that was driving her forward, forcing her fight, driving her on, giving her strength that *He* knew all too well. *He* held a torch, the temptation to turn it on, let her know why she was here. It was nearly time for an explanation, things were becoming a little clearer in *His* head. The time was getting closer...closer. *He* stood up; sending tiny ripples of water to splash against Jo-Lynn's legs and continued watching her face all the time. The image speckled, through the night sight strapped to his head but none the less effective. *He* turned and looked at the chair beside *Him* and saw the body of Rick Montoya, slumped half unconscious, bound to the seat. To *His* side were three steps leading to a small platform with a further seven steps, going up to a door, whose white luminescence was almost blinding through his night sights lenses. *He* walked up the steps and through the door bolting it shut from the outside.

Jo-Lynn sat for a moment, listening hard in the dark for any noise from Ray. She tried to shuffle her chair, dragging it toward the corner where she had a brief glimpse of her son. She inched the chair forward slowly. The sound resonating in the hollow cavernous room, followed by the sound of water breaking against the far wall, and her own efforts escaping from her lips as muffled anxiety. She wanted to call her husband, wake him; work out a plan to escape. She moved the chair sideways. One of the legs fell in to a rut, a divot under the pitch-black murky water causing Jo-Lynn to overbalance and fall sideways. Her face felt the embrace of water in the dark, as her head submerged. Momentary panic swept through her as her body remained tethered to the chair. Instinctively, as the chair began to topple, Jo-Lynn inhaled a deep lungful of air and closed her eyes. The sensation of water over her head whilst strapped to the chair, filled her with dread. She tried to lift her head, turning it to one side. The thought ran through her mind as to how long her lungful of air would last. The prospect of drowning in this hell spurred her on. Jo-Lynn tried to establish her bearings but it was almost impossible, down was up, up was down, everything was black. Her feet seemed to be above the water level, she hoped that she was lying on her back, bubbles began to escape from her mouth as the pressure inside her chest increased. She knew that soon she would have to exhale and after that, barring a miracle, she also knew it was just a matter of time until she would have to breathe in. She rocked the chair trying to unbalance it from its prone position, each effort resulting in more air escaping from her lungs. One last attempt finally moved the chair from her back to her side and with it the last gasp of air in her lungs, her face briefly felt the rush of cool air and in that fraction she breathed in, before once again being submerged. She wanted to scream; anger and hatred began building to an explosive level within her. The chair settled on its side. The top of her head was just above the water level now but her nose and mouth remained below the surface. She held onto her last breath and struggled and kicked with all her might, unwilling to let her life end without a fight. The tape that secured her shoulders suddenly gave and she was able to lift her head above the water. She breathed in through her nose, feeling water flow down her throat. She swallowed and tried to gulp the air filling her lungs.

The car bumped over the ramp as it drove on to Independence Bridge. The sensation woke Georgina from a brief doze. Sleep overcoming her almost as soon as she rested her head back against the restraint. Leroy drove along with the radio low; thought's buzzing through his head, all the time thinking, trying to obtain some sort of grip on the case. He was determined to resolve the case within his last three weeks but he was equally resolved to leave on the set date. He had lost Lia once and had no intention of doing so a second time. Georgina looked through bleary eyes at the dashboard and the windscreen ahead of her, for a moment she was back in her hire car during that sunny day six months previously. The Saturday of the basketball match. She remembered the tooth on the dashboard, the small child's tooth. The one time that the killer made contact with her. The whole incident forgotten or lost during the hunt for Charles Fleisher. The tooth would be sitting in a plastic bag tagged as evidence, never to be used, as no trial would follow the death of Fleisher. The ends of the case had all been wrapped up so neatly with his death. Dead men don't talk. She could see the tooth lying on Leroy's dashboard, so vivid was the image she almost reached forward to grab it.

'The tooth.' Georgina said.

'What?' Leroy didn't take his eyes from the road.

'The tooth...I need to see the tooth that was left in my car, remember?' There was an excitement to her voice, which over came the tiredness that she felt.

'You need to see this tooth *now* or in the morning.' Leroy said knowing which answer he'd prefer to hear.

For a moment Georgina remained silent while she pondered the possibilities. 'Now...if you don't mind?'

'I was afraid you'd say that.' Leroy swung the car around in one easy movement, receiving a blast from the horn of the driver behind until Leroy turned on the blue flashing lights in the grill and on the parcel shelf as they roared along the freeway back toward the police precinct. Georgina began to assemble several threads that could formulate an action plan. Her mind ran over several options but try as she did, everything was still too vague. They needed evidence and clues. They needed more than help if they were to save Rick and his family.

The e-mail arrived without bells and whistles but *he* was waiting patiently for it, all the time he was monitoring Jo-Lynn's progress as the image from the room was relayed to a monitor in front of him. *He* minimized the image, happy that she wasn't going to go and spoil things by drowning, and then opened the mail. He could sense Wesley Timms greed; it dripped of the page like hot fat even though it was an electronic screen. Prentice Fortune smiled.

'And the world will know my name.'

The tooth was small, a white molar with no sign of decay. Georgina held the plastic evidence bag closer to the light. The small evidence box was placed on the table in front of Georgina. Leroy was surprised that any evidence was left at all. The room was cold, lit with a buzzing neon tube that did little to encourage a warm ambience.

She stated at the tooth, lost for a moment, deep within her own thoughts. 'This tooth is quite small, could even be that of a small child or a women. Was the tooth ever cross referenced with Karen Fullers dental records?'

Leroy looked sideways at Georgina O'Neil. 'I doubt it. Nothing much was done but cover our backs over the Fuller incident.'

'Can you get the dental records?'

'Sure they're upstairs with the path' reports.'

Leroy turned to go back up the stairs from the vault.

'What about Fleisher's wife and family?'

'Narla Fleisher and Harley.'

'Can we check against them too. I also need the video tape that the killer sent us, you know, the Dalton one.'

Leroy stopped on the third stair up and shivered. He had a hard time forgetting the Dalton tape. 'It should be there with the tooth. All the evidence is there. What little there was.'

Georgina searched through the box. There were piles of 8mm videocassettes shot after the Fleisher incident, a sealed envelope marked *Polaroid's*. A knife blade dulled with dried blood but no standard format VHS videocassette. 'Definitely not here.'

'It's probably around somewhere...maybe misfiled.' Leroy continued walking up the steps. 'I bagged it myself.'

Georgina looked at the rows and rows of little brown boxes that were identical to the one she was holding.

'Great.' She placed the box back in its unoccupied slot on a shelf and sat on a table in the centre of the room. She continued to study the small tooth. The surface appeared unblemished, no scratches or indents caused by dentist pliers, no sign of stress caused by the killer's hammer, unlike the teeth of the other victims, all except Karen Fuller who never was a victim of the killer anyway. Georgina thought for a while. It was possible but highly improbable that there could be more than two people stalking Turtle Island. She was pretty sure that there was only one killer, Charles Fleisher had the misfortune to stumble right through their investigation and while that resulted in his death she could not feel an injustice had been afforded him. That left her still searching for the identity of the man labelled by the media as the *Dentist*. She wanted another viewing of the videotape that had been given to Barbara Dace. Recalling that name gave her the whereabouts of at least one copy of the tape. The TV studio had been showing carefully edited pieces, so they must have a copy.

Leroy walked back down the stairs to the evidence room. He held a manila folder between his fingers, rocking it back and forth within the rhythm of his walk.

'Dental records of one, Karen Fuller. I have run a check with the Fleisher's dentist for their records.' He handed the folder to Georgina.

She opened it and took out the history chart.

'They're pretty comprehensive, go way back.' Leroy said having briefly flicked through the records on the way down in the lift.

'This lady had great teeth, not one filling, not one extraction.'

'I want this tooth tested and checked against every other person involved in this case, no matter how tenuous the link, everyone from Fuller to Fleisher and his family... to, to.' Georgina began to think of all the sources from where the tooth may have come.

'To little Ray.' Leroy finished her sentence.

Georgina nodded. 'Get all the records together...Is there a reliable dentist, police surgeon, anyone local with the means to do the work fast?'

Now it was Leroy's turn to think. 'A lot of records are going to be on various lists, police, FBI, even my dentist on the Island. She is pretty dammed good, quite a techno junkie too. Her practice is outta Star Wars, lasers, microscopes, computers...yeah she's pretty good.'

'Okay, can you get that together? I gotta go visit Barbara Dace.'

Before he could complain, Leroy was watching Georgina moving swiftly up the stairs and out of the small storeroom.

Twenty-Eight

She heard the door being opened and could already feel his presence in the room with her.

Jo-Lynn's neck ached from straining to keep it above the cold water. Only briefly did she feel any sense of warmth, which was when she urinated. The pitch dark hid her shame and the fact that she enjoyed the sensation of warmth it briefly gave to her legs. She cried out for help through the tape around her mouth. Her words unintelligible but she hoped their desperation would not be lost. She felt hands grab her shoulders and powerfully lift her upright. *He* was right in front of her. How she wished she had a leg free, an arm free, something, anything with which she could strike out with. She wanted to tear this *mother's* face off. Gouge out his eyes, and even then she would not be happy. She could hear more tape being pulled away from a roll. The crackle of the glued surface as it freed itself from it's backing, quite distinctive, then she could feel it being wrapped around and around her head, over her eyes, the tape being pushed down securely around the bridge of her nose.

'I am going to turn the light on and take the tape from your mouth to feed you. Promise me that you won't try to scream when I take the tape away from your mouth. If you do scream I will kill you.' The voice was whispered.

Jo-Lynn felt something sharp pressed against her neck and guessed it was a knife.

She mumbled through the tape gag. The thought of having the tape removed from her mouth relieved her almost beyond measure. She felt fingers peeling the corner of the tape, gently. As the carpet tape pulled back, cold air rushed into the pores of her skin as tiny hairs were extracted, stuck to the glue. Jo-Lynn stretched her mouth, exercising it after the confinement of the adhesive gag. She heard a light-pull switch being tugged and could just see the flickering strobe of a fluorescent tube from a small gap under her taped eyes. Her throat was dry but she needed to speak to her captor, ask him why he was doing this? She wanted to know more than anything how her son and husband were. She tried to swallow.

'...I...I need to know, How my son is?' Her voice croaked.

'No talking.'

The smell of tomato soup being waved under Jo-Lynn's nose at first nearly made her retch but as a spoon was placed against her lips she realised how hungry she was. Her lips parted and the soup entered her mouth, lubricating her throat. She felt something cold pressed to her mouth, the smell strong. She found it hard to believe that what she tasted was only bread and butter. Jo-Lynn took a bite and while swallowing chanced speaking once more.

'How is my son, how's Ray? Please tell me, I promise I will be quiet if you tell me.'

'Your boy is alive for the moment. My grudge is not against you or your boy, but your husband has to pay for what he has done.' The voice echoed in the room, its slow distorted tone as chilling as the water around Jo-Lynn's knees.

Another spoonful of soup.

The voice continued. 'I promise neither of you will suffer, as long as you do as you are told.'

More bread.

She continued to eat in silence, not even sure if what she was eating was poisoned but the fact that she was being fed led her to believe that she was probably going to be in for a long stay and the fact that she was not allowed to see his face gave her fresh hope. From under the tape she could just see her legs, she wanted him to finish feeding her and hoped *He* would leave the light on, so that she could try to look around the room from under the tiny gap in the tape. Jo-Lynn took another mouthful of bread.

Now it was Wesley Timms turn to watch. He watched with glee as the counter started to move. The site was now live and with a few well placed e-mails was already starting to pay dividends both for him and the oh so ready advertisers with their little link buttons taking the ever eager customers to their corporate sites. Of course it had to be discreet, but Wesley was ingenious when it came to being devious. He watched Jo-Lynn being spoon-fed soup while on the phone to a major supermarket.

'Just think product placement…it's no worse than the movies, where we are spoon fed adverts throughout the feature.'

The line went dead.

'You win some, you lose some.' Wesley dialled the next number on his list.

Georgina borrowed Leroy's car hoping he was in no hurry to get home tonight. The memory of the small roads around the Island returned to her as she drove, and after only one mistake, Georgina found herself pulling up in the drive of Barbara Dace's house.

The reporter's four-wheel drive was parked outside the double garage, Georgina was pleased that it wasn't going to be a wasted journey. She rang the bell, a light shone through the frosted glass panel in the door. A small visible puff of air escaped Georgina's lips, highlighted in the soft yellow glow emanating through the door. Winter was approaching, even down as far south as she was, though the temperature compared to Pormorion was mild by any means. A silhouetted figure blotted out the light through the door as it approached. Georgina could tell from her actions that Barbara Dace was tying a dressing robe. A brighter light suddenly illuminated the passage and a voice.

'Who is it?'

'Mrs Dace, its Agent O'Neil.' Georgina pressed her identity badge against the frosted glass, hoping that its close proximity to the surface would render it legible.

'Hang on a moment.' Barbara replied, stopping before the door to check her appearance in the mirror. The importance of looking her best especially when confronted by younger, attractive women was paramount to Barbara, though she would not like anyone other than herself to know just how important. She tidied her hair with her fingers, pushing it back and wiped the slightly smudged lipstick from the edge of her lips, reapplying a fresh coat from an emergency stick that was housed in a drawer in a small table under the mirror. Barbara opened her dressing gown slightly at the top, exposing a fraction more cleavage, having paid for a little re-upholstery, she was dammed if she wouldn't use every tool in her armoury. Satisfied; she opened the door.

Georgina stood there, warrant card in hand.

'Hello, Mrs Dace.'

'This is a surprise.'

'I'm sorry it's so late.' Georgina apologised, stepping in to the threshold of the house, 'but I really need a favour.' Georgina got the sense that she had interrupted something, though she wasn't sure what.

It was a little after nine o' clock but the reporter was dressed for bed, or undressed as Georgina could clearly tell from the nature of the thin robe that failed in discretion.

'I was...I was just about to take a bath.' Barbara explained, reading the Detective's expression. 'So what can I do to help you?'

A noise from upstairs confirmed Georgina's suspicion. A low clunk followed by a creaking as somebody crossed the landing. Georgina watched Barbara's expression but it was clear that she was going to ignore the noise and was comfortable with the knowledge that she knew the source. Barbara held out an arm and guided the Detective into the lounge.

'So, what brings you back?'

'You don't know?' Georgina could not hide the surprise from the tone in her voice.

'Oh, I know, I just wanted to see *what* you knew.'

Georgina was too tired for mind games and cut to the point. 'I need a copy of the tape that was sent to you during the Fleisher case.' Georgina sat down; her eyes followed the invisible footsteps above her head.

'Drink...Coffee, Tea?'

Georgina shook her head

'I don't have a copy here at home, come to the studio tomorrow, I can duplicate you one.' Barbara studied the detective for a moment. 'Is that it, only my bath is going cold?'

'I'll be over in the morning.' Georgina stood, a creak above once more. 'Enjoy your ...*bath*.' Georgina smiled and left.

He waited until the door was closed and appeared at the top of the stairs, wearing a large towelling gown.

'She gone?' He asked.

Barbara smiled, 'She won't be back. Not tonight anyway.'

As Barbara Dace ascended the stairs, she let her robe fall open. She enjoyed watching him watch her. Tonight they would make a home movie together as they made love and then watch it after, before making love again.

It was a little before ten o'clock when Georgina pulled up outside the police station. She took a slight diversion and stopped off at the house where Charles Fleisher and Karen Fuller were killed. There were no lights in the house. Six months later it remained an empty shell, a shrine to the dead, devoid of life but retaining the lingering scent of death. Images of that night played through her mind like a movie. Memories that were always going to be close to the surface, just waiting for the dust to be wiped away and dragged out like an old photo album or video cassette. She could see the look of horror on Karen Fuller's face, the almost inevitable acceptance of her fate as Fleisher's writhing body thrashed around with the knife. Georgina walked up to the door but it was locked. Black and yellow tape still sealed the entrance, even though the case was now just a part of Turtle Island's history.

Georgina peered through the dirt-encrusted pane of glass that allowed light into the main room. But there was no light tonight, barely any moonlight and the house just sat there as a solemn, malevolent reminder to its past and her past. She wasn't sure why she was there, maybe it was just to get the scent back into her nostrils, maybe it was part of her exorcising the past. On the way back to the car she wondered how the Fleisher's daughter and wife were doing.

The melancholic mood prevailed as her mind skipped to Korjca's fresh, slightly rounded face. She knew as she left the house that this time there was to be no mistakes. No more chances for the killer to cause the small community or her pain.

'Thanks for coming back. I thought I was going to have to get a cab home.' Leroy was sitting behind his desk with his feet crossed and firmly planted on its over polished surface. He was holding a manila folder.

Georgina offered no apology or excuse. 'So?'

'So...' Leroy began. 'I'm waiting on a fax from my orthodontist. She was not best pleased at being disturbed during the evening but I used my charm.'

'And she's still helping?' Georgina mocked.

'I am a very charming man. I asked her to check her records to see if she treated either the Fleisher family or the Montoya's.'

As he spoke the fax bleeped and paper began to un-spool, being vomited outwards.

The binary cacophony audible in the background as letters transferred from code to something more legible on the shiny paper. Georgina sat on the edge of the desk next to Leroy's feet.

'Mrs Dace is having an affair. I think I interrupted something steamy.'

'Yuk, old people having sex.' Leroy rattled a pencil between his teeth as he talked. 'Anyway, what makes you so sure?'

'There was someone upstairs, bumping around in the dark. We both heard him, but Dace never flinched, pretended she heard nothing, there was no car, hers was on the drive. I guess his was in the garage out of prying eyes. So it's someone she doesn't want exposed.'

'I know who it is. The old dog' Leroy said with a mischievous smile. The sound of the fax ending transmission stopped Leroy. He half turned his body and tore the thin paper from the machine.

'So?'

'So what?'

'Don't tease, Leroy. Who is it?'

Leroy was reading the information on the fax. ' She was the local school dentist, so she treated both Harley and Ray. The tooth doesn't match either of their records. She says that the tooth, a molar, was showing some signs of decay and had a high level of discolouring probably associated with eating high concentrations of one particular food. She has no records for Max Dalton. That was a long shot anyway. I would have been surprised if she had. Dalton had only been in the area for less than six month's before he was abducted and killed.'

'I know this tooth hold's the answer to a lot of questions. It was placed in my car as a tease, for some perverted pupose.'

'Or maybe whoever is doing this, placed it there to waste our time, throw us off the scent.'

'No, it's definitely linked.' Georgina shook her head. 'It is not unusual for the perpetrators of major crimes to be fighting with themselves. Maybe part of him wants us to stop him. I just wish he'd left his name and address on a piece of paper instead, sure would have saved a lot of shit.'

'What about the tape?'

'Oh, I'm picking up a copy in the morning. You still haven't told me?' Georgina said moving around the desk and giving Leroy her most pleading, doe eyed look.

'Told you what?' Leroy teased.

'Leroy.' Georgina playfully punched Leroy on the shoulder.

'Ouch! Okay...okay.'

'Well?'

'I thought you would have guessed, being a detective an all.'

Georgina glared, pretending to be at the end of her patience.

Leroy shifted his feet from the desk. 'Captain Frusco.'

'You're kidding, I didn't know he had it in him. Sounds to me like its Barbara Dace who's got *it* in her though.'

Leroy grimaced, as a cough from behind made him suddenly feel very uncomfortable.

'Didn't know who had what in who, Agent O'Neil?'

Georgina turned to face the Frusco, unable to hide the red flush that was rising from her chest rapidly up her neck and to her cheeks. She decided it would be the better part of valour not to answer Frusco's inquiry.

'I don't have to ask what you're doing here, O'Neil.' Frusco's voice had a resigned acceptance to it. 'But while you're here keep your investigations to relevant issues, not office gossip.'

'Sir.' Suitably admonished Georgina wanted to slink away.

Leroy broke the awkward silence. 'We were just going through the evidence in the Fleisher case sir. Agent O'Neil thinks there are areas we missed.'

'Like what, LaPortiere? The Fleisher case is dead and buried along with Charles Fleisher.'

'The tooth that was placed in my car, I had no connection with Fleisher, I don't think he even knew I existed until...' Georgina let the sentence hang in the air

'We are not going to look to good if you undermine the Fleisher case, it's buried O'Neil. If you start digging around it's not going to reflect too well on any of us. Do I make myself clear?'

'Are you saying drop the evidence, sir?'

'No, O'Neil, I'm saying if you open that can of worms and start fishing you better land more than tiddlers.'

A moments' silence passed between them. Frusco let his message settle into Georgina's mind.

'Our duty is to find the person who has kidnapped Detective Montoya and his family.'

'And killed Korjca Piekarska.' Georgina added.

'That goes without saying. It's the Nanny's funeral tomorrow. I want you there, O'Neil. The cremation is at St Mary's, 10-30.' Frusco made his way to the door. He looked at O'Neil. The self-assured Agent that first came to Turtle Island was looking pale and tired. A shadow of the person that arrived six month's previously. 'The priest is a Father Reagan.'

'Okay.'

'Whoever is doing this might want to see the results of his actions. See the whole thing through, as it were. I want photographs of the mourners; needless to say discretion will be in everyone's best interest. I'll leave the photography to you, La Portiere.'

The detective nodded. 'I'll get a camera from stores.'

Frusco took out an envelope from his jacket and placed it on the desk between the two detectives. 'We received these an hour ago.' Frusco shook out three Polaroid photographs of detective Montoya, bound and bruised. 'Son of a bitch walked straight in and left them on my desk. The only fingerprints on the photos are Rick's.' The small mobile phone in Frusco's pocket vibrated. 'O'Neil, I don't need agents or officers fouling in an already murky pool.'

Georgina watched him leave. 'Was that a warning?'

Leroy shrugged. 'I get the feeling you rub him up the wrong way.'

'Good.'

Before driving back home, Leroy picked up a camera with a telephoto lens from the stores department. He threw the camera bag on the back seat of the car and sank wearily into the driver's position. Georgina sat in the front passengers seat. The effects of the day began to catch up with her. It had been a long day since her early morning run and she was looking forward to a good night's sleep.

Leroy drove the car out of the underground car park, a slight drizzle of rain greeted them. He switched on the wipers. The rubber blades smeared traffic film across the windscreen, momentarily obscuring the view.

'I'm going to run the tooth through the FBI's victims records, see if we can obtain a match.' Georgina said somewhat fatigued.

'You know you don't have to book in to a motel tonight...you could stay with me. There's plenty of room'

'Thanks Leroy, but I'm not sure it's the right thing. Especially with you getting back with Lia soon. We wouldn't want to jeopardise the situation in any way.'

'Hey, I was only offering a bed. You saying I can't resist you.' Leroy did his best to sound affronted.

'Maybe I'm saying, I couldn't.' Georgina was telling the truth. She felt tired and vulnerable and in need of a little comfort. The truth was she couldn't trust herself tonight. Tonight she'd have to make do with a hot bath and raiding the miniatures in the drinks cabinet. 'Don't look so shocked, fatigue lowers my standards.' Georgina mocked Leroy covering the tracks of her true feelings as usual.

They drove on in uncomfortable silence, until the Motel appeared; flashing it's broken pink neon sign.

'Should be no trouble getting a room, late October is hardly high season.' Leroy parked the car.

'Pick me up early?' Georgina asked.

'7-30 okay?'

Georgina nodded. 'Yeah, I want to get to the TV studios and get a copy of that tape before going on to the funeral.'

'I better not see you to the door, in case you hold me against my will and ask me to perform all variety's of deviant sexual acts?' Leroy said.

'Your loss, Leroy...your loss.' Georgina smiled. The whites of her eyes were losing battle to the network of bloodshot veins.

She got out of the car and pulled her luggage from the trunk. Georgina shut the passenger door but could hear Leroy bid her goodnight.

'Goodnight, O'Neil.' The Detective engaged drive and pulled away, leaving the weary agent struggling against both fatigue, the weight of her luggage and the case notes stuffed under her arm. She gainfully tried to retain grip on the suitcase as she headed toward the reception.

Twenty-Nine

Slowly she submerged into the water. It licked at her nose, trying to find passage into her lungs; there was a brief temptation to breathe in. She allowed it to lap gently against her upper lip. Parting her mouth slightly, she took in a small amount of water and projected it down the length of her body. Georgina wondered at the miracle of babies and their ability to breath liquid for the nine months before birth. The water was steaming hot, as hot as she could bare and within seconds of entering the bath she noticed her skin reddening. The radio was playing Van Morrison singing 'Crazy Love' and Van's voice was the velvet glove offering respite and comfort from the world outside the front door. She wanted to read, wanted to relax for a moment, just get away to a saner place or maybe just some other, any other, place. But her eyes were too tired to read and all that she had was the case report anyway. She picked up a sponge and squeezed the hot liquid over her face. Georgina watched the hot water cascade down toward her eyes until the last possible moment before blinking. A memory. Why memories choose certain times to return was as much a puzzle as the recollection itself. Maybe it was provoked by stimuli, the hot water; the momentary peace. Georgina didn't know, but the memory was there as fresh as the day it occurred. She was nine or ten, not much older, sitting in a bath of hot water, listening to her mother arguing with her father. The voices often travelled up the stairs. The sounds of a family tearing itself apart and all the time Georgina feeling she was somehow to blame. She found she was holding her breath for as long as they argued. The slightest action of her breathing would be the trigger to some sort of catastrophe. Then as the voices died she inhaled and submerged under the hot water, the water acting as a buffer against the resumed hostility, which invaded the house like some sort of demon. No one knew Georgina's mother was dying, no one knew that was the reason for her argumentative nature. Often Georgina would find her mother sitting alone crying, blaming herself for the arguments, the confusion raging in her head, a mystery. Georgina would sit under the water looking at the light bulb hanging from the centre of the ceiling, waiting until her lungs were ready to burst. Often, when she broke out of her artificial womb, she would find that the arguments had miraculously stopped.

Georgina opened her eyes, the view through the water so reminiscent of those childhood days. She sat for a while watching the tungsten world ripple, waiting; like the child she was, until the very last moment before re-emerging. If the world had not been cleansed, then at least *she* somehow felt exorcised for the moment. She breathed a deep breath filling her lungs with air and wiped the remnants of water from her eyes. Black mascara smudged in to her closed fist. Georgina leaned over the side of the bath and lifted the straight whiskey she had poured and took a sip before sinking down in the bath again, allowing the water to cover her shoulders. The only embrace she would have tonight.

The water was cold, colder than ever. Jo-Lynn waited in the dark. Cramp and fatigue were diminishing her resolve. Her hopes of being left with at least light were dashed when *He* taped her mouth again, turned off the light and left her in the dark once more. She was no longer sure if her husband was with her let alone her son. Right now she wanted to die, she wanted to die more than anything else, more than even seeing her son or her husband ever again. She knew she could do it, she could rock the chair and fall head first into the water, and then all she'd have to do would be breathe then it would all be over. Her hands were freezing...her legs were freezing. Never had she felt such despair and such a sense of sheer uselessness, if that was *his* objective then he had achieved it, but if she tipped the chair forward she would never know what had happened to her son and while she had given up on herself. She couldn't give up on Ray or Rick. No matter how much she wanted to die, there was no way she could give up on them. The umbilical cord was severed at birth but the maternal bond could never be severed, not while she held breath in her lungs. Jo-Lynn screamed and cried out but the tape muted her despair. She wanted to kill. She wanted to kill. Never before had she known, nor had been able to understand such cold hearted hatred. She believed in good. She had faith, believed that God would always be there, well where the hell was he now. She wanted to *kill*. Jo-Lynn felt a surge of hope. While she felt such rage she knew there was a chance. Given the chance, she'd rip *his* fucking head off....

Somehow she must have fallen asleep, though she could not remember slumber creeping upon her. Sleep has an anaesthetic quality and no matter how long she had been in the arms of its somnambulant cradle Georgina never once felt the coldness of the water. She had dreamt of freedom, warm sunny beaches. Running, moving. She awoke in the cold water of the bath, her body now a ridge of goose bumps as her skin searched for hot air. She pulled herself out of the bath and shivered, quickly wrapping a bath towel around her body to chase away night fingers. As she dried herself she felt totally alone.

'The last person on earth'

She lifted the near empty glass of whiskey and toasted herself in the mirror.

'Just me and a glass of whiskey.' Georgina nodded to her reflection and sank the last quarter in the tumbler. 'My old friend you warm me up on nights such as these.'

She threw the glass against the opposite wall watching it break in to a thousand fractured spears of glass. She wanted to scream at the top of her voice, cry out her frustration. Georgina wandered into the bedroom and flopped onto the bed.

An arm shook roughly at her shoulder. Jo-Lynn woke. And as soon as conscious thought replaced the sanctuary of dreams, she knew she must remember the feeling of hatred that had invaded her thoughts earlier. *He* started to take the tape from her mouth again.

'They don't have a clue. Lord knows I've given them enough. They're so ignorant. I could give them my address and they'd still take a week to get here.'

Jo-Lynn smelt toast. *He* placed a slice of toast near her lips. She could see the light from under the small gap near her nose.

'I need the toilet.' Jo-Lynn protested. 'I cannot eat until I have used a toilet.'

He pressed the toast closer to her lips

'Can't you hear me I NEED the bathroom.' she repeated.

He pulled the toast away and placed it on a tray, which held a mug of coffee. She heard something being opened and could then feel a rubbing sensation by her ankles. Suddenly one leg was free; more cutting then the next leg came unbound. She could feel *him* working around her back, *his* hand pushing at her shoulders guiding her upright but partially supporting her. Jo-Lynn never realised how weak her legs would be as they gave from under her, if *he* had not been supporting her she would have fallen in to the water.

He pulled her forward a few paces.

'How's my son. Please can I see him, or if I can't see him, can I hold him, please?'

Jo-Lynn felt the tip of cold steel against the top of her leg, followed by a tug as he cut her knickers away. *His* hands pressed down on to her shoulders, forcing her into a squat, all the time *he* supported her frame.

'You're kidding? I need privacy.'

He pushed down on her shoulders.

Thirty

Six O'clock. The alarm rang in Georgina's head a minute before the alarm next to her bed sounded. She reached out and switched the setting to the radio, allowing a little early morning music to gently pull her out of bed.

Three and a half miles away Leroy was already awake, sitting eating his breakfast, while familiarising himself with the controls of the camera. His telly was on in the background, which he glanced at between the pages of the manual that accompanied the camera. It was Barbara Dace's live report, which grabbed his attention. She was standing outside the Fleisher house, now boarded up, looking abandoned. The sun was just rising and her skin was looking bleached out by the harsh halogen used to light the scene.

'For those that believe that lightning doesn't strike twice, the events unfolding here on Turtle Island are a little too reminiscent of an incident which came to conclusion here inside this house six months ago. A little over half a year ago I stood inside the house behind me, only hours after Charles Fleisher had been gunned down after killing Karen Fuller, a local teacher at the high school here on Turtle Island. Many people then believed that the death of Fleisher would see an end to a series of kidnappings and murder, which saw the deaths of Max Dalton, Stephen England and finally Karen Fuller. But today I can exclusively reveal on Breakfast News that one of the Detectives in charge of the Fleisher case and his family has disappeared, presumably kidnapped at the hands of a copycat perpetrator. The body of the family nanny was found stabbed to death at the hone of Detective Rick Montoya. I have with me Lieutenant Norman Frusco, the police officer in charge assigned to Turtle Island.'

Leroy's jaw dropped open so far it nearly bounced off the table.

'What the...'

He listened as Norman Frusco shuffled into view, looking ill at ease in front of the camera, in comparison with his lover. Leroy tried to fathom why Frusco was publicising Rick's kidnapping.

Frusco delivered a prepared statement. Unfolding a crumpled piece of paper from the inside pocket of his even more crumpled jacket, he began to read.

'A little over two days ago Detective Rick Montoya and his wife and son were abducted from their family home here on Turtle Island. To the person that is responsible I have this to say. You have killed an innocent young woman, and are putting the lives of Detective Rick Montoya and his family at risk for no reason. We need to resolve this situation but can't if you don't contact us. We need to talk, we know you know how best to do that.'

Frusco folded the paper and continued staring uneasily into the camera for a few seconds before the camera shifted to the right and Barbara Dace for the close of the report.

'I will be back throughout the day following this story exclusively with the full co-operation of Lieutenant Frusco and the local police force. Barbara Dace reporting for MRTV.'

He watched the television with fascination, while preparing a tray with scrambled eggs, corn flakes and grapefruit juice with a glass of milk placed to one side. *He* tidied away used cutlery into the sink of hot water and carefully wiped the worktop clean with a sponge. All the time he whistled, seemingly happy and content. *He* lifted the tray and walked out of the small kitchen, still whistling as he strolled down the hall. From the room in front of *him* came the sound of a television tuned to the children's network and the sound of a small child laughing. *He* pushed the door open with his foot. Ray sat in the middle of the floor about four feet away from the TV.

'Don't sit too close Ray, it ain't healthy.'

Ray turned, smiling. 'Okay.' and shuffled back about six inches.

He smiled.

'You're late.' Georgina opened the door and stepped out of the small motel room.

The weather outside the front door was grey and drizzly but the air temperature was still mild.

'I know, I got delayed. Had to stop of at a shop for some film. The last person who had the camera was responsible for leaving a film in the camera.' Changing tack, Leroy asked Georgina. 'Did you watch any TV this morning?'

Georgina stepped out, closing the door behind her. 'Nope, just had the radio on. Some FM station that only played Elvis records.'

'You missed Frusco and Barbara Dace informing the world that we had a serial killer on Turtle Island, or as good as.'

'What?' Georgina stopped halfway between her door and the car.

The misty rain started to penetrate the fine layer of hair lacquer on Georgina's short raven hair. Leroy continued walking to the car, opening the door and half entering the vehicle.

'That's what I thought, and before you ask, no, I have no idea what he's playing at.'

Georgina opened the passenger door and joined Leroy in the dry, warm interior of the car.

'That's what happens when you start thinking with your dick instead of your head.'

Leroy smiled; he enjoyed listening to Georgina's barbed tongue.

'Not much point trying to pick up a copy of the tape just yet.' Leroy adjusted the rear view mirror slightly. A gesture that seemed more out of habit than for any functional purpose.

'The day is barely two hours old and already it's throwing up surprises.' Georgina pulled down the sun visor and stared into the vanity mirror. She pushed her hair back in to shape with her fingers and wiped the corner of her mouth with her index finger before pushing the visor back to its original position.

Leroy started the car engine. 'St Mary's is just a mile or so from Independence Bridge.'

He swung the car out of the motel. Georgina was not one of the world's greatest passengers but she was getting used to, and felt confident with, his style of driving, which was unhurried and smooth. She found herself wondering if peoples driving styles reflected their true personalities, it certainly seemed the case with Leroy.

'I sent the tooth by courier to the FBI's laboratory in Maryland late last night. Hopefully they should be testing and cross referencing it by now.' Georgina said as she stared out of the window.

Some cars passed, heading out of Turtle Island to start their day's work. Headlights on, tyres sloshing in the wet tarmac, squeezing out water from their treads. Georgina saw the camera case lying on the back seat of the car.

'You learnt how to use that thing?'

'I read the book.' Leroy's self assuredness never wavered, not over simple things or more complex frustrations. Georgina liked that; she felt that if she needed him in a back up situation he would be there.

' Thought you'd have a digital camera. This thing looks like it was used to catalogue the animals on Noah's ark.' Georgina said, lifting the SLR camera and peering through the viewfinder.

The car tyres bumped over the small ridge that joined the main land to Turtle Island via Independence Bridge.

'Do you think Rick's still alive?' Leroy glanced sideways, he could see Georgina's face; she was looking tired, only slightly refreshed from the night before. Though the black suit she was wearing did little to add colour to her complexion.

'Yeah, I think they are still alive. I also think that this is what our *friend* wanted all along. Which is why he wouldn't kill them straight away. Now would be a time for savouring their position, their *power,* for want of a better word.'

Leroy looked back. 'Did you get any sleep last night?'

Georgina pretended to ignore Leroy's question, choosing to look through the side window at a farmhouse, still lit with electric light, waiting for the sun to burst through the mass of grey that was blotting out its radiance.

'I take it that means no.'

'I got one or two hours.' Georgina said 'Sleep has been something of a recluse of late.'

Leroy remained silent this time, knowing an interruption would probably stop Georgina in her tracks. He waited.

Georgina rubbed her face wearily. Her index finger ran along the length of her nose before massaging her temple. She had the impression of the world closing in around her and found the constraint claustrophobic. At times she would have to stop whatever she was doing and just breathe. Breathe deeply, as though she had run out of air while diving under the sea. This was one of those times. She breathed deeply.

The church appeared, small, almost inconspicuous. The drizzle continued its spray of fine mist. Leroy parked the car in the spacious car park. Georgina stepped from the car into the wet day.

Rows of untended gravestones sat patiently waiting for loved ones to refresh their plots with flowers, never knowing if they would return at all. Grey slabs slowly turning green and sinking into the ground, as though clawed under by the occupants. The weather eating into the stonework, erasing the names that once resplendently heralded their existence on earth. Slowly their names and faces would disappear from the community they once lived in followed by the passing of time as their names became eroded by the wind, sun and rain, to be forgotten forever.

Georgina passed the sleeping incumbents, her footsteps barely an audible echo for those below. Leroy followed, camera bag slung casually over his shoulder. The weathered oak door was unlocked. Georgina entered the nineteenth century Catholic Church. The air inside the church smelled of death, the deads tangible gift to the living world, a smell of must and decay. A glow from the altar drew her eyes to the eight candles burning as a prayer to the parishes needy. Georgina walked up to the shrine and lifted a candle from a pack lying on a shelf above the two rows of burning hope. She lowered it against the flame of one of the stronger burning candles and lit a candle for Korjca Piekarska. Georgina knelt and said a silent prayer. Not so much because she believed in God anymore but more for Korjca's peace. She stared at the candle for a moment, watching the flame flicker as a breeze from the side played a song for it to dance to. She looked up to find Father Reagan standing by a closing door. Leroy leaned over her shoulder.

'I'm going to have a word with the priest, see if there's anywhere I can discreetly observe the funeral.' Leroy rested his hand on her collarbone, his fingers relaxed and warm. Georgina nodded acknowledgement. The priest was not how she had imagined him in her mind. He was young. Early to mid thirties she guessed. His hair had been stylishly cut and tended to with an amount of care that she immediately envied. Father Reagan was, on first glance of either Irish or European stock. Dark hair and pale skin. His vocation, no doubt the pride of his mother and a waste to the female race. He stood talking with Leroy. The priest's voice soft and reverential, its tone bouncing off the dark crevices around the church. Georgina heard her name mentioned by Leroy and saw him turn and point to her. The priest smiled, and gave a slight wave.

He has a nice smile she thought to herself. She stood and walked over to where the two men were standing.

Father Reagan held out a welcoming hand to Georgina.

'Hello.'

'Father.'

The priest smiled. A smile as welcoming as his warm and hearty handshake.

'Is it possible to see Korjca?'

'Certainly. You do understand that from the nature of her injuries we are not having an open casket before the service.'

Georgina nodded.

'But we do have a room where you may view in private. If you would care to follow me.' The priest held out his arm and guided Georgina toward an annex room to the left of the altar. Leroy ambled to the end of the church and out of a door, which led to some steps. He walked up the stone steps to the balcony, where he set up his camera. He checked the light, made sure the film was set to the right speed and became familiar and comfortable with the surroundings.

The priest opened the door to the small anteroom. The casket was set up on two trestles; dark mauve velvet material tried its best to hide the rough wooden legs of the supports. Georgina followed the priest; two steps behind, slightly hesitant. She didn't want to be there, she had no desire to see another dead body.

Father Reagan stood over the coffin and pulled the lid open gently, respectfully.

Georgina steeled herself, briefly closing her eyes and taking a deep breath before stepping forward. She opened her eyes. Korjca's pale skin still had its porcelain perfection, though the shape of her face seemed to have changed subtly. Georgina had seen this many times with corpses. Relaxed facial muscles have a tendency to pull back slightly; gravity taking its effect after rigor mortis passes. Her eyes were closed, her lips painted with a subdued pale red lipstick. A silk chiffon scarf had been tied around her throat covering the deep incision, which finally claimed her life.

Georgina's hand hovered in front of Korjca's face. She wanted to touch her and feel the warmth of life searing through her body, shake her awake. She lowered her hand and stroked Korjca's marble cold skin. The touch severed passion. The reality of death transferred through Korjca's skin to Georgina's fingers and much deeper within.

'Had you known Korjca long? I only ask because I know she had no family here and the few times she came to church she always seemed to be alone.' Father Reagan's voice came from behind Georgina, tearing her from her thoughts.

'No, not long, barely a day.' Georgina continued looking at Korjca's expressionless face.

'Do you wish me to leave you alone for a minute?' The priest didn't wait for an answer. He backed out of the room pulling the door gently closed.

Georgina waited for a few moments until she was certain she would not be disturbed then wiped her own lipstick away with her thumb leaving her lips bare. She then carefully wiped Korjca's mouth clean. Korjca's face cold and taut. A small amount of foundation transferred on to Georgina's wet thumb. She lowered her head, so that she could feel her own breath returning from Korjca's face, gently her lips brushed against Korjca's. She tenderly pulled the edge of Korjca's scarf back, revealing a row of bootlace stitching. No attempt had been made to cosmetically disguise her cause of death other than a small amount of foundation, which had been applied to the edge of the cut. A token effort to blunt the brutality of the attack.

Georgina wiped her eyes. She leaned forward, close to Korjca's face. Her nose brushed against Korjca's, while her hand caressed her forehead and hair. She felt her fingers entwine around a small lock of Korjca's hair. Georgina whispered *Forgive me,* and pulled four tiny hairs from Korjca's scalp. She never looked at the hairs but placed them inside an evidence bag and secured the bag deep in her jacket pocket. Georgina wiped her eyes and left the room.

The priest was sitting on one of the church pews close to the door she had just exited.

'Would you care for a drink or a coffee?'

Georgina looked drained once more. 'That would be nice.'

Father Reagan stood. 'Follow me.'

He opened a door, which led outside the church. A tiny path made of stone circled the church and ran to a small lodge fifty metres from the main church building. The drizzle had not stopped, there was a muted grey blanket covering the sky.

As they walked the priest spoke. 'I am not in the habit of bringing attractive young women home, much to my father's disappointment.'

Georgina's sense of humour betrayed her feelings of grief and she allowed a smile to spread from the corners of her mouth. 'Are you hitting on me, Father?'

'You should use that smile a lot, it is very attractive.'

Georgina could suddenly feel herself blush a little.

'You know, losing a friend or a loved one can be a time when suddenly you realise how vulnerable you are as a human being. You ask yourself lots of searching questions. Sometimes-painful questions. You wonder if there was anything you could have done to prevent a death or whether you had done enough for that person when they were alive. You ask if there is a god, and if there is, what sort of god could allow something like this happen. The one thing I get from nearly every person who mourns is a sense of guilt. It takes its form in many guises but I can see it. It lies in the eyes. A black spot, a deadness. It's not attractive and it would be such a shame to see it in your eyes.'

They reached the front door to the lodge. The priest put his hand to the door and it opened. 'I always leave it unlocked even during the night, much to my housekeepers alarm.'

'And your insurers?' Georgina said as she entered.

The priest looked heaven bound. 'My only insurer is God. Anyway, anything I have here on earth is but a temporary possession and could probably be put to better use by those more needy...except my computer and my CD player, oh and my DVD.'

Georgina smiled again, the priest was a man of contradiction; she liked him.

Father Reagan guided Georgina through to the kitchen. The room was in need of some decoration but only to bring it into the current decade. Other than that it was clean and meticulously tidy. There were shelves with recipe books, most of which seemed to be in pristine condition, a microwave, a cooker, fridge, freezer, all the usual utensils.

'Don't ask me to use anything but the kettle, that's Mrs Kingsley's domain. My housekeeper. She's the obsessive tidier. The one sin that I specialise in is sloth.' Father Reagan filled the kettle from the tap. 'Coffee?'

Georgina pulled out a chair from a large oak table and sat. 'One sugar, white.'

The gas lit under the kettle and began to send heat through the thin metal surface to the water inside, sending small bubbles of water to the cooler surface.

'Hope you have no objections to instant?' Reagan unscrewed a large jar of instant coffee.

She shook her head. 'Nope, I'm a home girl; fairly down to earth I like to think. No pretensions.'

'You should try confession, I only asked if you wanted instant.' He stirred milk into the brown powder and added the sugar, the same amount to each cup.

'I have this habit.' The Priest began. 'And before you say it, I know it's the monks who wear habits.'

He waited to see a smile, a little lightening up on Georgina's features. She obliged.

Reagan continued. 'As I was saying I have this habit. I always take the same amount of sugar as my guest. If they have one, I take one, two, two and so on. Once I had an old Irish builder sitting in the seat you're sat at. His wife had just died and he was feeling pretty cut up. He took five sugars in his coffee.' Father Reagan raised his hand and emphasised with his outstretched fingers. 'Five! He wanted to know how he was going to survive without her. They had been married for fifty three years.'

'What did you tell him?'

The kettle began to protest as the hot water expanded in its metal prison.

'I told him to wake up tomorrow and the next day and the next and that the pain of her death would never go away but he would grow to love her and her memory more and more.'

'Did that help?'

The priest reddened slightly. 'I was young and inexperienced then. He told me that I had no concept of grief. He was right. I used a stock answer not one that came truly from the heart. How do you tell an eighty five year old man living on his own in a foreign country when all that he loved had died, that tomorrow will be better than today. Deep down I knew it wouldn't. No matter how much he believed in God, tomorrow and all the following days would get tougher until his last breath. I know that sounds bleak but I'm a realist. The one area where I could practically help was with this man's life after his wife and that's what we did. If he were forty or fifty years younger my help would have been different.' The kettle began to boil over spitting hot jets of water onto the work surface.

'Like the amount of sugar you have in your coffee, different amounts for different people.'

The priest nodded 'Something like that.' and poured the steaming liquid on to the browned milk.

'So, do you believe in God?' Father Reagan asked.

'I see too much tragedy, too much suffering of the innocent. It kinda makes you cynical, but I respect those that do?'

'Father, mother?'

'Mother's dead. She died when I was fifteen. She had faith. My father is too much of a pragmatist to believe in anything that isn't tangible.'

The priest nodded, handing Georgina a mug of hot coffee.

'My step mom is three years younger than me.' Georgina continued. 'She still believes in God, but then again…she still believes in Santa.'

'Don't get on well?'

'Okay, I guess. I'm happy for dad. I know he wasn't trying to replace Mom and if I'm honest she's good for him. As long as she doesn't kill him in the sack.' Georgina sipped.

'What about yourself…Korjca? Was she…'

'She was someone I liked, who I never got the chance to know. I rang her on the night she was murdered.' Georgina breathed in, the memory still painful. 'I…I don't make friends easy. Too cynical I guess, but Korjca and I …I don't know, we kind of bonded but as usual I nerved out and left it until it was too late.'

'She came here on a few occasions to mass. I always remember a new face at congregation. Such a shame. And the Montoya's…a dreadful thing.' Reagan looked heaven bound as though searching for answers from a higher deity.

The first of the mourners began to arrive, just before ten o'clock. Leroy fiddled with the camera, checking the auto focus by firing off a test shot from his vantage point upstairs. Father Reagan informed Georgina that there was going to be a short service. He didn't expect many mourners. Korjca's mother was flying in from Poland and would return with her daughter's ashes.

Georgina watched a broken woman as she was helped out of out of a car, flanked by a funeral director and a younger woman. The younger woman was Korjca's sister, Anna.

The sight of the television vehicles came as no surprise to Georgina. They appeared an hour before the start of the funeral and set up. Georgina watched from the car.

'Jackals'

Barbara Dace was there, her cameraman John Keller in tow. There was every chance that the funeral was going to be a big media circus now that Dace had reported Rick Montoya and his family's abduction. Georgina sat trying to read case notes, trying to concentrate but all the time the word 'Jackals' ran through her head as she grew angrier at the infringement on the privacy and grief of Korjca Piekarska family. Georgina watched Anna Piekarska and her mother enter the church, followed by three cameras from rival television networks.

Anna Piekarska genuflected in front of the altar, years of conditioning pushing aside personal grief for the briefest of moments. Korjca's coffin, now sealed, was resting on two trestles in front of the altar. Both Anna and her mother had taken time alone with Korjca, just as Georgina had done earlier, now was the formal part of the ceremony. The part Anna dreaded most.

Korjca's mother, 'Ditta', sobbed continually. Ever since the phone call three days earlier. For Anna, her grief was different, it came in waves, unpredictably and uncontrollable when it washed over her, but her mourning was tidal, it ebbed and flowed. At times she felt as though she was in control. Anna looked at her mother knowing that she was not as strong, nor had the youth to comprehend or cope with the tragedy. Her mother had visibly aged in those three long days. Everything was so strange, so alien. There were many faces but neither Anna nor her Mother knew them. People she had never met, sat and cried at the loss of her sister, people who didn't even know who Anna or her mother was. One of them sat in the front row, discretely at the end of the bench by the aisle near the east wall. Soft daylight filtered down through the stained glass windows some twenty feet above. Anna sat staring at the stranger, who seemed to be using the shadows as a cloak of anonymity. The stranger stared ahead seemingly unaware of the scrutiny being forced on her but glanced sideways briefly to acknowledge Anna's presence. Anna guided her frail mother on to the pew. The older woman collapsed onto the seat, gravity having a wearing effect on her frailty. Anna glanced once more at the young woman at the end of the row. Her pale skin and dark hair were features she was more accustomed to seeing in Europe. She clutched a book in her hand, a bible, prayer book or hymnbook. The ringing of a bell, its short resonance echoing through the air, broke the silence, announcing the beginning of the ceremony.

Father Reagan entered the church from one of the small rooms at the rear. He led a small group of choirboys, who sang the opening verse of *'Walk with me, oh my Lord'*. They walked slowly to the altar, incense burning and being wafted through the musty dull air. Plumes of blue smoke hung frozen in the quiet stillness of the church, captured by candlelight. The only other sound was the crying wail of grief escaping from Ditta as Anna pulled her close, hugging her and at the same time stifling her own sobs. The procession of choirboys dressed in brilliant white smocks with round red collars continued to sing as they found their seats by the altar. A discreet organ played softly, seeming only to pick out certain notes to keep the choir on key. Father Reagan blessed his bible and kissed the foot of a stone statue of Jesus.

Leroy sat back and placed the camera into the small grey holdall. Every single member of the congregation including the choirboys were now silver halide images, captured on three rolls of film, though he sensed that it was a waste of time. The funeral had high media coverage and any killer or kidnapper would have to be madder than mad to show. Especially when it was being beamed live through the cable in to every house, flat or river house in Missouri. In fact he could have saved time by sitting at work and capturing the images off the videotape using an editing suite. He zipped the camera bag and made his way down the stairs. With luck the films would be processed before the end of the ceremony. There wasn't a single face that stood out, no one that appeared to be acting in a manner likely to cause concern, no one Leroy recognised from the past. Leroy left the church. He threw the camera bag on to the back seat of the car, the films secure deep inside his pocket. There was a photographic lab in the police station but Leroy wanted the photos fast so he could run a check against the records. Karl Frost on Turtle Island had a small photographic business. Leroy had used him on many other occasions and knew him to be reliable and discreet. He had processed many other films with much more sensitive material than a few mourners at a funeral. Leroy could have the prints within an hour and be on the way back to the station to cross check.

The shop was three doors away from Fleisher's real estate business. Leroy could not ignore a sense of certain paths crossing. He parked outside the glass-fronted shop. Family portraits adorned the display, advertising Frost's trade. A yellow gelatine sun filter was drawn across the window, protecting the photographs from the worst of the morning sun, which generally beamed directly onto the glass. Though the chance of much damage being sustained today was remote.

Leroy pushed the slight, wooden framed door open. A bell sounded deep within the premises. The shop was open planned with a few directors seats scattered and a coffee table with black portfolio's adorning them, containing samples of Karl's art. More pictures lined the walls displaying the range of the Photographer's skill. Advertising shots, industrial photography, weddings. A lone glamour shot, soft focused, a young black woman with startling electric blue eyes.

'Contacts', Leroy thought, though retouching or electronic manipulation was another option. She was sitting in a field of wheat, dressed in a near transparent white cotton dress. Water had been sprayed on her body to simulate perspiration, which had the effect of drawing her skin to the material. One leg was drawn up, allowing the short dress to expose the full length of her legs. A mill was spinning in the background, the blades blurred but she was in perfect focus. Leroy guessed it was a long exposure with her remaining perfectly still for the duration.

'How is she?' The voice broke Leroy's thoughts. He didn't hear Karl appear from the darkroom at the back of the shop.

Karl was a throw back to a lost generation. Though his hair was cut in a short contemporary style he was still pure hippy. His accent had a deeper southern twang to it than Leroy's. Karl originated from Arkan, a small town near Georgia. He like many other inhabitants was drawn to Turtle Island during the early seventies, the lure of the utopian lifestyle and the well-known freedom concerning various drugs being the siren that enticed him.

'Gone.'

'Hey, brutal...I'm real sorry.' The photographer stood beside Leroy. 'She's sure beautiful.'

The picture was now nearly seven years old. Lia was only eighteen when the picture was taken and had her heart set on a modelling career.

'Yeah.' Leroy sighed. He didn't want to explain the circumstances nor tell the photographer of his hopeful reunion. Tearing his eyes from the photograph Leroy placed the three films on the counter. 'I need these processed quickly, Karl.'

'You working on the nanny killing.'

Leroy nodded. An acidic smell began to filter through from the darkroom. Karl turned and pulled the door too. 'Been in the trade all my life, still can't stand the smell of fixer.' He fumbled behind the counter and returned holding a hand rolled cigarette. The moment he lit up, Leroy detected the sweet scent of marijuana. 'Want one, pure Moroccan, none of that chinky shit.'

Karl was a racist where the Chinese and Vietnamese were concerned. His experiences in Saigon tainted his life beyond reason. He had an

American bald eagle tattooed on his back, wings spread against a back drop of the stars and stripes, an indulgence of an extremely young and naive 17-year-old going to fight against the threat of communism. He had bought the whole MacArthur ticket, much to his embarrassment. After six months of creeping around the jungle trying to avoid the Vietcong followed by another six months of land mines, snipers, child suicide bombers and general shit, Karl changed his mind on virtually every aspect of his politics except his loathing of any one east of Florida or west of LA, if you fell within these boundaries you were okay.

Leroy declined, not that he didn't indulge in the odd joint or two, his approach to cannabis was as relaxed as Karl would be minutes after lighting the fat joint in his hands. Karl wrote out a ticket for the three films, his writing neat and precise, far neater than expectation would allow. He handed the docket to Leroy.

'Be a little over an hour. Guess you're in a hurry?'

'Fine, I'll pick em up on the way back through. So how's business?'

Karl dragged on the illegal joint. 'A little slow now the summer's over. Have to keep searching for new avenues to exploit. Nothing changes much.' He let the smoke fill his lungs, permeating through his bloodstream and interacting with the receptors in his brain. Karl began to mellow. Behind him the door to his studio opened sharply. An agitated looking young white girl, wrapped in a peach coloured shiny dressing gown, stood impatiently.

'Hurry up Karl, I'm freezing my little titties off in here.' The girl did not seem embarrassed by the presence of any one who might have been in the shop. The gown gaped at the front; exposing a flat boyish chest with little or no cleavage at all Her hand gathered the gown at her stomach retaining what little modesty she had. She did not bother to wait for a reply, turning and disappearing in to the inner sanctum of the studio.

'I hope she's not under-age, Karl?'

'She's seventeen, seen her birth certificate.' Karl exhaled. 'Seen her ass too. You know who she is?'

Leroy shrugged.

'Jessica Femoy.' Karl said her name as though it would be the key answer to all of Leroy's unasked questions. He looked at the detective hopefully.

Leroy shrugged again, still looking equally unimpressed.

'The Coulstan Milk girl. You seen her on the telly, man. She's the babe laying in the big bath full of milk.'

'Must have passed me by.'

Karl looked astounded. 'She's the biggest name on Turtle Island at the moment. Got a contract with Coulstan for three hundred thousand dollars. Agents spotted her when she was in the cheerleaders for the high school. Signed her up while she was only fifteen...' Karl waited to see if there was any sign of recognition. 'Anyway I'm doing her portfolio.'

'Oh. Do you want me to *gasp* or something?'

'You know, sarcasm is unattractive no matter who it comes from.'

Jessica called from the studio. 'C'mon, Karl, I am getting frostbite back here.'

'Okay, okay. Keep your panties on...for now.' Karl added as he opened the door back to the studio. 'Don't worry Leroy, your films will be ready.' Karl looked at his watch.

'Call back at around 12-30. Gotta go.' Karl disappeared behind the door to his studio.

On the way out Leroy glanced at the photograph of Lia once more.

He had lit the fuse. A signal had been sent out and was now broadcasting to the world, quite literally to the world, and the media would want to put a piece of Turtle Island into the homes of everyone that had a radio or television or computer or who ever bought a newspaper or magazine. The list was endless.

'Agent O'Neil...Agent O'Neil.' Barbara Dace called after the detective as she walked from the church.

Georgina slowed, allowing the reporter to catch up with her. She turned to see Barbara Dace jogging toward her holding a videotape.

'Save you a journey.' She held the tape out, passing it on like a baton in the relay. Her breath came hard, the result of smoking too many cigarettes.

Georgina could see Korjca's sister and mother standing with Barbara's cameraman, John Keller. The sister was talking with him. They seemed to be conversing with ease.

'She speaks English?' Georgina asked, nodding toward Anna Piekarska.

'She wants to meet you.'

Georgina looked puzzled. 'Why?'

'She has Korjca's diary.'

Georgina looked at Korjca's sister. The likeness between the two sisters was uncanny, the only discernable difference being Anna's slender frame and thinner face. Anna turned her attention from the cameraman and looked toward Georgina as though she sensed she was being scrutinised. No attempt at acknowledging the detective's presence was made by Anna; she just studied her with cold eyes.

'I want to speak to her in private.' Georgina added. 'At a neutral locale, not the police station.'

'She's staying at the Meridian.'

Georgina couldn't disguise her surprise, her eyes raised almost involuntarily

'It's all part of the deal. We paid her and her mother's flight, accommodation and expenses.'

'In return for?'

'Oh, purely altruistic reason's.'

'Yeah those; and the exclusive rights to their story.'

Barbara smiled. 'Well...we're not a charity honey.'

There was something about the smile, which got to Georgina. It hit a nerve. Maybe it was the first time that she had witnessed the true reporter in Barbara Dace.

A car honked its horn. Both women turned to find Leroy entering the car park.

'Which room?' Georgina asked.

'4072. Fourth floor.' Barbara looked at her watch. 'Shall I say about three?'

Thirty-One

Something brushed passed her legs. Something soft. It woke her. Jo-Lynn opened her eyes and the light nearly blinded her, at some stage *he* had returned and lit the room. She blinked rapidly in succession trying to get the pupils to adjust to the startling glare. She felt the thing brush past her again. Then felt its claws dig into her leg. Small wiry fingers clamped onto her skin, then clawed its way up her leg. She felt the tail sweep, in its rear guard action, confirming what she didn't want to know. Jo-Lynn looked down and stared in to the rat's beady eyes. The water clinging to its body only added to the revulsion that she felt. Inside her head she was screaming. Her throat was screaming but all that emitted was a dull muffled sound, which barely reached the tape that gagged her. She jerked her legs to try to dislodge it, moving them as violently as she could. The rat clung on, then made a run across her nightdress. She felt the tiny wet feet dance over her. The talon like nails piercing the flimsy material, making contact with her bare skin. Jo-Lynn jerked her body with all the force she could muster. The chair rocked side to side, nearly overbalancing. The prospect of falling back in to the water, now swimming with rats, - at least so in her imagination - made her straighten, forcing the chair to stabilise.

The rat clung on unconcerned and continued to walk over her. The matted fur moved with its body exposing pink flesh.

Jo-Lynn tried to shake the unremitting rodent from her. It seemed unaware of her presence almost nonchalant. The rat climbed to her collarbone and sat. Its nose sniffing the air, Jo-Lyn continued to struggle but the mammal would not dislodge. The fear that the rat would sink its yellow teeth into her petrified her. She imagined its teeth tearing at her cheek, gnawing down to the bone. Ripping away flesh, tearing skin in strips, like old wallpaper.

Jo-Lynn took a deep breath and threw her weight with all the force she could muster to her left. She was still screaming inside when she hit the water. The rat leapt from her shoulder and dived into the murky water, swimming away unconcerned. It's poor sighted eyes searching for the next landmass to anchor itself to. Jo-Lynn's right hand instinctively tried to reach her face. Her head was still submerged under the water but suddenly she realised her right arm was free. The tape began to unravel. She pulled frantically. The claustrophobia of her situation was overwhelming. Her hand then began to tug at the tape around her chest and shoulders. The air in her lungs seemed to be expanding, the pressure pushing up through her chest. She wanted to breathe. Her left arm just as suddenly freed itself; Jo-Lynn turned her body so she was facing down, her eyes bulging with fear. This was not how she wanted to die, not now, when she was so close to freeing herself. She pushed up, tipping her head back, hoping that the water would be shallow enough to allow her to break the surface and breathe. She could feel air on her face and exhaled knowing that if she was wrong it may be her last breath. The air rushed in through her mouth and nose. She breathed again and for a moment waited while she regained control, before submerging once more and turning. Her hands ripped at the tape that bound her legs. One of her nails bent back snapping under the force of her actions but she seemed oblivious to the pain as the nail detached from the skin underneath. Her legs began to kick. Anger began to combat frustration. She pulled one leg free and pushed down on the chair with it until her left leg also became free. Jo-Lynn pulled herself away and rolled onto her stomach, crawling forward on all fours, lifting her head and gulping in huge amounts of air, her mind was screaming obscenities. She turned around and sat up, her hands now pulling the last of the thick tape from her mouth and arms. She could barely take in enough air to her lungs. The water lapped around her shoulders, murky brown with a greenish hue. For the first time Jo-Lynn smelled the stagnant odour of it. The effort of her struggle had left her totally exhausted and for a moment she just sat there, trying to collect her strength and thought's.

The rat swam by looking for an island to inhabit in the water world. The sight of it no longer bothered Jo-Lynn; she was too tired to care, there was no sense of elation or freedom, she was still trapped. Jo-Lynn tried to stand, her legs unsure and weak beneath her body weight. A wave of nausea passed over her and for a moment she thought she was going to be sick. She crouched down, and then knelt in the water steadying herself with her hands pressed forward on the floor. She cast her gaze around her cell for the first time. Her chair was lying upturned in the water, its hind legs emerging through the water. Graffiti daubed the walls along with newspaper cuttings and Polaroid images. Another seat was in the centre of the room. Unoccupied. There was no sign of Rick or her son. The thought that she might have been left, abandoned, occupied her mind for a few seconds but she dismissed it. If that were what had happened she reasoned to herself, then she would have to be more than resourceful to escape. A head filled with panic would not be helpful.

Thirty-Two

The hotel rooms in the Meridian Hotel were a cut above Georgina's dingy motel room. Slightly more than thirty bucks a night she thought to herself. She was apprehensive about meeting Korjca's sister. She had left Leroy back at the police station trying to run the photographs against a huge data bank. A fruitless job which both of them knew held no chance of success. Nobody seemed out of place at the funeral. In fact there was only seven faces that Leroy did not know, most of the mourners coming from Rick's immediate circle of friends colleagues and families. Of the seven, two were Korjca's sister and mother. Leaving just five faces. The five that Leroy was now trying to put names to through police and FBI records.

The bellboy asked Georgina which floor she would like.

She entered the lift.

'Fourth floor, room 4072.' She smiled at the youth dressed nattily in a dark suit and crisp white shirt with an immaculately tied black bow tie. His hair was sort and extremely neat, held in place with hair lacquer or gel. Georgina guessed the bellboy was in his late teens, probably his first job. The doors closed, and there was an embarrassing silence. There was neither sense of motion in the lift nor any sound to betray its machination, only the red LED display silently changing between floors. 2...3...4... the doors opened.

'4072 is right along the end of the corridor through the double doors, ma'am.'

Another dilemma. Does she tip? She chose not to, merely smiling and saying a feeble 'Thank you' as she exited. She could feel the flush of embarrassment rise from her chest, up her neck and through the now reddened cheeks of her face. She hated servitude.

The plush deep pile carpets absorbed any sound her shoes would make. Modern art paintings adorned the walls at intermittent spaces, mostly collisions of colour, abstract. Georgina thought she could discern shapes or outlines but wondered if the paintings were nothing more than colourful Riechstat inkblots. She pushed the double doors and they opened with silent ease. Everything about the hotel seemed to be geared toward noise reduction or total silence.

4069. She was close; her sweating palms had converted to a nervous stomach. She wanted to know the diary's contents. Georgina felt that somewhere within the pages were the answers to questions that she has asked herself during the solitude of night and space. 4072. A deep breath, before knocking.

As he suspected the photographs drew a blank, Leroy leaned back in his chair stretching the muscles in his lower back, too much sitting down in the job, too much driving, too much pen pushing and too many hours spent in front of flickering VDU's spent doing futile searches. He wanted to ring Lia. The photograph of Lia at Karl Frost's served as a painful reminder to what he once had, undervalued and subsequently lost. He fumbled through his pockets for the scrap of paper, which had Lia's aunt's phone number, the phone ringing halted his search. Leroy picked it up.

'Hel-lo. Leroy LaPortiere?' Leroy didn't recognise the voice at the other end of the line, a woman from the FBI forensic laboratory. 'Hello, Mr LaPortiere. My name is Judy Wells. Agent Georgina O'Neil sent a tooth, with reference to the investigation that she's undertaking.'

'Uh-huh.'

'We have made a match. Is she there?'

'Nope. She's out for a few hours.'

'Well, she asked me to pass the information on to you as soon as we found anything, if she was unavailable.'

'Okay.' He placed a pencil on the jotter pad in front of him ready to write down the information.

'The tooth belongs to, or rather belonged to a Jordan Montoya from Chicago. She was killed in a car crash. The tooth matches DNA from her medical records and is a match from her dental records.'

The nib of Leroy's pencil began to bow under pressure and snapped backwards.

Georgina shouldn't have been surprised to be greeted by Barbara Dace. The reporter showed her into the hotel room.

'Bang on time, Agent O'Neil.'

'Don't like to waste tax payer's money.' Georgina replied curtly.

Anna Piekarska was sitting on the edge of a sofa in the huge lounge. Her eyes told the story of her recent grief. She had not cried at all during the funeral but as soon as she got back to the room she found she could not stop.

'Hello.' Georgina held out her hand.

'Forgive me, I am not in much mood for receiving visitors.' Anna apologised. 'My mother is asleep. The doctor has given her some sleeping tablets.' Anna laughed a scornful snort. 'Magic pills that make the world go away.' Her emotion was raw. The envy in her voice for her mother's drug induced sleep, unmistakable.

Georgina pulled her hand away, no contact having been established.

'I see you have the diary.'

Barbara sat next to Anna, as the young Polish woman tentatively opened the book.

Georgina took a seat opposite. 'Only read what you want but there might be something in there that could help us find whoever did this.'

Anna tried to smile, a pain filled smile. Her fingers ran over the cover, passing a page between them before she focused on the first lines of hand written text. Korjca's writing was neat the pages, smudge free. Written, then forgotten. 'This is the diary of Korjca Maria Piekarska. My life in a strange world....' Anne looked up 'It starts on the day Korjca left home to come to America.

This morning is the start of a new life. My rudimentary knowledge of English seems to have held me in good favour and I have found employment with a family in America. They have just moved to a new home from Chicago and need a nanny for their young son. America seems such an exciting place...it seems that anything can happen here...' Anna's voice began to tremble, quavering under the pressure of emotion. She coughed and cleared her throat before continuing. *'I am so excited...'* Anna took a sip from a glass of water. Georgina noticed a tape recorder whirring on the table. A small black voice activated dictation machine. Anna continued. *'I have slept my first night away from my home. The family I am to look after are lovely. I have a large bedroom with a television and dvd recorder. They have even bought me some films, plus a small CD player that has a radio. The boy, Ray is friendly, though a bit shy. It is sad that he lost his sister.'*

Anna continued reading the diary to the intense silence of the detective and the reporter.

'I need confirmation.' Leroy said to the FBI forensic agent.

'No trouble, Mr LaPortiere. Do you have a PC with Internet access?'

Leroy stared at the PC on Rick's desk. He done his utmost to avoid learning or using computers but knew enough to get on line and access the Net's seamier side.

'Yeah. Send down the information.' Leroy gave Agent Wells his e-mail address and sidled over to Rick's desk and powered up the machine.

An electronic voice prompt shouted *POST* as soon as the browser kicked in. Leroy guided the cursor to his electronic mailbox and opened it. Then waited for the download to begin.

'You have 314 messages.' Computers could be sarcastic when they wanted to be. Leroy's backlog of unopened mail was entirely of his own doing. He groaned. 'Oh man, I don't need this shit.' He scanned

down the list. Half the e-mails were from people he had never heard of, some were from dubious Internet sites. The rest were work related but non-important. Everyone knew if they had anything-important dealing with a case, never to send it to Leroy via e-mail. The FBI's e-mail had not yet arrived. Leroy started opening his *post,* the first message was from an unknown sender or at least an e-mail address he didn't recognise. It was from a prisoner in the state pen that Leroy had caught and convicted of robbery with intent to endanger life and property. Leroy remembered the case. The man had tried to rob a gas station before flooding the forecourt and one of the sales assistant's with gasoline, only he had used the diesel line. Leroy shot the man in the knee. He opened the message and read it.

Hope you die a painful death, motherfucker

'Huh, fan mail.' Leroy chuckled to himself unfazed by the message. He continued opening all sorts of messages some with attached files, others that were no more than blatant advertising. His mind began to go numb with the banality of it all. As he opened his one hundred and third message he was quite unprepared for the shock that greeted him. An anonymous e-mail which the sender had obviously taken a lot of time and trouble in removing any traceable aspects.

'Let's face it, you have no idea who I am. I could be sitting next to you. I could have been in the church today watching you all scrabble about for answers. I could be cutting all their little heads off...the boy has such soft skin. Cuts very easy. She tastes nice. I have kissed her more than twice and when drugged, my fingers found her oh so, so...accommodating. The stupid fuck of a detective is such a disappointment though...Enjoy the photo's. See you real soon'

Leroy opened an attached file expecting to see pictures of Rick and his wife and son but all there was, was a web address. He ran the cursor over the text hyperlink, clicked and was taken to a web site. A black background appeared, followed by an animated splash of red across the screen. Then four Polaroid's began to download on to the screen. Three of them faces Leroy knew very well. The forth a photograph of Korjca taken soon after she had been killed. A Wav file began to transfer. Leroy picked up the phone and dialled an internal number.

'Captain Frusco.' Leroy waited while Frusco's secretary put him through.

'Sir I've got something I think you should see.'

'I called Mama last night. I know she misses me, though she will not say so to me. She worries needlessly that I have not settled but nothing could be further from the truth. Ray is a lovely boy and very easy to look after, though the first three or four weeks were a struggle. Jo-Lynn

is so nice. At the weekend they took me to a country park and we camped in a trailer until Monday evening. Everyone had such a good time.

March 10. Something strange happened today. I had dropped Ray off to school and returned home for a bath. One thing I think I shall not get used to is the hot weather. The doorbell rang, as I was about to get in so I put on a robe and went downstairs to answer. A young man was standing at the door looking very anxious. Very nervous. I took the small bottle of mace from the hall table before opening the door. He said he wanted to see Detective Montoya. All the time he kept looking over his shoulder. I could feel his unease but was weary of letting him in, so I told him that Mr Montoya was out at work. He said tell Detective Montoya that Stephen England called. In the evening when Mr Montoya returned from work I told him of his caller and he became agitated, telling me to forget that I had seen the man.

March 11. There is great excitement. A body has been found in the river. Talk at the school from the mothers and nannies, is that whoever he was, he was murdered. I know Rick is working on the case but he doesn't talk about it to me. Though everybody on Turtle Island seems to know something or have a different story.'

Anna took another sip from the glass. She knew there was another six month's of entries to plough through of varying lengths. Occasionally she would glance up and study both the detective and the reporter's face for reaction, both seemed to be deeply engrossed. Apart from the occasional mention of family members, Anna felt she was reading the diary of a stranger. Georgina shifted on her chair; she looked at her watch. Anna had been reading for about an hour and a half and moved through months of a fairly detailed record of her sister's life. 'Would you mind if I had a break for a few minutes please?' Anna asked

'Of course not. I could do with a break myself.' Georgina said, standing and stretching her legs.

Barbara switched off the tape recorder.

Georgina felt the rush of excitement when Anna mentioned Stephen England in Korjca's diary. She saw that Dace recognised the name too, and fought hard not show that she spotted the connection. This was their first real break.

Frusco was leaning over Leroy's shoulder staring at a computer screen. He chewed on his thumbnail, pulling away a bitten piece of nail and biting down on it. 'Can we trace him through the internet provider?'

'This page will have certain traceable aspects but they can be falsified. Also, in the scheme of things, if *he* wants to hide himself, which I'm sure he does, then this page is a thousand times smaller than a needle and the Internet is a million times larger than the proverbial haystack.'

'Damn.' Frusco pushed himself away from the back of Leroy's chair, which he was leaning on. 'One way or another we're going to get this fucker and nail his sorry ass.'

'There's also a wav file.'

'A what?'

'It downloaded automatically. Some sort of sound file.'

'Can we play it?' Frusco sat back against the edge of Leroy's desk.

'Yeah.' Leroy reduced the current screen and opened a wav player.

A virtual hi-fi appeared on the screen. Leroy clicked on open file and searched through his hard drive for the downloaded file. It had automatically saved as *Torture.wav*. He double clicked the file and pressed the play button once the file had loaded in the player. The voice was slowed, distorted, but coherent.

'You are so slow. So far behind me. I have given you all the clues, all the chances you need.' The sound of someone screaming ended the file. Leroy closed the file and returned to the main screen with images of Korjca and the earlier victims.

'Can we work on the message to get rid of the voice distortion?'

'I don't know. It's in digital form so I guess that it's possible.'

'Send a copy to voice analysis.' Frusco picked up his coffee. 'Fuck technology! It was easier in my day; these sicko's just used to send you bits of bodies. You knew where you stood.'

Leroy ran the cursor over the image of Korjca with her throat cut. The pointer changed to a hand indicating a link to another page or web site. 'Shit.' He double clicked and a page started to download.

WELCOME TO DEATHCAM. *Your chance to watch a killer doing what he does best...*

Underneath the melodramatic headline was a list of familiar names starting with Max Dalton, Korjca Piekarska and finishing with Stephen England by the column of names was another line that said 'LIVE DEATHCAM'. Leroy guided the pointer to it and double clicked the mouse. The screen went blank as the browser started to search for the page. The arrow cursor changed once more to an egg timer.

'What's happening?' Frusco asked impatiently.

The screen started to fill with images, like a jigsaw, one piece at a time. First the headline, then the text and finally what appeared to be a live feed to a water filled basement. Leroy read the headline.

TWO DAYS TO GO. *Be witness to America's first public execution in over a hundred years. Vote now who gets it first. THE BOY, HIS MOTHER, or HIS FATHER.*

Click on the person of your choice.

There was a counter under each name and an accompanying photograph. The counter had already fifty thousand 'hits' against Jo-Lynn's name and a similar figure against the other two.

'Oh my God.' Frusco visibly paled. In the corner of the main screen his eyes were drawn to some movement. The picture was not too clear but clear enough for him to tell who it was. Jo-Lynn's head could be seen emerging from the dark, peering nervously toward something to her right.

May 13th. The arguments go on until late in the night. I hear them but in the morning Mr and Mrs Montoya act as though nothing has happened. Little Ray sleeps through it all. The workmen arrived today to start digging the pool. I think one of them has taken a liking to me. He is not too shy. He stares at me quite unashamedly. I wish he would ask me out. I need to get a life outside of here.

The more Georgina heard from the diary, the more she realised its importance. A much clearer picture was beginning to form.

Anna read on.

'May 14th. A man called today. I don't know why but I took an instant dislike to him. It was very early in the morning, but Mrs Montoya was already on her way to work and Mr Montoya had been working all night, another body has been found. People are becoming very afraid. The man barged his way into the house claiming to be a friend of Mr Montoya. His eyes were all over me. He said 'Tell Rick, Charles, needs to speak urgently at his office.' As he left he ran his hand across my back. He smiled an awful sneer and licked his lips. I was too ashamed to tell Mr or Mrs Montoya of his behaviour but gave Jo-Lynn the message when she got home. She seemed upset.

15th May. We are having a barbeque on Saturday. I am very much looking forward to it.

Leroy placed the cursor over the picture of Max Dalton and clicked. A grainy film started. There was no sound, just the image of Dalton tied to a chair in a basement. Somebody dressed from head to foot in black, from a ski mask down to black gloves, was walking in front of the camera, barely visible in the gloomy interior. The camera zoomed in on Dalton's face. He is terrified. His nose is broken, with light catching off a protruding piece of gristle through lacerated skin and his right eye is a mass of red. The white of the eyeball is engulfed in a sea of blood. A man walks toward Dalton with something in his hand. At first neither Leroy nor Frusco can quite tell what it is, until it is held up for the purpose of the camera. As the blades start to flash it became all too clear. Both Leroy and Norman Frusco had used one before, and knew how lethal an electric carving knife could be. The camera panned down to Max's right hand. Within thirty sickening seconds both hands had been removed and the killer was starting work on the man's feet.

Leroy could hear the screams even though there was no sound. Once Dalton's feet had been removed the killer moved the knife into Dalton's mouth and sliced through the tongue. Blood showered the killer who seemed to be getting more and more psyched up with each new atrocity. The camera followed every move. For his finale, the killer set about Dalton's mouth with a hammer. Smashing every tooth he could hit then finished off with pinking shears, removing what was left of Max Dalton's lips.

Captain Frusco pushed away the Pizza box, which he had delivered for dinner. 'Well that's cured my appetite.'

Leroy stared at the screen in disbelief. 'He doesn't think he's gonna get caught.'

'No.' Frusco shook his head. 'No...He doesn't *care* that he's gonna get caught. And that's what makes him so frightening.'

Leroy's fist smashed against the screen in front of him. 'Who the fuck is he?'

Frusco picked up a phone next to the pizza box. 'Call Agent O'Neil. I don't care where she is or what she's doing I want her here now.'

'She's at a hotel, The Meridian. With Korjca Piekarska sister and her diary. Anna Piekarska is translating it, it was written in Polish or some language. She thinks it might have important information in it.'

'Why wasn't it brought in here as evidence?' Frusco demanded.

Leroy looked sheepish. 'We have no translators. Only Kwoiskizchi or whatever his name is and he's in Florida on vacation.'

'Mickey fuckin Mouse...Well get O'Neil here, with the diary and the Polack.'

Barbara Dace picked up the ringing telephone. The break was a welcome interruption for Anna who was feeling exhausted. The strain of the past few days was beginning to show.

'It's for you.' Barbara passed the phone handset to Georgina.

'Hello?'

'It's Leroy. Frusco wants you back here. All sorts of shit's occurring. Our killer has set up his own web site and is promising to kill either Rick, Jo-Lynn or the boy live, online.'

'What?'

'I know, I know. Just get back here as soon as you can and bring the diary. It's now states evidence, Frusco knows about it.'

'Shit.'

'More crazy news as well. Your guys at Quantico dental records came up with a match and this is a doozy.'

'Who Leroy? I don't play guessing games for fun.'

'Jordan Montoya.'

Georgina didn't say goodbye. She placed the receiver down on the cradle.

She grabbed the Diary from Anna and physically pulled her from the chair. 'I'm sorry but you're gonna have to read this to me as we drive to the police station.'

'What? You can't do that.' Barbara stormed.

'Watch me.' Georgina was dragging a bemused Anna Piekarska along the hall to the lift before she could protest, with Barbara Dace following. The three women rode down in the lift to the basement and Georgina's parked car.

'I don't have time to argue with you Barbara. There have been developments. Frusco needs the diary and Anna to translate.'

'But the deal was I'd get the scoop. So far that amounts to squat.'

Georgina opened the rear passenger door and manhandled Anna into the car before jumping in to the drivers seat, leaving Barbara standing breathing in the fumes from the over rich petrol mix of the car. As Georgina drove up and out of the basement she apologised to Anna.

'I'm sorry to treat you like this.'

Anna looked on bewildered from the rear seat.

John Keller caught up with Barbara in the basement car park. His camera was in the carry bag over his shoulder.

'I don't care what you do John, just get me to the police station faster than yesterday.'

Keller opened the door to the Cherokee jeep and they climbed in.

'Did you hear those passages relating to England, Fleisher and Rick?' Keller asked.

'O'Neil's a cool cookie. I am sure she made the connection.' Dace smiled.

Before she had buckled up, Keller had the car in drive and was up into the drizzly night and the evening rush hour traffic. Barbara looked for Georgina O'Neil's taillights. The Cherokee zipped through the traffic, handled with consummate ease by Keller. Dace switched on her cell phone then dialled the TV station.

'Jenny, it's Barbara, put me through to Chris.' She cupped the mouthpiece as she began to explain what was happening to her cameraman. 'Securing a slot for the ten o' clock bulletin. I think this is about to blow big time.'

'Jesus, Barbara where the hell have you been?' The urgency in her boss's voice told her news was breaking at the station as well as with her.

'Got a potential scoop here Chris, to do with the Montoya kidnapping. We need an eight minute slot.'

Keller turned his head and mouthed *eight minutes'* in surprise. Knowing that at the moment they barely had enough new material to cover two minutes.

'Never mind. Get back here as soon as you can.'

'But I'm....'

'The killer's gone online and wants to talk with you at 8pm sharp over the Internet. Can you believe this, his agent...you heard me right, his agent just rang to arrange the interview.'

Barbara looked at the clock inset on the Jeep's consol. 7-37pm. She felt her heart turn. 'Leave O'Neil, John. Get back to the TV station, NOW.' Keller screeched the jeep to a halt, looked over his shoulder and swung the car left onto the opposite carriageway as soon as there was a clearing in the traffic.

'Read some more from the diary.' Georgina passed the book over her shoulder to Anna. She was focused on the road ahead but her mind listened with intent to every word from Anna.

'Sunday18th May. The barbeque was great fun. We had a basketball match. The women verse the men. We won. Thanks to the FBI agent that is working with Mr Montoya. Her name is Georgina.'

Anna began to falter as her eyes raced ahead reading the next couple of lines.

'She is quite beautiful. It was a shame that they had to race away. Mr Montoya did not return home Saturday. The arguments seem to be getting worse. They were talking about the man who called on Wednesday. The voices were angry and his name bounced from both sets of lips as a tennis ball. Charles.

Monday 19th May. Jo-Lynn has shocked me today. She confided in me that she was thinking of getting a divorce. She seemed very upset.'

Georgina continued to drive, taking mental notes. She wasn't surprised to hear that the Montoya's marriage was going through a rough patch. She remembered Jo-Lynn's remarks by the hole in the ground that was going to be the swimming pool. Between Rick's job, the death of a child and her own time consuming career, Georgina had figured that something would give. What concerned her though was the remark's linking them to *Charles*. She wondered if it was Charles Fleisher or some other person named Charles. Could it be co-incidence? But co-incidence was a phenomenon she placed just above religion in the believability stakes. The large police precinct appeared in view as she turned the car into Biston Boulevard. She slowed down on the approach to the underground car park and swiped her pass card through the reader. The barrier waited for the electronic instruction to be issued before rising.

Anna continued reading.

'May 20th. It would seem that Mr Montoya and the FBI Agent have caught the Turtle Island killer. There have been a lot of TV cameras here today. It feels like a dark cloud has lifted from the island.

The car stopped.

Georgina turned. 'We're here.'

Thirty-Three

Jo-Lynn tried to keep moving to stay warm but the skin on the soles of her feet were soft and splitting from over-exposure to the water, making walking painful. She hobbled up the short set of steps and sat near the top by the locked door. At least it was dry there. Her eyes scanned the room, three chairs, water and a strip light. The Grand Floridian it wasn't.

Her mind was working, trying to fathom a way out, wondering what had happened to her husband, trying to come to terms with what she had done to deserve this predicament. *He* had not visited her for a long time. She couldn't judge how long, a day, sixteen hours…eight hours? Bouts of sleep had come in-between, disturbing any accurate estimate. She tried to comfort herself with the thought that maybe her husband and son were being held somewhere dry and warm. She pulled her legs up to her chest to try and gain extra warmth from them. The soles of her feet scraped against the rough surface, leaving a smear of blood from the split skin. She looked around at the door behind her. A flat metal panel faced her, secured to the frame of the door with rivets. There was no visible lock or handle and less than a five millimetre gap between the door and the frame. No way out. She sighed. Near the top of the wall directly opposite where she sat, about eight feet from the ground was a metal grill. Too small for a body, it fed the room with its supply of fresh air. To the left was a standpipe with tap attached. There seemed to be no way out other than through the door. Jo-Lynn shivered, cold air danced over her spine, chilling her.

7-52pm. Barbara Dace ran up the stairs to the third floor and along the slim corridor. Her breathing laboured as she cursed her twenty a day habit. Two clear glass doors lay ahead; she pushed through one and entered the open office. Small blocks of desks, or *working units* as they were known in management speak, occupied virtually every available space, leaving small paths in-between to walk from A to B. On each desk was at least one computer monitor. The room was alive, a hubbub of activity and noise. The air bristled with excitement; it virtually jumped off the walls like forked lightning ricocheting in a box.

Chris Hurley was the first to notice her arrival.

'Thank God you're here.' Hurley ran across the room to greet her. He pulled her along to her workstation and sat her down behind her already glowing PC.

'How long we got?' Barbara asked. It was a general question, which somehow in the melee obtained an answer.

'Seven minutes.' Hurley's personal assistant answered. He was at another computer with a large group gathered around.

Hurley bit into his lip. 'Shit. Not long. Right, listen Barbara; this is what's happening. We got E-Mail earlier today; at first we thought it was from some crank. He said he was the Turtle Island killer's agent and that his *client* wanted an interview with you tonight. We were going to dismiss it but he gave us a web site to check out.' Hurley shivered as the image of its contents replayed in his head. 'What you can see on the screen at the moment are some link pages from the site.'

Barbara looked at the screen. 'His agent?' She said incredulously.

'I know. Wesley Timms. Apparently he doesn't know where this psycho is, but has made contact via the Internet. Our lawyers inform us that he hasn't even broken the law.'

'Glory be the new revolution.'

The Death cam page had been accessed. The live feed showed a woman, partially clothed, crouched on a set of stairs asleep. Barbara turned.

'That's...'

'Jo-Lynn Montoya.' Hurley interjected. 'And there's worse to come.'

He scrolled up the page to the hit counters and the pictures of Rick, Jo-Lynn and Ray. Under Jo-Lynn's name was a figure of one hundred and eighty thousand, three hundred and thirty four followed by a button that read *YES*. Barbara quickly read the page.

'Four minutes.' Hurley's PA shouted.

'On some of the other pages there are short films of him torturing and killing some of his victims. He's somehow set up a whole site dedicated to his crimes and managed to get it on search engines and linked to various other sites, Christ he's even got sponsors. The count under Jo-Lynn's name has increased by over fifteen thousand in the past half hour.' Hurley leaned over Barbara's shoulder, moved the mouse pointer onto the file heading marked *open* and clicked. A small box appeared on the screen. Reading from a printed piece of paper he copy typed a web address and clicked *Okay*.

'Two and a half minutes.'

'Is this thing set up properly?' Hurley asked. His question aimed at the desk with his PA.

'It's working fine.'

Barbara noticed for the first time the small triangular object on top of her PC. A small lens in the centre reflected light in a multitude of subdued colours. For someone who spent most of her working day staring in to a lens, Barbara felt distinctly uncomfortable.

'Is this what I think it is?'

'He only wants to speak to you. This is going to be the biggest thing that has happened to this station since....' Hurley was lost for a comparison.

'One minute.'

The computer linked to the web address. The title 'DEATHCAM' confirmed the location. A small orange highlighted box stood out from the black background. Static fuzz filled the box.

'Thirty seconds.'

'Why has he chosen me?'

'Who knows? You're a local media celeb. Maybe he's very parochial.'

Barbara laughed blackly.

'Ten seconds.' Hurley's PA began a countdown.

Barbara took a gulp of water from a plastic cup, which had thoughtfully been placed by her computer. From the corner of her eye she could see John Keller moving closer. His camera perched on his shoulder to record the event.

'Five...four...three...two...one.'

Barbara drew on her breath to steady her nerves. She knew that this was the opportunity of a lifetime, possibly an award winning opportunity. Reporter of the year had been awarded for less. She stared at the small static area on the computer monitor.

'Maybe he doesn't keep eastern time.' Hurley's PA quipped.

The foggy dancing white balls of interference suddenly cleared and an image began to form. Barbara could feel the nerves in the pit of her stomach jumping and pulsing. The picture became clear though it was like watching an old silent movie. *He* was sitting in a chair. The light around him was dull. When he moved forward the image on Barbara's monitor jerked as the processor struggled to assimilate all the information. *He* was wearing a black ski mask. The whites of his eyes shone through the darkness, staring and intense. The resolution of the image was too poor to see eye colour but they appeared to be dark, almost black.

'Hello, Mrs Dace. I'm glad you could make it.' His voice was going through some sort of processor, distorting it; the hairs on the back of Barbara's neck began to rise. 'I'm a big fan of yours.'

Barbara wondered what sort of reply he was expecting. Thanks, reverential gratitude, respect. *He* didn't give her a chance to think of a reply.

'I assume you have had a chance to see my work. Are you a fan of mine? Don't worry that's a rhetorical question.' All the time *he* was staring fixedly in to the camera, his eyes unblinking, compelling. *He* was sucking her in with his intensity. 'Some of my best work for the whole world to see, and tomorrow, Mrs Dace, I'm giving America the chance to witness my art, live. Imagine that? Imagine the thrill of letting the world see.' His voice hissed and crackled.

'Why do you want to speak to me?' Barbara asked, wanting to gain some control over the situation. Taking the focus away from his self-massaging ego.

'Do you mean, what is the purpose of my contacting you, or, why did I pick you? There are different answers to both and I wouldn't want to disappoint you.'

Even though they were only connected via a USB cable, Barbara felt the link with the killer to be tangible. She felt uneasy with the fact that *he* was replying to her, her questions, and the words that came from her mouth. As much as it was anathema to her Barbara had to keep him on her side. She knew she had to placate him without patronising him.

'I was wondering what the reason was for your contacting me now, at this present timel, but the answer as to why you picked me would also be interesting?'

'I have contacted you before Mrs Dace. Remember the video? You made me a star then, so I figured that I should repay the compliment and make you a star, in turn by telling the world of my accomplishments I will achieve what I want. You see, I'm killing two birds with one stone.'

'And what is it you want to achieve?' Barbara asked picking up on the inflection that he put on the later half of the sentence. 'Is it just notoriety?'

'I could say fame, but that would be a lie. Anyway by the time this hits the news tonight, you will have done that for me. No, what I want is justice?'

'Justice for what?'

'Oh, I can't give away the ending. That's going to be the fun part.' *He* laughed, inhaling at the same time, producing a high-pitched squeal. The laughed cut into Barbara's nerves the way the sound of fingernails being scrapped down a blackboard does. 'You have seen my web site. Quite a piece of work. The site has been submitted to all the major search engines. As you can see from the amount of people visiting it, word is already spreading. Word spreads like a virus on the net. Words become a plague when something is hot. I have e-mailed every major TV station in America, Europe and the Far East. They're starting to run this story. And they will all be heading for this tiny little Island, as they do the count goes up from the little people, the people who have a dark streak, my supporters. The count goes up and the fate of the Montoya family is decided. I promise you now; I will kill only one, the person with the highest vote. Tonight America votes.'

'Wha...'

The screen in front of Barbara went blank before she could finish her first word.

Hurley leaned forward. 'Okay, Barbara?'

She nodded.

'Right, let's get this report up and ready. We're going to cut in on the movie with a newsflash and run a trailer for the full interview for the ten o'clock. Come on people, lets get to it.' Hurley clapped his hands, snapping his dazed staff out of their bewilderment.

Georgina sat alone in the office. She watched the Videotape of Max Dalton's torture. She compared it with the film footage of the web site. Her eyes ached and her head was less than one hundred metres behind but closing fast. She had reached the point where all she could do was replay the evidence over and over, but the thought process was too exhausted to start gelling anomalies or adding coincidences and compiling facts. It seemed as if there was suddenly too much evidence, too much to compile and make sense of.

Captain Frusco made his way to the TV studio. The whole case unsettled him. Evidence of Rick Montoya's meetings with Charles Fleisher and Stephen England had opened un-thought of, unspoken implications. The counter under the names of Rick Montoya, Jo-Lynn Montoya and Ray were increasing, like a time bomb ticking away. In the last hour eighty thousand visits had been made to the site, word was getting out. The small Island was rapidly becoming global.

The prospect of sleep, even an hour's break was somewhere on par with holding a winning lottery ticket. The computer clock on the bottom right hand side of Georgina's screen ticked over another minute but somewhere between glances an hour had elapsed. It now said 21-57. Her mind kept coming back to the tooth that was left in her car, the child's tooth. Jordan Montoya's tooth. Why her...Why the Montoya's? The questions kept invading her thought process. The door to her right opened, Leroy struggled in holding a tray with a flat square box and two polystyrene cups of coffee.

'Great Pizza...again.' Georgina sighed.

'Gotta keep the cholesterol level up.' Leroy placed the tray down and patted his stomach, which was a tribute to the lifestyle that being in the homicide department affords.

'You know this is the first case I've worked on where I've actually put weight on. Two pounds.'

Leroy flipped open the box to a less than enthusiastic fanfare. 'Ta-da.'

'Pepperoni and Chilli?' Georgina said looking at the pizza.

'With anchovies and mushrooms.' Leroy added

'May I ask you a question, Leroy?'

'Yeah, sure.'

'Are you pregnant? Because that is the most disgusting combination.' Leroy pulled a triangle of pizza free from the box. The molten cheese stretched, refusing to break it umbilical link with the rest of the Pizza. He moved the box to one side to reveal a second box, which he handed to Georgina.

'Here you are.' He scooped a hot stringy piece of cheese, which was welding to his lip, and placed it inside his mouth. 'As ordered, one regular cheese and tomato with bacon'

Georgina licked her lips in fake expectation. 'Mmmn.' She took a bite from the pizza and mumbled through the masticated food. 'The ten' o'clock bulletin.' She was pointing to the dead TV screen sitting on a shelf snuggled between piles of books and papers.

Leroy leaned forward and through a scattering of coffee cups, pizza boxes and reports, located the remote control. His index finger found the on button with automated efficiency. They watched the ads roll by, before a warning was aired about the content of the news bulletin *'which many people may find distressing'.*

'How's Anna?' Georgina asked.

'I dropped her back to the hotel. She tired and confused.' Leroy shrugged

'Well, it's good to know we're not an elite group.'

Frusco grabbed Barbara Dace by the arm, stopping her in her tracks and turning her. 'You can't run the video. You have to cut the interview.'

'I won't be told by you what I can or cannot do, Norman. This is the biggest thing to happen here and just for once we have got the edge. Even if we pulled the whole story from the bulletin he'll get his publicity. He's timed electronic mail to hit the desks of every major network in the World.'

A make up girl intervened between the police captain and the reporter as though he wasn't there and started dusting Barbara's face, taking the shine from her skin.

'Anyway, even if I could, which I wouldn't, it's not my call.' She nodded towards the cameras. Standing by one was Chris Hurley. 'He's the boss.'

'Thirty seconds Barbara.' The floor manager shouted. 'Places everybody. Run the VT.'

Frusco ran over to where Hurley was standing. 'You've got to pull the interview.'

'Yeah sure.' Hurley replied ignoring Frusco. 'Good luck, Barbara.' He shouted over Norman Frusco's shoulder. Hurley stepped to one side and started to walk to the director's room. Frusco followed.

'I mean it, Mr Hurley. I can get a warrant.'

Hurley laughed. 'Get one.' then opened the door. Before entering the editing room he looked back. 'Any moment now the whole world is going to come crashing around this little Island, Mr Frusco, and we have got a jump ahead of them. So tell me Captain, what's the fucking point? You're the boy with his finger in the dam, Captain.' Hurley disappeared behind the door. Frusco turned to see Barbara introduce herself to the waiting world knowing Hurley was right.

Leroy pressed the record button on the video and sat back with his Pizza. Georgina had started to draw a tree chart. At the top was Charles Fleisher's name, next to that was Rick Montoya's and his family. A third box had no name just a question mark. From each box ran a line leading to another box. Under the Montoya's she wrote Korjca Piekarska and Jordan Montoya. She drew a line down to a fresh box and wrote their professions, Police, Lawyer, Nanny and School. Underneath Charles Fleisher's box she put in his wife, Narla, and his daughter, Harley's names. A line continued from Fleisher's name to a box where she wrote Real Estate Agent then underneath that the name of Karen Fuller, Fleisher's victim. From the question-marked box, she wrote *killer* and under that his victims. Max Dalton aged 29and Stephen England aged 31. At the bottom of the page she drew a large box and entered the word DIARY. She started to connect lines from the names of people who subsequently she had found out knew each other either by profession or through their private lives. Georgina thought about the connections. Karen Fuller taught Harley Fleisher at the same school that Ray attended. She was also having an affair with Charles. Korjca Piekarska had met Charles once and noted it in her diary. Somehow he had dealings with Rick Montoya. She put a question mark against the link connecting them. The tooth of Rick's deceased daughter fell into the possession of the killer. Stephen England also visited Rick Montoya and had been seen by Korjca. Her diagram was beginning to look confused under a mass of connecting lines. But the one thing that was emerging from the jumbled mess of lines was that more of them were connecting to Rick Montoya than anyone else.

And now for our world exclusive interview with the man who claims to be the Turtle Island killer, known as the Dentist.

Leroy's hand grabbed at Georgina's shoulder and shook her gently. She looked up at the screen.

Georgina mouthed ' The Dentist? Who comes up with this shit.'

The image of the Montoya's kidnapper appeared for the entire world to see.

Maureen Cochran drew her blinds, locking out the world. For a moment she stood in darkness and listened. Happy that all was quiet she made her way across the room and switched on the light. The television was on low, meant as nothing more than an accompaniment for a lonely lady, but late breaking news bulletin unsettled her. It seemed that death was returning to her little island. The world was going crazy and finally it had caught up with her and tracked her down to the small island, which she thought was a sanctuary against the madness. At times like this she regretted not having married, there were no children to whom she could phone in the middle of the night when her sense of security was warped. She just had herself and that would have to make do. Life was different when she was younger, she had a string of men queuing outside her door, much to the disgust of her father and the eternal shame of her mother. An only child, Maureen had no contemporaries to base her behaviour on, she just knew she liked men and never for a moment dreamed that she would ever be left living her life alone and afraid, but now all the men seemed to have disappeared, either married or dead. She threw another log on the fire and watched the flames lick around it, sparking, jettisoning tiny lighted embers onto the hearth. Maureen shivered; it wasn't the cold that was getting to her bones though. She sat on the sofa and watched the news report on the television, cursing herself, knowing that she wouldn't be able to sleep later.

Part Three

With the fear comes the consequence

Thirty-Four

As night turns black, a thousand souls shall be claimed by the corrupted and they shall feast in my decadence.

Anon 1573. *The Book Of Lost Souls.*

The roads began to clog up with traffic within an hour of the newscast. Without warning Turtle Island was thrust into the World's attention and it wasn't ready. Cars, trucks and rigs stretched from Independence Bridge to Campbelltown in a slow moving procession searching for what was to become a scarce commodity; Hotels, Motels, bed and breakfast accommodation or anywhere where a bed could be found or put, even car parks. The police, already stretched to breaking point with the murders, now had to cope with a media invasion unlike any other seen before.

Gary Clarkson put his mother to bed and headed back into the general store. The rain had continued falling throughout the day and still fell with relish from the sky. He spent half an hour explaining to his mother that he was going to open the store and a further half hour reassuring her that she had nothing to be worried about. Sure there was a killer out there somewhere on their little island upsetting the ph level of life but *they* were safe. He wandered through the darkened shop and turned the closed sign to read open and unlocked the door. As he walked back the lights flickered on signalling to the arriving masses that one little piece of Turtle Island was at least ready for the coming onslaught. He busied himself filling shelves from the stock room until the first of the night's visitors arrived.

Frusco spent a sleepless night co-ordinating proceedings, calling in the National Guard to cope with the increasing traffic problems brought about by the invasion. By sunrise, the news crews of every major network had established a base on or near the Island and were beginning to make reports.

Leroy found two comfortable chairs and pushed them together for Georgina to catch a few hours sleep. He pushed himself into a third chair, resting his feet on a table, despite being uncomfortable, fatigue made sleep an easy but fleeting friend. He was woken by the sound of Georgina's alarm on her wristwatch. Daylight was creeping through the blinds; she continued to sleep until the last ring of the alarm, which finally managed to stir her. Georgina opened her eyes. Her arm was pinned under her head and her face was squashed into the side of the armchair. She had a raincoat for a blanket and her own jacket on top of the raincoat, her back ached and her legs felt heavy. She twisted around, her skirt protested, cutting into her stomach. Leroy moved his feet from the table and hoped that his morning glory erection would die before she noticed. He shuffled uneasily on the chair trying not to draw attention to himself.

'Hi.' Georgina's voice was dry, slightly gruff. She coughed to clear her throat. The taste of the Pizza came back to haunt her. Georgina rubbed her face and had to study her watch with intense concentration, before she could manage to decipher the time in her muggy brain.

'Six o'clock.' Leroy helpfully offered. He leaned forward and stretched his neck knowing from experience that the pain would disappear within an hour.

'God, I need a shower.' Georgina said relishing the idea of being able to freshen up.

'Well, I didn't want to be the first to say.' Leroy joked.

Georgina pulled a cushion from behind her and flung it at the detective.

'Hey, if you're lucky I won't mention your boner to the guy's in the canteen.' Georgina replied with lightness in her voice that hadn't been there for some time.

Leroy looked down at his crotch. 'How did you know?'

'I didn't, but you just confirmed it.' Georgina laughed

'Shit.' Leroy stood and turning his back, adjusted his trousers. 'Excuse me.'

Georgina stretched her body and slid out of the chairs. She pulled the zipper to her skirt up. 'I'm gonna get a shower and something wholesome for breakfast, before I even look at anything.'

'Good Idea.' Leroy picked his jacket up from the floor.

The two detectives left the small office. The computer monitor was still online. As they passed Georgina noticed that the figures on the counter had changed dramatically.

When Jo-Lynn woke she was aware that her feet and nightdress were dry for the first time in days. She was hungry. It had been a long time since the bread and soup. It had been a long time since *he* was there. She looked at the soles of her feet. The wounds were beginning to close, though they were still red raw near the edges. She pressed against the torn skin. The pain that shot up her legs went straight to her pain receptors in her brain. The dirty water had infected them. Jo-Lynn stood but nearly fell straight over. Biting into her lip to stop her screaming. She pulled her nightdress up to just above her waist and tied a knot in it, determined to keep it dry, then frailly stepped down into the water. It seemed to be colder than ever and twice as murky. She stayed near the edge, close to the stairs, remembering the rat, and surveyed the room. The rats appeared to be gone. She moved to the centre of the room, to where her chair was. Each painful step was a mile. Jo-Lynn righted the chair then started to drag it over to the wall with the vent. Half way across, the chair legs bounced against something, and for a moment would go no further until she tugged hard to free it. When she reached the vent, she stood on the chair seat and tried to peer down the small shaft where what little fresh air there was, was coming from. She could feel the air on her face but there was not one chink of light. Maybe it was night she told herself. Her mind went back to the obstruction in the middle of the floor. She climbed down off the chair and limped to the area. Bending down she searched with her hands through the muddy water. Her fingers scraped against the stone floor until they came to a tiny dip. She knelt down, pulling her nightdress higher above her breasts tying it with a knot, once more determined to keep it dry even at the cost to her dignity. She leaned an arm deeper into the water. Her fingers became her eyes, trying to gauge exactly what she had stumbled across. She could feel a metal ring. Jo-Lynn traced along the edge until she was sure. Hope began to rise for the first time since she was kidnapped. She was sure she had found some form of a trap door.

Matthew Gates sat looking at his computer screen eyes wide open, heart thumping through his chest. His friends were equally quiet; five of them were crammed into the small bedroom.

'See, I told you.' Matthew said looking behind him for approval from his friends, Ralph Ramierez, Matt Colman, Jimmy Freedan and Paul Connor.

His friends stared at the screen with disbelief. The group of boys, all of them just in their teens were for once at a loss for words.

'Are you sure this is real?' Jimmy asked, his face a mass of freckles that almost joined to make his skin looked orangey brown.

'It's real man, didn't you see the news?' Paul said pushing between Karl and Ralph for a better view. 'Wow, you can see her tush...oh man, I don't believe it, she's just turned round.'

The gaggle of boys fought hard for a better viewing position around the 17-inch monitor

'Yeah.' Ralph said. 'I saw the news but they didn't show you this.'

'D'you think it's for real?' Matthew asked, briefly glancing a look behind.

'We can vote on who he stiffs next, her, the boy, or her old man? Then he's gonna do it live on the net tonight.'

'Yeah, he might even fuck her man, before he does it.' Jimmy said, adding. 'She's a hot looking bitch.'

The door to Matthew's bedroom opened. Matthew's mother entered holding a tray with a pitcher of orange juice and four glasses. Still dressed in her dressing gown. 'Now you guy's don't be late for school.'

Matthew quickly clicked on to his previous saved page. The image of Jo-Lynn was replaced with Madonna's home page from an unofficial web site. She placed the tray down on the desk next to her son, unaware of either her son's computer activities or the fact that his four friends were getting a choice view of her breasts as she lowered herself to put the tray down. Jimmy Freedan fought hard not to faint; his whole body throbbed with excitement as he managed to glimpse one of Aileen Gates nipples.

'I'm gonna take a shower Matt, keep an ear open for Bob. He's coming over to drop me off to work this morning. If he comes tell him I won't be long and show him to the lounge.' She stroked Matt's face and kissed his head, then ruffled his hair before leaving. Much to his embarrassment.

'Okay, Mom.' He watched her leave.

'Your mom is fit, man.' Jimmy said

Matt looked at his friend .'Seriously sick.' before clicking the forward icon on his browser. The screen appeared but Jo-Lynn was no where to be seen

'Ah man, she's gone.' Karl moaned.

'Maybe she's just outta camera.' Ralph offered. 'Taking a pee or a dump.'

'That I don't want to see. Cheers Ralph, trust you to raise the tone.' Matt said dryly, forcing a spate of suppressed laughter from the other boys.

'Hey, we should vote.' Paul said, which surprised Matt, as Paul was the studious quiet thinker in the group.

'Yeah, lets stiff the bi-artch.' Jimmy repeated.

Matt clicked on the icon at the bottom of the page. The voting page appeared with the three faces of Rick Montoya, Jo-Lynn and Ray.

'Look, she's in the lead.' Jimmy said barely able to contain his excitement.

'Yeah by two thousand votes, then it's the boy.' Matt looked at the counters below the photos. 'Who shall we vote for?'

The four boys in unison replied as one. 'The bitch.' And laughed.

Across the country in bedrooms, offices and games rooms people were starting to vote by the thousand, snared into what appeared to be something between a game and reality.

Matt's hand hovered over the left hand button on his mouse while he positioned his cursor under the picture of Jo-Lynn. Only fleetingly did he feel any responsibility when he clicked to the roaring approval of his friends.

Georgina stood under the piping hot water for what appeared to be an age, allowing the pressurised water to sooth her aching shoulder muscles and ease away the tension in her neck. Her mind was whirring away, thinking about the case. She kept coming back to the diary.

'Rick Montoya knew Charles Fleisher...Why? What did Stephen England want and how did he know Rick?'

She rinsed the shampoo from her hair and continued thinking, mulling over the options. Fleisher's name kept returning like a bad penny. Whatever she personally thought about his implication in the killings of Dalton, and England she knew one thing for sure, Charles Fleisher had killed Karen Fuller and was responsible as surely as if he had put a gun to her head, ruining the life of his daughter Harley to the bargain. Then the bad penny that kept returning suddenly dropped. Georgina stepped from the shower cursing to herself. The missing link was right in front of them all along and not once did they see it. She wrapped a large bath towel around herself and ran out of the women's shower room across the hall straight into the men's locker room, past the protesting naked foot patrollers and squad car drivers called in for early duty to cope with the influx of America on to their little island.

'LEROY...LEROY.' She blurted excitedly, looking over the shower stalls and doors trying to find the detective, apologising to every white and black ass that wasn't her partners. Leroy was standing under the showerhead facing the door, with soapsuds through his hair, running down his slightly overweight chest and stomach. Georgina stopped at the door and for a few seconds took in the full picture of his nakedness before speaking.

'Leroy, I think I may have found the link.'

Leroy peered through a half open eye hoping soap wouldn't run down into it. He thought he had heard Georgina. He wiped his face clear of suds and blinked. Sure enough she was standing there, right in front of him. A clear glass partition was not enough to save his modesty.

'What the...'

'Get dry and meet me in your office.' She had turned before Leroy managed to complete his sentence. 'Oh and by the way Leroy... nice

Johnson.' She smiled then walked out of the locker room to complete shocked silence.

By the time Leroy reached his office, Georgina was already sitting behind his PC. Files from the *'Fleisher killings'* lay scattered on the floor and over what little spare desk space was left.
'Do you mind telling me what all that was about in the locker room?' Leroy looked for once ruffled, and genuinely pissed.

'We have been so dumb. So caught up in it, that we missed something that was so obvious.' Georgina took a deep breath of apathy, disgusted at her own oversight.

'So enlighten me.' Leroy said. His patience already stretched to the limit without the need for any more guessing games.

'It was so obvious.' Georgina found it hard to reconcile her revelation. 'Children, Leroy, children.'

'What are you talking about?'

'I've checked through the files.' She spread the folders out. 'We got films of Fleisher abusing his daughter. Some of the films include other people. How many of those have we followed up and investigated?'

Leroy shrugged his shoulders

Georgina gave a hollow laugh. 'None...not one.'

'Wait, wait, what are you saying, that this is some sort of paedophile ring?'

'I don't know.' Georgina seemed to be asking for support. 'But it gets worse. I think Rick is involved somehow.'

Leroy physically staggered. 'No way. No way, he loved his kids.'

'I know this sounds hard but he is linked with Fleisher and Stephen England. Korjca mentions that they both visited the house in her diary. We're going to have to interview Harley Fleisher. She's the key and as hard as it is we're going to have to view all of Fleisher's tapes.' Georgina shivered at the prospect of having to view the vile molestation. Abuse of children sickened her but she knew it was vital that every tape was viewed for clues.

'I think Frusco should know.' Leroy said, his mind churning over the possibilities.

'There are only twelve and a half hours until eight o'clock.' Georgina threw her pencil across the table, time was running out and they had no idea where the Montoya's were being kept.

'Okay. You interview Harley Fleisher; I think she'll be more responsive and open to you. I'll start viewing the tapes. If I find *anything* I'll call you.' Leroy said.

Thirty-Five

The first thing Georgina noticed was the *For Sale* board pitched in the centre of the lawn. A *sold* sticker had recently been plastered through the bright red lettering. The board was slightly crooked as though it had succumbed to a battering by the weather. Georgina wanted to straighten the sign and fought the urge as she passed. She pulled her identification from the inside pocket of her jacket, making sure that she re-buttoned it, covering the brown leather holster containing her pistol. She rang the doorbell and held the ID out to be clearly inspected. Narla Fleisher opened the door, wiping the corner of her mouth with a drying cloth. Georgina noticed that Narla was extremely pregnant. Her overlarge shirt was straining against the girth of her stomach.

'Hello, Mrs Fleisher. My name is Agent Georgina O'Neil. We met briefly six months ago.'

The flicker of recognition passed over Narla's eyes followed by a look of concern, which Georgina immediately picked up on.

'It's all right, Mrs Fleisher; there is nothing to worry about, no need for concern. I just want to ask Harley some questions.'

'May I ask what it is concerning?' Narla was guarded, naturally protective to her daughter.

'You may have seen on the television about the kidnapping of one of the detectives and his family that were working on the case here six months ago.'

Narla nodded. 'Yes I heard...It's terrible, but I don't know what Harley can do to help.'

'There are certain aspects to this case that are beginning to overlap with the trouble here last year. We just want to make sure that we cover all the angles.'

Narla stepped aside. 'You better come in. Through to the kitchen if you don't mind. I was just about to serve Harley her breakfast.'

'Thank you.'

'Maybe I can help.' Narla said, two steps behind the FBI agent.

'I'm sure you can, but for now I need to speak to Harley' Georgina turned and smiled. 'Should I be congratulating you' Georgina said, looking at Narla's bump.

'You can if you want. It was Charles parting gift to me...he drugged and raped me. Narla looked hurt for the briefest of moments then she nodded. 'I'll just go and get her.'

Georgina looked around the kitchen. It had a homely feel. The smell of coffee hung in the air invitingly, temptingly. The radio was on low in the background, tuned to a local station playing a mixture of new country and old blues, interspersed with hammy adverts for used car lots and air conditioning companies. Postcards adorned the fridge, attached by magnets. The sound of toast springing from the toaster made Georgina jump, she turned to look at the offender and came face to face with Harley Fleisher.

'Hello...' Georgina hand clutched her chest to steady her pounding heart. 'The toast...kinda gave me a fright.' she tried explaining.

'I remember you.' Harley said. She passed Agent O'Neil and collected a piece of toast to butter. 'I saw you at the hospital.'

Georgina smiled. 'Good memory.' She privately hoped to herself that her memory on other matters would be as concise. Harley buttered the slice and applied a thick layer of honey, too thick for Georgina's taste. She bit into it then offered Georgina the other slice, which she accepted.

'Coffee?' Harley was the perfect host and much more mature than her eleven years suggested. Georgina guessed that after what she had been through in the last year that it was not surprising that she had to grow up. A child robbed of her childhood by her father and by circumstance beyond her control.

Georgina could relate to that on one albeit very different level. She nodded. 'Coffee would be nice, one sugar, white please.'

'I hope you have been looking after our guest.'

Georgina span around to see Narla enter the kitchen.

'Sorry to have left you to Harley's *terrible* company but...' She patted the large mound developing near her stomach. 'This baby dictates my life these days.'

Harley made a horrible grimacing face, showing the openness and ease of the relationship between mother and daughter.

'She always needs to pee or puke.' Harley said with a large amount of mischief.

'Why, thank you Harley. I'm sure that's far more information than Miss O'Neil needed to know. Even though, sad to say, it is true.' Narla laughed not at all annoyed or embarrassed by her daughter's behaviour.

Harley poured some coffee from the pot and passed a mug to Georgina.

'Thank you.'

Harley smiled. 'I guess you're here to ask me about my father.' There seemed to be no trace of anger, sadness or bitterness in Harley's voice.

'If you don't mind?'

Harley shook her head while biting through her toast. 'Why should I?'

'Is there somewhere comfortable we could sit?' Georgina directed the question at Narla.

'Only this could take an hour or so. I have arranged for a call to be put through to Harley's school, informing them that she probably won't be in today.'

Harley's eyes lit up. 'Cool.'

'Yeah, sure the sitting room.' Narla waddled ahead, leading the way.

As they walked through a set of double doors that led directly from the kitchen to a well-furnished lounge, Narla said quietly to Georgina. 'Go easy on her. She may seem to have coped with everything okay, but sometimes you only have to scratch the surface to find a lot of pain. She's had counselling but what amount of psychobabble can repair the damage that bastard done.'

'I know your talking about me.' Harley said walking close behind. Her face buried in another thick slice of gooey honey on toast. 'People always whisper when they're talking about me.'

'And what about you?' Georgina grasped Narla's arm.

'I have other things to worry about,' She patted her stomach. 'like my children. My job is to make sure that they're okay now.'

Five VCRs worked constantly, hooked up to five different TV screens, each playing a different tape, a different image but the one thing they seemed to have in common was the content of the image. Leroy and Norman Frusco sat watching images that they hoped never to witness again in their lives. Frusco sat next to Leroy. A stack of tapes was collected and sitting to one side on a melamine table in the darkened room. There were moments where the fast forward button could be pressed but they were few and far between. Leroy stared at the screen in front of him. The tape had been labelled with a felt tipped pen, *C and H, Mouth*. It was hard for Leroy to judge, but Harley appeared to be no more than eight or nine when the film was made. The only other thing that was apparent apart from the sickening nature of the film was that there was a third person filming Charles Fleisher's acts of oral sex with his daughter. Leroy pressed fast forward until the end of the tape.

'Eight down, thirty-four to go. I'm not sure I'm gonna make it to the end of this.' He reached behind and took the next tape from the top of the nearest pile.

'This one should be a doozy.' Leroy flipped the tape around so he could read the title. 'It's called S and H, G and C-h-tel.' He put the tape in and pressed play. 'Jesus.' The word slipped out of Leroy's shocked mouth.

'What is it?' Frusco leaned to one side to see what had caused Leroy's reaction. He looked at the screen, at the familiar face that belonged to the man pinning Harley down to the bed. Charles Fleisher's reflection could be clearly seen filming the debauched scene in a mirror to the side of the bed. Norman Frusco was shocked to the bone. The last person he had expected to see was one of the victims. He watched Stephen England clambering naked, over the top of the small girl. Leroy stopped the tape; not wishing to see anything more than was absolutely necessary.

'You know, I felt sorry for that motherfucker lying in the hospital like a vegetable.' Leroy's voice was low, full of anger. 'It seems O'Neil was right.'

Leroy turned the tape back on. He pressed the fast forward button. The machine clunked and the images on the screen sped up like actors in an early silent feature, they looked comical but this was no comedy. The tape whirred on until static fuzz replaced them and the principle participants changed. Leroy pressed the play button. The man was Charles Fleisher, lying naked on the bed. The girl this time was older, though not much older. She was standing by the bed; Stephen England grabbed her from behind. Both were naked. England moved her forward closer to Fleisher. He pushed down on the back of the girl's head forcing her closer to Fleisher. Leroy wound the tape forward again.

'There's another person filming.' Leroy said.

'Harley?'

Leroy almost laughed. 'No, she's not there. This is a different day. Fleisher's hair is much shorter, his pubic hair is shaved in the first film, see, here, its grown back.'

'That's a little more detail to observation than I really want Leroy.' Frusco said trying to lighten the moment.

'Lot's of these sick fuckers like to feel their little girls real close, they don't like hair getting in the way.' Leroy looked at his captain briefly before returning to the screen. 'If the camera goes back to its original position we should catch a glance of him or her, in the mirror.'

'Who's the girl?' Norman asked.

The girl on the screen was now sitting on top of Fleisher's chest. England's hands pulled her forward toward his face. The camera moved to a close-up of the girls face. She turned as though someone had called her name. Leroy had seen the face before. The green eyes, her straightened black hair, her brown skin, and the smile that she was forcing showed the final confirmation, the missing tooth. Leroy's heart sank further than he felt possible.

'Jordan Montoya.'

A knock at the door interrupted them, both Leroy and Norman Frusco pressed the stop button on their respective videos, and the craven images were replaced by a blue screen.

'Come in.' Frusco shouted.

A fresh-faced young officer tentatively poked his head through the small gap in the door.

'Sir, all hell's breaking loose out there.'

'Okay, I'll be out...to be honest I could do with a break.' Frusco stood and arched his back. His neck audibly clicked indicating the tension he was feeling.

Thirty-Six

The residents of Turtle Island woke to pandemonium. Blocked roads, police checks, TV crews, and helicopter flights buzzing constantly over the rooftops of the houses, fields and boathouses.

Norman Frusco had, with the mayor and governor's blessing, ordered in the National Guard to save his own force being stretched to an unbearable limit. To all intent and purposes Turtle Island was under siege and the prospect of being able to carry out any sort of investigation was severely hampered. Frusco had been awake all night trying to police the worsening situation. He drank his fifth cup of strong, black, coffee within two hours and dissolved another two *'Sta-Awake!'* tablets in a glass of water, as he took a ten minute break from the wall to wall pornography to catch up with events on the island. The television was on constantly. The change over of staff for the morning shift was beginning; tired officers straggled away for an hour or two's sleep before continuing work.

Frusco watched Barbara Dace on the small screen; somehow she still managed to be looking fresh. She was beginning to become a national celebrity, having spent the evening giving interviews to networks and foreign stations. The monitor next to the television was still linked to the Death Cam web site. Frusco clicked on the reload button to refresh and update the site. He watched the figures change and wondered how people could actually vote to end a life.

Georgina sat next to the young girl. 'How are you coping?'

Harley Fleisher shrugged her shoulders. 'Okay, I guess.'

Georgina wanted to be tactful but at the same time knew that being direct would save time. She couldn't begin to imagine what was going on in the mind of the little girl sitting next to her, though she could see that Harley was resilient, but Narla's caution hovered in Georgina's mind. The last thing Georgina wanted was to add to the psychological damage that already existed.

'I've spoken to doctors and all sorts of people.' Harley began without further prompting. 'They keep telling me I've nothing to be ashamed of...' Harley looked squarely in to Georgina's eyes. 'You can't help but feel though it's your own fault, that maybe somehow I...I don't know, I just feel as though it is all my fault. I didn't know, I used to think that what was happening to me was normal. I thought it happened to every little girl or boy. Daddy told me it was special love…'

'At the time did **you** feel he was lying?'

Harley looked puzzled. 'No. I know now though that what he did was wrong.'

'He was wrong Harley and yes, he was very ill.' Georgina changed tack. 'I see that you're going to be moving soon. Are you happy about that?'

'Yeah, its really cool. I've already got friends where we're going. I kinda want to leave here. There are memories here that I want to forget. The doctor…a child psychologist.' Harley continued. 'The doctor said that it was important that I should try to remember the good times I had spent with dad. That he will always be here.' Harley pointed to her head and her heart.

'I know there are things that you want to forget, Harley, but some of those things might help me to catch bad men that might hurt other children. This person may have been someone your daddy knew, maybe someone he introduced to you.'

Harley looked unsure. Georgina sensed a flicker of reticence. Harley sat back in the chair. She looked down at her feet; lost for a few seconds.

'Okay.'

Georgina opened the small folder she had brought with her and fished through it until she came upon a group of photographs. She pulled them out and laid them on the table. One by one, face up. Six colour photos, all close up portraits. Stephen England, Max Dalton, Detective Rick Montoya, Jordan Montoya, Ray Montoya and Jo-Lynn Montoya.

'I want you to tell me if you have ever seen any of these people, Harley? Look carefully and touch any of the photos of anyone you recognise.'

Harley sat forward and studied the photographs. Within seconds of glancing at them, her arm stretched forward and her index finger stabbed at five of the photos, dragging them forward.

If she could just get her fingers around the small metal ring, Jo-Lynn thought she might be able to pull open the trap door. She had been working at the ring for what seemed like hours and was pretty sure that *he* would be back soon. She had lost count of how many hours or even days it was since *he* had been there. She needed something hard to get under the rusted metal ring, some sort of tool to prize it upwards so she could gain purchase. As she struggled with it, her fingernail bent back, half ripping away from the skin beneath. She screamed out in frustration and pain and fell back into the mucky water. Jo-Lynn landed seated in waist-high water. She put her torn fingernail to her mouth, trying to ease the pain, not wanting to look at the damage. As she sucked on her finger, the glint of her wedding ring caught her eye; she had an implement she could use, the solitaire diamond set in the centre of the ring.

A noise at the top of the stairs caught her attention. *He* was coming. She got to her feet and ran, as best she could, to the landing by the steps to where her nightdress lay. She pulled it over her head catching the broken nail and cursing the pain. Jo-Lynn huddled into the corner, pulling her knees up.

She pretended to be asleep but watched from the corner of her eye as the door at the top of the stairs opened. *He* appeared; walking carefully down each step. His face was covered with a ski mask, which merged seamlessly with a black polo neck jumper. His hands were gloved, holding a tray. The aroma of the food hit her nose before she had even seen it. His hands were full. A thought ran through Jo-Lynn's mind. She could pull him over but would she have enough strength to struggle with him and escape. She stayed curled watching his slow thoughtful approach, step by step. Fate was walking down the stairs. Her fate.

John Borland watched from the comfort of his bedroom. He watched the drama unfolding. He was aroused. When wasn't he aroused? But this was different, this was real; real life, real death and he got to choose. He got to vote. John Borland voted more than once. He was hooked up on-line permanently for the past 18 hours, stopping only to eat, defecate and re-supply himself with fresh tissues. Occasionally he would look out of his window at the snow-covered landscape of Troy Falls, Minnesota. He would look at the sleepy town and plan.

The answers were there all along. Leroy cursed their laziness, his own. So much of what had happened could have been prevented. Leroy watched the hungry videocassette recorder swallow another tape and steeled himself. The pile of un-viewed tapes had diminished and now there were only three left including the one being seated in the recorder. As the image flickered, Captain Frusco broke Leroy's concentration.

'Who's this?'

Leroy leaned across and stared at the picture. A naked man in his late thirties to early forties was walking around a bed. Leroy didn't recognise the young boy lying on the bed.

'This is gettin' messy... who is that?' Leroy tapped his pencil on the screen, the lead tip stabbing the man in the back. 'Put it on hold a moment?'

Frusco hit the pause button. The image was not too well defined but with a little tinkering and image enhancement Leroy knew that if the man had a record then they could make a positive match.

'Key player?' Frusco asked.

'Any unknown face is a key player. It's odd how camera shy the adults are compared to the focus they put on the children. Can we get this enhanced?'

Frusco nodded. 'If the lab can't handle it I've got a couple of favours to call in over at MRTV. They've got state of the art equipment there.'

Leroy pulled the tape from the machine. 'Okay. If anything else breaks, call me.'

As Leroy left the small darkened room he switched on his mobile phone and dialled Georgina's number

'So where was your mother when your father first started to come into your bedroom?' Georgina's voice was soft but direct. She aimed her question wanting answers but at the same time aware of the girl's sensitivities.

Narla interjected, she was standing at the door holding a tray with fresh drinks. 'I can answer that, I am an insomniac, always have been. I have two ways of sleeping, Miss O'Neil. Both of them come from a bottle, both of them taken in the right quantities result in unconsciousness.'

Narla placed the tray down on the coffee table and handed a glass of orange to Harley and a fresh cup of coffee to Georgina.

'I know this is tough Mrs Fleisher, but I need to hear Harley's version of events.'

'Sure, but there are areas I'd rather you didn't stray into for too long. If you don't mind, I will sit here. I promise I will try not to butt in.'

O'Neil nodded. 'Harley, when did you father first start visiting your room at night?'

Harley thought back, though the memories were fresh she wanted to make sure that she answered correctly. 'I don't really know, maybe I was five or six when he first started coming in. He told me he loved me, then he would kiss me...you know....' She paused, breathing slowly before continuing. 'Then it was every night. There didn't seem to be anything wrong, to me this was how all daddies behaved.'

Narla sat back in the seat opposite, an anguished look etched on her face.

'He made films and introduced you to other people...'

'My special Uncles. Daddy told me to keep them a secret and not tell mummy. I guess by then I knew something was wrong but it had been going on so long I just wouldn't admit it to myself.'

'You know this girl?' Georgina pointed to a photograph of Jordan Montoya that Harley had chosen.

Harley didn't answer but chose to nod affirmation.

'You know her daddy?' Georgina pressed on, even though she could tell Harley was beginning to clam up. Harley looked at Georgina; painful tears were welling in her eyes.

'I know this is tough.' Georgina placed her hand on Harley's arm.

Harley shook her head. 'Not sure…there was so many faces, so many different men.'

'How many *special uncles* was there, Harley?'

Harley wiped away a tear then looked away. She tried to count and remember the faces. The faces she wanted to forget, the faces that often returned in her dreams when she closed her eyes.

'Eight, maybe nine. I'm not certain, I never counted'

'Do you know their names, any of them?'

Harley nodded. 'Some, first names only.'

Georgina's heart began to race. She was close to a breakthrough.

'My daddy used to talk with them all the time on computer.'

'Your daddy's computer was checked out; we found nothing. We even looked at his work machine.' She could feel her heart begin to sink.

'That's because he used my computer to talk to them.'

'Your computer?'

'Yeah. My computer. Daddy bought it for me for my seventh birthday.'

'Where is it now, Harley?'

Harley pointed to the ceiling and whispered conspiratorially. 'It's in my bedroom.'

'Can I see it?'

'Sure.' Harley jumped up and grabbed Georgina by the arms, pulling her from the sofa. 'I use it all the time to talk to our new neighbours in Texas. Mommy said I hogged the line, but she only said that because she wants to talk to Dexter. They get very slushy.' Harley pretended to gag.

'Who is Dexter?'

'Mommy's new boyfriend. So she went and got a broadband connection.'

Thirteen stairs and a short hop across a tiny landing brought Georgina into 'Harleyland'; wall to wall posters, Will Smith, Ben Afleck, Matt Damon, Mark Wahlberg, Brad Pitt and Leonardo di Caprio. It looked like the average room of any eleven-year-old girl whose hormones were beginning to kick in.

'Wow. Some poster collection.' Georgina said impressed.

'Yeah, Mommy lets me hang them. When we're out shopping she would often buy me one. She's great, really cool.'

Georgina's sight rested on the cream coloured PC mounted on an antique wood desk.

'Sorry about the bed.' Harley apologised, quickly pulling the quilt up and straightening the pillow. 'I usually make it when I come home form school, that's if Mommy hasn't come in and blitzed the room. She a 'clean' freak.'

Georgina made her way to the desk.

Narla appeared at the door. 'Everything alright?'

Georgina wasn't sure who the question was aimed at so she decided to let Harley answer.

'I'm showing...' Harley was unsure about using the detective's Christian name or her formal title and by the time she had made up her mind Georgina stepped in.

'Harley's showing me her PC. We never got to see it before. I'm hoping that there is information in here that can help us.' Georgina patted the computer monitor. 'We didn't know until now that Charles used this PC for Internet access.'

Harley moved in beside the detective, sitting down in the chair in front of the computer screen. She fired up the PC. Narla entered the room and watched with Georgina and Harley as the computer went through various checks before launching. Harley dragged the mouse across the screen, rested the pointer on the start icon and clicked. Two lists appeared, filled with various programs. She ran the cursor down until it rested on a line marked AIA.

Georgina recognised the logo for American Internet Access, she had seen it in various magazines and billboards but had never delved further. The opening screen appeared, a gaudy mauve background with the flag of the union fluttering in the foreground. A box marked 'Sign on' and another that read 'password' were to the right of the flag. Harley moved the cursor to the sign on box and clicked on an arrow. Another list appeared, this time a row of six names; people who shared the account with Harley. Georgina noticed that Charles name was absent from the list.

'Who are these people?' Georgina asked.

Narla read the list over Harley's shoulder. There were no names that she recognised apart from Harley's, which sat at the top. Harley pointed to the first name under her own and dragged the cursor down the list watching each subsequent name become highlighted.

'They're all dad's. You can open up to 12 separate accounts with this ISP.'

Narla looked puzzled. 'ISP?'

'Internet Service Provider.' Harley said barely hiding her disgust at her mother's ignorance.

Looking suitably shamed Narla shrugged her shoulders. 'I guess I should really keep up with all of this, but it was more Charles territory.'

'Do you know any of the passwords to access the accounts, Harley?'

'He never let me in the room when he was on-line. I tried; you know all the usual things. Our names, pet names, nicknames, house names, birthdays. Backwards and forwards and then I got lucky.'

'You managed to guess the password?'

'Yeah, it was *Lucky*.'

Georgina smiled. 'Very clever.'

Harley leaned forward and typed *Lucky* in the password box and hit the enter button, within seconds Georgina was in.

'Choose the name underneath your own, Harley.'

Harley clicked on the name, *Frank Timms*.

Georgina placed her hand over Harley's and guided the cursor to a column marked *file*. She pushed down gently on Harley's finger and clicked, another list appeared. Georgina guided Harley down to a line that read Personal Filling Cabinet and double clicked. The screen changed and an animated filling cabinet appeared with the middle drawer opening. A folder popped up out of the cabinet and opened. On top of the folder was the name Frank Timms.

'If I'm right this should hold every e-mail and attachment that *Frank Timms* has downloaded.' Georgina ran down the long list of e-mails, reading the subject titles. 'Maybe you should wait downstairs, Harley. There may be things here that you really don't need to see.'

Harley looked at her mother. Narla didn't say anything but nodded, gesturing for her to go downstairs. The girl stood without protesting, and walked silently down to the kitchen.

Georgina's hand hovered over the mouse for a moment, before she clicked and opened the first e-mail. The sound of her phone ringing stopped her from opening it. 'Yeah.' She answered distractedly, her eyes reading the long list of electronic post, scanning for anything that she might recognise.

'Hi, Georgina, it's Leroy. We got another break, a John Doe on one of the tapes. I'm on my way to get the image enhanced to iron out the fuzzy edges. I think we can get a positive ID on this guy.'

'Where are you now?' Georgina asked, her finger finally clicking the mouse. The e-mail opened.

'I'm taking it to the TV station. The guy's in the lab are still snowed under trying to find out where the web site is that our mutual friend is operating. Frusco's pulling in favours with Barbara Dace.' Leroy replied.

'Tell the lab rats to start looking at AIA as being the net provider. Things are starting to...' Georgina fell silent as her brain started to decode what she was subconsciously reading.

'Georgina?' Leroy shook his phone. He hated cell phones at the best of times and cursed their poor reception, which always seemed to occur when they were needed most.

'Georgina?' Leroy repeated.

'...Listen Leroy, I'm gonna call you back, something's come up.' She closed her cell phone, snapping the small trap door shut that covered half of the black plastic phone. Her eyes furiously read then re-read the message.

Thirty-Seven

She could have grabbed his ankles as he walked down the stairs. 'Why didn't she do it?' Arlene Trimiota cursed the lack of fight and recourse in the lawyer. She had heard all about the death cam site and as soon as her husband had left for his shift, hauling tobacco across the country, she fired up her computer and went on-line. Arlene had been trying to access the site for over four hours when she suddenly found herself inside. Since then she stayed on-line, determined not to break connection until she had witnessed an execution. Her husband, Earl, had bought her the PC to stop her getting lonely at nights when he was away *haulin' bacca' 'cross the States*. Earl had a laptop fitted in his cab with a cell phone connection that ran from the truck. Many a night the two of them would spend an evening apart but linked via their modems, and many a night Arlene would spend on-line talking filthy to some guy in Alaska or Albuquerque. God knows, there was even a guy in the Soviet Union, only they don't call it that no more. But today she was gonna stay watching this lawyer woman and see if she gets it.

'Damn Woman.' Arlene complained watching Jo-Lynn's failure to take action against this man who was holding her captive. Arlene admitted to herself, more than a little perverse enjoyment in watching the black woman's predicament. 'Your fancy job don't help you out none now does it honey.' She watched the man step down the final step, tray held out in front...

Jo-Lynn knew that now might be her best chance. *He* had left the door open. Somewhere down the passage that led off from it, she could hear a television set on. The sound of children's laughter drifted through. Above the canned recorded joviality came the solitary laugh of a small boy. The laugh she knew so well. She could hear Ray. The sound of her son fogged her mind, ending any remote possibility of trying to escape. Jo-Lynn was suddenly paralysed with raw emotion. She found herself accepting the tray of food and watching *him* turn and walk back up the stairs. The word escaped from her lips like a pathetic newborn kittens mew; a name. The reason she had kept her sanity. 'Ray.'

He was approximately half way up the steps. The sound of her voice made him stop. He turned to see the shambles of a woman, shaking uncontrollably. Tea spilling out of her cup onto the plate of beans, the toast upon which they sat eagerly sopped up the hot liquid.

Her voice a little stronger this time. 'Ray.'

He continued his journey, allowing a laugh to escape his lips as he neared the top.

Jo-Lynn summoned up all the strength that she had in her body, breathed deeply and this time screamed. 'WILL.' Just as *he* slammed the door shut.

She wanted to throw the tray to one side, smash it into the wall but part of her told her not to. Part of her was saying 'Eat the food, drink the tea. If you are to escape you will need to be strong.' She knew to listen to that part of her rationale. It was her instinctive side, the side she had come to know well and rely on in her job. Jo-Lynn sat and started to eat the beans on toast and a mug of tea; it tasted like the best meal she had ever eaten. She cherished each mouthful, savouring what seemed to be a multitude of flavours, the tea, hot and sharp tasting, each sip quenching her thirst. With the final swallow of the last chewed mouthful came a moment of sadness; Jo-Lynn finished off the last dregs of tea in her mug and sat for a moment in contemplation. She twisted the ring on her finger, using some of the melted butter left on her plate to lubricate it and slowly pulled the ring upwards and off. She lifted her nightdress until it rested on her shoulders and tied it so it wouldn't fall into the water, then stood up and entered the thick brown murky pool and headed for the trap door. Finding the edge of the door under the water, Jo-Lynn started to rub her wedding ring along the lip, hoping to free it. She could feel the ring grind and knew that the rusted edge was doing irreparable damage to her wedding band but not to the large solitaire diamond. She kept scraping it along and occasionally would tug, waiting for a little movement…hoping.

The early morning drizzle had finally given way to a full-blown downpour. The rain bounced off cars and overfilled guttering and down pipes, running along the gutters in little ravines, spurring at the sewer inlets before going deep down into the underground system. Leroy pulled his car to a halt, what should have been a ten minute journey was stretched in to twenty five minutes as he tried to navigate through the milling throngs of journalist's and TV crews that failed to have their spirits dampened by the weather. Turtle Island was fast becoming a carnival and Leroy could only see the media circus hindering their progress but here he was knocking at their door asking for favours. He entered MRTV's prestigious building and asked at the reception to speak with Barbara Dace. A request that was met with utter refusal until Leroy produced his badge. Within minutes he heard a lift bell ring and saw Barbara Dace exit. She was beginning to look tired, only having caught two hours sleep since the story broke. Leroy noticed the ever-present cigarette in her hand as well as a carton of coffee. She drew on the cigarette

'Breakfast.' She explained and washed the carbon monoxide down with a glug of caffeine.

'Most crucial meal of the day.' Leroy replied smiling.

'So, Mr LaPortiere, what brings you here? I'm sure it wasn't to discuss my dietary habits, which...' She drew on the cigarette once more. '...are even beginning to disgust me.' She exhaled a plume of blue smoke, which passed Leroy's cheek.

Leroy produced the videotape.

'Got an image, it needs cleaning up, clarifying. I was hoping you could help.'

The expression on Barbara's face changed to one of surprise. 'I thought you had specialists to deal with that sort of thing?'

'Yeah, we have but they're kinda busy. I need this right now.' Leroy tried to look apologetic while retaining a mood of authority.

Barbara took the tape. 'Okay, as long as we get to transmit what ever you have on that tape.'

'If you transmit this then you'll loose your license.' Leroy wagged the tape in the air

'No, I just mean the face. I take it that this is John Doe or am I mistaken?' Barbara continued walking to the open lift.

'He's a player. We can't be sure if he's the key player yet though.'
Barbara stepped back into the lift. 'I'm waiting Detective, I'm waiting.'

Norman Frusco tapped the National Reserve pilot on the shoulder and asked him to swoop down to the house where Charles Fleisher was found. From the air the picture became whole and with the clarity came a sense of shock. Turtle Island, his Island was in danger of becoming grid-locked. The helicopter twisted and snaked along the river that amputated the Island from the mainland. The river that made Turtle Island into the anomaly that it was, surrounded by water and the water surrounded by land. The rain on the windscreen threatened to obscure his vision totally. The operation of the wipers had become almost pointless, merely smearing an opaque landscape. Frusco watched a detachment of troops scouring the land below, searching from house to house, moving on, crossing the next field. All the time he was hoping that Agent O'Neil and Leroy were having more luck than him.

The editing suite was a large air-conditioned room stacked with pieces of technology that baffled Leroy. Barbara Dace sat behind a large desk that housed three video players and two twenty one inch monitors. A man she introduced as Andy White sat next to her. He took the tape from Barbara and slotted it into the machine furthest from him. He opened a fresh tape and slotted it in the machine to his right.

'What am I looking for?' Andy rattled a biro between his teeth constantly. His hair was nearly shoulder length and he dressed in a grungy style, faded worn out tee-shirts and equally faded denim, with worn out trainers. Leroy knew it must cost a lot of money to look that bad, he guessed that the job of video editing paid well. The tape began to play; Leroy leaned forward and pointed to the man about to climb on the bed next to the young boy.

'That's the man. Can you enhance the image so we can get a clearer picture of him?'

Andy looked at the blurred out face and upper body on the screen. 'This image has already been doctored. Someone has gone to great lengths to hide this man's identity.'

The tape played on. The man started to masturbate in front of the boy, grabbing the child's hands and placing them on him.

Andy rewound the tape back to the point where the man climbed on to the bed then slowed the image down to one frame per second, stopping every now and then, hoping to get a better view of the man's face.

'I'm sorry to have to ask, but to get the very best image of the man I think it would be best to view the whole film. Do you think you can do that?' Leroy asked the technician.

'Believe me, if I didn't have to I wouldn't, but if it helps to catch this guy...I take it it's the net guy?'

Leroy shrugged. 'To be honest; we really don't know. Suddenly it seems like some sort of sick cancer had enveloped this whole Island. He may only be part of a much bigger problem.'

'You know we're not miracle worker's.' Andy said scrolling the images a frame at a time. 'There's a whole mythology surrounding the abilities of image enhancement. Movies and books generate the idea that all we have to do is take any blurred image run it through some non-existing software and ...hey what's that?' Andy stopped mid-sentence and looked at the screen. The man was partially facing the screen with his back turned toward the camera. Although the image had been doctored it was clear that he was either wearing something or had some sort of disfigurement covering his back. Andy moved the mouse cursor and clicked on a tool bar at the top of the screen. The pointer icon changed to a lasso with a small box underneath. Andy placed the new icon over the area of the man's back and clicked the mouse and dragged the lasso icon. A section of the man's back was highlighted.

'What they've done is quite crude but still effective.' Andy clicked on the toolbar again and ran his cursor down a list, stopping at 'filter noise' and clicked once more.

'I'll be damned...It's a tattoo.' Leroy said.

The area on the man's back became slightly clearer.

'Can you improve on that, so we can see exactly what it is?'

'Give me an hour.' Andy turned to the detective.

As she worked at the jammed door Jo-Lynn began to notice the increased noise of air-traffic as the sound of helicopters and light planes echoed through the air duct in the wall above her. She ran the edge of the ring along the seized joint for what seemed to be the hundredth time and tried to prize free the ring that was set in to the door. A groove had been worn around the small handle, all she needed was something to wedge under the small gap and she would be able to pry the handle free.

'My God, I can't believe this is real.' Maria Codez sat back in her chair, her office colleagues were either glued to their own screen, logged on to the same site or gathered around any available monitor, watching the drama unfold. What made it so real to Maria was that Jo-Lynn was a senior member of the small law practice that she worked in. Coffee was placed by Maria's side by a tearful secretary. The atmosphere in the office was solemn and the usual hum of activity had been replaced with intense concentration as the employees of Sagem Carter willed Jo-Lynn free. Maria flicked back to the voting screen. A clock was ticking inexorably toward eight o'clock. Maria could not believe that nearly eighteen million people had actually voted to see her friend executed.

Georgina continued reading through the long list of e-mails, opening each communiqué and scanning it for relevant information. Some were innocuous, some had links to other web sites, others contained downloads of child pornography, pictures that Georgina had to look at, images that defied humanity. She made a note of various files on a note pad in front of her. Some names kept appearing, though names used in this secret underworld were undoubtedly pseudonyms.

Narla Fleisher rubbed her eyes, weary of reading from the screen. 'I don't know how kids stay on these things for so long, it must drive their eyes crazy.'

Georgina scrolled down the page of the latest opened e-mail to the sender information and transfer coding. Something registered in Narla's brain. A subliminal message, a name she recognised as it flashed past her eyes.

'Stop a minute could you?' Narla grabbed Georgina's arm.

'What is it?'

'Go back up the page.' Narla watched as the lines of text reversed from the bottom of the screen. The name appeared again.

'Stop, stop.' Narla pointed to a name sandwiched between lines of coded text.

'There...John Kiers...I know that name.' Narla bit her into her lip, trying to force her brain to remember. Georgina looked at her, hoping that this was the break she needed, everyone needed. Narla stood up, walking away from the computer, needing to put distance between herself and the flickering screen for a second. She gazed out of the bedroom window, racking her mind.

'Kiers, Kiers, Kiers.' Narla repeated the name, hoping that hearing it echo through her head would jar a distant memory. An image flashed in her mind. A face. 'Oh my God.' She sat on the edge of the bed. 'I've nearly got it. I can see his face.' Narla leaned forward and put her hands to her face, covering her eyes and closing them in the same instant. The face was still there, floating in her minds eye. A picture of Charles smiling and shaking hands with John Kiers joined it.

'That's it...' Narla said. 'He used to work with Charles a long time ago. God, yes. We had dinner with him once. I remember him now.' Narla shuddered. 'He was really...overpowering...You know?' Narla lifted her head and stared at Georgina. 'A real creep. We were eating and he was trying to touch me, you know, under the table. He had this *'butter wouldn't melt'* look on his slimy face. It seemed to be part of a game with him. I don't even think he was doing it because he fancied me. I just think he enjoyed making me feel uncomfortable.' Narla stared into her distant memory, lost in thought. Georgina opened her mobile phone and began to dial, as soon as the last digit was entered an operators voice spoke.

'I'm sorry but all lines are temporarily busy. We are experiencing severe demand on this network, please hang up and try again later.' Static followed, cutting the line dead.

Georgina closed the phone. 'Great. Can I use your phone?'

'Of course.' Narla pointed to a handset sitting next to the computer. Georgina picked up the phone but was greeted with the same white noise of static. She slammed it down.

'Shit! The lines are down.' She looked at her watch, it was nearing midday. 'Okay, stay cool, O'Neil, stay cool.' Georgina tried to calm herself down. She was faced with a decision, to stay where she was and continue sifting through a backlog of computer files, hoping that the phone lines would clear, or get in her car and play a hunch. She picked up her files, phone and keys and started heading out the door. As she walked down the hall to the stairs she scribbled a phone number on a piece of paper.

'I want you to keep ringing this number. If the lines come back on, ask to speak to Detective La Portiere.' Georgina passed back the scrap of paper into Narla's waiting hands. 'Tell him to run a check on John Kiers.' O'Neil's voice quivered as she was running down the steps and out through the front door. 'Oh, and whatever you do keep the Internet connection logged on.'

The traffic jam started two miles out of Narla's house and was solid both ways, going onto the mainland and crossing Independence Bridge to the island. Georgina begrudgingly brought the car to a halt. The rain hammered down from the sky, bouncing like bullets off the windscreen. There would not have been any point turning a siren on even if she had one. To her right there was no grass verge with a high bank and the cars to the left formed a formidable wall of steel leaving her no place to go drive other than remain static in the roadblock. For a moment she contemplated driving down the median in the centre of the carriageway, but she could see metal crash barriers erected forty yards ahead. Georgina picked up the mobile from the passengers seat and tried ringing Leroy once more. She was greeted with static fuzz this time and no message from the operator. She flicked the radio on and tuned to a local station.

'*The word, Bob, is that it's chaos out there. Believe me if your thinking of travelling anywhere today forget it.*'

'*Yeah Mike, our eye in the sky has just passed over the incident and Arlene in the chopper tells me that the traffic is queuing back a solid five miles in either direction. Wouldn't want to be in that Mike.*'

'*No, Bob. More after Celine Dion and the love theme from Titanic.*'

Georgina frantically searched for another radio station. Being in the traffic jam was bad enough, but watching the time tick away until the Montoya family were slaughtered before the eyes of the world, left Georgina cold with fear.

'*WkFM, You're listening to WkFM and I'm Phil Slaver taking you through to drive time, not that anybodies going anywhere today thanks to the jack-knifed articulated wagon and the thirteen car pile up that followed...*'

It was as she was being informed by the radio that Georgina noticed the thick plumes of black smoke rising into the air, a mile or so north.

'*First reports mention up to 18 casualties, three of which are confirmed fatalities. Rescue attempts have been hampered by the heavier than usual traffic, the weather and the loss of telephone communications in the area, which I have been informed is a temporary fault which should be rectified in three to four hours. Full report in the news after Celine...'*

Georgina clicked the off button, knowing that she was going nowhere fast. The rain continued a relentless assault against her windscreen. Her wipers smeared the latest collection of bugs across the constantly smudged screen. She turned her engine off and opened the door. Lifting the tailgate, she searched through her bags in the boot and found what she was looking for. She took the bundle of clothing and threw them into the passengers seat. Georgina sat in the driver's seat once more and turned on the air-conditioning to full blast, slowly the windscreens started to mist. She turned the radio back on, Celine was in full effect as Georgina started to take off her jacket and unbutton her blouse. She pulled on the hooded sweat top quickly, not because she was worried about being seen stripping in the vehicle but because she was more concerned with the plummeting temperature as the air-conditioning did its thing. She pulled up the sweat pants and then unzipped her skirt, her shoes was lying discarded in the foot well, the only problem Georgina had was in tying the laces of her running shoes. The confines of the car made it nearly impossible without eating part of the steering wheel. Celine finished singing and after three minutes of adverts, the news bulletin arrived as promised. Georgina sat and listened to the worsening picture developing a mile or so up the road. The death toll had risen to five, the result of a truck and trailer spinning out of control and crushing a car and its occupants, before careering across the verge and coming to a rest, blocking both north and south bound lanes. Georgina wrote a hasty note and pinned it to the dashboard before abandoning her car and starting to run through the metal jigsaw of stationary vehicles. The rain pressed against her face, immediately soaking her jogging top, although it wasn't cold, air vapour puffed out through her mouth and nose at regular intervals. The police precinct was at least five miles away; Georgina guessed that at her current pace it would take her at least 40 minutes. She injected a little speed, hitting seven-minute mileing; hoping she could sustain the pace for the distance. Georgina ran along the narrow grass verge, occasionally weaving around overheated cars that had pull over to cool down. Sporadic wolf whistles followed her progress, something that managed to bring a smile to her face, those neglected muscles almost protested at being woken from their dormant stasis, bringing light relief to an otherwise dour situation. After twenty minutes she began to notice drivers standing outside their cars, even though it was still lashing with rain. The curious were craning their necks for a better view of the overturned truck and trailer.

The windshield was sitting in the road some thirty yards from where the truck came to rest. The blackened cab, was now nothing more than a twisted carbon filled shell, with molten plastic and metal dripping through the open aperture. Georgina spotted a burned-out vehicle. She guessed it was the one from which the majority of the fatalities came. She mentally blamed another five deaths on the monster that was bringing chaos to Turtle Island. The emergency services were still tending to casualties, dousing the vehicles with foam. The Police were starting to erect a huge plastic blue screen to cordon the area from the prying eyes of the morbidly curious, who were gathering in silence by the scene, watching as though they were watching something reverential. Georgina held onto her warrant card and cut through the crowd, attracting the attention of an officer who was trying to get some of the traffic to reverse off the bridge.

'Sorry ma'am, you can't come through here.' The policeman held up his hand in an effort to stop her. Georgina flashed her FBI identification.

'Officer, do you have communication with your HQ.'

'Yeah, the radio link's still operational.'

'Thank God. I need to get a message through to Captain Frusco.'

The policeman stepped back and smiled. 'Well that shouldn't prove to be too difficult.'

He turned and called out. 'Captain, there's an FBI agent here who wants to speak with you.'

Norman Frusco walked out from behind the blue screen.

Thirty-Eight

The bell never stopped ringing. Every two seconds the slightly swollen door would jar against the frame; followed by the bell announcing yet another customer. During a quiet moment Gary Clarkson stopped for a brief coffee, whilst making it, he stopped and breathed the scent of money from his hands. Food, maps, alcohol, bumper stickers, everything flew from the shelves. The afternoon brought the first of his regulars in through the door in deeply paranoid panic mode. Clarkson was shrewd enough to put aside his regular orders, he didn't mind ripping off the tourists but a living still had to be made when the fuss eventually died down. Regulars came in the store in bunches, whispering conspiratorially until the strangers had left the shop before talking openly about their fears.

Rick's throat felt dry. He couldn't move, yet nothing bound his limbs. He couldn't see, yet he was not in darkness. It took every effort of concentration to move his eyelids barely a millimetre. His mind was active, working, torturing him with thought, memory and guilt. He wanted to shake the voices from his head but how could he, he was literally powerless. Jordan Montoya was sitting next to him in the jeep, it was a bright sunny day. Rick waited for the traffic lights to change from red with his foot hovering over the accelerator. Jordan was quiet, she had been quiet for months, almost mute. A Camaro pulled up next to Rick's car. The blast from the cars horn broke Rick's reverie. Rick turned to his left and saw Prentice Fortune sitting behind the wheel of the Camaro. Next to him was his girlfriend with the emphasis on *girl*. Dorette Nelson was thirteen years old, she smiled at the detective and then her head disappeared from view as she ventured toward Prentice Fortune's lap. Fortune rolled his head back as the lights changed colour. Rick turned to his daughter.

'Do me.'

'Dad.'

'Do me.' He repeated. Rick engaged drive as he felt his daughter's fumbling hands tugging at his zipper.

Rick tried to roll over, he wanted to shut the world out, but he was a prisoner. He could hear a door close by being opened, followed by footsteps. Somebody stopped by Rick and crouched down close to him.

Rick's eyelids were suddenly pulled back, exposing his eyes to a harsh white light. He couldn't talk, his tongue flopped inside his mouth and a grunting noise emanated. As Rick's eyes adjusted to the light he began to focus on Prentice Fortune's features.

'Hello, Rick.' Fortune picked up an object from the tray he was carrying. It was a staple gun. With great precision, Prentice Fortune lifted Rick's eyelids, pulling back on the lashes and pressed the gun, pinning his eyelids open. The click reverberated through Rick's head but the paralysis saved him from the pain, though not the fear.

Rick made a whining noise.

'Ssh!' Fortune placed the stainless steel tray next to Montoya's lifeless form. Sitting on the tray was a syringe filled with a dark yellow, almost burnt amber liquid. 'You know now that there is no escape, not for you Rick. No way out.' Fortune could barely contain himself. 'I wanted to set up something really elaborate. Something big.' Fortune stood and walked to the end of the room, out of Rick's limited field of vision. Another bright light switched on.

'Smile Rick…you're dead.' Fortune stood behind a video camera. He zoomed into Rick's features exposing the grotesque mask of pain and torture. Fortune walked back to the tray and picked up a pair of pinking shears. 'When you want me to stop, just nod. Oh no, you can't. Well make that mewing noise and it will all be over with one little injection. No pain, I promise…just fear.' Prentice Fortune opened and closed the pinking shears, the metal rasped together. 'Don't worry, you won't feel a thing.' He pulled Rick's top lip and placed it between the blades of the shears. Rick remembered the cars pulling away from the traffic lights almost in unison. He remembered jerking and thrusting, not watching the road and finally the clash of metal as both cars collided. Rick pulled Jordan's head away from him as he fought to regain control of the car. Through the grinding and crunching of metal he could hear Dorette's scream as Prentice Fortune's car hurtled through Garland Bach's main window. The scream was cut short as the car impaled itself into scaffolding. Rick's jeep hit the kerb and rolled, following Fortune's car through the shop.

Prentice Fortune closed the blades together, slicing through skin and tissue with ease. Rick mewed.

'You're no fun.' Fortune picked up the syringe. 'But a promise is a promise.' He stuck the needle into Rick's neck and pushed the plunger evacuating its contents into Montoya's bloodstream. 'Let's hope your family is more fun than you.'

Rick felt a surge of warmth.

'Cos you know what,? I lied. I'm gonna kill them too.

The last thing Rick felt was fear.

Jo-Lynn continued to rub hard with her diamond ring against the embedded trap door. Slowly it freed itself from its setting, opening up the possibility of access to the entrance that lay below the surface of the water. The sudden movement sent her sprawling backward into the dirty water. Her wedding band flew from her grasp and landed somewhere nearby under the hundreds of gallons of water. She briefly submerged, swallowing a small amount of murky brown liquid, which made her immediately want to vomit. She wasn't certain, but the level in the room appeared to rising slowly. The seat of the chair she was sitting on had disappeared under a film of semi opaque water. Jo-Lynn scurried over to the trap door and grabbed hold of the lever under the water. Her fingers scrabbled around for the small metal loop. She pulled hard at the ring hoping to free the door but the weight of the water made it impossible. It was then that she noticed the small trickle of water running down the wall through the air vent. On closer inspection she realised that it wasn't an air vent but an access point for rain. As she looked around the room, Jo-Lynn realised that she was being held in part of a storm drain overflow chamber, probably underneath a house. The chambers led to the main sewerage system, through the access door in the centre of the room. Houses that were in prone to flooding would have a chamber built adjacent to the house on the vulnerable side. If a river flooded or there was heavier rain than the normal drain system could cope with, then the owner of the property would open the chamber and sewer access point allowing huge volumes of water to cascade into it, before being funnelled and dissipated through a network of adjoining pipelines leading to the water processing station or a drainage outlet pipe miles away, often into the ocean. Jo-Lynn watched the water continue to trickle out through the grill. As she moved her head, a reflection high up on the wall caught her eye. Jo-Lynn tilted her head back and saw the tiny camera lens that recorded her every move. The world continued to watch her, through satellite, cable and ISDN lines. The horror of the invasion into her predicament left Jo-Lynn feeling stunned, followed by a numb disbelief. She moved back to the dry sanctity of the stairs, defeated. Her hope dissipated, the feeling of isolation compounded by the echo of water dripping in to the ever-swelling pool. She was suddenly aware of her virtual nakedness, wondering who had been watching her attempts to escape, scrabbling around in the water, naked, trying to keep her only garment dry. Was it just *him* or were there others? Her hope of being rescued was below zero. Jo-Lynn sat down to contemplate her options, which she knew were limited. The food tray was still resting on the step where she had left it after finishing her meagre meal of soup and bread. The bowl was a children's patterned variety, made of lightweight plastic. Certainly no weapon, the spoon was constructed from a lighter grade of plastic. Jo-Lynn picked the spoon up and snapped the rounded head from it leaving just the handle with a jagged neck. Was *he* watching her now, sitting laughing at her feeble attempts? Jo-Lynn considered the outlook. She hadn't seen Rick or her son for days, possibly weeks; she was not sure of the time span that had passed. She was intelligent enough to know that she part of a bigger plan; otherwise she would already be dead. Was it simply ransom? She dismissed kidnapping, knowing that it was rare for entire families to be taken. Who would pay the ransom? Where was Rick, where was her son? She had heard Ray laughing. Why didn't he seem concerned? Jo-Lynn looked at the camera and wondered again if her abductor was watching. She decided there was one way to find out. She wanted to gain *his* attention, and the only way to do that was to put her self back in control. Jo-Lynn knew she was about to take the biggest risk of her life and if she miscalculated and *he* wasn't there watching her every move, then she would at least be free and in a way would have won. She stood trembling with fear and cold, though fear was the overriding emotion. Her stomach lurched like a ship on rough seas. She walked down to the water, her cracked feet aware that each step could be her last. The pain from each step a sharp reminder of life, pain for once assuring her that she was alive. One way or another she hoped that what she was about to do would finalise her situation. She looked up at the camera; cold, dirty, muddy water lapping around her thighs, took a deep breath then exhaled, inhaled and repeated the process twice more before plunging head first into the murky pool. Under the water she could see nothing. She tried not to think about the condition of the water or whether its rodent inhabitants had returned. Her body sank down a little way before her natural buoyancy returned her to the surface, where she remained floating, holding her breath, hoping that *he* could see her. If *he* did not return she had promised herself that she would let a final breath go before inhaling the water. She realised that the only power she had left was to deny *him* his moment and if the only way she could do that was by sacrificing her life then she figured that her chosen method of death would be far more preferable than any nightmare that *he* might dream up. Time slowed inexorably to the point where she did not know how much of its precious gift had elapsed or indeed, how much remained. Her lungs began to strain under the pressure of the forced inertia. The water moved around her face, something warm brushed against the skin of her cheeks but Jo-Lynn's eyes were shut, unable to greet the rat's return. The presence of her body in the rat's domain, a curiosity. She was an oddity to him. A strange invader. Desperately, she began to exhale the very last breath that had entered her body. The rat watched her with indifference for now, the tiny air bubbles that escaped Jo-Lynn's mouth and nose no more than an amusement, a pre-occupation, very rarely would he attack 'live' prey for food, live prey normally fought back and he was in no mood for a scrap. He could wait.

He returned to the monitor, pulling the mask down over his face as he walked to the seat in front of the three monitors and separate computer systems. One monitor relayed the *live* image from a little further than two hundred yards away. He sat in the seat and moved the computer mouse, activating the computer from the screensaver slumber that was on a constant link to his web site. Then he pressed the refresh button hoping to see an update on the figures on the counter that invariably was going to lead to an execution, in a little over five hours. The error message sent the mouse hurtling toward the screen. *He* moved across the desk and lifted the phone to be greeted by a dead line. The system was crumbling under the strain and interest that he had created. His finger tapped a Morse rhythm on the receiver button hoping to re-establish a link, but with no joy. *He* ripped out the landline connection and connected the machine's modem to a jack socket on his cell phone, which linked to a laptop computer. *He* called up the network-dialling box and entered his password, *Jordan,* then once again tried to establish a connection, hoping that the signal could establish a link via satellite. While *he* waited *he* glanced at the live feed from the flood chamber. His finger toyed with a small joystick, moving the camera around the chamber. The all seeing eye scanned the stairs and moved down them one by one, until it met the waters edge. Something semi round came into view, something that was floating, something that looked like a heel, a bare naked heel. *He* pulled back on the joystick allowing the camera to zoom out. As it did so, the rest of Jo-Lynn's body became visible. Floating, motionless. The control of the joystick pressed into *his* skin, pressing against the soft fleshy part of *his* palm, making a small white indentation, until the skin ruptured and the metal rod entered his body through the fissure. *He* pulled back sharply, freeing the foreign body from his hand, then ran from the room, pulling open the door fiercely, sending it rocking back on its hinges. The sound reverberated down the long passage. *He* continued running down the hall, past three doors to his left and two to his right. From one of the rooms came the sound of a television, at the bottom of the corridor was another door, which he opened with equal force and began descending down a flight of steps. *He* was feeling a rush of adrenaline and apprehension. These sensations pumping him to a new height of frenzy. *He* reached the steel door, as he pulled back the bolts that secured the heavy door, a voice from the top of the stairs jolted *him* into stasis. *He* remained motionless, *his* heart threatened to leap out from of *his* chest. A boy's voice temporarily paralysed him.

'Daddy?'

'Get in. This weather's really foul.' Barbara Dace cursed the blackening sky.

John Keller lumbered into the waiting helicopter, weighed down by his camera and enough baggage to suffice a fortnights holiday somewhere drier and sunnier than Turtle Island in the winter.

The rain was gathering momentum, splashing large droplets against the windscreen.

'We're still ahead of the pack.' She shouted to the pilot over the whirr of the rotor blades above her head. Within minutes the Borland Ziborski hovered over the crash scene. Paramedics were scrambling from another helicopter parked in what appeared to be the only available gap near the grass verge bordering the tar macadam surface of the highway. Barbara could clearly see the jack-knifed lorry and what remained of the vehicles that were helplessly swept along in its wake. A white car was now blackened with carbon scorch marks running from the rear of the car to the driver's seat. Firemen were attempting to cut away the roof of the car using hydraulic cutting tools. The clamps being placed through the broken glass panels so the jaws of the cutters could slowly eat their way through the blackened twisted hulk.

Barbara tapped John Keller on the shoulder and pointed to the rescue attempt. From their position it was difficult to tell if there were any occupants still alive. She guessed, looking at the other victims in the horrific scene that the rescue team wouldn't be wasting their time trying to free the dead.

Each corner of the roof was severed with speed and efficiency, until the lid of the burnt out can was peeled back like a used sardine can, ready to be hoisted away.

'Get in close, John.' Barbara told the experienced cameraman what he didn't need to know, but he knew Barbara too well to be insulted. He zoomed in until the rectangular roof filled the camera's viewing area, then waited to see the sardines inside the tin. Firefighters moved around the driver's side, they appeared to be talking to the driver, who must have miraculously been alive. One of the firemen was pointing forward. The last of the cutters were pulled away and a group of four rescue workers each elected to grab a corner of the severed car roof. As the roof began to open, Keller felt a trickle of sweat run from his forehead, over his eyelid and down the corner of his eye. He blinked away the salty invader from the corner of his eye and in that blink the roof was carried away, exposing four blackened occupants inside the car. Keller's mind tried to assemble the scene inside the vehicle. He couldn't hear the fireman telling the driver not to look behind, but he could see the reaction of two of the hardened rescue workers as they staggered away from the car. John Keller could also see, quite clearly see, the bodies of two children, scorched black. Fire had ravaged their tiny bodies until they were shells that had begun to merge with the molten interior. The driver appeared to be almost free from any burns whatsoever. John Keller could see that he had lost some hair from the back of his head, he could also see what he thought to be the man's wife lying forward with her head tilted virtually all the way back, her eyes wide open and a bloody grimace spread across her features. He had seen enough, Keller moved the camera away from the car, choosing to get a panoramic view of the chaos that had brought Turtle Island to gridlock. As he moved past the crash site and in front of the hastily erected blue screens, Keller caught a brief glimpse of two familiar figures. He used the zoom facility on the camera. This time he tapped Barbara on the shoulder.

'Take a look.' He offered the reporter the viewfinder to look through. Barbara shifted across the seat and peered through the tiny eyepiece.

'O'Neil and Frusco.' Barbara turned her attention to the pilot. 'Frank, I don't care where you put this bird, but take us down.'

The wind from the rotors blew the blue plastic tarpaulin taught, threatening to rip the freshly hammered stakes out of the ever-softening ground. The rain was pushed with even greater force into Georgina and Norman Frusco's face and body. Frusco shielded his eyes as he looked up at the approaching helicopter, Georgina turned away, trying to avoid the worst of the spray until the blades stopped whirring. Keller was out of the chopper first. His camera was already cradled on his shoulder, filming the devastation on the ground. Barbara Dace made a beeline for Captain Norman Frusco, her lover.

'What's wrong Norman, phone not working?'

'For the past few hours, actually, no.'

'The world's going mad.' Barbara tried to light a cigarette but the elements conspired against her. In frustration, she threw the wet cigarette to the ground. 'Got a patch going spare, Norm?'

Frusco searched through his pockets. He pulled out an unopened pack of twenty cigarettes, he fished again inside the deep pockets of the soaked trench coat and returned hold yet another pack plus a couple of nicotine patches.

'One or two?'

229

'Jesus, the way I feel today, there ain't enough patches in the world.' Barbara took the two patches from Norman. She peeled the backing paper off the first patch, pulled at the neck of her blouse and slapped the patch on the top of her left arm. 'Got any gum?'

Frusco smiled. 'Only nicotine gum.'

'You know, Norm, I think we were made for each other. How come I never met you thirty years ago.'

'I was waiting. I'm just reaching my peak now.'

Barbara leaned forward and delicately moved one of the few remaining strands of hair that had blown down across his face and gently placed it back on his head. The hair didn't even make an attempt to hide the huge bald expanse in-between.

'Captain, there's a message for you on the radio.' Georgina's voice interrupted the moment.

Frusco gave Barbara the pack of nicotine gum and turned toward the erected blue PVC walls. Barbara opened the pack of gum and shook one of the small tablets out of the cardboard pack. She offered the pack toward Georgina. Georgina shook her head. Droplets of rain were disturbed from her hair and searched for another surface to cling to. O'Neil and Dace stood in uneasy, wet, silence, awaiting Norman Frusco's return.

Leroy rubbed his eyes. He had finally finished watching the last videotape from Charles Fleisher's sordid collection. It left just the one unknown face, the tattooed man. Leroy lifted the phone. He looked at his watch; nearly three hours had passed since he last talked with Andy at the TV station. He had been promised an hour but he was as much to blame; searching the videos had robbed time from him, time he could ill afford. Leroy pressed the receiver, a constant dull tone emitted from the handset. He pressed the receiver button once more. More of the same.

'Shit.' Leroy cursed. He pressed the *on* button of his cell phone. This time a signal came through. Pulling a business card from his pocket, Leroy proceeded to press out the number on the small illuminated pad. The connection rang for three short rings before a woman answered the phone.

'Hello?' The voice was stressed, slightly out of breath and the background noise roared through the earpiece denting Leroy's eardrum. She sounded puzzled and nervous at the same time.

'Georgina?' Leroy asked unsure.

'Yeah.'

'What the hell's that noise?'

'I'm in a helicopter on my way back to you.' She was shouting. 'The phones are back.'

'What do you mean, back?'

'The lines have been down all afternoon, it's crazy out here.' She fell silent for a moment then said. 'Whoa!' loudly. 'Jesus H. Christ, I'm gonna die.'

'What in hell's name is going on?' Leroy demanded.

'Don't worry. I'll be with you soon to explain. The roads are jammed solid, what with the crash an' all.'

'What Crash?'

'It don't matter now...' She fell silent once more

'Georgina?'

'Oh man, I think I'm gonna puke. Listen gotta go. Be with you in...the pilots telling me two minutes, no he's not, he's telling me I have to quit using the phone. ...sorry gotta go.'

The line disconnected, leaving Leroy listening to static. He closed the flip pad to his cell phone and replaced it inside his pocket. Stopping only briefly to pick up the scraps of paper, he had scribbled notes on, Leroy headed out of the small basement room.

He bounded up the steps two at a time, not stopping for the lift, nor to catch his breath.

The precinct was a hive of activity. Within seconds of his entering the main processing floor, all of the telephones began to ring at once, a phenomenon, which brought a huge cheer from all the detectives and officers. Leroy moved through the crowded floor, heading for his office. He pulled up his chair behind his desk. The computer monitor was still on and the link to Death Cam web site engaged. The numbers under each figure were almost unreadable, millions of people were passing a judgement of death on complete strangers with the moral conviction of killing a computer animated sprite. Leroy felt sickened, wanting to shout through the screen to everyone that this was real; this was not a game. A young fresh-faced policeman appeared at the door, almost shyly poking his head through.

'Detective LaPortiere?' He said unsurely.

Leroy nodded

'I have a message from the Captain. He said he wants you to ring him urgently. The police officer was gone within the blink of an eye. Leroy picked up the phone and used the speed dial to contact Norman Frusco. 'What now?' He said to himself, almost fearing the answer.

'I've some bad news, Leroy.' Frusco gasped between breathing fits. 'Ned Freeman, the pleasure boat skipper...he...he just dragged up another body. Apparently a black male.'

'Rick?' Leroy asked, concern mixing with apprehension.

Frusco was standing on the riverbank looking down at *The Ingénue*. A group of police divers were scouring the riverbed using their bare hands. Frusco shrugged his shoulders. 'We only just found this guy about ten minutes or so ago. The divers are still trying to get the body out of the water. Ned found the body over an hour ago. He couldn't contact us cause the phones were down. Agent O'Neil is on her way to you, bring her out here with you.'

Within in a minute, Leroy had grabbed his coat and was stepping out onto the roof, watching a helicopter approach the landing pad.

The large circled *H* on the roof of the police headquarters was a welcome site for Georgina O'Neil and one that could have come earlier. Gripped tightly in her right hand was a white wax paper bag, inside, the contents of her breakfast, partially digested; melted by the acids in her stomach. From the moment she vomited to the landing, Georgina clutched the bag for dear life and kept her eyes closed. She tried to concentrate on the case. Building a mental image of John Kiers, hoping police records or the FBI's files would have something on the man, but try as she might, her mind could do no more than fight with her inherent phobia of flying, and Kiers was pushed to the back of her mind until she could strike contact with earth. As she stepped out, much to her relief, she was met by Leroy who was waving and remonstrating above the scream of the engines and rotors, which were slicing through protesting air currents.

'We gotta get back in. Head back to the river. They've found another body.' Then Leroy added solemnly. 'A black man.' Knowing that Georgina was aware of the implication.

Georgina looked at the helicopter, at that precise time there were very few things in the world that could have persuaded her to board it again but the prospect of finding Rick Montoya's body was one of them. Hopefully the site where the body was found might generate clues that would lead them to their man.

The pilot handed Georgina a fresh sick bag as she boarded, which she reluctantly accepted before climbing back on board.

Thirty-Nine

Jo-Lynn felt the sensation of being carried from the murky pool and rested gently on the wooden decking at the foot of the stairs.

He placed his head against her chest, listening for a heartbeat. Panic sent his own heart into a pounding rhythm that filled his head, confusing him even further. Was it his heart or her heart that he could hear? His hands fumbled for her wrist, a pulse; a pulse...surely that was a way to tell. Her chest was not rising; air was not escaping from her lips. *He* slapped her face hard crying out in frustration.

'Bitch.' No reaction.

His fingers made contact with the soft warm skin of her wrist, searching for a pulse. His eyes stared frantically at her, then moving from her arm to her neck, he found what he was looking for, a strong healthy rhythm, boom, boom, boom.

Jo-Lynn opened her eyes. 'Fuck YOU.' Her other hand moved swiftly.

He did not see the jagged edge of the broken white plastic spoon but felt it as it travelled deep into his cheek. She used such force that half of it embedded through the soft fleshy tissue, breaking off another smaller segment, which she followed up by sticking into his throat.

Stunned and shocked *he* fell backwards into the water, his hands groping at the balaclava, trying to exorcise it, to retrieve the foreign bodies protruding from his skin.

Jo-Lynn was up on her feet faster than she could imagine possible, and already had a three-step advantage heading for the door at the top of the landing. She knew it wasn't locked this time. *He* had entered in too much of a hurry, desperate not to be deprived of his spoils by allowing her to die, face down in the water. When *he* had carried her to the platform and laid her down, *he* for the first time had shown concern for her welfare, though the sentiment was lost on Jo-Lynn.

Her hands shot out in front of her pushing against the steel panelled door. Tortured, angry, pained screaming followed her up the stairs.

Jo-Lynn knew *he* was close behind. She was too afraid to look behind, fearing that seeing how close *he* was would paralyse her.

The door opened and Jo-Lynn was faced with another set of steps, leading up a dark corridor. Light shone down from a hall above, Jo-Lynn ran as hard as she could, ungracefully scrambling up the stairs. *He* was close behind, screaming and cursing obscenities. During this melee Jo-Lynn realised that she recognised the voice of her captor; her blood ran cold.

As soon as her foot touched ground, Georgina's cell phone began to ring, as did Leroy's. Norman Frusco's was walking up the grassy incline to greet them. The gale blasting from the rotors played havoc with Frusco's thinning hair, which he tried vainly to keep under control whilst operating the minute cell phone with his free hand. The news was the same to all three detectives. The killer's live link had gone off-line, replaced by film of him killing and torturing Stephen England and Max Dalton. The voting was now closed.

'Looks like we're into the end game.' Frusco said, his words as chilling as the breeze around them. Georgina looked at her watch.

'But it's only four o'clock.'

'Yeah, four o'clock eastern time.' Leroy interjected, his voice struggling to be heard over the blades. 'But right now it's eight in California.'

The scream from the rotor blades suddenly died as the pilot cut the engine.

'No, he's got her close by.' Georgina said, adjusting the level of her own voice to the more tranquil silence that was befalling Turtle Island.

Barbara Dace and John Keller joined the detectives at the front of the copter. Keller had his lightweight camera hoisted on to his shoulder and was filming.

'I can feel it in my bones...he's close by.' Georgina shivered. 'So where's the body?'

'A little down this way, back to the river.' Frusco began to lead them down the slope to the river's edge, where were greeted by two familiar figures, Ned Freeman and Nemo his dog, both of them waiting patiently. The Ingénue was moored, tied and staked to the embankment. A team of divers were in the river, which was running like a torrent, struggling with ropes trying to attach them to the foot of the body. Rain continued to pepper the surface of the water like a million bullets ripping through the black surging, gushing stream.

'I don't get it, we searched every house around here.' Leroy said puzzled

'Yeah, every house until we found Fleisher, then we gave up.' Georgina answered with bitterness in her voice, the realisation of not following up all the clues to the case now painfully bitter in her mouth. She had panicked and allowed herself in-turn to be panicked by the escalating situation in the case. Inexperience which she knew was going to come back to haunt her when the case finally wrapped. It was rare for such a monumental degree of mistakes to be overlooked by her superiors, and as she headed down the hill her fears were confirmed.

The assistant director of the FBI's child crimes unit was half-hidden behind a large black umbrella, which he carried to shield himself from the increasing volumes of rain falling from the sky. She recognised his stance in a moment. The way he carried himself, the way his body moved, albeit half hidden. Georgina thought it was impossible to feel sicker than she already did but like so many times in the past, she was proved to be wrong. Her stomach turned once more.

'Agent O'Neil.' The man looked out from under the umbrella. His steel grey hair and cold blue eyes added the correct amount of solemnity that his position carried. His skin was fair though slightly tanned, wearing the expression of a man at ease with himself. Georgina could feel her eyes welling up and she had to fight extremely hard to control her emotion.

'Father.'

Assistant director, Wynan O'Neil, frowned, the familiarity he wanted in his private life was out of place in the field. Work was no place for family domesticities as far as he was concerned, especially in the territory in which they found themselves. This was a place for professionals, nothing less. Georgina wanted to hug her father, but the man standing in front of her wasn't her father. Her father would be the man who would later visit her motel room and try to explain as gently as he could that she was to be the subject of an investigation by the FBI, regarding her conduct during the case. He would be the man who would at first comfort her and then support her. Support her anger and her rage, before channelling it into a strategy that she could use as defence. But now he just looked at her with those cold blue eyes. 'Agent O'Neil, it appears we have another body.'

Georgina wiped rain from her face, pushing her matted hair back from her eyes.

Leroy regarded the confrontation between the two as odd and sensed a feeling of discomfort displayed by both.

Norman Frusco barged past the small group, determined to get on with the business at hand, letting time or the lack of it be his only hindrance. Wynan O'Neil turned, following the captain and black detective, leaving his daughter momentarily standing alone in the rain.

He plunged his hand into the cold water and rolled the body over, so that the white staring eyes bore into his. Wynan O'Neil looked at the skin, which was once brown but now had a bluish-grey hue to it. The flesh was puffy, split in places; raw open wounds gaped perversely, almost pornographically at him. Assistant director O'Neil stepped back to allow two policemen with boat hooks to pull the naked body from the water. He watched a small Jack Russell bound about in the rain, barking excitedly, while his owner (he assumed) sat silently against the side of his boat peeling an orange. Leroy walked toward the body, now extracted from the water and laid on the muddy riverbank, his emotions a turmoil of apprehension and anxiety. He felt Georgina's hand slip into his as they approached the corpse. The rain had not let up and the day was turning to hell on earth as time ticked away. With all the breaks, all the leads they had been given over the past twenty-four hours they were still no closer to finding the culprit. From a discreet distance, John Keller, focused on the detectives faces, hoping to capture the anguish and emotion. Barbara Dace recorded a monologue for a voice over. Her years of professionalism exercised to the full, as she fought with her memory and vocabulary to construct a piece of journalism 'on the fly'.

Georgina squeezed Leroy's hand as the body was laid before them on the rain sodden, muddy bank.

'Is it Rick?' Georgina asked.

A canvas cloth had been placed over the dead man's face by the police divers. There was something bizarre about the need to do such a thing, maybe it was a gesture of respect for the dead but what dignity could be afforded a naked corpse whose body was swollen with water absorption and half eaten by rats, crocodiles and other wildlife; certainly not enough from an oil stained rag. Norman Frusco joined the detectives as Leroy crouched down on his haunches and gently lifted the veil. The staring white eyes bulged in their sockets, swollen with body gases, water, infection, mites and maggots that crawled beneath the skin feeding on what sustenance they could find. Their movement animated the features of the corpse into something even more grotesque. Leroy ran, slipping and sliding from the body to the waters edge, he wanted to be sick. His stomach turned and threatened to expel its contents but by breathing deeply and slowly Leroy managed to retain control. Georgina replaced the cloth.

Leroy shouted through the barrage of increasing rain but his voice was almost lost against the cacophony, though neither Georgina, nor Norman Frusco needed Leroy identification to know who the victim was.

'WILL...WILL.' Jo-Lynn screamed. Pushing open doors as she passed room after room. There was a television in each room, most of them seemed to be tuned into children's networks or linked to the Internet, not that she had much time to linger, taking in details. Her priority was singular, to get her son and only then to get out alive. Nothing else mattered. She knew *he* was not far behind and that he had the advantage of knowing the territory. She opened the fifth door along the long narrow hall and called once more.

'WILL.'

Silence.

Jo-Lynn turned, suddenly aware that she was alone. There was no chasing monster, no pursuing demon. Where had *he* gone?

'Maybe…' she consoled herself, '…maybe he's dead or dying.' She knew she had embedded the jagged implement deep into *his* throat, it could have pierced his windpipe or an artery?; it was not inconceivable. Just as she was about to turn and try the last door, a voice whispered.

'Mummy?' It sounded unsure.

From the recess of the darkened room the small figure of a child stepped forward. The boy squinted against the harsher light from the corridor and put his hand to his eyes to shield them so he could gain a better view.

'He told me you had left me.' The boy began to sob 'He told me you had gone away for ever.'

Jo-Lynn held her arms out to welcome her son in a loving embrace, an embrace that she so desperately needed. As she held her son, Jo-Lynn saw Ray's eyes widen and knew, somehow could sense, the silent presence behind her even before she heard the rasping gargled breathing. Cold fear ate deep into her bones threatening to immobilise her.

He laid the ski mask on her left shoulder.

'Poor son of a bitch.' Wynan O'Neil sheltered beneath the dry haven of the umbrella.

'Don't feel too sorry for him.' Georgina was crouching over the body, rain bounced off both her and the lifeless, uncaring face of the corpse. 'A more fitting end I couldn't have wished for.'

'Jonathan Marland Kiers, ex partner of Charles Fleisher, pederast, abuser of women, drug taker, all round nasty fuck.' Leroy filled the senior FBI agent in on some of the corpse's finer personality disorders.

'And not our man. Kiers has been dead for days, maybe even weeks. Gentlemen, I don't want to rain on this parade but we have a little over two and a half hours before our man completes his agenda.' Norman Frusco was already walking back to the helicopter as he spoke.

'Yeah, but where do we go from here?' Leroy asked no one in general. Georgina joined him by his side.

237

'This is a nightmare, Leroy.' Georgina shivered, as the rain grew steadily harder; making contact through her clothes to her skin, adding to her misery. She watched her father walk away, leaving the body to be zipped in a PVC body bag.

Two boiler suited men struggled with the dead weight on the slippery surface as they carried John Kiers to the back of the coroner's van.

'Can there really be a hell bad enough for someone like him?'

'At the moment, in the scheme of things, John Kiers is not even the bad guy.' Leroy answered.

Barbara Dace slid down the small incline toward the detectives. She had urgency about her approach, which was immediately apparent. She was calling to the detectives, beckoning them to her.

'Andy's gone.' She said breathlessly as she drew nearer. 'Andy's gone...and there's a fire in the editing suite.' The words came in hurried, excited bursts. 'All the tapes, everything...whoosh, up in flames.'

The three of them broke into a sprint running toward the waiting helicopter; Frusco and Wynan O'Neil were already on board. Wynan O'Neil still immaculate, cool and dry, Frusco, wet, agitated and determined. By the time Leroy, Dace and Georgina got to the machine the rotors were spinning, sending freezing air down on their wet clothes.

'It's gonna be cramped.' Barbara said, as she entered the tiny confine. 'Bunch up tight.'

Norman Frusco moved in closer to Wynan O'Neil allowing Barbara to sit next to him. Leroy, Georgina and John Keller occupied the other row of seats. The rain continued to lash down making visibility even worse than before, but the helicopter rose from the ground without hesitation, swooping low over the fields, passing the blocked roads, which were finally starting to move. Georgina looked over Keller's shoulder at the scene below. The jack-knifed lorry was being hauled to one side as cars were starting to filter around the gap. The large blue screening was erect with a row of five tarpaulin-covered bodies lying behind it, awaiting carriage to the hospital morgue. Georgina's cell phone rang; the shrill making everyone's hearts beat a little faster. The pilot called from over his shoulder. 'You'll have to turn that off.'

Georgina opened the phone and answered. 'Yes?'

'I said you'll have to turn that off, Miss. It interferes with the instrumentation panel.'

The pilot reiterated, with little patience.

It was Harley Fleisher. 'I have found something, I think you should know.'

The helicopter lurched.

'TURN IT OFF, NOW!' The pilot demanded.

'Put me down then.' Georgina shouted.

'What?'

'Land this helicopter. I don't care where, just land it.'

Puzzled faces looked at Georgina as she continued to listen to her caller. She spoke into the handset. 'Hang on. Call me in a minute.'

The connection fuzzed and cracked, cutting out. Georgina couldn't be sure whether she had been heard. She gestured to the pilot to hurry up and land.

The helicopter began a quick decent, heading for the middle of a rain soaked field. Water glistened in huge puddles. The fear of getting bogged in, made the pilot hover some three feet above the muddy earth.

'You'll have to jump.' He shouted.

Georgina looked at the distance and the ground below, at least it would be soft she consoled herself.

'Wait here.' She unbuckled herself and leapt out of the open door. Georgina landed on all fours; telephone clutched in her muddy hand and immediately ran away from the copter to a quieter location where she could safely take the call. The giant helicopter roared away and sat motionless in mid-air, suspended in its own powerful stasis. Georgina turned from the wind, which carried with it the relentless rain and placed her finger in her free ear so she could hear the conversation better. Georgina listened.

John Keller filmed Georgina as she ran across the field waving, beckoning the helicopter to lower to allow her access. She rolled on board the cramped floor space and before she could utter a single word they were flying through the air, heading toward a plume of thick black smoke.

Georgina noticed Norman Frusco's hand rest on Barbara's knee and squeeze a comforting embrace. The look that passed between them was brief but long enough for Georgina to pick up on.

'That bastard, Andy. What the hell is he playing at?'

Georgina managed to sit up on her haunches. Her feet rested just under her bottom, while she held onto Leroy's leg for stability. The feeling of unease and the motion was still playing havoc with her senses. The copter lurched sending Georgina's hand higher on to Leroy's thigh.

'So, who called?' Leroy asked trying to take his mind of the physical contact between them.

'...Harley Fleisher.' Her thumb and fingers gripped a little tighter. Leroy didn't know if Georgina was trying to silently pass a message to him or whether she was just trying to gain a better purchase for balance. Georgina looked at her watch. The hands were moving toward the six.

Jo-Lynn wanted to run. She wanted to barge past the monster standing in front of her but even though he was wounded, he was bigger, faster and more powerful.

'Why…Why?' She stared at him. She saw the face of evil and eyes that were burning with hatred. A man no longer inhabited the body that stood un-bowingly in front of her. She saw the face but what life there was inside was living in hell. *He* clawed at the broken plastic embedded in his throat, his fingers grasping the barely protruding fragments, unable to free them. He coughed and a small spurt of blood trickled down his throat from the wound.

'It's too late.' *He* began. He pulled at his neck and studied the blood around the tips for a moment before continuing. 'You know what's so funny?' He didn't wait for an answer. 'It doesn't matter what happens from here on in. I have already had my justice. Ask Rick why he let me be the first with Jordan?'

Jo-Lynn felt numbed by his statement, then sickened at the full realisation of it. 'Always loved children.' *He* sniffed the blood on his fingers and smiled. 'Jordan was special. Firm, just beginning to bloom.' *He* breathed deeply in fond reminiscence. 'So, so fine.' Without warning, his hand shot out, fist clenched and made contact with Jo-Lynn's jaw. All around her, the walls began to close in and *his* words echoed in her head. Jo-Lynn's limbs began to tingle then slowly go numb. They no longer wanted to support her frame. She staggered backward two steps and bounced off her son, who tried to steady her. The floor rushed to greet Jo-Lynn as her body finally collapsed. *He* watched as her head cracked against the flooring, jarring back painfully. A small trickle of blood ran down the swollen and split skin on her forehead, gathering in a tiny pool on the floor. As *he* bent down to lift Jo-Lynn to her feet, Ray ran past, down the corridor, screaming at the top of his voice. *He* was going to turn and give chase but what was the point; he knew the boy could not escape. *He* lifted Jo-Lynn. The exertion opened the wound on his neck slightly further. His breathing rasped as he carried her, walking down the stairs back to the flood chamber. Before finally blacking out, Jo-Lynn thought what could have caused her husband to act with such total madness.

Forty

T'he whole island had stopped breathing, momentarily holding its breath. The only thing that moved was the relentless deluge of rain and the frantic efforts of the police to resolve the case before it was too late, everything else stood still, locked in a time capsule of observation. Islanders and mainlanders alike were glued to their television sets barely daring to blink, as rival TV networks fought for the best coverage and the latest scoops on events. The skies above buzzed with helicopters, small aircraft and every conceivable form of electronic media and communication.

She was placed in a chair and bound by her hands and feet. Water swam around her thighs, brown, putrid smelling water. The first thing Jo-Lynn saw when she woke was the video camera standing on a tripod some six or seven feet in front of her. The tripod was opened to its fullest extension and the camera was near the ceiling pointing down at her. There was a red light blinking on the side of the camera, divulging its raison d'être. To the left was a bright halogen lamp, aimed directly on her, cables had been duck taped to the ceiling, some of them drooping precariously as though arranged in haste.

Rick Montoya's voice came from behind a glaring light trained on her. 'I thought of many ways in which to tell you. It wasn't supposed to end like this. I never meant to hurt Jordan…never. I'd do anything to have her back.'

Jo-Lynn's eyes began to adapt to the harsh light aimed at her. She could see Rick sitting in front of her, his hands behind his back.

Rick lifted his head and stared into Jo-Lynn's eyes. Rick's face was a mass of swelling and bruises; dried blood was encrusted around his mouth in a stream of red that had ceased flowing hours before. His teeth and gum were exposed in a horrific grimace.

'What are you saying?' Jo-Lynn pleaded to her husband for an explanation.

'I couldn't tell you. I knew you would never understand.' The silhouetted figure moved the light, turning it to expose his mutilated features. Rick began to sob. Gargled words belched out of his mouth in an incomprehensible babble.

The water around Jo-Lynn's legs suddenly felt very cold as hope drained from her body.

Movement from behind her husband caught Jo-Lynn's eye. There was someone else in the room. A second man. He stepped out of the shadows. 'You see, Rick and I had a nice little cottage industry going. Not that it was just about the money. Oh no, the money was a fringe benefit but the real excitement, the real excitement...' *He* repeated. 'came from the endless stream of delicacies that came our way . Jordan she was so fine.' *He* seemed lost for a moment in melancholy. 'Then your husband got an attack of moral righteousness. A very bad thing. This world has no place for morals.' He smiled, seemingly genuinely enjoying the moment.

As *he* moved forward, Jo-Lynn noticed the hammer in his hand. She whispered, almost cried. 'Who are you?'

He waded through the water, stopping in front of Jo-Lynn and bent down until his face was parallel with hers. Jo-Lynn could still see the plastic spoon embedded in his throat, blood eased around it, dribbling down his neck.

'How remiss of me, do you want to introduce me Rick, or shall I introduce myself.' He placed the hammer by his feet, his hands moved up her thighs, resting at her hips. Jo-Lynn did not think it possible to feel colder but his touch turned her to ice.

'Better I do it myself, as Rick is having a little trouble speaking clearly. Prentice Fortune, at your pleasure.'

Water reigned down on the fire, from both the sky and the fire departments hoses, but neither seemed to be having an effect on the inferno blazing thirty feet in front of John Keller's lens. Barbara Dace stood alongside some of the crew of the TV station. The shocked silence between them shattered by the occasional small explosion from inside the burning building as gas canisters and pressurised equipment gave way to the fearsome heat.

Norman Frusco laid a sympathetic hand on her shoulder, Barbara reached up and held on tightly to his hand, any attempt to hide their relationship dismissed, as she watched a lifetime of work and history ascend to the inferno.

Georgina grabbed hold of Leroy during the commotion and dragged him to the rear of the helicopter. The rotors now subdued. He could see from the strung out look in her eyes that Georgina was close to breaking point.

'What's up?'

Georgina laughed, a short snorting laugh. 'What's up?' The question deserved an answer that could take her days to work out let alone begin to tell. 'I...' She began but stopped. Her eyes bore deep in to Leroy's, searching for part of the answer before deciding whether she could continue. 'I need a friend out here...'

Leroy smiled.

'Someone I can trust.' She held his gaze until it passed the point of discomfort or embarrassment for both of them. 'I...' She paused again. 'I know certain things, things that, that I find difficult to believe in. But none the less seem to be true. Things that if they are true are going to blow this tiny little island apart.'

'More than this.' Leroy gestured to the burning building and the chaos surrounding them. Georgina flinched as a tiny explosion, a gas canister surrendered to the heat.

'This is all part of the game. The distraction to keep us from getting too close, from knowing the answers.' Georgina looked at the burning building and the firemen trying to salvage the modern complex. 'Did you know that as part of the design of newer buildings, fire doors and the layout of corridors and rooms are to prevent the rapid spread of flames?'

Leroy looked puzzled, almost insulted. 'Of course.'

'There are three separate fires burning here.' Georgina pointed to flames pouring out of a broken window on the third floor of the complex and then to another fire burning from the rear of the ground floor. 'Plus the fire burning in the video editing suite where this was supposed to have started in the basement.'

Leroy shrugged. 'So...It's not impossible. The fire could be spreading through open doors, the air-con system, windows...I don't know.' He tried to explain.

'The fires are isolated, too far apart. From a distance it looks as though the whole building is an inferno.' Georgina began to walk away from the building. Leroy chased after her.

'Hey, wait a minute!' He ran to her and continued walking by her side. 'So?'

'So, I was brought here because I couldn't solve the mystery...or because there was a very high probability that I wouldn't? Jerk me around long enough, tantalise and tease me with enough, but not too much information, nothing incriminating and hope that by the time I have it all figured out it will be too late.' She reached the helicopter.

'I really don't know what you are talking about.' Leroy said.

'The time, Leroy, the time.' Georgina stressed. She took hold of his left arm and pushed the sleeve of his coat back up his arm, exposing his watch. 'Fake Rolex, class Leroy.' Georgina studied the face and dials.

One hour left. She climbed on board and tapped on the back of the pilot's helmet. Small skull and crossbones were painted on the helmet with an inscription, *Fly the Friendly Skies* in gothic calligraphy.

The pilot turned. 'What's up?'

Georgina buckled herself in. 'We are.'

The pilot handed a sick bag over his shoulder, which Georgina accepted without comment.

Leroy scrambled on board as the helicopter started to rise from the ground. Georgina leaned forward and helped pull him in. Leroy sat on the floor catching his breath. Georgina leaned forward and shouted to the pilot above the noise of the rotors.

'GET ME AS CLOSE AS YOU CAN TO 14162 HARPENDERS GROVE.'

Leroy recognised Narla Fleisher's address. As they pulled away, Georgina saw her father and Captain Frusco running, waving. They were trying to beckon down the helicopter.

'Keep going.' Georgina shouted.

The engine roared and the helicopter swooped away leaving Captain Frusco, Agent Wynan O'Neil, Barbara Dace and John Keller looking toward the sky, and the rain that continued to pour down from it onto their frustrated faces.

'Tic-toc, tic-toc, tic-toc. You know the beautiful thing about this, is that all along I have been playing them at their game and I have won.' Prentice moved. He became a silhouetted figure behind the harsh glare of white light once more.

The cold, stinking pool of stagnant water now lay just beneath Jo-Lynn's breasts. The room was beginning to fill from the flood chambers.

She noticed the small red light on the camera indicating that he was recording the *event*. The man in front of her was a perfect stranger; the man bound to the chair immediately to her left was no longer her husband and even more so a stranger now. Jo-Lynn blinked; against the light, the blinding white halogen light placed directly ahead of her. Jo-Lynn began to doubt her sanity. The feeling of sheer blinding terror began to overwhelm her and she began to shake violently.

Fortune bent down and retrieved the hammer. 'Less than an hour, but hey, fuck it, you know…' He looked Jo-Lynn deep in the eyes. 'I can't be bothered to wait.' He stepped back and lifted the hammer.

'For god's sake.' Rick cried out but no one understood.

Prentice turned and glanced the hammer across Rick Montoya's skull. Montoya slumped forward in his seat, restrained by the duck tape securing his body to the seat.

'Now that was fun.'

'Why are you doing this?' Jo-Lynn screamed.

Fortune unfolded a knife. The blade dirty and rusted and proceeded to slash through the duck tape holding Rick to the seat. Montoya's body slumped forward and splashed into the water face down. Fortune dragged the chair sideways and sat next to Jo-Lynn.

'Let me tell you about your husband.'

'Please help him.' Though she despised the though of what he had done, part of Jo-Lynn was still struggling to accept what Prentice Fortune had told her as being the truth.

'We'll see...the more you interrupt, the longer this will take. The longer this will take, the longer Ricky boy drinks sewerage. By the time I am finished telling you all about your adorable husband though, I am sure that you will want me to kill him anyway. Hell, you'll want to kill him yourself.'

Forty-One

The sight of the helicopter landing in the middle of the street induced a mixture of curiosity, excitement and panic. Georgina barely waited for it to touch down before her feet were running along the road to 14162 Harpenders Grove. Leroy followed, puffing slightly as he fought to catch up. Narla was already waiting at the door, an anxious look embedded on her face. Georgina made it to the door ahead of Leroy.

'Where is she?'

Narla nodded with her head, indicating upstairs. As Georgina passed, Narla turned

'She'll only tell you, she won't even tell me.'

'Looks like I'll sit this one out.' Leroy said, watching Georgina take two stairs at a time.

'Coffee, Mr LaPortiere?' Narla asked, then added. 'It's already brewed.'

'That would be fine.'

'How do you like it?'

'Sweet and white.' Leroy replied.

'Don't tell me; just like your women.' Narla joked, she didn't know why she joked; she certainly didn't feel funny.

Georgina grasped the handle to the bedroom door and pushed it open. The sound of a printer continuously working was audible just above a CD, which was playing through the speakers of Harley's computer, where she was sitting. Kelly Clarkson was going through another therapy session. The computer screen was on and Georgina didn't need to guess what the image flickering on the small monitor was.

Harley didn't turn. '104 Headbridge. It's a mile or so upriver from the three bridges. The house is an old wooden constructed colonial style.' She leaned forward and clicked her mouse. The image on the screen changed and the house appeared. Georgina moved closer 'What...Where did you get this?' She was dumbfounded and for a moment her legs felt leaden, then her heart started pumping as adrenaline began to surge through her.

'I found it in a folder marked *homework,* except I knew it wasn't mine. It wasn't even on this computer it was on a web based online storage account. I tried all of the names listed with various e-mail web based accounts. Dad wasn't too imaginative about the password...*Harley.* Guess he thought no one would ever find it.'

Georgina sat beside the young girl. 'What else is in there?'

'You know, I remember the house. My father took me there, a couple of times, we were always at different places, different houses he had on the market, usually furnished though, but I remember this one because it was empty, except for bed and a few other things..' Harley closed her eyes to recollect. 'There was a load of camera's, videos...you know.'

Georgina put her arm around the fragile child. Harley clicked on the image and the live feed to Jo-Lynn returned.

'That's a flood chamber. It's at the back of the house but connected by stairs, first to the basement then directly into the house.' The noise of the printer suddenly stopped. Harley stood and walked over to the tray by the printer and collected a pile of printouts. She rearranged the order, tapped them into a neat pile before sliding them into a bright fluorescent orange folder and then handed them to Georgina.

'Catch them.' She looked pleadingly. 'Please.'

'What's in here?'

'Everything I could find.' Harley looked sad. The hidden emotion was drawing to the surface, the turmoil of abuse and victimisation, the indignity and suffocation of her childhood. Georgina flipped open the folder. She sat back on the bed so that she was eye level with the young girl.

'Sometimes I knew that the things they were doing to me was wrong. Daddy always said that they would stop if they hurt me...but they never did and after a while it kinda felt funny.'

Georgina held her breath. The silence in the room echoed.

'Was it wrong?' Harley asked, confusion written across her face. 'Was it wrong to sometimes like the feeling?'

Georgina placed her arm around Harley's shoulder and pulled her closer to her and hugged her. She couldn't look into Harley's eyes for fear of breaking down. 'No...of course it wasn't, you must never think that.'

Photographs, pictures that she had never seen before; faces. Faces she recognised. Ordinary people, vile people. Georgina shivered. She was leaving the bedroom and running down the stairs. As she reached the foot of the stairs, Narla was handing a cup of coffee to Leroy.

'No time, Leroy. Gotta go, now.' She took the cup from his grasp and placed it down on the floor.

'Where to?' He asked.

'I need the quickest way to Headbridge.' She looked down the road but the helicopter was gone. 'Shit!'

Narla raced to her jacket hanging in the hall. 'Here take my Jeep, it's parked in the garage.'

Georgina didn't need a second invitation and snatched the keys from Narla's hand.

'Press the remote.' Narla called after them. 'It operates the garage door.'

As she ran, Georgina depressed the tiny black button attached to the key fob. Within seconds they were safely inside the vehicle with the engine roaring to life. Georgina screeched out of the garage, with Leroy holding on to the dash to steady himself.

'Be careful…it's new.' Narla vainly called after them. Knowing that they would never hear.

After a few seconds racing along the highway, Georgina took the folder off her lap and handed it too Leroy.

'Seems there was a lot more on Harley's computer that we first thought.'

Leroy opened the brightly coloured folder. His stomach turned but this time it was to do with Georgina's driving.

'Have you a weapon?' She asked crunching the gears as her foot prematurely disengaged the clutch.

Leroy patted his side. 'Browning.'

'Browning?' Georgina said surprised

'It's not regulation issue. It's for my own personal protection. You?' Leroy enquired.

'Berretta. It's back at the motel in the safe.'

'Oh, fine.'

'I know. I meant to pick it up.'

Leroy looked at the clock on the dash. 'Is that thing right?'

Georgina glanced. 'Fuck' She stepped harder on the gas pedal. 'Fifty-five minutes. How much further?'

'About five minutes to Independence Bridge, then another eight, maybe ten minutes, that's if everything is clear.' Leroy answered, remembering back to the chaos of the crashed lorry and the gridlock of vehicles.

The RV4 accelerated, pressing both Georgina and Leroy back further into their seats.

Leroy took out his phone. 'I call ahead, see if it's clear.'

'You can't.' Georgina stressed. 'Open the folder.'

The photograph was not printed in the best quality, but the image was well defined and in focus, there could be no disputing who the man with Harley was, the balding head, slightly ruddy complexion, puffy overweight face and neck. Leroy knew Norman Frusco at a glance, the picture would have to have been a hell of a lot more unclear for there to have been even one grain of uncertainty.

'Looks like we're on our own.' Georgina could see the iron ruttings of the bridge, half a mile or so away, down the straight road.

The rain was now beginning to fill the sides of the road and in one or two uneven places was forming in larger pools that coved the expanse of tar macadam. The wipers continually cleared the windscreen but the left one seemed to smear more than clear. Red taillights ahead suggested traffic. Georgina prayed that it wasn't still the congestion from earlier. As they drew nearer the reality became an alternative scenario that she didn't want to think about. Leroy saw the flashing light. The deputy was standing in the centre of the road wearing a waterproof cagoule that unlike the officer, appeared to have failed in its duty. He was swinging his torch from left to right slowing all the cars crossing Independence Bridge.

'What we gonna do?' Georgina asked as they neared the tail back. There were five cars ahead in the line before it was their turn.

'I dunno.' Leroy said, and then added. 'Keep cool. Hopefully Frusco doesn't know what sort of car to look for.'

'No, but there won't be many cars out here with a black guy and a white girl.'

'Okay…okay.'

The last stationary vehicle; a silver Toyota Celica was now fifty yards ahead of Georgina.

'Think fast, Leroy, think fast.'

'You know I thought you would appreciate the irony of it all.' Prentice Fortune whispered in her ear. The breath from his lips clouded as a fine mist in the cool damp atmosphere. Jo-Lynn could feel the warm air caress her ear. Her spine retracted in an involuntary spasm, ending a shiver through her bones. This was the only confirmation to her that she was still alive; any sense of feeling in her body had been numbed by the freezing cold water, there was no space for emotion anymore in her mind, all that was left there was a vacuous hollow and resignation that she was going to die after all she had been through; her life was going to end in a flooded basement. The water covered her chest and was beginning to move up her arms toward her shoulders.

'What does it feel like to know that your husband used to rent out your little girl, your pride and joy. Did he come home to you after energised and give you something to remember. Well, he gave me something to remember when he killed my girlfriend. Sweet as honey, but Ricky boy killed her, killed Jordan too. One mad moment, one rush of blood.'

'Let me go please, I'll do anything you want.' Jo-Lynn did not want to hear any more of his corruption.

'Don't flatter yourself honey. You look like shit, you smell like shit and your way too old. You know you really shouldn't have tried to run away. I was going to make it quick, spare the pain. Give my viewers a bit of an adrenaline rush. But now...' *He* sighed as though the effort of completing the sentence was too much. 'Now I think, slooooooowly is the order of the day. What do you think?' *His* hand moved around to his back. Jo-Lynn heard the scrape of metal as *he* withdrew a different knife from a sheath, it rubbed against the leather housing it was encased in. The knife was long, about 11 to 12 inches from tip to butt and the teeth serrated, almost barbed. The blade edge was extremely thin, around two inches across the width at the widest point.

'A cut here, a cut there. I would imagine that the blood going into the water should get the rats into quite a frenzy. If you are extremely lucky I may get heavy handed, or too excited, if not...I'm sure the rats will finish you off...eventually.' *He* grinned. Perfect teeth, white, straight, and no gaps.

Jo-Lynn's eyes widened. She wanted to rise to the bait but the glint from the knife disturbed some sub-conscious desire for survival that even now existed when hope was all but gone.

'I wonder if you taste as good as Jordan did?' Prentice Fortune's tongue slithered out and ran a trail of wetness across her cheek. 'Ooh, not too fresh.' He mocked in a campish tone.

'Come on Leroy, we're getting closer. Any minute now and they'll be able to see in.'

Leroy crouched down in the rear foot well. Georgina desperately tried to cover him with a picnic blanket that she found lying on the rear parcel shelf. She started to slow the car as the policeman played god, beckoning some cars through and asking others to pull over to the side. Leroy's hand wrestled his pistol from its holster, just in case.

'Come on, come on. Let us through.' Georgina was biting her pinched lips. She could see the policeman's rain splattered features through the darkening evening gloom. He looked about as pissed with the detail as he could possibly be. Georgina hated herself for doing it but she unbuttoned her blouse by three buttons and stretched open the material to expose a little bargaining power. She was loathed to think that most difficult situations could be resolved with the flash of a pert breast but where men were concerned, especially dumb asses standing in the pissing rain on a no win duty, it appeared to be a fact of life. She stopped the car and wound down the window. It was an officer that she hadn't seen before.

'Excuse me, ma'am.' The dumb ass shouted above the rain and the noise from the car engine. 'Can I ask where you are heading?'

'Is there a problem officer?' Georgina noticed his eyes were already fishing through the gap in her blouse; so predictable. Though in the wet, torchlight night, she had to admit to herself that he looked cute. 'I work at the hospital, I'm just going home.' Georgina lied, hoping that he was as dumb as he looked. The rain was now bouncing so hard off the car's roof that Georgina had difficulty hearing the officer.

'Hey, small world, my girlfriend works there.' A smile briefly flashed across his soaked features. 'Maybe you know her. Julie Cardonez?'

Georgina gripped the steering wheel tighter and her foot hovered over the accelerator.

'Julie Cardonez?' Georgina repeated, as though searching through her memory for a face to fit the name. 'I'm kinda new there so…Julie?'

The officer nodded, sending a shower of rain down to the ground from the plastic protector fitted over his cap.

'Dark hair, kinda sexy…brown eyes.'

'Yeah, that's her.'

'Yeah, I've spoken to her a couple of times but not much. As I said I'm new there.' Georgina noticed the cop's eyes flick this way and that, as they all but left his sockets and jumped into her bra.

'You need my ID.' Georgina turned knowing full well that her blouse would gape even further as she pretended to fish about in her handbag. He let her pretend for a few seconds revelling in the view before saying.

'Nah, you know Julie, maybe we'll meet up some time.' The officer stepped back. 'Have a good evening.'

'Hopefully.' Georgina straightened in the seat.

The officer banged on the roof of the car to see them off. Her heart began to beat rapidly as she engaged first and pulled jerkily away. She looked in the rear view, waiting to be stopped but as she pulled away she realised that they had made it onto the Island. Leroy waited for a minute before peering out from the rear foot well. 'Phew that was a close thing, lucky you knew his girlfriend.' He sat up and moved on to the back seat, stretching his stiffened legs as he moved.

'I have no idea who he was talking about.' Georgina began to laugh. 'I know it's not very PC, but I played the stereotype game.'

'What?'

'Her name, Julie Cardonez. I just described a typical Latin American girl, nothing specific but as I described rudimentary, albeit stereotypical, features. His mind was filling in the blanks. It's a psychological test that is used on schizophrenics to gauge reaction to short term memory loss syndrome. That mixed with the fact that it's raining like the end of the world and that he was cold, wet, and probably had a 'boner' from looking at my breasts. I dare say that it has been the most entertainment he's had all evening.'

Leroy laughed. 'You are a cruel lady.'

Georgina thought 'I'm a desperate lady.' but remained silent. She stared ahead at the relentless torrent that showed no sign of abating. Rivulets were cascading along the gutters, filling the sewerage system and beginning to flow back on itself, but this time returning with an unsavoury cargo from deep beneath the road.

'104 Headbridge.' Leroy said out of the blue. Georgina turned.

'What?'

'104 Headbridge.' He stated. 'It should mean something.'

Georgina turned sharply to the right, any glow from florescent street lighting now disappearing to the total blackness of dead country. The road became a little rougher. Georgina switched on the headlights to full beam, though the effect barely dented the opaque concentrate of night. The glimmer from the clock mounted in the facia of the car ticked on as another quarter hour sank away to its shameful retreat.

'Thirty minutes.'

'Yeah that's if this motherfucker's gonna keep his word. Why should he care about clocks, he's a psycho.'

Georgina fumbled inside her coat and propelled a cell phone at Leroy, who caught it instinctively. 'Call Narla, make sure Harley is logged on to the DeathCam site.'

'Oh, very educational.'

'No time to fuck about Leroy, we need to know if he's back on air.'

His fingers were already scrolling through the phones address book ready to press the autodial.

'I know…I know.'

Narla remained at the window watching the rain streak down the glass pane. The shrill from the phone nearly caused her to loose her reasoning.

'Jesus.' She pounced on the phone, eager to silence its intrusive cry. 'Yes…She's upstairs.' She placed the handset carefully on the glass-topped table. She ran through the lounge and stopped at the foot of the stairs, where she called up to Harley.

'Harley?'

She waited, knowing that her daughter would be sitting on the bed with her iPod on, listening to some obscene *gangsta rapper* or erasing brain cells playing for hours on her Playstation.

'HARLEY?' She shouted this time, before setting foot on the first step and begrudgingly deciding that she would have to walk the whole flight. As she reached the top, the door to Harley's bedroom opened.

Narla was sure that this was a little trick Harley done just to get under her skin.

Harley had the IPod on. 'You call?'

'The phone Harley, pick up the phone.' Narla exaggerated the movement of her mouth as though trying to communicate with a deaf person. Harley nodded. 'No need to shout.' She smiled knowing this really grated, but Narla was still young enough to know that this was all part of the game. Harley pulled off the headset and the music blasted from the tiny speakers. 'Who is it?'

'Detective LaPortiere said he needs some information.' Narla waited by the door.

Harley sighed as though the very act of having to impart even more information was too much like hard work. She half-closed the door to her bedroom. Narla stepped closer, the creaking floorboard on the landing *ratting* on her.

'You may as well come in rather than hover outside being surreptitious.'

'*Surreptitious.*' Narla blushed. Narla entered and sat on the edge of the bed.

Harley placed the phone to her ear.

'Uh-huh…yeah…hang on.' She leaned forward and flicked the mouse that was sitting idle on her worktop. The screensaver on the computer changed to the familiar bar of her Internet browser and below that the live feed to Jo-Lynn Montoya.

He looked at his watch, twenty-five minutes until eight o'clock. Twenty-five minutes until Showtime. Fortune positioned the tiny camera for optimum view and moved the harsh halogen lamp that was now beaming directly into Jo-Lynn's face. In the past half hour the water level had risen by six inches, maybe more. The lead from the lamp stretched upwards and disappeared into the darkness above, maybe into a light socket, it was difficult to tell from where Jo-Lynn was sitting. She felt relief when he dragged Rick from the water and dumped his body unceremoniously on the decking. Rick hadn't moved since and she had no way of knowing if he was dead or alive. If what Fortune had told her was true maybe it no longer mattered.

Occasionally she caught glimpses of Prentice Fortune as he fiddled with the lights and the camera. Everything had to be perfect but she could sense his frustration at the rising water level. This is not how it was supposed to end; this was a chink in his plan that he never catered for. Jo-Lynn tried to move her legs. She knew he used duck tape to strap her to either leg of the chair. She used all her might and anger and pulled and stretched the tape binding her legs. The water must be having an effect on the glue, she reasoned to herself. She tried pulling her hands but they seemed more firmly secured to the back of the chair and remained dry. She gave another effort, this time concentrating on her left leg which she thought had a little give, and sure enough her ankle moved. Jo-Lynn moved to her right leg and again strained hard against the grey tape.

A staircase waited at the bottom of the long hall. It waited for Ray, beckoning him and appeared to be the only way out. He stopped when he reached the landing newel post and gripped tightly onto the rail, then leaned forward craning his neck so he could see and listen. Silence.

'You know what? I can't wait.' Fortune pulled the knife from its protective leather sheath. 'Five minutes, ten minutes who really cares? They're all out there, watching this live on their little TV's and computers anyway.'

Panic filtered through Jo-Lynn's numbed senses. This was it. She strained with all her might against the loosened tape on her leg. She knew something would have to snap either the tape or her leg. At the moment though she wasn't taking bets as to which. She could feel the edge of the tape piercing her skin, but it no longer mattered. Nothing mattered anymore; nothing, except survival. As Prentice Fortune approached, she began screaming and shifting violently on the chair. Cold malice spread through his features. She knew he was enjoying himself. He waded through the silt water, his trousers clung obscenely to him; it was obvious he was enjoying it on more than one level.

Snap! Her foot come free. Just one foot. He drew nearer but not within striking distance. Jo-Lynn wanted to be sure to hurt him, even if it was to be the last thing that she would do. She wanted the satisfaction of knowing that she at least caused him pain.

And then *he* was upon her. So close she could feel the heat from his body.

He pressed the knife tip to her throat. 'Smile…you're dead.'

Jo-Lynn looked into the dead eyes that were so prominent through the mask, it was as though she was looking at a shark about to attack. The tip of the blade pierced her neck and slowly began to enter her. Knowing that she had less than a second to make her move, Jo-Lynn pulled her leg back and with all the force she could muster and raised her knee deep into his groin. The action sending her backwards into the water and him falling like a stone in the opposite direction. The knife flew from his hand as he made an involuntary reaction against the pain. *He* screamed as he rolled over in agony taking in mouthfuls of brown water. As he fought to regain his composure he yelled. 'You're gonna die.' But before *he* barely finished speaking, a siren buzzed through a speaker high on the far wall. Prentice Fortune looked up at it.

'NO…No, no, not now.' Fortune held his head with both hands trying to shut out the noise and more importantly the meaning of the noise.

Jo-Lynn tried to roll on to her front. Her hands and feet now trying to thrash wildly as the air slowly began to force its way from her lungs. She felt him rush past her, the movement, sending currents toward her face. Her ears detected the faint sound of a siren. She knew she needed to move to the platform at the bottom of the stairs and somehow get her head above water. She pushed heavily on her free leg, forcing herself upright through the water. Jo-Lynn's head emerged and she grasped the fetid air, inhaling it into her lungs as though it were nectar. She balanced precariously and scanned the room but there was no sign of *him*. Now desperation flooded her as surely as the water in room she was in. This really was her last chance, if she had to break her arm to free herself form the binding attaching her to the chair she would, she was that determined. She pulled and stretched and pulled and stretched and shook violently, wriggling and forcing the tape to give. As she pulled tiny speckles of blood began to break through the surface of her skin around the binding but the tape had to give. She screamed in anger and frustration, cursing the tape, cursing her situation and swearing at her lack of strength. Jo-Lynn lowered her head and began to gnaw at the tape, her teeth biting ravenously, hardly caring if she was eating her own flesh; now the only thing that mattered was survival. A tiny strand of tape pulled free and suddenly she had something to make purchase with, her teeth attacked again; all the time the water continued to rise. The slow trickle through the inlet was now a continuous flow. In the last quarter hour the level had risen over three inches. Jo-Lynn pulled, then pulled again. Then she stretched her arm as hard as she could, hoping to break the bondage before setting to it with her teeth once more. Another effort, more tape spat from her mouth into the filthy brown water and then finally her arm burst free. Within seconds she had freed her other arm then her leg and was collapsing head first in to the water, exhausted by the sheer effort. As Jo-Lynn hit the water's surface she remembered the knife.

'Go girl, go.' Maria Codez sat on the edge of her chair watching events unfold. The whole office sat in stunned silence. No one had wanted to go home. The emotions in the office were beyond anything that they had experienced before. Codez was rooted to the spot, she didn't want to blink but her contact lenses kept drying out and reluctantly her eyes batted for the briefest of milliseconds. She was almost tempted to ask if she had missed anything. As Jo-Lynn freed herself, the whole office erupted, everyone in Sagem Carter cheered.

Forty-Two

'I can't see a damned thing.'

'Trust me...drive straight on.' Leroy tried to peer through the blackened night, but he knew that even a rabbit with carotene overdose would be as blind as crooked boxing referee on a night like this. The four-wheel drive bounced through a few potholes before finally lodging itself firmly in a crater. The tyres span uselessly, churning mud and the last vestiges of grass in the waterlogged field.

'Great. Now what?' Georgina looked at Leroy. 'Maybe you could push?'

Leroy opened the door. 'We don't have time.' He set off on foot. 'Georgina, c'mon. We ain't got long.'

Catching a final glimpse at the clock inset on the dashboard, Georgina headed into the pouring rain and the black Missouri night. As she ran, following the darkened figure ahead, Georgina auto dialled Harley. Her footing was treacherous, many times sinking into the muddied field. The phone went through the routine of dialling, oblivious to its owner's desperation. The line connected.

'H...hel..lo Harley?' Georgina gasped, trying to wipe cold stinging rain away from her eyes while she ran. 'What's...the ...sit...u...ation?' The syllables were interrupted by pants of exertion.

'She's still alive I think, though the feed went dead a couple of minutes ago. Something happened. They had a fight, then *he* ran away and the live feed went down. The detective was lying on the floor near the foot of the stairs...he wasn't moving.'

Georgina didn't know if it was good news, though she was pretty sure that *he* would want to claim his pound of flesh.

'G...g...good...shit!' The line went dead as Georgina slipped down a grassy bank, her ear pressed the disconnect button as she fell. Mud and wet grass plastered itself to her. As she fell her mobile phone bounced out of her hand, landing somewhere in the darkness

'Fuck.' Georgina tried to halt her fall but scrambled messily, grasping air, awaiting impact with the sodden ground, which inexorably rose to meet her. 'Uh!' She rolled down a sharper incline, calling out in surprise, hoping Leroy would hear. Suddenly her body was encased in freezing cold water and her voice shut off by water rushing in through her mouth. Between shock and fear, lay panic. Georgina instinctively coughed out the water, before her head submerged beneath the blackness.

Leroy stopped and turned, taking a moment to look around. He called out low through the driving rain. 'Georgina!'

A light ahead briefly distracted him. It flicked on and off seven times in succession before plunging finally into darkness and the still of the night. The house disappeared but at least Leroy knew in what direction to head. 'Georgina?' He waited but knew he had to move onwards toward the house, alone if necessary.

Georgina was carried along, her head jarred off something that seemed too hard to be an embankment. As her senses returned, she could smell the stench of effluence, decay and death. This was no river; it was a tide of decay, the overspill from the abattoir combining with the flood and sewerage outlets. Somewhere it would meet the river but for now Georgina was carried along on a fast moving current of death. Too cold and weak to swim against its relentless force, she hoped that she would be able to grasp something and hold on until she could pull herself out. In the near distance she saw a light flicker on and off several times. She held her breath to try to stop her teeth chattering but it was as though her whole body was being frozen, her fingers and feet had already begun to loose their feeling. Her head banged off something hard. Before blacking out, Georgina sensed the motion of falling.

Georgina awoke knee deep in water with a torrent bouncing off her back, over her head. The ground beneath her hands and knees was solid, not a riverbank but something man made. She looked at her watch, blinking away water, trying to focus. Her head pounded and when she placed her hand to the point of pain it returned covered in blood. She staggered forward out of the Niagara that was bouncing off her and collapsed, letting the current, now much subsided carry her along until she came to a halt. For a while she sat there dazed and concussed, trying to think straight, trying to see straight. Georgina noticed rows of strip-lights along the ceiling in what appeared to be a storm tunnel or flood chamber. Her watch read eight o'clock and a wave of uselessness threatened to overwhelm her. She hoped against hope that Leroy had managed to save Jo-Lynn.

Leroy moved forward carefully, the light came once more. Encouraged, his pace quickened, he was now a couple of hundred yards away and could see the outline of a child silhouetted against the drawn blinds when the light was on and instantly recognised Ray Montoya. He began to run faster, his hand reached inside his jacket and unclipped the retainer on his holster allowing access to his weapon. About 100 yards from the house an automatic movement sensor picked Leroy's presence and a one thousand-kilowatt halogen lamp floodlit the entire house, which in turn triggered one at the back of the house. Like a rabbit motionless in car headlights, Leroy was temporarily frozen. Immobile and blinded, he felt extremely vulnerable. To his left there was nothing but open space, to his right there was nothing but a lightning tree, the branches reaching out, screaming at the injustice of a life cut short, at the same time offering protection. Leroy began to run toward it, half way to it he heard a loud rapport. Another thunderclap and a burst of white lightning, though this time it was followed by a searing pain and Leroy fell to the ground. The lights went out.

Inside the house, Fortune was a mass of confusion. He placed the rifle down and breathed in the smell of cordite from the spent round. His finger circled the tiny hole in the reinforced pane of glass, the sharp edge drew blood just as he had drew blood, and for the briefest of moments he felt a sense of satisfaction but soon his mind was returning to more serious matters than one rogue policeman. The boy was nowhere to be found. A noise from the room next door brought his mind back into sharp focus; the night was not over yet, not by a long way.

Jo-Lynn scrabbled around under the water, her hands feeling for the knife. She had seen it fly from his hand and made a mental note of approximately where it had landed. She began her frantic search not knowing how long she had until he returned, and suddenly there it was, her fingers ran across the blade, knocking it slightly further away. She scurried after it, panicking that it would fall irretrievably from her grasp, but she found it and held on to it for all her life was worth. Jo-Lynn ran through the water to the decking and her husband. With mixed and confused emotions she checked frantically for a pulse. A steady rhythm, Rick was still alive. The next part of her plan was something she had been thinking of ever since she realised the function of the chamber she was in. She knew that there was a lever somewhere that opened the trap door to allow the floodwaters to enter the sewage system below. The only obstacle now was to find it. The only place in the room she had not access to was the space underneath the stairs. She ran through the water as fast as her legs could carry her, driven by fear and hope, the water the only impediment to her progress. Jo-Lynn stumbled and fell once but got up straight away. Sunken away, on the far wall beneath the stairs was, as she had hoped, a lever mounted on a board. She didn't stop to analyse the finer points of the mechanism. She grabbed hold of the cold metal handle and pulled down with all her might, nothing seemed to happen. An enormous wave of despair started to fill every pore of Jo-Lynn battered and beaten existence. As she turned and looked with desperate hope at the centre of the chamber, a hydraulic 'phut' sound made her heart begin to race. Something was happening.

Georgina thought she heard a gun being fired, the sound echoed down the tunnel making the water around her feet ripple. But now there was silence. She wanted to do something, wanted to act, to do her duty, *serve and protect,* the words came to her mind but never had she felt so impotent. She looked around, nothing but endless tunnels, sending water and worse to an unknown destination. Nothing overhead but the occasional working strip light followed by florescent tubes that danced through the night, flicking on and off. She wondered for a moment whether they were permanently on or was it her presence that activated them fooled into thinking that she was a sewer worker. A noise a few yards down the tunnel made her look upward. She stood and wandered down, sloshing through the water, trying not to think about the smell of the floating effluent. She wondered if the FBI would pick up her cleaning tab and smiled at the surreal nature of her predicament. The strip light on the ceiling illuminated the rough brickwork and a small oblong inset within it. Without warning the oblong swung outwards and a deluge of water followed and with it a loud claxon wailing in distress. Georgina was covered in water once more; hardly able to breathe she staggered backward, searching for air. The water pinned her to the wall and all she could do was cough and splutter, hoping that the deluge would stop before she needed to breathe again. Georgina thought she saw a blur of something fall with the water. The sound of a heavier splash impacting on the water confirmed her suspicion.

The klaxon rang through the house.

Fortune turned, the boy could wait. He knew that the boy would never be able to open the front door, and the windows were constructed from toughened glass, he could not break them, not a boy. He slung his rifle over his shoulder, now was the time to finish what he started. He entered the hall and stopped at the door to the cellar. As he unbolted it, another alarm sounded. He couldn't believe it. Prentice Fortune's hands unfastened the retainers, urged on by a sense of panic. He would not be denied his moment of triumph. He ran down the stairs as soon as the door was open, then along a narrow passage to another door. This time a steel reinforced door, more bolts. Fortune began to curse his own security. The last bolt pulled back, he grabbed hold of the handle and yanked the cumbersome door before taking the final set of stairs two at a time. Instantly he knew she was gone. The final few gallons of water poured through the opened trap door. Fortune stepped forward, close to the opened hatch, then knelt down and placed his head into the opened space, looking, searching.

The chair lay below, being carried along with the current.

He shouted through to the network of tunnels.

'You won't escape.' His voice echoed. As he straightened into a kneeling position, he heard movement from behind and a voice.

'Yes I fucking will.'

Fortune turned just in time to see the large blade enter his shoulder and run downwards fully to the hilt, sinking into his flesh. Jo-Lynn pushed with all her might and he toppled backward through the open hatch.

Georgina watched the body, arm and legs splaying widely, grabbing air, as it hurtled through the opening. She stepped back a few paces to make sure he did not catch her as he plummeted to the ground. His body impacted on the water like a mistimed high diver, displacing showers of water in all directions. As soon as the body landed, Georgina was making her way toward him, reaching in her back pocket for the nylon ties, which she preferred using to the cumbersome regulation handcuffs. He was lying still in the water; the tip of the blade had pushed all the way through his shoulder with the tip of the blade exposed through the back of his jumper. His hands were floating above his head, Georgina wasn't even sure if was still alive but was in no mood to take the risk. She knelt on the body submerging it in the knee-deep water, as she did so she noticed the tip of the blade protrude even further through the back of his shoulder. Quickly, she grabbed his right arm and pulled it to the centre of *his* back. As she repeated the action with the left arm, Prentice Fortune pulled the nylon tie from her hands. He rolled over and dragged her down into the water. Georgina spat out water and fought for air. Fortune was still felt powerful despite the knife embedded in his shoulder. Georgina grabbed hold of the handle of the knife and pulled down with all her might. The knife moved downwards, cutting flesh, breaking bone. Prentice Fortune yelled with pain. A spurt of blood shot out of the wound streaking across Georgina's jacket. She yanked upwards and the knife came free in her hands. Georgina didn't wait; she couldn't afford to wait. She plunged the knife deep into Prentice Fortune's throat and heard a sickening crack as the serrated blade severed his windpipe. Fortune staggered backwards with his arms outstretched and toppled backwards for a final time into the water. Even though he was dead, Georgina set about securing his feet and arms with the ties, before slumping exhausted and dizzy into the water. She sat for a while submerged to her waist staring at the body of the dead man, not even curious as to who he was, just relieved to be alive.

'Hey?' Georgina shouted up through the gap. She waited but heard no reply, so she shouted a second time but louder, much louder.

'HEY!!! ANYBODY UP THERE?'

A face appeared through the sluice door opening. A face Georgina recognised followed by a second much younger face. Jo-Lynn smiled, the burden of her nightmare already beginning to recede as she hugged her son, their faces touching.

Georgina looked up. 'I think I need some help down here.'

'My son has already called the police.' Jo-Lynn said with pride before emotion overwhelmed her. Jo-Lynn pulled away from the opening and began to cry. At first silently, then with rage.

Forty-Three

Georgina began to move back down the tunnel. She knew that Jo-Lynn needed time by herself with her son. Jo-Lynn's sobs echoed down the tunnel. She cradled Ray, kissing him, making his face wet with her tears, and slowly the rage she felt turned to joy. Joy like she had never experienced before, not even when he was born, and the tears and sobs finally merged into a laugh of relief. Ray sat on his mother's lap, confused, tired and in a state of shock.

Prentice Fortune sat propped against the wall of the sewer; the fluorescent tube above flickered on and off waiting to expire. Georgina looked up at the open hatch and called. 'Jo-Lynn?'

Jo-Lynn Montoya crawled to the edge of the hatch.

'Did you find Rick?'

'He's up here with me…' She could see Prentice Fortune propped against the wall. 'Is he dead?'

Georgina took a deep breath and shrugged. 'Hopefully.'

Jo-Lynn's turned, searching for her son and was chilled to the bone when she heard the malevolent rasp of her husband's voice.

'Lose something?' Rick towered over Jo-Lynn holding their child.

Cold abhorrent fear consumed every ounce of Jo-Lynn's body.

Rick swayed unsteadily in front of her, clasping Ray to his body. 'I can't let you leave, not knowing what you know now.' His arm held Ray securely.

'What…what are you doing? Surely we've been through enough.'

'I can't let you go.' Rick repeated.

'Don't be stupid Rick, everyone knows. The police are on the way. It's over, Rick. Everything's over.'

'No.' Rick threw Ray as though he was a rag doll, not even stopping to watch as his son bounced hard against the wall. The boy collapsed into it with a sickening thud and slid down to the floor unconscious. The pain and confusion inside Rick matched the rank picture of evil in his eyes. Rick lunged at Jo-Lynn. She took a step back and fell through the open hatch.

'NO!' She screamed as the ground disappeared from under her feet and suddenly she was falling through the air uncertain of if her son was alive and if she would live through the fall.

Georgina heard the cry echo through the tunnel, followed by the sight of Jo-Lynn falling through the air. She hit the water hard.

'Jesus.' Georgina ran to Jo-Lynn, wading through the water and pulled her to the side. She rolled Jo-Lynn over so she was face up.

Jo-Lynn was still conscious but barely. Behind her came the sound of another person entering the water. A heavier much splash.

Georgina realised that it was detective Rick Montoya, though the man that hauled himself upright from the water bared no resemblance to the man she once knew. She also was aware that she was no match for him when dragging a half conscious woman through knee-deep effluent. 'Come on, we've got to go.'

'The knife...get the knife.' Jo-Lynn tried to stand and though half conscious was still smart enough to remember the knife she plunged into Prentice Fortune. She pointed to the knife, now deeply embedded in Fortune's neck. Georgina swam the short width of the outlet and with all of her strength yanked the knife from Fortune. Jo-Lynn was already moving as fast as she could up the sewer outlet. Fortune rolled forward face down into the water, his body becoming engulfed in a sea of waste. Georgina moved fast to catch up. She had no compulsion about Fortune. Lights above flicked on and off as they moved down the tunnel. Georgina soon caught up with Jo-Lynn, both of them knowing and hearing the manic demented screams of the detective pursing them.

'We've got to keep on moving. We'll be out of here soon.' Georgina didn't want to look behind, she could hear the sound of water splashing and knew that Montoya was on his feet and closing the gap between them. Jo-Lynn stumbled, Georgina was unsure if she had passed out or whether her legs just gave way, but suddenly Jo-Lynn was a dead weight and dragging them both down to the surface of the water. The demented rage f Rick Montoya echoed down the tunnel. The chill from his angler like a cold breath on the back of Georgina's neck. He was closing fast and she was stumbling along the passage, her feet trying desperately to find purchase in the watery environment. Georgina dragged Jo-Lynn as best as she could but knew that if either of them was to survive she would have to let her fall to the water. Georgina could feel the cold blast of night air rushing to greet them. The exit from the sewer tunnels was only yards away. The sound of water being displaced by the rushing angry sound of Montoya approaching made her briefly look over her shoulder, an act she instantly regretted. The fury of the man was made all the more evident by a loud voracious scream. Georgina put her arm around Jo-Lynn and dragged her onwards. 'C'MON' She shouted in Jo-Lynn's ear. The sound of Montoya approaching grew louder. Georgina imagined that she could feel his very presence upon her and was too paralysed to turn this time for facing the truth. She had no gun, just the knife, which she clutched onto desperately. Georgina heard the familiar sound of a gun being cocked, ready to fire. Paralysis once more slowing her movement as she imagined Rick Montoya steadying himself to aim and fire a bullet directly into her. The sound of the gun engaging in the tunnel clear and succinct over the rushing water and ensuing pandemonium. Georgina's legs began to betray her, slowing down, becoming molten lead. The bullet exploded through the tunnel like an express train roaring past her head. Instinctively she grabbed Jo-Lynn and dived head first into the water. She swam forward, not knowing or seeing her destination. The muted sound of gunfire rang out again. She swam forward as far as she could until her lungs gave out. Finally gasping for air, she surfaced, dragging Jo-Lynn with her. They were at the entrance to the flood chamber.

'Stand to the side.' The order was bellowed to Georgina and Jo-Lynn from the bank. Confused, Georgina acted on instinct and did as directed. They pushed themselves as hard as they could to the riverbank.

Leroy LaPortiere tried to stabilise himself. He raised his pistol again and fired off a third round. He watched the projectile thunder down the tunnel, followed by another, then another and another. Leroy kept on firing until the clip was empty, until there was no reason or need to fire anymore. Nothing came out of the tunnel but silence, then eventually, the floating body of Rick Montoya. The already ravaged face was pulped by three direct hits, leaving impacted craters where his features used to be. There was no doubt that detective Rick Montoya was dead, but Leroy gingerly entered the water, reloaded a clip and fired another three rounds into the head of Rick Montoya.

Leroy pulled Jo-Lynn Montoya out of the water first and then Georgina O'Neil. They both lay on the muddy riverbank, exhausted by the night, by the cold, and by the events.

Jo-Lynn got to her feet first. 'My baby.'

Georgina noticed blood staining Leroy's trouser leg. 'You're hurt?'

Jo-Lynn moved to the mouth of the tunnel, breathed deeply and shouted with all of her might.

'WILL?'

Barely half a second passed before Ray's voice roared back. 'MOMMY.'

'Are you okay, baby?' Her voice echoed down the tunnel.

Ray's voice came in sobs, no longer able to be strong. He just wanted to be hugging his mother. 'Help me, Mommy.'

Jo-Lynn fell to her knees. 'We're coming, baby...we're coming.'

A hand rested on her shoulder, Jo-Lynn turned to see Georgina smiling at her. 'I'm sure he's fine, a fighter just like his mother.'

A helicopter swooped past. The bright halogen lamps set around the house were triggered illuminating the area. Somewhere in the near distance was the sound of approaching emergency response vehicles. Leroy sat down on the muddy grass and returned his gun to his holster. Blood continued to soak from his wounded leg through his trousers.

'You want me to apply some pressure to that.' Georgina said, indicating to the thigh wound.

'Yeah' Leroy tried his best to smile. 'I always knew you were dying to get inside my pants.'

Georgina hunkered down and pressed the palms of her hands firmly onto Leroy's bleeding thigh. 'As long as you know, I am not making a pass.'

Leroy sat down on the ground and lay back, looking at the black night and the falling rain.

The hours that followed were, in Georgina's mind, unnecessarily excessive and tortuous on top of the ordeal they had encountered but she was often part of that procedural team herself on many occasions and understood the reasons why, even if she couldn't sympathise with them. Wynan O'Neil stepped from the helicopter and made his way to the house. The door was wide open now. The FBI director found Leroy, Jo-Lynn, Ray and his daughter sitting in silence in the kitchen, too exhausted to talk. Ray had scouted around the house and produced some quilts and blankets; Jo-Lynn had turned the televisions off that were hooked up to the computers in an attempt to disconnect from the real world and gain some much needed privacy. She sat cradling her son, rocking back and forth both of them still shell-shocked. It would be a long time before the healing process would begin. Georgina sat on the floor in the kitchen still applying pressure to Leroy's leg wound. He would survive, there was a lot of blood but the bullet was a through and through, missing the femur and artery. Eventually the paramedics arrived for Leroy and another ambulance followed for Jo-Lynn and Ray.

'I just want to thank you. I know that sounds inadequate but...' Jo-Lynn stared deep into Georgina's eyes. Georgina felt like an impostor, in her mind she hadn't done anything.

'It's...it's more than adequate.'

'You know, I really can't believe that Rick could do this.'

Georgina looked at Jo-Lynn hugging her son, who was now sleeping standing on his feet. Jo-Lynn lifted the child and rested him on her hip and walked out into the rain and the waiting ambulance.

'I'll visit you tomorrow.' Georgina called after Jo-Lynn. Her voice echoed through the hall and rattled out of the building, out into the rain sodden night, where it was lost amongst the black sky and the white halogen lights of the assembling television crews.

'Ready to go home, Georgie?' Wynan O'Neil took of his long coat and draped it around his daughter's shoulders.

Epilogue

'The impending inquiry will of course give you chance to redress any question or matter you feel is warranted. I can't begin to tell you what a god-awful mess this whole affair has been. We have no choice but to suspend you on full pay pending the decision of the enquiry'

Georgina sat in the large office, staring through Director Ebbley, out beyond the reinforced glass walls of his sixth floor office. Her father, Wynan O'Neil, sat next to Ebbley. Remaining silent for the entire hearing. He listened to the proceedings with interest, only showing signs of detachment and professionalism. Georgina's finger ran over the small scar on her forehead, it itched from the removal of the stitches and promised to leave an angry red line which, *'would diminish with time.'* or so she was assured. Harold Ebbley had given the same speech at least once a month for the past fourteen years in his post as Director of the behavioural science unit. He had given it so many times it sounded flat and said with little heart or conviction.

'It has been three weeks and there is still no sign of Captain Frusco even being charged.' Georgina replied in an equally flat tone. The passion in her own voice lost, stranded somewhere else, wrapped up in bureaucracy and politics.

'The situation there is delicate, and as you know complicated by recent events.'

Events, Georgina knew what recent *events* were, and in her mind gilded an already poisoned chalice.

'The photos you gave us were fake doctored digital images. As far as we can tell, Prentice Fortune and Rick Montoya were both responsible for manipulating images, as was Andy White from the TV station. Rick was getting Andy White to doctor the video images. From what we can gather, Montoya, Fortune, Kiers, Dalton, England White and Fleisher were the only people involved in the affair that we have any credible incriminating evidence for. And some of that evidence went up in smoke in the fire.' Ebbley let the sentence hang in the air. 'Maybe we will never know the full story.'

Ebbley's voice drifted away inside Georgina's head, once more an incoherent mumble. She picked up one of the colour photos from

Director Ebbley's Birchwood desk. The television station was almost raised to the ground, now nothing more than a pile of smouldering black ashes. Littered amongst the skeletal walls and empty doorframes was the molten videotapes and images White was working on. White was still missing. The case was a mess and far from ever being truly solved.

'…we will have to sit back and slowly continue trying to piece together this together, but the truth is we may now never know.' Ebbley's voice snapped back into focus.

Georgina laughed to herself, though the ironic smile never escaped Ebbley's attentive eyes. Georgina O'Neil stood and handed over her badge and her weapon. Wynan O'Neil blinked once but remained concentrated on his daughter's face.

'Take the break, O'Neil. We'll be in touch.'

Winter still hung in the air in Maryland. It seemed like an age since summer. Georgina had just about had enough, she was mentally and physically exhausted and the temptation to walk away from the FBI was overwhelming. She lay on her bed, her nose pressed close to the quilt and she breathed in the comfort of home, the smell of her and her house, the smell of loneliness. Now more than ever she needed somebody. Her mind strayed to Korjca, to her slightly rounded face and fresh complexion and as she wondered and imagined. Four strands of Korjca's hair were wrapped around Georgina's fingers; sleep entered and closed the world outside her head, to allow fantasies breathing space. She woke in a dark cold room, disorientated. Georgina sat bolt upright and tried to gather her thoughts and wits, but for a few long seconds she was somewhere else, somewhere terrible. Familiarity slowly broached, entering through the dark. As she reached for the phone on the bedside locker it rang. Her hand hovered above it briefly before she garnered the courage to lift the receiver.

'Hello.' Her voice left vapour trails against the moonlight coming from the shuttered window.

'Hi.' He had a deep honey brown voice, which she instantly recognised.

'Hi, Leroy.' She did not even try to hide the relief in her voice. 'How are things?'

'Thought I'd call see how you were. I heard about the inquiry.'

Georgina barely contained a disgusted grunt, which managed to sound like a stifled sneeze to Leroy.

'Suspended until further notice. It's procedure, so they tell me…I need a friend.' The end of her sentence even surprised Georgina, the words fell from her lips like betrayers kiss and in an instant left her floundering. 'Can we meet?' Georgina hoped that there were no signs of desperation in her voice.

'How about lunch tomorrow? On me. I'll pick you up around twelve

Twelve, Georgina sat on the bed in the cold, dark room. 'Make it two. I don't get up early these days. Don't sleep through the night too well.'

'Are you okay?' Leroy asked. The silence down the end of the phone that greeted him added to his concerns.'

After a pause, Georgina answered. 'Not really. See you tomorrow.'

'See you then.' Leroy lingered for a moment before placing the phone down on the receiver, as did Georgina. Both of them listening to the silence and to their own breathing.

<u>END</u>

Exclusive 1st Chapter

Read the rest of this thrilling new Georgina O'Neil novel, Dark County.

Published by Caffeine Nights Publishing.
In all good book stores, 2008.

Dark country

By

Darren E Laws

The second book in the Georgina O'Neil crime thriller trilogy

Prologue

1957, Talinha, Texas.
The Teenarosa Motel.

Jonah Fintall banged on the dust-laden window once more. Small microbes of dirt bounced back into the dry atmosphere. He turned to his left where Officer Mike Reynolds was standing, impatiently fighting off the sweat from streaming down his forehead into his eyes. His complexion was ruddy, but seemed to go hand in hand with his overweight stature.

'See, it's like I told you, she's not answering.' Jonah pressed his face closer to the glass and peered through the grimy film to the room inside. 'I can see her in the bed, she hasn't moved all morning.'

Officer Reynolds wiped the sweat from his face using a handkerchief that was already soaking wet. 'It's not a crime to ignore fans, Mr Fintall.'

'I know, I know. But what about the girl?'

'The girl?'

'Yeah. Her daughter. She booked in with her two nights ago. A little-un. No more than two or three, I'd say.'

The police officer looked at the motel manager and then at the door. 'You got a key?'

'Got spare keys to all the rooms.' Fintall searched in his pocket and removed a solitary key, which he handed to Reynolds.

Officer Reynolds puffy fingers grabbed the key and placed it in the lock. 'You better be right, Mr Fintall.' He banged loudly on the door and waited a full minute. Jonah Fintall was still looking through the window.

'Any movement?' Reynolds asked hopefully.

Jonah shook his head. 'I don't like the look of this. Had a suicide here three, maybe four years ago. Had to throw away a whole bunch of bedding. Blood just wouldn't shift no matter how much you scrubbed.'

Reynolds placed the key in the lock and slowly turned the handle. The door sprang free. The smell of dry air and death poured through the opening. Reynolds stepped back and placed his back against the doorframe, his head tilted upward trying to find a clean cool stream of air. 'Mrs. Dark…Mrs. Dark, are you okay in there?'

No answer

Reynolds steadied himself and wrapped his chubby fingers around the grip of his regular issue pistol, flicking the holding strap off his holster and withdrawing the weapon in one easy movement. Jonah Fintall moved away from the policeman but remained peering through the window. Reynolds turned and weapon drawn entered the motel room.

'Mrs. Dark?…Mrs. Dark?' Sweat finally breached his eyebrows and ran into his eyes. Officer Mike Reynolds blinked. The salt concentrate in his sweat stung. His hand trembled slightly but Reynolds breathed deeply a couple of times to regain his composure. 'Mrs. Dark?'

No reply.

The officer drew closer to the bed. The outline of her body was clear through the linen sheet. The odour of decay in the hot room was evident. Reynolds leaned forward and tapped the woman's foot with the nozzle of his gun. There was no response. He turned and looked at Jonah Fintall, who was now standing in the open doorway, watching the proceedings. Reynolds could not hide the desperate look of fear etched on his face. He walked around the side of the bed until he could see a mop of tousled blonde hair protruding from beneath the sheet. By the side of the bed on the cabinet was an empty medicine bottle with a few white pills scattered, some of which were on the floor. Reynolds trod on something, which cracked under the weight of his heavy boot. He looked down to find some more tablets and the white powdery remnants of a pill crushed under the sole of his boot. 'Mrs. Dark?' He whispered, his voice low, almost in fear of waking the dead.

The door to the bathroom was closed. Reynolds moved closer to the body in the bed. He reached forward, fingers outstretched, until they grasped the bed sheet. Reynolds pulled the sheet down. Amy Dark did not react; she did not mover or give any signs of life. Her eyes were closed as though asleep, her features soft, showing no troubles or angst with her sleep.

'Mrs. Dark?' Reynolds voice was soft. His hand moved forward closer to her shoulder. 'Mrs. Dark, its Officer Mike Reynolds from the Talinha County Police.'

He made contact with her body, first his fingers, then his hand as he gently rocked her body. Her body moved as one, as though she were a mannequin. The cold, unforgiving feel of her body registered in Reynolds brain. Amy Dark was in the throes of rigor mortis and had been dead many hours.

Reynolds turned his head to face Jonah Fintall. 'Oh my god, she's dead.'

Fintall's face briefly lit up. 'This place will be a shrine.' He whispered.

Reynolds pulled the sheet back exposing the body of Amy Dark. She was wearing a nightgown. 'This don't make sense, who dresses for bed and then commits suicide.'

'I could open it up as a bona-fide tourist attraction.'

Reynolds looked at the motel manager. 'You ever see that film called 'Psycho', buddy?' He wasn't even sure if Fintall had heard him. If he had, the bloated motel manager chose not to answer.

There was a muted sob from behind Officer Reynolds. At first he thought it had come from the body. He had heard of such things, gasses escaping corpses in low groans or moans. But this was a definite cry. The cry of a young child.

'The girl.' Fintall said, as he entered the room. The smell of corruption slowed his pace. As he passed by the body of Amy Dark, Jonah Fintall glanced briefly at her. There was nothing dignified about her death, it was obvious her bowels and bladder had passed excrement and urine on her death as the body's muscles relaxed. It was not the image he would have liked to remember the queen of Country and Western music.

The cry came again.

Reynolds turned to the bathroom door. 'I'm coming, honey. Just hold on.'

Officer Reynolds placed his gun back in the holster and secured the safety strap. He edged toward the door and with more confidence than when he entered the motel room, walked straight into the bathroom.

'Poor little m…'

The sound of the gun firing was like an explosion in the room. Fortunately Reynolds knew little of it, before the bullet snuffing his life like a candle severed his spinal cord. Reynolds fell to the ground, never to get up, just the brief realization of a hot stinging sensation. Fintall had no desire or curiosity to wait around. On hearing the shot, he turned and ran for all his life was worth. His whole body felt saturated with sweat and much to his shame, urine. Fear had relinquished his body's automatic hold over his bladder and for the first time since he was a boy, Jonah Fintall had wet himself. As he ran, he felt spurts of hot piss drenching his legs and trousers. His bowels threatened betrayal but nothing was going to stop him from running. Nothing, except the second shot which he heard in its entirety. The blast knocked him sideways, punching the wind from his stomach. Fintall's legs wobbled unsteadily but he kept on running. He could see his small office and living quarter's only yards away. Soon he would be safe. He had a gun in the office. Soon he would have the gun in his hand and be on equal terms with his assailant. He never heard the third shot. His head split like a ripe banana filled with minced meat. Jonah Fintall managed to run three more steps before his legs finally stopped receiving signals from his brain, the brain that was now lying in segments in the dust, forced through the exit wound in his forehead.

1984

Wink Winkler, Texas.

Fortune's End Trailer Park

'Ssh now, baby, hush.'

Caroline Dark walked back and forth across the mobile home. She had seven steps each way before being confronted by a wall or a room divider. The baby continued to cry. The wail from its tiny lungs filled the confines of the small trailer.

'Come on Genna, give you mumma, some peace.'

Caroline was drained and close to breaking point. Six weeks on the road, living out of a coach, instead of a string of low rent motels and hotels had paid a toll on Caroline Dark's health. She wished now that she had never listened to her manager and boyfriend (when it suited him), Bobby Oates. The very idea of touring with a young baby in tow was little short of mad. And where was Bobby now? Caroline sighed…she wished she knew. It had been two weeks since he had last been in touch. Two painfully long weeks of endless shows and upping sticks and moving on to the next town and of course it had to be by trailer. "The surest fastest way to make bucks." She wished she had never listened to him. If it were not for the support of her band and the two roadies then the tour would have finished just outside Toledo when Bobby left. Caroline sat down on the quilted seating at the end of the trailer and looked out of the window. At least she was home now for a night or two. Home such as it was; was a cheap trailer home sited in the cheapest trailer park she could find. This was her night off, her one free night before another string of shows taking her through Texas to Louisiana. Caroline's reflection stared back, and so haggard and unfamiliar was her face that for a moment she thought someone was outside staring in at her. Her eyes were heavy and ringed with dark circles, blackened by interrupted nights of lost sleep as Genna started to cut her first teeth. Caroline's skin was dry, flaking in places, dehydrated by the harsh sun and wind that had been battering Texas…..

Printed in the United Kingdom by
Lightning Source UK Ltd., Milton Keynes
140358UK00001B/13/A